**Every move
could be
your last.**

STALKING ANDI

A jacket tossed over his shoulder, Luke followed Andi onto the porch and yanked the door shut. "What's that?" he asked in a tight voice.

"What?"

He was staring at the willow wreath she'd hung on the door, his willow wreath. Her heart clutched as she saw him gingerly pluck a white card from the ring of sticks.

"Another note?" he asked and her heart went cold. All the happiness she'd felt seconds earlier, the fantasies had shriveled.

Carefully, just touching the edges, he turned the card over.

Little birds should be careful who they choose as a mate. Tsk, tsk. There is no such thing as faithfulness. Be careful. Seabirds can die, too.

Andi started quaking deep inside. "What is this? Why are they doing this?"

"To scare you," he said grimly.

She shook her head.

"Our note writer is threatened by me," he observed. "Not sure what he means about being faithless. Maybe he thinks our relationship has gone on longer than it has."

"All this about birds. Trini and me . . . and now seabirds?"

"Some kind of clue," Luke said.

"It's getting personal and he's pissing me off." That was true. The shivering inside her body, the fear, was morphing into anger. She was furious about what had happened to Trini, about her brother's involvement, about creeping around and trying to terrorize her and now . . . *now* bringing Luke into his sick, twisted game . . .

Books by Nancy Bush

CANDY APPLE RED

ELECTRIC BLUE

ULTRAVIOLET

WICKED GAME

WICKED LIES

SOMETHING WICKED

WICKED WAYS

UNSEEN

BLIND SPOT

HUSH

NOWHERE TO RUN

NOWHERE TO HIDE

NOWHERE SAFE

SINISTER

I'LL FIND YOU

YOU CAN'T ESCAPE

YOU DON'T KNOW ME

THE KILLING GAME

Published by Kensington Publishing Corporation

The
Killing Game

NANCY
BUSH

ZEBRA BOOKS
KENSINGTON PUBLISHING CORP.
http://www.kensingtonbooks.com

ZEBRA BOOKS are published by

Kensington Publishing Corp.
119 West 40th Street
New York, NY 10018

All Kensington titles, imprints and distributed lines are available at special quantity discounts for bulk purchases for sales promotion, premiums, fund-raising, educational or institutional use.

Special book excerpts or customized printings can also be created to fit specific needs. For details, write or phone the office of the Kensington Sales Manager. Attn.: Sales Department. Kensington Publishing Corp., 119 West 40th Street, New York, NY 10018. Phone: 1-800-221-2647.

Zebra and the Z logo Reg. U.S. Pat. & TM Off.

First Printing: July 2016
ISBN-13: 978-1-4201-3466-7
ISBN-10: 1-4201-3466-3

eISBN-13: 978-1-4201-3467-4
eISBN-10: 1-4201-3467-1

10 9 8 7 6 5 4 3 2 1

Printed in the United States of America

PART I

***

OPENING

Prologue

I like games. All kinds. Crossword puzzles, jigsaw puzzles, chess, Sudoku, Jumble, cryptograms, board games, video games, card games . . . I'm good at them. I'm also good at mind games. Deception, trickery, and lying come as naturally to me as breathing. There have been times when my emotions have taken over and nearly tripped me up, but now I have my rage and hate under control, for the most part. Still, emotions are part of the fuel that drives my favorite game: murder. Killing is the best game, by far. There is no comparison. The high that comes afterward is better than sex.

The first time I killed it was because someone had become dangerous to me. The second time was just to see if I could get away with it, and I did, and it left me miles above the earth, so far out of reach it was like I lived on a distant planet. Untouchable. King of the universe. I had to return to earth eventually with its banality, a hard landing. But then I began plotting and planning again, constructing more games in order to buoy myself into the stratosphere once again. The world is so gray and mundane without puzzles, twists, turns, and mysteries, without someone's life balanced on a razor's edge.

My latest game has begun. It's about retribution and acquisition, but no one is to know. There's some misdirection mixed in to the plot, to keep the cops at bay, and it's got some moves my quarries will not expect. I'm really, really good. I tell myself to be humble, but it's difficult. The only way to lose is to get caught, but that'll never happen.

This one's going to take awhile, require a few extra steps, a few more deaths, but I'm into playing the long game. Makes the winning so much sweeter.

I've already made my opening gambit.

And her name's Belinda . . .

The ferry plowed across surprisingly rough gray waves, its running lights quivering against the black waters of Puget Sound. Belinda Meadowlark sat with a book at a table inside the upper deck, but though she read the same passage three times, it was Rob's handsome face she kept seeing superimposed on the page. Unable to concentrate, she finally closed the hardback with a decided *thump*. It was a story about love and revenge, and she couldn't see how the ending was going to be anything but disappointing. She lived for happy endings. Always. Maybe because she'd had so few of them.

But that had all changed when she met Rob. He was gorgeous and funny—did she say gorgeous? OMG! He was a god! He'd struck up a conversation with her at the bar in Friday Harbor the previous April. OMG! When she recalled the way he sought her out, it still caused a hot thrill to run right from her hoohaw straight up to her breasts. My, my. She could feel it even now, just at the thought, and her cheeks reddened and she looked around, almost certain someone would notice. She damn near had to fan herself.

But there were only a few people on the ferry tonight and the ones that were had stayed on the lower deck.

Rob . . . She smiled as she recalled the way his lustrous brown eyes had looked her over. "Do I know you?" he'd asked curiously, tilting his head in that way that made her want to grab him and squirm all over him.

Of course he didn't know her. She was no beauty and she could stand to lose a few pounds, where he was casually handsome and looked totally fit. He'd been wearing short sleeves, even though it had been brisk with a capital BRRR the day he'd been standing outside the hotel, watching the passengers disembark from the last ferry. Belinda, who lived in Friday Harbor, had immediately tagged him as a tourist.

"I don't think so," she told him regretfully.

He slowly shook his head, wagging it from side to side. "No, we've met . . ."

"I would have remembered," she admitted, suddenly wishing it were true. He looked good enough to eat and he smelled a little like Old Spice and something darker and muskier.

He snapped his fingers. "Belinda," he said. "And your last name's . . . some bird?"

She goggled and gasped aloud in shock and delight. "Meadowlark!"

He grinned. "I remember now. You were pointed out to me at some event around here a year or so ago."

She racked her brain, trying to think where she'd been that he would have seen her. "A year or so ago?"

"Right about then, I think."

"I don't know what that would be," she murmured dubiously. "Maybe the clambake?" The owners of one of the restaurants near the harbor came from the East Coast and put on an annual clambake, adding salmon to the menu to make it more Pacific Northwest, but it was really kind of a small affair, and she'd only been there a minute or two before she had to leave.

"That sounds right," he said after a moment of thought. "Well, what are you doing now? Can you have a drink? I'm buying."

"I—need to go home . . . first."

"Come back. I'll be in the bar here." He jerked his head in the direction of a small place called the Sand Bar. "I don't know anybody else around here. My buddies all took off sailing, but I'm not heading home till tomorrow."

"Where's that?"

"California. I'm based out of Los Angeles. I sell sports equipment up and down the West Coast."

Belinda had immediately thought about the pounds she needed to lose and she'd been deeply embarrassed.

"Go on home," Rob encouraged, "but come back. What do you like to drink? I'll have one waiting for you."

She didn't drink, as a rule, but she didn't want to seem unsophisticated, so she said tentatively, "A cosmopolitan?"

"Perfect." He smiled at her again, a flash of white, then had headed toward the bar. She'd almost followed right after him, but she'd forced herself to go home first, then had looked in the mirror in despair. How could *he* be interested in *her*? It didn't make sense. But then, he was just trying to pass the time and he'd seen her and knew her. It couldn't be from the clambake, though. She wanted it to be, but she'd barely arrived at the beach when her mother had called and demanded she help with Grandpa, who was raising hell at the nursing home again.

Who cares? she'd told herself at the time as she squeezed into her best jeans and the purple blouse, real silk, that made her breasts look good and had a sexy shimmer in dim light, which the Sand Bar had in spades. Sometimes it was so dark there you felt like you had to raise your hand to within an inch of your face to see it.

She'd hurried to meet him, slipping a little on the wet concrete walk that led to the Sand Bar's front door, her new boots kind of pinchy and uncomfortable, but they looked good.

Inside, she followed the dull path of carpet to the darkened main bar where, luckily, a pink neon beer sign in the shape of a crab helped her make out some forms.

"Belinda!" Rob called, standing up at a table in the back of the room.

She threaded her way carefully toward him, decrying her bumpity-bump hips as they brushed the tables. When she neared him, he reached out and grabbed her arm, guiding her the last few steps to a black Naugahyde bench. He sat right down beside her, their thighs touching, and he turned on his phone and used it like a flashlight to show her her drink.

"It's really dark in here," she said apologetically.

"I kind of like it." And his hand had slipped along her forearm, sending her nerve endings into high gear.

She honestly couldn't remember all that much about the rest of the evening, except that he drove her home and kissed her lightly on the lips at the front door of her crappy apartment. She'd told him she was a teacher's aide, and had said she was working on her degree; she remembered that much. And she did recall throwing herself into his arms and planting a sloppy kiss back at him.

Embarrassing!

But he'd laughed, squeezed her, and said that he would keep in touch.

She'd thought that would be the end of it, but he was as good as his word, texting her from every city he visited. Two weeks after that first encounter he was back, and that time she'd let him into her bedroom. Actually, she'd practically dragged him in, and he'd made love to her so sweetly she'd fought back tears. Luckily, she hadn't broken down and cried. How juvenile would that have been? At the door he'd kissed her hard enough to make her toes curl.

"When will you be back?" she'd asked, dying inside at the thought of not seeing him for a while. She would die without him. Just die.

"Next Saturday night. Take the last ferry out of Friday Harbor to Orcas Island," he told her.

"The last ferry? I could come earlier," she said eagerly.

"No. The last ferry. Go to the upper deck. I'll have something special for you."

So, here she was, cruising along. The sun had sunk into the sea and there was a quiet somnolence to the humming engines and near-empty boat. She couldn't concentrate on her book. She half-expected something amazing to happen, like he might suddenly appear or something, but so far there'd been no surprises.

Bzzz. She jumped when she heard the text.

I see you, little bird.

She looked around wildly, eagerly. He was here? *Where?*

And then she spied him on the outside deck, peering through the window at her. He lifted a hand in greeting, his grin a slash of white. Abandoning her book, she ran to the door, sliding it open, and was greeted by a slap of cold sea air and a buffeting wind. When she rounded the corner he'd disappeared from where he'd looked at her through the window. "Where are you?" she called, but the wind threw her words back into her throat.

"Right here."

He was behind her, grabbing her around the waist.

She laughed in delight and tried to turn to face him, but he wouldn't have it. She realized he was humping her from behind.

"I want you, little bird. Right here. Right now."

"Are you crazy?" She giggled. "Anybody could come up on us!"

"But they won't. Come on."

And there she was sprawled facedown on the wet deck and he was yanking down her jeans and pulling up her hips, jamming himself inside her, pumping hard and fast. It hurt like hell and she couldn't help the little yelp of pain, though she tried to stifle it. She acquiesced, her eyes sliding around in fear, hoping against hope no one would discover them.

She was relieved when it was over. "Good, huh?" he breathed in her ear, one hand gripping her breast almost painfully.

"Good," she murmured, reaching for the jeans that were pooled around her ankles. She was in an ungainly position, on her hands and knees, when he suddenly swooped her to her feet, finally turning her to look at him.

"My pants," she whispered, trying to grab them with her right hand.

"You don't need them where you're going."

"What?"

"Birds need to fly."

And then he picked her up with furious strength and tossed her over the rail. She was so stunned she didn't cry out until the water closed over her head. She gulped in a deluge, flailing, dragged down by the jeans tangled around her ankles, unable to kick with any strength. By the time she could make a sound, the ferry had churned away into the blackness, and the wind shrieked louder than her voice. She screamed and screamed, but she was no match for the gales that tore across the surface of the water.

The last sight she had on this earth were the ferry lights, growing smaller and smaller, finally winking out.

Then she sank beneath the cold, black water one final time.

Chapter One

Andi gazed down at the toes of her black flats, her most comfortable work shoes. The right heel was scuffed from long hours resting on the carpet of her Hyundai Tucson as she'd pressed down on the accelerator. She supposed she really ought to put some polish on it. It wasn't going to get better by itself.

She sat in a chair with smooth oak arms and a blue cushion, her vision focused on the commercial gray carpet that ran the length of the reception area. Minutes elapsed, their passing accompanied by a flat hum in her ears. She'd been in this same suspended state for over three months, ever since Greg's death. Friends and family had consoled her over losing her husband, murmuring words of encouragement and hope, and she'd tried to acknowledge their kindness.

But what if you don't feel anything? What if your husband's infidelity creates a different truth? What if your grief is from the shock of change and not the actual loss of your spouse?

The only person she'd told her true feelings to was Dr. Knapp, her therapist, the woman to whom Greg had steered her when she'd been so depressed, and that was *before* his death.

But you loved Greg once, didn't you?

She reopened her eyes. After four years of marriage, three failed IVF procedures, one ugly affair—his, not hers—where Greg's lover had turned up pregnant—oh, yes, *that* had happened—her love for him was a whole lot harder to remember.

She looked around the waiting room. A twentysomething woman with dark hair and the drawn, faraway look of the utterly hopeless sat across the room. Andi wondered if some terrible fate had befallen her. She suspected she'd had that same look on her face when she'd learned the last IVF implantation hadn't taken. And she may have looked that way when she'd learned Greg's Lexus had veered off the road that encircled Schultz Lake and plunged into the water. One moment she was lost in her failure to start a family, the next she was a widow.

Greg's two siblings, Carter and Emma, were grieving and sympathetic to Andi's loss until they learned she'd inherited 66 percent of Wren Development, the family business started by Douglas Wren, Carter and Emma's grandfather, whereas they'd only gotten 17.5 percent apiece. Andi had become the major stockholder upon Greg's death. Now they couldn't stand dealing with her, especially since she'd become part of the company. Couldn't stand that she was "in the way." Her business degree didn't matter. They just wanted her gone.

The inner door opened and a nurse in blue scrubs said, "Mrs. Wren? Dr. Ferante will see you now."

Slinging the strap of her purse over her shoulder, Andi followed after her through the door she held open. They walked down polished floors that squeaked beneath the crepe soles of the nurse's shoes. She hadn't wanted to make this appointment, but the gray fog that wouldn't lift from around her wasn't normal. And the weight on her chest was killing her. Her therapist had prescribed pills for her, but they hadn't seemed to help and she'd stopped taking them.

But she'd been so tired that she'd made an appointment and had blood work done. This was her follow-up.

Dr. Ferante was a middle-aged Hispanic woman with short, curly black hair, white teeth, and a brisk, friendly manner. Andi sat down on the crinkly paper on the end of the examining table and waited for some answers.

Now, she studied the woman who'd been Greg's doctor first, after the family's longtime physician had retired. Greg hadn't known what to think of his first woman physician, but Andi had sensed Dr. Ferante was a straight shooter.

"So, am I going to be okay?" Andi asked, smiling faintly, though it was an effort.

When Dr. Ferante didn't immediately answer, Andi's heart clutched a bit. Oh God. She hadn't believed she was really sick.

"You're pregnant."

Andi's mouth dropped open. "What! No. I'm not."

"I ran the test three times."

"I can't be. I *can't* be."

"I assure you, you are. You're a little over three months, best guess."

Andi stared at her. She couldn't breathe. Couldn't *think*.

"I even checked to make sure your results weren't mixed up with someone else's," Dr. Ferante went on, "though it would be highly unlikely. The lab's extremely careful and has a wonderful reput—"

"I don't believe you!"

Dr. Ferante cut off what she was about to say and nodded instead. "I understand this is overwhelming. You've been through a lot in a very short time. But I think this is good news, right?" she said gently.

"But the IVFs failed."

"You've said you've been lacking in energy. That you haven't been able to focus. This is why. This and your grief," she said. "Call your gynecologist and make an appointment."

Andi couldn't process. Boggled, she quit arguing with Dr. Ferante and allowed herself to be led toward the door. Her brain was whirling like a top. Three months . . . the baby, of course, was Greg's. They'd had that attempt at reconciliation after the horror of learning about Mimi Quade's pregnancy, which Greg had furiously denied being any part of. Greg had died before any testing could prove otherwise, and in the three months since, there had been no contact with Mimi or her brother, Scott.

Andi's hands felt cold and numb and she stared down at them as if they weren't attached to her arms. She climbed into her Hyundai Tucson and sat there for a moment, staring through the windshield. Then she pulled out her cell phone, scrolling to her gynecologist, Dr. Schuster's, number. When the receptionist answered, she said in a bemused voice, "This is Andrea Wren and I've been told I'm pregnant, so I guess I need an appointment."

"Wonderful!" the woman said warmly. Carrie. Her name was Carrie, Andi recalled.

"I'm having trouble processing this. I just want to be sure."

"How far away are you? Dr. Schuster had a last-minute cancellation today, but the appointment's right now."

"Oh God. I can be there in fifteen minutes. Will that work?"

"Just," Carrie said, then added, "Drive carefully."

Andi aimed her car out of the medical complex and toward the familiar offices of Dr. Schuster's IVF offices, which were across the Willamette River to Portland's east side. She made the trip in twenty-three minutes, gnashing her teeth when it took several more minutes to find a parking spot. Slamming out of the SUV, she remote locked it as she hurried toward the covered stairs on the west side of the building, refusing to wait for the elevator. She hadn't felt this much urgency since before Greg's death.

When she entered the reception room, her face was flushed and her heartbeat light and fast. She scanned the room and settled on the woman at the curved reception counter. Carrie, who was somewhere in her forties, with straight, brown hair clipped at her nape, about Andi's same shade and length, though Andi's was currently hanging limply to her shoulders. She'd combed it this morning, but that was about as far as she'd gotten after showering, brushing her teeth, and getting dressed. She'd thrown on some mascara, the extent of her makeup.

"Go on through," Carrie urged her, coming around the desk to hold open the door to the hallway beyond. "Second door on your right."

"Thank you."

She seated herself on the end of the examining table. Suddenly her body felt hot all over, and she sensed she was going to throw up. It was as if her mind, having accepted this new truth, had convinced her body. She knew where the nearest bathroom was and ran for the door. Too late. She was already heaving. She grabbed the nearest waste can, with its white plastic kitchen bag, moments before losing the remains of her earlier coffee and a muffin.

When her stomach stopped feeling as if it were turning itself inside out, she grabbed some tissues from the box of Kleenex on the counter and wiped her lips. Then she leaned under the faucet at the small stainless-steel sink and washed the sour taste from her mouth. Pregnant, she thought again, struggling to process. *Pregnant!*

Her eyes fell on a pictorial representation of a woman's body in the last trimester, the position of the fetus, the swelling of the mother's abdomen. Tentatively, she placed her hand over her still-quivering midsection.

The doctor bustled in a few minutes later. She was in her fifties, with thick, steel-gray hair that curved beneath her chin and looked surprisingly chic and healthy. Behind frameless glasses, her eyes were a startling light blue and peered at you as if you were a specimen in a jar. Dr. Schuster worked hard to effect pregnancies, but she didn't exhibit a warm and fuzzy manner.

Andi confessed, "I threw up in your trash can."

"We'll take care of it. I understand you think you're pregnant?"

"My doctor, Dr. Ferante, just told me I was."

"Okay."

She gave Andi a routine exam, and once again her blood was drawn. The doctor looked thoughtful but wasn't going to give out any answers before she was ready. It was another ten minutes before she returned to the room and, holding Andi's file to her chest, said with a slight softening of her manner, "Yes, you are pregnant."

Heat flooded Andi's system. She didn't know whether to laugh or cry. "Greg's been gone for three months."

"That's about how far along you are."

"After all this time . . . all the effort," Andi said now, swallowing.

"When the stress is off, sometimes it happens like this."

Andi knew that. She just hadn't completely believed it.

She and Dr. Schuster talked about what was in store in the next few months: a healthy diet, light exercise, plenty of rest. At the reception desk Andi consulted the calendar on her cell phone and lined up future appointments. She left the medical offices in a state of wonderment, driving back toward her house, the one she'd just sold, feeling like she was living a dream. She wondered briefly if she should have held on to the house, but it was too late now. She'd purchased one of the older cabins on Schultz Lake, the very lake that was the scene of Wren Development's latest endeavor—a lodge at the north end that had just begun construction—and her real estate agent had delivered the keys the night before. She'd sold the house she'd shared with Greg because that part of her life was over.

She pulled into her drive. Andi still had some packing to do and the new buyers were giving her through the weekend to move. She'd managed to box up most of her belongings, forcing herself to fill one box per day or it would never happen, but now the push was on. Even though she was pregnant, she had a renewed sense of energy. What had seemed like an insurmountable task now felt doable.

Pregnant . . . !

Her cell buzzed as she was climbing from the SUV. She looked down to find a text from her best friend, Trini.

Tomorrow at the club?

Andi and Trini had a long-standing Tuesday/Thursday morning workout schedule, which Andi had completely abandoned after Greg's death. Now she texted back You bet and immediately received All right! along with a winking emoticon happy face.

Would she tell Trini about the baby? No . . . not yet. Ditto Carter and Emma. She needed some time to process this. It felt too precious to reveal yet. She had no doubt Carter and Emma would be horrified. She was already the interloper, and now Greg's *child* . . . She could already hear them talking about her behind her back, perhaps mounting a lawsuit to claim back the company; that would be just like them.

Her pulse fluttered as she thought about when she would deliver the news. She was three months and not even showing. She had time. Greg's brother and sister were trying to put a good face on the fact that she was both majority stockholder and a capable business associate, but it was taking all they had. Since Greg's death they'd been too involved in other business problems, chiefly the quiet war Wren Development was having with the Carrera brothers, who were trying to take over all the properties surrounding Schultz Lake, to put all their concentration on Andi's position in the company. The Carreras were thugs who used fair means or foul—mostly foul, actually—to achieve their goals; they had tried to put a moratorium on building, not for any reason other than to stop the Wrens. Greg, Carter, and Emma had been handling the project, which involved slogging through and complying with all the county ordinances on the one hand, and dealing with twins Brian and Blake Carrera on the other. Greg's death had put Andi in the thick of it even while she moved through life as an automaton, but the project had gone forward anyway.

Andi's emotional fog had allowed Greg's siblings to run things any way they wanted these past few months, but she'd set up a meeting with them for later today at the site. Even through her numbness, she'd been irked at the way they'd dismissed her, and now that she'd surfaced, she planned to take control of her life and her place in Wren Development.

And what a way to surface . . . *she was having a baby . . . a Wren heir.*

The house Greg had insisted on buying for them was over three thousand square feet, a big, square contemporary settled among other big, square contemporaries. Andi parked in the driveway next to the Sirocco Realty sign with its red, diagonal "Sale Pending" banner. She'd already signed papers and the house had closed, so she had through this coming weekend to move, and it was just a matter of schlepping boxes and getting her furniture taken by truck. She couldn't wait to move into the cabin.

She hit the remote for the garage and looked at the wall of boxes waiting for her. She'd left a small trail to the back

door and traversed it now, letting herself into the sleek
kitchen with its stainless appliances and sink, deeply veined,
dark slab granite, and glass-and-chrome cabinets. No more
stainless-steel cleaner, she thought with a sense of freedom.
Her cabin was rustic. Not "decorator" rustic. More like old-
time, maybe-there-are-mice-in-the-walls rustic.

She was going to have her work cut out for her and she
didn't care.

Of course everyone had told her to wait. Selling your
home wasn't the sort of decisions to make when you were
still grieving. She didn't see how she could explain that
she'd never liked the house anyway, that she'd been dragged
along by a husband who earnestly believed his wishes were
her wishes, and who argued with her whenever she disagreed, certain he could make her see that her opinion was
faulty, that she just needed to see his side. She'd learned to
rarely fight with him, to pick the few battles carefully for
which she would go to the mat. Whenever she did, Greg
would roll his eyes and smile, like she was a crazy woman,
and finally lift his hands as if she'd been blasting him with
artillery fire, drawling, "Oh . . . kay," in a way that meant
he would acquiesce, but she would be sorr . . . eee, no doubt
about it. His behavior had put her teeth on edge more than
once, but she'd never seriously considered divorce until
maybe Mimi. She understood Greg had thought their
marriage was stronger than she had, but his perception was
always different than hers, so she'd let him believe what
he wanted. People were individuals, and as the French said,
vive la différence.

And there had been those times when she and Greg
did see eye to eye, most of those times being when they
were discussing Wren Development and Carter and
Emma's involvement. Greg thought both of them would be
poor stewards of the profitable company founded by his
grandfather, and Andi had agreed. Of course, she'd believed

Greg would be the person in charge, never dreaming she would be the one left holding the reins.

She stalked past the heaps of boxes in the foyer and dining room. She didn't know where she would put everything in her two-bedroom cottage. Half of her belongings were going into storage as it was, and she'd made a pledge to herself that she would empty out the storage unit before a calendar year had passed, using, selling, or giving away everything inside. She had until Sunday evening to move. It was Wednesday, so that gave her five days.

Andi hurried up the stairs. She didn't want to be late for the meeting with Carter and Emma and have to explain what kind of doctor she'd visited. Until it became too obvious to hide, she would keep her condition a secret.

Her steps hesitated in the hallway as she passed the doorway of the spare bedroom she'd planned as a nursery. It was painted a bright yellow, and there was a chest of once-scarred pine drawers, a piece of Greg's from his childhood, that Andi had repainted white. That was as far as their plans for a family had gone. She'd wanted to wait until she knew what sex the child was before decorating further.

She wondered now if Mimi knew the sex of her baby. She'd tried so hard not to think about Greg's mistress and her child, whether that baby really was Greg's.

Shaking her head in disbelief, she went on to the master bedroom, which was done in tones of cream with touches of green, its heavy Mediterranean furniture Greg's choice. He would never have gone for the Schultz Lake cabin even though Wren Development was building the new lodge, heralding a new era for the whole lake community. It wouldn't matter how many people were making the cabins their primary residences. In Greg's world, that wasn't how it worked.

But now Greg was gone, and Andi was in the thick of the lodge construction. As for the rest of Wren Development's projects, she didn't really know much about them; she hadn't been privy to all the ins and outs of the company.

Glancing into the mirror, Andi checked her outfit—gray slacks and jacket over a white silk blouse with its looping bow. She decided her clothes looked presentable enough for the meeting. Her black pumps could use a polish, but she didn't have time and had no idea what box the polish might be in. They would suffice and only had a slight heel, nothing like the crazy three-inchers some of the young women wore to the office. Jill, the Wren Development receptionist, always looked like she was about to teeter over, popping ligaments and tendons along the way. Andi had never been one for super high heels in any case, but with her pregnancy, her footwear would definitely be heading into the supersensible range, a facet clotheshorse Emma could pick up on, if she was ever sober enough to notice. Greg's sister was flirting with a serious drinking problem, though no one seemed to be addressing that elephant in the room either.

Ten minutes later she was on her way toward the lodge, where her meeting was scheduled for eleven thirty. She glanced at the clock on her dash again and saw it was eleven straight up. Could she stop by the cabin and still be on time for the meeting? Not really. But the keys to the cabin were in her purse and she hadn't had time to check things out until now. She might be a little late to the meeting, but so far neither Carter nor Emma even viewed her as a viable partner, so . . .

The cabin was down a rutted lane, like most of them were on the west side of the lake. Tiny fir branches and needles made a carpet that crackled as she drove away from the main road. A low September sun sent slanting rays into her eyes and she squinted as she angled beneath the arc of a natural arbor, formed by the sweeping branches of Douglas firs on either side. The greenery created the frame for a beautiful picture as Andi drove forward toward her new home at the edge of the lake. At least it would have been beautiful if the cabin hadn't looked so decrepit. The moss-covered roof was first on her repair list, and the weathered gray board-and-batten siding needed to be repainted. The front porch listed a little, causing the southernmost post to dip, and therefore the roof above it.

She pulled to a stop and hurried up the two wooden steps, aware that one board was loose. She'd gotten the property "as is" on a short sale and was prepared to make repairs. Digging in her purse for her new keys, she had to untangle them from her old ones. Then she threaded the key into the lock, only to have the door open before she even twisted it.

Unlocked?

Andi frowned. Had her realtor forgotten to lock it? Or . . .

She checked the dead bolt and realized the jamb was broken out, making it impossible to lock it satisfactorily. *Huh*. She was pretty sure it hadn't been that way before.

Her stomach clenched. She was worried her home had been broken in to by vandals, but a cursory glance from the porch into the living room/dining nook showed the place was undisturbed. Carefully, she stepped inside, walking through the first two rooms to the kitchen. It sported old, scarred linoleum and chipped gray Formica. The pine cabinets, with their black, rustic hinges, were just as sorry and beaten up as they'd been when she'd seen them the last time, just before closing. No vandalism she could detect.

She retraced her steps and headed down the short hallway toward the bedrooms. The second bedroom still smelled musty, and the dust on the bedstead and sagging mattress, "gifts" from the previous owner, looked as if it had been there since the ice age. The hall bath looked okay, and as she crossed into the master bedroom, she let out a pent-up breath.

Then her eyes fell on the brown envelope lying atop the bare mattress on the bed. ANDREA was spelled out in block letters on its face. Andi's brain tried to tell her that Edie, her realtor, had left it for her, but no one addressed her as Andrea.

Her heartbeat quickened as she walked forward and picked up the envelope by its edge. Sliding a finger under the flap, which wasn't glued down, she carefully pulled out the hard white notecard. More block letters:

LITTLE BIRDS NEED TO FLY.

She stared in confusion. What? She lost her grip and the card fluttered to the floor. Immediately she bent to pick it up, trying hard to be careful, but it took an effort to get it back in the envelope without smearing her own fingerprints on it. Her mouth was dry, spitless. She didn't know what the words signified, but they sounded ominous. A play on her last name, she guessed, but *what did they mean?*

And who'd left it for her?

Gooseflesh rose on her arms and she scurried out to the safety of her car.

Chapter Two

I've made my first move. I want my opponent to get a first clue, a small inkling, nudge, worry, that the game's afoot. I look around my special room and see the boxes of board games from my youth, dusty now from disuse. The old grinder, desktop computer where I once spent hours in play now sits idle. I don't need any of them any longer.

I dream and strategize and plot. My vision is far in the future.

But there's much to do.

The echoing sound of hammers greeted Andi as she drove along the chunky gravel that made up the temporary driveway to the lodge. The structure currently rose three stories, a skeleton of wood and steel that the framers were pounding at furiously. When the building was finished, the exterior would be shingles, the roof slate, similar in style to the lodge at Crater Lake National Park, though not nearly so grand in size. It had been Greg's idea for the homage to the 1930s lodge in southern Oregon, and Andi had loved it. Carter had been less enthusiastic about the idea, though he'd acquiesced in the end. Emma hadn't really cared one way or another, apart from how much it was costing them and when they would see some income.

Carter was already at the site, leaning against his shiny black BMW, ankles crossed, wearing a green golf shirt and tan chinos, his expression unreadable. He turned on a smile when he saw Andi approach, but like always, she got the feeling it was an effort for him. Greg's little brother could be charming, but he was a shade too impressed with his own good looks for its spell to last long, except maybe on the string of pretty and vacant girlfriends he had as a retinue. He was smart, though, and had kept the project on track since Greg's death. Andi wasn't really sure what Carter thought about the lodge and lake community as a whole. Meanwhile, his sister could offer well-thought-out insights, at least when she was sober and when she was interested, but that was less and less lately. Today she was nowhere in sight as Andi pulled to a stop and got out.

"How're you doing?" Carter asked.

"Fine."

The note was fresh on her mind and she wanted to tell someone, anyone, about it. She opened her mouth to do just that, but then Carter asked lightly, "No recent blackouts?"

The words shriveled on her tongue. "What?"

"The blackouts. Since Greg's death? Oh, come on. It's the fucking elephant in the room."

Her heart started pounding painfully. "I've lost focus a few times. I didn't realize it was such a problem."

"You don't remember passing out in the conference room?"

"Carter!" She almost laughed, but then realized he was deadly serious.

"Andi, you were out for fifteen minutes. Emma thought you were drunk, but then, she thinks everyone's drunk."

"It wasn't fifteen minutes." Andi recalled the strangeness, the dizziness . . . and yes, the disorientation in the conference room. "I was dehydrated . . . I lost time . . . I was . . ." *Pregnant.*

"This is why, Andi. *This* is why you can't run the company like I know you want to."

"I don't want to run the company. Where do you get that? But I'm majority stockholder and yes, I want to be a part of it."

"It's hard enough with Emma, and she's family."

Andi felt her face grow hot. He was exaggerating, but she should have told her doctors about her lapses in focus. "I've been to a doctor," she said.

"Good. What'd he say?"

"*She* said there's nothing wrong." A lie, but she wasn't about to tell him the truth.

"Your guru shrink tell you that? You need to go to a real doctor."

"Dr. Knapp is a psychiatrist," Andi answered tightly, "and I didn't see her anyway. Where's Emma?" she asked, looking back toward the road.

"Did you check Lacey's parking lot as you drove by?"

Lacey's was a shitkicker bar about a half mile from the lodge on the north road. It had scarred wooden chairs and tables, a clientele with a taste for Jack Daniel's and hot, oily fries, country and western music on the jukebox, and a tiny outside area for smokers that was always in high demand.

"I didn't come that way. I came from my cabin." She'd rather eat larvae than say anything about the note now.

"Ah, the cabin. It's yours now?"

"I'm moving in this weekend."

"You sure you're all right?" he asked, peering at her in a penetrating way.

"You're the one in a bad mood."

"You noticed. Well, no shit. You're late, Emma's God knows where, and I've got a meeting with Harlow Ransom this afternoon." When Andi didn't immediately respond, he said, "The county planner?"

"I know who he is."

"Somebody's gotta knock some sense into his head. If Ransom has his way, we won't be able to subdivide the larger lots and those north shore cabins'll remain the squatter palaces they are."

He was specifically referring to a series of cabins similar to the one Andi had just purchased that had been sold to Wren Development in a block. No one had done any upkeep on them since the 1940s and they were all still standing by the grace of God. The Carrera brothers had made an offer for them, but the cabins' cantankerous ninety-year-old owner had bullishly resisted, selling out lock, stock, and barrel to the Wrens before suffering a fatal heart attack.

"I thought we were clear on that property."

"Ransom's always sided with the Carreras," he said. "This is what I mean, Andi. You have no business in the business. For all kinds of reasons."

"So, is Emma coming?" Andi asked tightly.

He shook his head and brushed imaginary dirt from his slacks as he straightened. "Doesn't look like it, does it?"

"Are you going to the office later?"

"I doubt it. Ransom isn't the only person I have to see. Why?"

"Well, actually, I thought maybe we would meet Emma there later, then, but I guess not."

"Just go home and we'll take this up tomorrow."

"Fine."

They both went silent. She expected him to take off, but instead Carter yanked his cell phone from his pocket and, tight-lipped, stabbed out a number. After a series of rings, he pressed the Off button, and muttered tightly, "Emma's 'not available.'" There was a good chance he was right about Emma. Her drinking was escalating.

"I'll see you, and damn well better see Emma, in the conference room tomorrow at ten," Carter said, wrenching open his driver's door. He drove away carefully, herding his baby over the rough gravel, before punching the accelerator once the BMW was safely on the blacktop two-lane county road that circled the lake.

Andi stayed rooted to the spot for long moments. Carter pissed her off, but he'd shaken her with his comments about her loss of focus. She thought about the prescription Dr. Knapp, her "guru shrink," as Carter had called her, had given to her, the antidepressants she'd taken for a while but had let slide. Maybe she'd reacted to them. Maybe that was the problem. Except the conference room episode had been recent.

She yanked out her cell and called Dr. Knapp but learned she couldn't get an appointment until the following week. Well, fine. She was moving this weekend anyway. She would tell the doctor about her pregnancy when she saw her, and she'd also tell her about the note left at her cabin.

You should tell the police.

And what would she say? *Someone broke into my cabin and left a message that said* Little birds need to fly? They would probably tell her it was a prank.

But by whom?

She bit her lip, then called Edie at Sirocco Realty but learned the agent was out of the office. When Edie's voice mail came up, Andi said, "Hey, this is Andi Wren and I went to my cabin this morning and the front door was open. It looks like the latch is broken. I don't remember it being that way before, but maybe. Anyway, someone was in there and left a note on the bed in the master for me. Give me a call and let's talk."

After that she got in the Tucson and took the north road on her return to her house in Laurelton. A whisper of apprehension slid down her spine as she drove along the hairpin

turn where Greg had driven off the road. His Lexus hadn't
made the last bend and he'd broken through the guardrail
and flown off the edge of the cliff that rimmed this, the
highest point above Schultz Lake and one of the most
dangerous spots on the road. The guardrail had been replaced,
but Andi couldn't help throwing a quick glance over the
edge, the view of firs and pines blocking all but a scintilla
of green water far below.

Ten minutes later she cruised past Lacey's, checking the
parking lot for Emma's car, but of course it wasn't there.
Lacey's wouldn't be the kind of place Emma would choose
for her drinking. Too low-class. Andi thought about stopping
in for a burger and fries herself, a craving she'd developed
in the last few weeks—one she understood better now—but
with nutrition high on her mind, she turned off the lake road
and onto Sunset Highway toward a place near the Wren
Development offices simply called The Café. She ordered
a chicken salad sandwich on thick-sliced wheat bread and
ate half of it at the bistro, taking the second half back with
her to her house, where she spent the next three hours packing up the last of her boxes.

She then whiled away the rest of the afternoon and
evening reading her myriad of baby books, the ones she'd
initially packed away but had now dragged from their
boxes, dreaming about renovating the second bedroom of
the cabin into a nursery. Edie texted her around four to say
she'd sent someone to the cabin to check on the lock and
that she would call her in the morning. Andi gingerly pulled
the envelope with the note from her purse, then put it in the
bag she used for her laptop. She ate the second half of her
sandwich for dinner and then packed up the meager items
left in her refrigerator, putting them in another empty card-
board box: ketchup, mustard, a small carton of half and
half cream, and a jar of dill relish. The rest of the refrigerator

detritus she tossed out, ready for the last collection of her garbage.

Lying in bed that night, she pushed thoughts of the disturbing note aside and concentrated on the joy of her pregnancy. She would go over everything with Dr. Knapp soon enough. Her thoughts turned to her friends and family, her brother, Jarrett, her mother, Diana, who lived across the country in Boston, and of course, her closest friend, Trini, whom she was seeing the next day. She wondered when she should tell them about the baby. She almost didn't want to say anything at all, worried that it would break the spell somehow.

With no clear answer in mind, she drifted off to sleep.

She was awakened by a summer storm and flung back the covers and crossed to the window, watching lightning streak across the sky before hearing the rumble of thunder. Electrical storms were rare in Oregon and thrilling. Fascinated, she eagerly waited for another flash.

The storm reminded her of one evening vacationing at one of the cabins with her mother, father, and brother. Jarrett had shaken her awake to watch the lightning with him. Their parents were already on the back porch overlooking the lake, each with a glass of scotch. It was the summer before her parents split up, but she was blissfully ignorant of any familial disharmony as they all waited for the next brilliant flash.

Jarrett had pointed to the black water. "If you were out there in the middle, you'd get zapped and you'd be dead."

"It's a good thing we're not out there, then," her father rejoined, his voice slightly slurred.

"Like in a boat," Jarrett stressed, "all by yourself."

"I'd never do that," Andi told her brother indignantly.

"Of course you wouldn't," Mom responded.

Jarrett had ignored them both. "If you wanted to get rid of somebody, that's how you'd do it, and no one would ever know. Take 'em out in a boat in a lightning storm."

"Timing wise, that would be impractical," her father said, though it came out *impragdigal*. "You want to kill somebody you'd need a better plan."

"Jim," Mom warned.

"Come on, Diana. We're just talking. Your coddling knows no bounds."

And then he'd tossed the rest of his drink onto the floor, splashing Mom's pant leg in the process before stomping off to bed.

Now, Andi crawled back into her own bed and wondered at the vagaries of memory, how sharp that one was, though her father had been out of their lives for years, succumbing to liver cancer five years earlier. Her mother called sporadically from Boston, where she'd moved after the divorce from Andi's father. Soon, thereafter—too soon, in Andi's opinion—she'd married a man named Tom DeCarolis whom Andi barely knew. Her mother had given birth to two more children with him whom Andi knew mostly through dutiful Christmas cards. Diana Sellers DeCarolis had drifted out of Andi and Jarrett's life and into a new one across the country. Jarrett had moved to California for a while, tried a few different colleges but had returned to Oregon several years earlier and now worked for a wealthy restauranteur. She didn't see much of him either. He'd called her after Greg's death, but the conversation had been stilted, more because he'd once dated Trini and, after their ragingly dysfunctional relationship's blowup ending, he didn't seem to know how to deal with his sister any longer.

Now Andi stared up at the ceiling and listened to distant thunder, remembering uneasily that Jarrett had occasionally passed out unexpectedly when he was younger as well, although she was pretty sure his blackouts had been heat-related. A hot room with little or no air flow had contributed to the problem, which was common for lots of people. Nothing malignant about it. Still, she should probably ask him if he still experienced blackout periods.

She finally drifted back to sleep and woke with a heavy feeling that dogged her while she was getting ready to go to the club. She pushed her worries aside, concentrating instead on her pregnancy, as she drove to SportClub Laurelton and headed for her favorite treadmill. Light exercise, Dr. Schuster had said, and Andi planned to follow her advice to a tee. In black sweats and a dark gray tank, she kept a steady pace just under a jog. With her gaze on the television news program overhead, she tamped down the questions that circled endlessly through her mind. The current broadcast was from a blond woman who was delivering a stern reminder of the fire hazard that still was in evidence; they'd had little to no rain throughout August and September.

Sweat beaded on her forehead, but Andi doggedly pushed forward, internally monitoring her body's vitals. Her heart rate was elevated some, but she was still breathing fairly easily, unlike the man who'd taken the treadmill to her left and was now running full tilt, each step accompanied by a *huh* of effort, so that she heard *huh, huh, huh, huh, huh* in counterpoint to the newscaster.

She thought about her cabin, wondering how many boxes she could fit in her car. Most of the boxes were filled with Greg's belongings; of the two of them, she'd had lesser "things" when they'd entered into their marriage, and she hadn't amassed tons more since.

The blond newscaster turned over the program to an earnest-looking, dark-haired male reporter who was standing in front of the Multnomah County Courthouse in downtown Portland. ". . . hearing is slated for nine a.m. for Ray

Bolchoy, who's been accused of allegedly creating false evidence to prove twin brothers Blake and Brian Carrera used coercion to gain control of property around Schultz Lake . . ."

Andi looked up sharply. She knew about the Portland homicide detective who believed the Carrera brothers were responsible for several mysterious deaths around the greater Portland area. However, she hadn't known his hearing was today. She wondered if the DA had enough evidence to convince the judge to go to trial. She didn't know if Bolchoy was guilty of falsifying evidence or not, but she knew the Carrera brothers' tactics were just short of criminal . . . maybe flat-out criminal.

There was a picture of the gray-haired Bolchoy with a much younger man whose rakish good looks Andi had seen before. Bolchoy's ex-partner. ". . . Lucas Denton," the reporter said, reminding Andi of his name, "who gave up his career as a homicide detective when Bolchoy was put on administrative leave . . ."

Next a clip was shown of Denton talking to a different reporter outside a strip mall office beneath a sign that read "Denton Investigations." "I'm not discussing Ray's intentions with the media," Lucas Denton said, clearly annoyed at being caught outside his place of business. "All I know is that I didn't like how things came down, so I quit."

"But do you think Bolchoy's guilty?"

"We're all guilty of something. I'm guilty of wanting the Carreras to go down for their crimes."

The reporter kept the microphone close to Denton's mouth, though he tried to turn away. "Did Bolchoy falsify evidence?"

"Now you're not listenin' close, are ya? I'm not discussing Ray's intentions with the media."

"People say he's hard to know, but that you, his homicide partner of several years, were as close to him as anyone."

"We weren't dating, if that's what you want to know," Denton said dryly, unlocking his office and stepping inside.

That reporter looked like he'd sucked on a lemon, and Andi found herself smiling. The onscreen view returned to the earnest-looking man outside the courthouse, who concluded, "Ex-homicide detective Lucas Denton, who turned in his badge over his anger at the way his partner was treated, has turned to private investigation. Meanwhile, Ray Bolchoy awaits a hearing on whether there's enough evidence to charge him with a crime."

Once more the blond newscaster took over. "And that hearing's today. Stay tuned to this channel and we'll keep you posted."

Talk of the Carreras sent Andi's thoughts to the ten cabins on Lake Schultz's north shore, not far from the lodge construction, that ninety-year-old Mr. Allencore had sold to the Wrens. The Carreras had made a play for the self-same cottages and had both been coldly furious when stubborn Mr. Allencore had gleefully refused them flat-out. He'd died several weeks after the final papers were signed, and sometimes Andi wondered, in a small, secret, paranoid spot of herself, if the Carreras had contributed to the old man's death. The brothers weren't above intense pressure, and she suspected they'd been none too happy when the cottages were outside their grasp. A few well-placed threats and the old man's heart could have given out, although by all accounts it had simply been his time.

The Carrera brothers . . . There were stories and stories about them. Though neither had done anything strictly illegal yet—that they'd been caught at anyway—one of the twins had definitely contributed to a fatal car accident he had walked away from but that had resulted in a young woman's death. That was Blake Carrera, she believed, and his cavalier attitude had infuriated the public to the point that he'd been compelled to issue an apology, though he'd sworn it wasn't his fault. No alcohol or drugs were discovered in his system. It was just an unfortunate driving error when his wheels had locked on a slippery road and he'd spun around and slammed into her car. No criminal charges were filed and, as ever, the Carreras had slipped away from the long arm of the law.

Someone changed the channel and, as if her thoughts had wished it, a brunette woman newscaster popped on the screen with another picture of Ray Bolchoy's grizzled, glowering face. The newscaster was talking about the upcoming hearing as well. "Detective Bolchoy's scheduled court time is nine a.m. today. The expectation is that he will not go to trial, that the evidence against him isn't strong enough. We'll see."

"Thank you, Pauline," a smooth male newscaster said in a tone that suggested he didn't think much of his coanchor. Though he opened his mouth to say something further, someone once again switched the channel to a different station, this one airing a morning program on which the hosts were learning how to incorporate kale into every dish.

Ray Bolchoy. The seasoned Portland Police Department homicide detective had gone after the Carreras hammer and tongs, seeking to pin something on them. He was connected to the woman Blake Carrera had inadvertently killed somehow, Andi thought. Andi slowed her treadmill. She dabbed at her moist face with the towel around her neck. Normally she could go much further, but these were not normal times. And where was Trini? Andi had saved the empty treadmill on her right by throwing her jacket over one of the arms, but now she swept it off, though no one seemed interested in working out on the machine. She decided

she would wait around for a few more minutes, then hit the
showers and get ready for the conference meeting with
Carter and Emma.

Should you tell Trini about the baby?

She wasn't sure. Trini had been no fan of Greg's. A free
spirit, she'd objected from the get-go to Greg's stiff, linear
thinking. Though she'd been there for Andi when he'd
died, had been shocked and sorry he was gone, she hadn't
been able to completely disguise the fact that she was also
relieved Andi was unshackled.

Someone switched the television station yet again; there
appeared to be a war going on between two out-of-view
club employees on what should be shown. There again was
Bolchoy, looking grim and slightly belligerent. The
fiftysomething detective was walking beside his lawyer
toward the courthouse. A bevy of reporters followed after
them. Andi could appreciate the fact that the detective had
tried to do something to make the Carreras pay for their
crimes, even if he'd failed. The fact that the brothers had
been able to steamroll their agenda time and again made
many people question whether they had someone helping
them on the planning commission. Andi would bet on it.
But that person was still in the shadows, and Bolchoy was
on his own.

Reaching for her water bottle, Andi shot a glance at the
huffing runner beside her. He was lean and long-limbed.
She could just see his profile.

Without turning toward her, he asked, "Wha'dya think
of all that?" He lifted a chin toward the screen in between
*huh*s.

Andi took a drink from her water bottle, her gaze back
toward the television. She didn't want to engage with him
or anyone else. The picture had changed to a view of Schultz
Lake. The reporter was explaining how the lake, which sat

on the westernmost edge of Winslow County, just outside
the Laurelton city limits, had always been a mecca for out-
door sports enthusiasts—camping, canoeing, kayaking,
hiking—but over the past few years its rustic cabins and
winding trails had been undergoing a change to more high-
end housing and full-time residents. The area wasn't that
far from Portland's city center and it was even closer to
the Nike campus. Its main drawback to full-time living was
the winding two-lane access road that took at least twenty
minutes to connect with Sunset Highway, the artery that ran
from Hillsboro, Laurelton, and all points west into the city
center. Still, people liked living on the lake and the extra
twenty minutes of commuting was a small price to pay.
Consequently, the values of the lots were skyrocketing.

Andi had tuned out. She knew all this information backward and forward. But then the latest newscaster said,
"Wren Development is building a lodge at the northernmost
point of the lake and they plan to keep the 'summer camp'
feel of the cabins closest to the lodge. To quote deceased
CEO Gregory Wren, 'We want to keep the architecture and
nostalgia, just with modern amenities. Our competitors,
Blake and Brian Carrera, have a different plan in mind.
Their mow-down mentality doesn't take public input into
account. I haven't seen their design, but take a look at their
Portland developments and see for yourself. They're con-
structed of chrome and glass, not shingles and timbers.'"

The man on the treadmill next to her snorted his disgust.
He'd turned his machine off as well, and his steps were
slowing with the belt. Out of the corner of her eye she saw
him wipe his face with his towel. He was still breathing
hard, but his *huh*s had disappeared when he'd stopped
running.

She considered heading for the showers without waiting
for Trini.

". . . brothers Blake and Brian Carrera have filed suit

against Detective Ray Bolchoy for falsifying evidence, along with other members of the Portland Police Department, Detective Opal Amberson and former Detective Lucas Denton." Another picture of Bolchoy, looking dour and cranky. ". . . among others the brothers believe were all part of a smear campaign against them and their development company, Carrera Limited," the newswoman reported.

There followed more shots of Detective Opal Amberson, slim, black, and fierce-looking, and more of Lucas Denton. Andi assessed Denton thoughtfully. He was rangy, dark-haired, with a slight smile that probably invited a lot of confidences. He looked capable. More than capable. Andi had seen lots of photos of both Amberson and Denton. They'd been and still were Bolchoy's staunchest defenders. Denton had left the force over what he believed was the department turning its back on one of their own. She mentally applauded him.

The newswoman finished with, "More later after we learn whether Ray Bolchoy's case is headed to trial."

"Bolchoy's guilty all right," the man now standing on the treadmill said. "Tried to frame us and it blew up in his face."

Andi turned to stare fully at him. Curly, dark hair and a scar across his chin. Oh God. She'd seen his picture a hundred times, too. "You're Blake Carrera."

"It's Brian, actually. And you're the Widow Wren."

Her heart lurched. "You know me?"

"Sure. You're the beauty with the cheating dead husband. I hear you ended up with the lion's share of the company."

"You . . . planned this?" She could hear the thread of fear in her voice as she indicated their side-by-side treadmills.

"Let's just say I knew you came here," he said around a cold smile.

He was too thuggish to be called handsome. There was something cold about him, and his dark eyes were black, emotionless pits. *Why?* she almost asked, but she knew the answer. "Schultz Lake."

He held out a sweaty palm. "Right the first time."

She ignored his outstretched hand. She almost asked him how he'd known when she would be here, but the answer was evident: he knew her routine.

"My friend Trini is meeting me," she heard herself say.

"Good for her," he said.

"I've got to go."

"So soon? We've barely had a chance to talk."

"All talking should be done through our lawyers."

"Sure, sure. But maybe you can pass on some information to your brother- and sister-in-law. Tell them they should be more reasonable. That lodge you're building? It doesn't look like it's safe, y'know? Anything could happen to it."

Andi gazed at him in shock. She had to resist the urge to cradle her abdomen. "Did you just threaten me?"

"I'm just saying, all of you should be more reasonable." He spread his palms. "Given a chance, we could really be good friends. We have common interests, after all."

"Our tactics are vastly different."

He flipped his towel over his shoulder. "Friendship's your best bet. You don't want us for enemies." He winked at her as he strolled away.

Andi's heart was climbing up her throat as she stared after him. With an effort, she jerked her eyes from his retreating figure and back to the newscast, but it was over. She glanced again at his retreating form as he sauntered nonchalantly away, probably whistling. Her knees quivered and she wanted to sit down, but just then Trini came rushing in, her short, tough, gymnast's frame a hard bundle of muscle as she jumped onto the treadmill Carrera had just vacated.

"Sorry I'm late," she said, pushing up the speed so in

seconds she was running as fast as Brian Carrera had been. "Why aren't you jogging?" she asked, her almond-shaped eyes giving Andi a sidelong look.

Andi wasn't sure she was ready to explain to Trini what had just transpired. She wasn't certain herself, but it sure as hell felt like he'd threatened her. "I just finished a workout."

"Oh, come on. Just a few more minutes. I've got news!"

"Go ahead. I'll hit the shower in a few." She didn't want to chance running into Carrera again anyway. Her heart was still galloping.

"How're things going with the project?" Trini asked.

"What project?"

"The lodge, silly. The *big* project."

To date Trini hadn't shown the least bit of interest in anything the Wrens were involved in. She'd not only been against Andi's marriage to Greg but she'd taken off on a long hike with friends through the Himalayas about the time of Andi's wedding, missing the event entirely. And she'd never asked about anything to do with the company.

"You really want to talk about the lodge? That's your news?"

She smiled. "Not really. I want to tell you about my new guy."

"Fire away."

"Well, he came to my Pilates class. Not my usual type. Much more buttoned-down . . . kinda like Greg. I can't believe it myself. It's crazy!"

Andi didn't know what to say. Her head was full of her confrontation with Brian Carrera. Now that it was over, she was feeling shaky with reaction. She finally squeezed out, "Wow."

"I know, right?"

Trini was a Pilates instructor. A gymnast in her youth, she'd majored in health and fitness and had always leaned toward physical fitness and sports. She also had a healthy sexual appetite but couldn't seem to settle down with one guy for long. She went for bodies over minds, where Andi, a business major, had been attracted to men with smarts and senses of humor. Physical attractiveness definitely played a part, but it wasn't the top attribute that drew her in. Greg had been smart and good-looking, maybe not with as refined a sense of humor as some, but she'd been attracted to him. Trini's interest in Jarrett had been more true to form; Andi's brother was a far cry from the buttoned-down type.

"I want you to meet him soon," Trini said, unaware that Andi's mind was elsewhere.

"Sure."

"Not yet. Some things have got to work out first." She laughed, a breathless catch in the back of her throat that was totally unlike her. "You know, one little thing where we're total compadres? He doesn't like shellfish of any kind. Not allergic, like me, just doesn't like the stuff. So happy. Even Jarrett was always ordering shrimp, and I was always freaking out that he'd try to kiss me."

Andi nodded. Trini had told that story a hundred times.

Trini woke up to Andi's distraction. "Where's your head, girl?"

"I'm just tired. Mind if I head out? I've got some things to do."

"Whatever works. But I want you to meet him. Maybe this weekend?"

"Okay, but I'm moving."

"Right, right, right. And I'll help you. I told you I would. And anyway, you still have to eat, so maybe we'll catch a meal together."

"I'll text you," Andi said. Trini had a tendency to promise all kinds of things and then seldom ever came through.

"You're really going to like him," she called as Andi

headed for the locker room, her eyes searching for any sign of Carrera. "I'm telling you, he's more your type than mine."

She seemed to be alone. At least she didn't meet anyone as she slipped into the women's room. There was no one about, so Andi went to her locker and pulled out her bag of clothes, then took a quick shower and redressed.

Her mind was a jumble of images, her emotions raw. She thought about the baby and the note and those tense few moments with Brian Carrera, and Ray Bolchoy and Lucas Denton . . . private investigator.

Determinedly, she set her jaw. She had to protect her baby and herself. And who better to protect her than the man who'd quit his job with the police in solidarity with his friend, who believed the Carreras had literally gotten away with murder?

At her SUV she reached for her cell and made a quick search of Lucas Denton's Internet information. His office was in Laurelton, close by. She flexed her fingers over the steering wheel. She had some errands to run, and there was a good chance Denton would be at the hearing this morning. Putting the vehicle in gear, she backed out of her spot at SportClub Laurelton, feeling better for having a plan.

Chapter Three

Early Thursday morning Luke Denton slowly surfaced and immediately realized he was gonna have one helluva hangover. He was lying on his back, on his bed, and he cracked one eye open at the same time his hand encountered warm human flesh lying beside him. That got him awake. He inched his head around enough to see the bare back and arm of Iris Holchek, his ex-girlfriend.

Well, ain't that a kick in the pants.

She didn't appear to be wearing much of anything. He did a quick tactile survey and was relieved to discover he was shirtless but still in the aged denim jeans he'd worn the night before.

The. Night. Before.

See, this is the problem, Denton. When she broke it off, you should have been an asshole and refused to talk to her anymore. You know you never wanted the relationship. And during those first few weeks of hell after Bolchoy's screwup, she gave you the perfect out. But, oh no, you had to be nice to her. Too polite. Now what the hell are you gonna do?

As if hearing his thoughts, Iris turned over and opened her cool blue eyes. "Hey, lover," she said.

Uh-oh.

"I've been waiting for you to sleep it off, so we could . . ." Her fingers started trailing along his arm and slipped under the covers, tippy-tapping their way down his abdomen toward . . .

He reached down and clamped a hand over her wrist. "Might I ask what you're doing here?"

She smiled that cat-and-cream smile that had once heated his blood but now sent every nerve ending on red alert, and not in a good way. "You were way friendlier last night."

"Last night I was strategizing with friends about Bolchoy."

The chill was immediate. She yanked her hand back and regarded him coldly. "The man's going to jail. I just don't see how you can throw your career away over him." Flinging back the covers, she got out of bed and angrily picked up a scrap of black lace thong underwear that she stepped into, her back to him. Then she shimmied into a tight black dress that he remembered had cost such a fortune he'd thought it was a joke when she'd told him the price. It was her money, so his comment was out of line, but her anger over his disbelief had made him see how the gap between them was expanding, not contracting.

"He's got to go to trial first, and that might not happen."

"I told you. Corkland is putting him away. Gleefully. Bolchoy is a black eye on the department, and no one at Portland PD can save him. That's the mood of the country, lover. Police do bad things, they go to jail, just like everyone else."

"Whatever Bolchoy did wasn't a bad thing."

"Keep telling yourself that." She stepped into tall pewter heels and searched around for her bag. "Meanwhile, my boss is dropping the hammer on him."

She was referring to T.J. Corkland, the district attorney

who had a serious hard-on to put Bolchoy away. Iris worked
in the DA's office and she was just as eager to put Bolchoy
behind bars as her boss, though her reasons were slightly
different. Corkland thought it would look good politically to prove that the police weren't above the law; Iris just
wanted Luke to see what kind of a scumbag his ex-partner
was. She blamed Bolchoy for Luke quitting the force, when
in actuality, Luke had already been pretty fed up with the
powers that be above him who made all the decisions. Bolchoy had overstepped his bounds, allegedly manufacturing
evidence that proved the Carrera brothers' guilt—he'd
probably done it, too, Luke thought with a grimace, knowing his ex-partner's penchant to run around the law—and
the wrath of the department had descended upon him. No
one had Ray's back except Luke and Opal Amberson, and
they'd been warned against picking the wrong team. The
result was Luke quit, and Opal damn near did.

Iris had not been happy when Luke left the department.
After screaming at him for all she was worth, she had
broken up with him, flooding Luke with relief, which her
sharp eyes had caught. She'd been instantly hurt, though
she'd never said anything to him about it, and let's face it,
he hadn't wanted to go into it either.

That had been nearly a year ago. Luke had spent the next
couple of months wondering what the hell to do with his
life. Private security/investigation sort of found him, not
the other way around, and he was still working through
the hours to get his license. This had pissed off Iris no end.
She couldn't *believe* he'd given up being a detective with
the Portland PD for some kind of "half-assed" private practice. Though they'd gotten under his skin, he'd ignored her
rants and had set a course for himself with a determination
that was new to him. Iris was no longer his girlfriend, so he
was a free man and could do whatever he damned well

pleased. Becoming a private investigator was what he chose.

Last night he'd met with Opal and Yates and DeSantos, and they'd all gone down to Tiny Tim's, which was little more than a hole in the wall, with some of the cheapest beer around. Tiny Tim himself, over three hundred pounds, eschewed all the microbeers and cutting-edge cuisine Portland was so famous for these days, and served up favorite standards like Pabst, Bud, and Coors, along with greasy fries, jalapeño poppers with basic ranch dressing or tarted-up with raspberry jam, onion rings, and hot dogs or hamburgers (lettuce and tomato extra, which the clientele didn't often opt for). Tiny Tim's also held a liquor license, and that was where Luke had made his mistake, going for Johnnie Walker Red, sometimes Black, once in a great, great while Blue, depending on how much money he wanted to spend. But last night it wasn't about money and/or quality, it was about quantity, and Luke had had his fill and then some.

"Are you going to the hearing?" Iris asked, drawing on a line of lip gloss with her left index finger.

"I think I'll wait for the CliffsNotes."

"You're not going for the friend you defended so much you *quit your job*?"

"That would be a yes . . . I'm not going."

"I don't believe you."

"You've never understood the finer points of why I quit."

She thrust one fist on her hip. "Maybe you can explain it to me."

"Doubtful," Luke said as he climbed out of bed.

Two bright spots of color bloomed on her cheeks, little red flags of suppressed fury. "You oughta be more grateful to me for pulling you out of that *bar*. If you'd gotten in your car, you'd be in jail just like your good buddy, Ray."

"I wasn't driving. I took Uber."

"You kissed me when we got back here," she declared, practically in a shout.

The noise caused his head to throb. "I was drunk. I was worried about Bolchoy. I'm still worried about him."

"You kissed me!" she repeated.

"I do remember," he snapped, his patience shredding. "You took off my shirt and *you* kissed *me*. I don't know what you want, but whatever it is, it doesn't look like I'm giving it to you. So, I guess I'm saying thank you? For seeing me home?"

"You're such an asshole."

"You're not the first to point that out."

"Jesus, Luke." She glared at him. "When are you going to wake up?"

"I'm awake."

They glared at each other. Luke was the first to break away, his attention distracted as he considered what time it was. He might go to the hearing, but he had an eleven thirty appointment, so maybe not. And Iris didn't have to know until he showed up, or didn't, anyway.

"Bolchoy's going to prison," she said again. "He falsified evidence and Corkland's got him dead to rights."

Luke shrugged. He didn't know exactly what Bolchoy had done and he didn't care anyway.

"Why are you going down for him? He didn't ask you to. If you go back to the department and talk to your lieutenant—"

"I'm not going back."

"—he'd give you your job back. I'm just trying to help you."

"I don't want the job back. I told you. I'm going to keep doing what I'm doing."

"I can't play this game forever, Luke. I mean it." Tears stood in her eyes.

He shook his head. "I gotta get to work." With a

headache threatening to break into a crusher at the back of
his skull, he brushed past her to his walk-in closet, the one
nod to luxury in his two-bedroom/one-bath apartment.

"For God's sake, Luke . . ." she trailed off.

"Iris, go home. Or to the courthouse, or wherever."

"You just can't wait to get rid of me, can you?" she
asked bitterly, sweeping up an airy black scarf that she
threw around her shoulders. Her makeup wasn't even
smeared, and he wondered how the hell she managed that.

"We've been through this scenario before. A couple of
times."

"We need to talk. No matter what you think, we need to
talk."

"I'm all talked out." He pulled out another pair of jeans
and a white shirt, freshly pressed, and took them to the
bathroom. Iris followed him and tried to hold open the door
with the palm of her hand. "Iris," he warned.

"Listen to me. Just listen." She pushed back on the door
when he tried to close it with slow but steady pressure.
"You can't help Bolchoy. He doesn't want to be helped. He
wants to be right, and he's wrong. He forged the Carrera
brothers' names on those confessions. He *admitted* he did
it. This case is not subject to interpretation. You know it and
I know it. It's going to trial."

"The Carreras have intimidated and coerced and threatened. They zero in on their next real estate acquisition and
drive everyone out. They don't care how. They pretend to
offer a fair price, but they never follow through. Anyone
who thwarts them ends up in some kind of 'accident,' or
some other misery befalls them. That's what I know."

"You can't be a one-man vigilante on this. The judicial
system will get them eventually. Go back to Portland PD,
or finish with that law degree. Luke, come on . . . don't let
this get in our way."

He yanked open the bathroom door so hard, she fell

forward and had to catch herself. "I've got a different job now."

"Private investigating?" she said with a sneer. Her eyes widened a moment later when he clamped his hands on her shoulders, turned her around, and steered her toward the front door. She actually tried to dig in her heels and grip the sides of the door frame. "My purse!" she yelled and, with a pungent swear word, he was forced to let go of her.

"Don't move," he warned in a cold voice as he turned back and swept the purse from the nightstand, returning a few moments later and slapping the clutch bag into her hands.

She gripped it in one hand, then raised up both in surrender. "This is ridiculous. Honestly, Luke. Come on."

"You don't like what I do. You don't like my friends. You don't really like me."

"That's not true—"

"Darlin', this is over."

To his consternation, her skin pinkened and he sensed that she was about to cry. She didn't do it often, but she was about to do it now. "I love you," she said tremulously.

He shook his head, unable to come up with an answer to that one. The movement aggravated the headache forming like a storm. He eased Iris out the door, and this time she went meekly, as if all the stuffing had been smacked out of her. It made him feel bad, but not bad enough to change his mind. He needed to be separated from her. For good.

Turning the lock on the door, he headed back to the shower, stripping off his jeans. He stood beneath the hot spray for a good ten minutes, then dressed in the fresh clothes on the counter. He rolled up the sleeves of his shirt to midforearm, then combed out his wet hair, the light brown strands unnaturally dark from the water. He stared into his own blue eyes, registering how harsh the light felt.

Evil drink. What good had it gotten him? Bolchoy wasn't going to go free. Iris had been right about that.

"Rule number one, buddy," the older detective had told Luke when they'd first been partnered. "Stay the fuck out of my way."

Luke had been taken aback. It was his first job as a detective and he'd been assigned to homicide, a real coup. Or, at least he'd thought so in the beginning, until he realized everyone was having a good old hah-hah at his expense because he was teamed with Ray Bolchoy. Nobody, but nobody, wanted to be partnered with the gruff old-timer. Better to stay back in robbery or work missing persons, or vice . . . *anything* but homicide with the stubborn, single-minded detective.

In those early days, Luke had learned that Bolchoy had a lot of rules, although most of them were superseded by rule number one. Luke tried hard to stay the fuck out of his partner's way, though a few times he'd made the mistake of getting underfoot in an investigation, at least according to Bolchoy, and then there'd been hell to pay. It took years before Bolchoy trusted him enough to truly treat him as a partner, so many in fact that Lucas's brother, Dallas, had urged him to quit long before he actually had.

"Be a writer," Dallas had told him. "Your partner's a crackpot who's nearing retirement but won't retire. Unless they force him out, you're stuck with him for more of your life than you need to be. It's worse than a marriage. Go back to writing that stuff you did in college."

Easy for Dallas to say. Yes, he liked writing, but he wasn't a great writer. He knew that. His best attempts were filling out reports. He had a technical mind, and it was restful putting things down in chronological order. But a writer? Of fiction? *Yeah, sure, Dal. I'll get started on that right away . . .*

He drove to his office in a dark mood, annoyed by the

uncommon humidity that seemed to hang in the air like an invisible shroud. It wasn't his nature to be gloomy, but Iris, and the hovering hangover that hadn't fully presented itself yet, were getting to him. He parked his truck in the spot behind the back door that led to his office. The door was rust-colored, from paint and maybe just because it was, and it was one of many other rust-colored doors that lined the back of the strip mall. He'd rented the one-room space alongside the Asian fusion restaurant for next to nothing. The scent of curry occasionally wove through the air, which had a tendency to draw him like a cartoon finger of aroma, beckoning him inside, but otherwise his office was exactly what he needed.

He sat around and shuffled papers and kept an eye on the clock. It was early. Still time to hit the hearing. He wanted to support Bolchoy, but he didn't want to get snagged by more reporters; they always pissed him off. Still . . .

He headed out at eight fifteen, fighting the snarl of traffic that took him east on the Sunset. He almost didn't make it in time and then had to pay for parking three blocks away. It was hot and his shirt was sticking to him. He hurried up the steps, but sure enough, that piranha of a reporter, Pauline Kirby, was standing in his way.

"Mr. Denton," she called loudly. "How do you think the hearing will go for your friend, er, ex-partner, Ray Bolchoy?"

"I'm hoping the judge sees there's no reason to go to trial."

"So, you don't think the charges against Bolchoy are credible?"

"What I think doesn't matter." He tried to move past her, but she kept with him, step for step.

"But you believe in Bolchoy's innocence."

Innocent wasn't a word he would choose for Ray Bolchoy.

"We all just want this in the rearview," he said, then ducked inside.

He took a seat toward the rear and waited while everyone got set up. He saw the Carrera boys seated across the aisle from him. They both wore those supercilious smiles he detested, but he tamped down his frustration as he watched the defense and prosecution put up their evidence. It was difficult at first to tell which way the judge was going to rule until the prosecution couldn't come up with the false confessions Bolchoy had allegedly turned in. Luke gazed in surprise at his old partner, who sat stoically beside his lawyer. He suspected Bolchoy had done exactly what he was accused of. He was a man out for justice, whether it was legal or not. But if there was no evidence then maybe . . . ?

It took the judge less than ten minutes to rule there wasn't enough evidence for trial. Luke felt like shouting and would have, except for the pounding in his head. Instead he settled for a victory smile he made sure the Carrera brothers saw. They both sported stone visages with cold glares.

Luke left the courthouse and sneaked around the crowd to avoid the Kirby woman, though she spotted him and tried to chase him down. He ran through a McDonald's drive-through on his way back to the office and picked up a coffee with cream. His headache was a dull throb, barely discernible. The joy over Bolchoy's victory made everything else seem less of a problem.

Of course his old partner was still out of a job. Maybe the union would get him back in, but the captain had never liked him and the feeling was mutual. Bolchoy was nearing retirement, but he didn't seem any too anxious to give up the work he loved. If he wanted his job back, Luke hoped he would get it, though he thought it was unlikely.

Luke wheeled into the parking lot at 11:19. His 11:30

appointment was with Helena Garcia, a skittish woman
who felt her husband, Carlos, a Colombian native who had
become a naturalized citizen, was planning to kidnap their
young daughter and take her back to his home country. The
fact that said husband was a pretty happy guy who'd started
his own landscaping company after working years for
another firm and, from what Luke had discovered, was
gaining clients all the time, didn't speak to her fears very
well. Luke had tried to tell her as much, but she'd just
gotten mad at him, and then, for a moment, when she'd
snatched up his stapler and drawn her arm back as if to hurl
it at him, he'd wondered if maybe she was the unstable one
and was projecting her own plans to possibly kidnap their
child on Carlos.

She'd managed to put the stapler down, but it had taken
her awhile. Too long, in Luke's biased opinion. He'd carefully tried to counsel her. "Your husband doesn't seem to
have any reason to leave the country. I talked to a couple of
his clients. Called them up and asked what they thought of
his work, and all I got back were glowing reports."

"It's all a fake!" Helena was a redhead with a tempera-
ment to match.

"I picked the clients at random. I could go down the list
and call every name you gave me. Maybe there's somebody
who doesn't like him, but . . ." He'd trailed off, leaving her
to hopefully see the waste of time ahead of him.

But she hadn't. "I have to take Emily away. It's the only
way to keep her safe."

"Now, Helena, that's a bad idea."

He'd further explained that *she* would be breaking the
law, not Carlos, and he'd thought he'd gotten through to her.
Then, yesterday, she'd called up screaming. Carlos had
apparently picked up Emily from day care without telling
Helena, and when she'd gone to collect her, Emily wasn't
there. She'd immediately called Luke on his cell phone,

read him the riot act up one side and down the other. Then she'd returned home to find her husband's truck in the driveway and Carlos and Emily inside the house sharing bowls of ice cream.

She'd called Luke back to tell him, but she hadn't apologized for her rant. Now Helena was due to meet him at his office and sure enough, almost on the dot, he saw the silhouette of a woman outside the obscured glass of his office door. He expected her to just bust in, as she was wont to do, but this time she hesitated. Maybe she'd thought over her behavior after all. Curious, Luke got up to open the door, but then the handle twisted and the woman entered, along with a blast of blinding, hot September air that damn near broiled him where he stood. He had to lift a hand to shade his eyes in order to see her.

His visitor wasn't Helena. This woman's hair was soft brown and long, swept into a loose ponytail at her nape, held by a dull silver clip. Her eyes were green with thick, dark lashes, a certain wariness lurking in their depths, and her nose was straight and a trifle pointy in a way he kind of liked. Her mouth could have been kissable except for the way it was currently drawn into a thin line of disapproval or worry. She was medium height, with a taut body that looked as if she spent time at the gym, but just now she wore lightweight tan pants and a cream-colored blouse. She held a laptop bag in one hand that seemed to be her purse.

"Lucas Denton?" she asked.

It was the hottest day of the year when she strolled into his office, as cool as cherry ice cream.

The line ran through his mind unsolicited. He was torn between laughter and annoyance. *Damn you, Dallas.* He thrust out a hand. "It's Luke."

She held on to the doorknob a tad too long, as if she

were about to make an about-face and leave. It took her a
moment to shake his hand, but the handshake was firm.

"Andrea Wren. And it's Andi."

"Wren," Luke repeated. He reached around her and shut
the door, cutting the heat and blinding sunshine.

"Sorry," she apologized.

"No problem."

"Yes, I'm from those Wrens," she admitted as Luke
walked back behind his desk. He gestured to his client
chairs and she chose one, smoothed the back of her skirt,
and settled herself on the edge.

"I'm going to guess this has something to do with the
Carrera brothers."

She tried to smile but it didn't reach her lips. "This
morning I was approached by Brian Carrera. Threatened by
him, actually. I know your story, and I wondered if you
would help me find a way to put the Carrera brothers away
for good. Legally."

Luke was trying to place her. Not the sister. That woman
was a bit shorter and heavier. "You're Gregory Wren's
widow?"

"Yes."

"How were you threatened?"

"I was at the gym and he was on the treadmill next to
mine. Your . . . ex-partner's case came up on the TV and
you were interviewed."

"Ah." Luke made a face.

"Brian started talking to me, and I realized who he was.
He said something to the effect that it would be better if we
all got along. How the Carreras were good friends and bad
enemies."

"Well, that's definitely true."

"I don't want to go to the police. With this lawsuit
against your partner, it seems like they're all just covering
their . . . covering for themselves."

"They are covering their asses," he agreed. "But they also do their jobs. The Carreras don't play nice. You're right to be concerned."

"That's why I'm here."

He noticed how flawless her skin was. "Did Carrera say or do anything else?"

"He told me that I need to make sure my brother- and sister-in-law understand that part, about being better friends than enemies."

"I'd like nothing more than to put the Carrera brothers away for the rest of their natural lives," he stated flatly.

That netted him her first real smile. She'd set the bag beside her chair, but now she reached into it and gingerly pulled out a white letter-sized envelope with ANDREA printed on the front. She carefully unfolded the paper from it and slid it across his desk.

Written in block print was: LITTLE BIRDS NEED TO FLY.

"What's this?" he asked.

"I just bought a cabin on Schultz Lake and last night this was waiting for me, on the bed. This morning Brian Carrera was on the treadmill next to me."

"You think he left it for you?"

"I've never had any contact with him before, so why is he targeting me? How did he know about my cabin? But I don't know who else would have left the note. It feels like a threat. I just . . ." She trailed off. Luke tried to hand the note back to her, but she shook her head. "Keep it."

He stared down at the message. "It's a play on your last name."

"The lock on the cabin's front door was broken, so anyone could have wandered in. Or maybe they broke in. I don't know. I called my real estate agent and she was going to send someone out to repair it."

"What do you want me to do?"

"I want you to find out who sent me the note. If it was the Carreras, I want to stop them, make sure they can't get away with threatening me, or any one of us."

"But no police."

"No police." Her green gaze was steady, but he sensed the tension coiled within her. "I don't know what the range of your services is, but I may also need protection."

"Personal protection?"

She shifted in her seat. "I have . . ." She seemed uncertain how to continue. He waited, knowing sometimes silence worked better than questions. "I have an issue I learned about yesterday that I'm still working out."

"What kind of issue?"

She was silent so long he thought she might not answer him. Then she drew in a breath and expelled it in a rush. "I'm . . . pregnant," she blurted out. "About three months. It's my husband's. I'm still adjusting to the news, and I really don't know what to do about the Carreras, but I want to feel safe. I want my baby to be safe."

As Lucas absorbed that information, the smell of eastern spices drifted to his nose. It apparently reached hers, too, because she turned toward the aroma like a bloodhound with a scent.

"Any chance you and the baby might like some Thai-ish food?" he asked, hooking a thumb toward the wall that separated his office from the restaurant.

"Thai-ish?"

"Asian fusion."

She relaxed a bit for the first time. "The baby and I would love it."

Chapter Four

They headed out together and he was locking the door to his office when he remembered Helena. She was late, not the first time she'd forgotten the time or been a no-show. Still . . .

"Go on in and get out of the heat. I gotta make a call."

"No, I'll wait."

"Okay, but . . ." He trailed off as he looked across the front lot and saw Helena slam the door on her Ford Escape. She saw him, too, and barreled his way. "I had a client scheduled for eleven thirty," he explained to Andi. "I thought you were her, but there she is now."

Andi looked past him toward Helena, whose red hair was flying out behind her like a cape as she stalked toward Lucas. "Hmm. I'll get that table," Andi said and wisely headed inside.

Helena flicked a glance at Andi's retreating back as she approached Luke. "Who was that?"

"Someone I'm meeting for lunch. You were late."

"Barely. Carlos wants full custody of Emily and it's your fault!"

"Whoa . . . whoa . . . How is it my fault? And since when are you getting a divorce?"

"Since I filed papers last week. Now, all of a sudden, he wants to be a daddy, and he's never been there for her!"

That was patently untrue, but Luke knew better than to say so. He guided Helena back to his office and hustled her inside. "Make it quick," he told her.

"Why? So you can meet your *date*?"

"Helena, Carlos hasn't shown any indication that he's anything but a model parent. I never found anything that said otherwise. I'm not a lawyer, but—"

"You didn't try hard enough. Now he's going to take Emily away from me!"

"He can't do that. Neither of you can."

"I've got to get away from him. He's a crazy man. You just don't see it."

"Don't do anything rash. You need a good lawyer. Why did you file for divorce? You never said anything about filing."

"What does it matter?"

"Well, because now things can escalate. You've thrown down the gauntlet."

"I don't know what you're saying. If I don't do something, Carlos wins. He'll take Emily back to Colombia and that'll be it. You've got to help me!"

"Myrna Mintz is an excellent divorce attorney. I'll give you her number."

When Luke turned toward his desk, his eyes fell on the note left for Andi. LITTLE BIRDS NEED TO FLY . . . He was momentarily distracted until Helena grabbed him by his sleeve. "I don't want a fucking lawyer. I want my daughter safe with me."

"Helena," he warned.

"If you won't help me, I'll get someone who will."

"C'mon. Take a moment."

"You haven't helped me at all. You just tell me what not to do."

"I don't think Carlos is trying to kidnap Emily."

"Good-bye, *Luke*. Thanks for nothing." With that, she stomped out of the office and slammed the door. Luke carefully put Andi's note back inside the envelope and tucked it beneath a few papers that were already inside his in-box.

Asian World was a rectangular room with a series of booths arranged in blocks with wooden half walls, painted black. The half walls rose three feet above the red Naugahyde bench seats, offering privacy. The smell of the restaurant's dishes made Andi's mouth water. She figured that was a good sign. Hunger. Even with everything that was going on, her body was signaling that she needed to take care of herself.

She wasn't sure what she thought of Lucas Denton. He'd seemed approachable from the pictures she'd seen on television and in the paper, but in person he exuded a strength of character that hadn't come through on screen. She'd been shocked by how much she wanted to just fold herself into his arms and let him take care of her.

Good. God.

An Asian waitress waved to her to take any seat, and Andi chose one of the booths near the front door. The thin metal blinds were drawn across the window against the heat, but there was a tiny vertical strip along the edge where she could just see Luke's client slam out of the office and stalk toward her Escape.

Whatever her deal was, things must not have gone well.

"You like something to drink?" the waitress asked her, dropping off a menu. "Tea?"

"Two menus, please, and um, water would be great."

She left abruptly, but Andi called after her, "Do you have decaf tea?"

A brief nod without a look back said she'd been heard.

The door opened and Luke stepped inside. He spied Andi immediately and slipped inside the booth across from her.

"That was your eleven thirty?" she asked.

He glanced at the large watch he wore on his left arm. "More like a twelve ten."

"We're on the clock, then. I assume I'm footing the bill for lunch."

She said it matter-of-factly, and for some reason it pissed Luke off.

"Now see, that attitude really stinks. I was planning on going Dutch, unless you really want to fork over your hard-earned money."

"Dutch is fine."

"Relax," he told her. "We're going to get the Carreras."

"Are we?" To her consternation, she suddenly felt tears burn her eyes. *Oh God . . . oh, please, don't let me cry.*

"Are you all right?" he asked.

And that's when the waterworks started.

She couldn't believe this was happening, especially in front of Luke Denton. It was mortifying. She desperately tried to keep from crying, but her throat grew hot and her eyes filled with tears. She ducked her head, horrifically embarrassed, and when he said, "Hormones," she started laughing, swiping at the wet tracks on her face.

"I don't think that's strictly true, but I'll take any excuse."

She picked up her menu with its pictorial depiction of the available dishes.

"No excuse," he said. "Fact."

She couldn't look up from the menu yet. She needed some time to collect herself. She finally managed a brief glance in his direction and was disconcerted to find him staring back at her. His eyes were blue, a deep cerulean shade she was a sucker for, and his hair was brown, a couple of shades darker than her own. He had a dimple and a really nice smile. She had the deep, dreaded feeling that she'd made a mistake with him. He was the kind of man/boy type she generally couldn't stomach, the kind that oozed charm and cleverness, when in reality they were just a shade or two above empty-headed. But Denton had quit the force in his loyalty to his partner, and that showed character.

"Do you know what you're going to order?" she asked him, aware he hadn't looked at the menu.

"Yeah. Do you?"

"No."

"You look like a salad type." He hitched a thumb to the specials written on a chalkboard. "I've heard the green papaya salad is good."

It felt like things were getting away from her. "I can order for myself."

"That is not in doubt."

"Have you had the salad?"

"Nope."

"What are you having?"

"I like a lot of curry," he said.

Her stomach did an uncomfortable twist, and suddenly the prospect of any kind of food was iffy. From being starved, she was now uncertain she would make it through the meal without disgracing herself. A fine sheen of sweat broke out on her forehead. "The salad could be good."

The waitress came by and asked for their order, and Luke ordered the green papaya salad for her, then picked out a few items for himself, all with curry in the title, then turned to Andi, whose stomach gave a hard wrench.

"Excuse me . . ."

She walked quickly toward the back of the restaurant, relieved when she correctly guessed where the restrooms were. She locked herself inside the unisex unit and leaned against the door, willing her stomach to relax. Man, it was as if her hormones had just been waiting for her to catch on. Holy God.

She had to splash water on her face and fight back the urge to retch, but finally she got herself together. She looked at her wan reflection in the mirror.

What are you doing?

She'd had a boyfriend once who'd been the same type of character as Lucas Denton—amused, detached, maybe a little too cute—and she'd broken off that relationship after only a few months. But she could feel her heightened interest now, and it kind of pissed her off.

She returned to the table. Luke leaned on his arms and said, "You sure you're all right?"

"Fine."

"Okay. Tell me about Carrera. Word for word, as much as you can remember, about what he said to you this morning."

"Didn't I already tell you?"

"Give it to me again. The whole conversation. As much as you can remember. Everything."

With an effort, Andi pulled herself together. She'd hired him and she was going to go with it. "The news was on at my club and someone kept switching the television station. Bolchoy's hearing was on . . . and you . . . but then there

was this archived segment with my husband . . . Greg . . .
who was saying that the Carreras build steel-and-glass
buildings but that the Wrens were constructing a lodge
more in the vein of the one at Crater Lake. Something like
that."

The waitress returned with their meals and Andi looked
down at hers, very aware of her jumpy stomach.

"That interview was about a month before Greg died,"
she added, dragging her gaze from the food.

"Brian Carrera was on the treadmill next to you?" Luke
asked, digging into his meal.

"Yes."

"And he was watching the newscast, too?"

"Oh yes. Greg was going on about how the Carreras
were the wrong choice because they would destroy the feel
of the area." She shook her head. "Again, it was something
like that."

"What did you say?"

"I ignored him. I didn't really look at him. I didn't know
who he was."

"He just happened to be on the treadmill next to you."

"Well . . . yes."

"Did you get there first or did he?"

"I did. When he took that treadmill I put my jogging
jacket over the treadmill on my other side so I could save a
place for my friend, Trini."

"Could he have picked any another treadmill?"

"He did it on purpose. There's no doubt in my mind."

"You're not going to faint, are you? You're white as a
sheet."

"I don't faint." *Liar.* "At least not usually," she amended.

"It sounds like Carrera set this up to talk to you. Warn
you. Threaten you. Get a reaction."

She nodded.

"What was the threat again? As close as you can remember."

"Something like, 'Maybe you can pass on some information to your brother- and sister-in-law. Tell them to be more reasonable. We make better friends than enemies.'" She carefully tucked her fork into the salad. "And then he said, 'That lodge you're building doesn't look safe.' And then I said, 'Did you just threaten me?' and he said we had common interests, and I said, 'We have vastly different tactics.'"

Luke was listening, but he was also eating with an appetite she suddenly envied. It felt like her whole body was in rebellion. She realized she'd counted on sailing through her pregnancy with no problems at all, which was unrealistic, to say the least. But whatever it took, it was worth it.

"Anything else?" he asked.

She shook her head. "I wish I had said something about the note they left, but I was too stunned and blindsided."

"You're sure they left it?"

"Well, no . . . but logically, I get the note and the next day Brian Carrera's on the treadmill next to me?"

"You don't have any other enemies?"

"I didn't even really know I had these. I haven't been involved in the business until recently."

Luke nodded. "The fact that it's a play on words for your last name, which is part of the corporation name, points to the Carreras in a way. They're attacking Wren Development and the Wren family as a whole. But it's strange for them. Unless . . ."

"Unless?"

He shrugged. "I've followed the Carreras for a long time. They're money-motivated thugs. *Little birds need to fly* suggests they want you to leave, and that makes sense, but they usually don't have that much imagination. His threats to you this morning? They were on the nose. 'We're good friends and bad enemies.' That sounds just like them."

"So?"

"I don't know. I don't like the idea that someone has some deeper, hidden message. The note inside your cabin was directed at you, whereas Brian coming to see you at the gym today was in order to make you the messenger. It's psychologically different."

"I guess you're right." She put down her fork, unable to eat.

"You don't like it?"

"No, it's . . . the pregnancy, I think."

"Ah." He regarded her soberly. "I'm not trying to scare you. I'm just spitballing here."

Andi's pulse had elevated. Her mind was jumping all over the place. "You think they're specifically targeting me."

"I don't know. I shouldn't have said that."

"No, say what you're thinking. Please. I need to know."

"I think you might be a target," he said carefully.

"That's why I came to you." Her voice was rising. "They left me that message. They . . . chose me because I'm the majority stockholder."

"Wait . . . don't jump to conclusions. It could be more personal."

Andi gazed at him. Perplexed, she asked, "What do you mean?"

"Could they know you're pregnant?"

"No!"

"I just thought maybe they're targeting you because they think you're the most vulnerable. That you'll cave easiest."

"They don't know about the baby because *I* just found out." Andi stood up and Luke stood, too.

"That's not it, then. Shit. I'm doing this wrong. I shouldn't have said that. Bolchoy would have my head if he were here."

Andi felt dizzy. "I've gotta go pack my house."

"I'll take you home. No packing. You need to lie down."

"I'm fine . . . really . . . I just need to rest a while."

Luke threw some cash on the table and Andi felt like she was moving through water as she pulled up her bag. She heard his terse, "I've got it," and then he was guiding her back to his office. She realized he hadn't given her a chance to pay her half.

Andi sat on her couch amid the boxes, feeling like an idiot, while Luke glanced around, taking in the signs of her packing. "I'm fine," she said with more conviction than at the restaurant. "I don't need to lie down." She'd been scared that she was facing another blackout, but she'd known almost immediately that it was a reaction to the news and maybe too little food that had accounted for her faintness. Luke had gotten her a glass of water as soon as they'd entered her house and she'd bounced back.

"When is this move taking place?" he asked.

"Movers are coming tomorrow afternoon. A lot of this is going to storage. My cabin's too small for most of it."

"The movers are taking everything. You're not lifting anything yourself."

A part of her was irked that he sounded so authoritative. Another part wanted to just close her eyes and say, "Thank you, thank you, thank you." It had been too long since she'd been able to lean on anyone.

"Yes, the movers are doing the heavy lifting. My friend, Trini, said she'd help," she added, though all Trini had said was that she wanted Andi to meet her new guy. That was the extent of their weekend plans together, and that one was iffy at best.

"You said you just found out you're pregnant."

"After I sold this place, yes. The cabin's small, but I wanted to move."

He nodded.

"Do we need to write up a contract or something?" she asked. "This has all been kind of weird."

"First, I want to get clear what you want me to do. Keep an eye on the Carreras. Keep them from threatening you and carrying out those threats. Find out if the Carreras are behind the note that was addressed to you, and offer you protection."

"Yes. Right."

"What about the broken lock—at the cabin?"

"I think it's being taken care of."

"Let me know."

She nodded. "Okay."

"What about a meal? You didn't eat anything."

"I had a few bites. What I really need is my car back. I appreciate your driving me home, but I'm okay. Really. I'd like you to take me back to it."

"You sure?"

"Yes. Please." Andi got up from the couch. She felt vaguely light-headed, but as he'd pointed out, she hadn't eaten. "Maybe a little food is a good idea."

"We can pick up your car and follow each other somewhere."

She thought she should disabuse him of this protection thing. It felt . . . self-indulgent . . . but she said instead, "There's The Café near the Wren offices."

They were heading outside to his somewhat battered Ford truck. Luke asked, "What's the café's name?"

Andi broke into a grin as she climbed into the passenger side of his vehicle. Seeing her face, he asked, "What?"

"Never mind. Let's get to my car and I'll show you how to get there . . ."

Chapter Five

Sometimes it's easiest to let the game begin on its own. I've tried forcing the start a time or two, but it's better to see what move your opponent makes first. I'm watching several players. I have them ranked already. One of them will be there at the end . . . the others are way stations. Incidental stopping points. Sidebars.

So much to do. Tumblers must fall in place.

Unconsciously, I start to pleasure myself just thinking about it, but I stay my hand.

I need to draw out the ending until it's excruciating.

My blood races hot. I can feel myself slamming into her already, my fingers on the delicate bones at her neck. It's so easy to crush little birds.

Little birds . . . so incredibly perfect.

Detective September Rafferty shaded her eyes against a persistent afternoon sun and watched a hawk glide over the scrubland at the end of Aurora Lane. Pointing, she asked, "Where does that field end up?"

Her partner, Gretchen Sandler, flicked a look in the same

direction, westward from the end of Aurora Lane's cul-de-sac toward distant trees against the horizon. "Dunno."

They were standing outside the home of Jan and Phillip Singleton, who'd apparently poisoned each other after living together most of their lives in mutual hate. They'd had the fortitude to take the poison while seated across from each other at the table and just waited for each other to die. Unbelievable. But that was the story their granddaughter and her husband, Frances "Fairy" Walchek and Craig Walchek, wanted them to believe. Maybe it was even true . . .

Jan Singleton's sister, Carol Jenkins, late seventies, with bleached, flyaway blond hair that showed a lot of scalp underneath, looked from one detective to the other, dragging her gaze away from the house her sister, Jan, had lived and died in. She then followed September's gaze. "Schultz Lake," she said.

"I didn't know we were so close to it." September scanned the faraway trees, figuring it was about a mile away. "That's where they're building that new lodge."

"Oh yeah, now it's the big deal." Carol sniffed and held a Kleenex to her nose. It could have been from emotion, but her sister had been gone a while, so September thought it might be to cover up a sneer.

Gretchen squinted, her almond-shaped eyes screened by thick black lashes. Gretchen's hair was a wild mass of black curls that she sometimes wore back, but today the strands were sticking to her face. She brushed them back with one hand, held on to a clump of hair impatiently, and said to Carol, "So, Fairy and Craig . . . They're out on bail and you know they're still insisting they had nothing to do with your sister and her husband's deaths—"

"Frances. Her name is Frances."

"*Frances* and Craig claim they had nothing to do with

their deaths," Gretchen reiterated, "and that after Harold died—"

"My brother," Carol said.

"—of natural causes, the Singletons moved his body to their basement, which is, by definition, abuse of a corpse in the second degree, a Class C felony. But the ME couldn't find anything in Harold's bones that said he'd died any differently, so it's not a homicide. Still, there are four bodies down in that basement." She swept a hand toward the house that had held the cache of human bones she was referring to: Great-Uncle Harold's, both Jan and Phillip Singleton's, and an unidentified adult male's, the main reason Gretchen and September were on Aurora Lane today.

Carol declared, "Well, I should say. Jan couldn't hurt a soul and she'd never hurt Harry in any case! He's our brother and we loved him."

"Must be long-distance love; he's been gone a while," Gretchen pointed out.

Carol's face turned purple. "Harold didn't communicate for years at a time. It was just his way, and anyway, we were never the kind of family that had to check in all the time." Neither September nor Gretchen responded to what was so blatantly obvious, which seemed to piss her off. "I've told you this a thousand times. I don't see how you could let Frances and that filthy *hippie* out of jail. He's responsible for everything! He's the one who killed Jan and Phillip, and he got Frances involved!"

"You think they killed your sister, your brother, and your brother-in-law and left all their bones in the basement."

"Yes," she answered belligerently.

"Harold died years before of natural causes, and your sister and brother-in-law kept on cashing his Social Security checks. After Jan and Phillip poisoned themselves, Frances and Craig saw a good thing and kept to the same program, pocketing three Social Security checks every month, forging your sister's signature. It's fraud, not murder."

Except for the bones of the male who'd died at around age eighteen. Those had been jumbled in with all the rest, and there was no explanation for them. September looked back to the Singletons' house. Several months had passed since the discovery. Fairy and Craig had been taken in for questioning, and they'd told September and Gretchen that Gran and Gramps—Jan and Phillip—had never reported Uncle Harold's death—possibly from heart failure as medical records showed years of cardiac decline—and instead had stowed his bones in a basement closet to keep collecting his Social Security checks along with their own. But Gran and Gramps really didn't like each other all that much—couldn't stand each other—and had resorted to a double suicide at the table where they'd shared so many meals.

Everyone said that was impossible. They would be too ill to stay seated, couldn't have had the nerve to wait there and die. But upon a complete examination, it was determined the two had also taken a shitload of sedatives, and maybe it could have happened that way. Aunt Carol believed her niece and her filthy hippie husband were "lying through their meth-ruined teeth," which was also false because Fairy and Craig hadn't tested for anything stronger than marijuana and had perfectly nice teeth. Impossible as it seemed, it looked much like Fairy and Craig had said: Gran and Gramps had been pretending Harry was still alive for years in order to keep his Social Security payments and then had eventually killed themselves. Fairy and Craig had followed suit once Gran and Gramps were gone, adding their bones to the pile with Uncle Harold's and pocketing their Social Security checks along with his. Fairy and Craig were facing jail time for a whole host of charges, but it didn't appear they were murderers. To say Aunt Carol was biased was putting it lightly. She blamed Fairy and Craig totally for the entire scam, which, truthfully, might have gone on for decades had Aunt Carol not wondered what the hell had happened to her sister and contacted the authorities, blowing the whistle on the miscreants.

It was while the pile of bones was being tagged and bagged that extra pieces were discovered: the skeleton of an as-yet unidentified male, someone who, if they'd lived, would be about September's own age now, had been part of the basement jumble. The crime lab had recovered trace DNA from the bone marrow, and there was dirt concentrated on the bones, suggesting the body had been buried once. But the identity of the bones was still a mystery, one September and Gretchen had been tasked to solve. Gretchen had initially predicted they would wrap the case up in a matter of days, but it had dragged on into the fall, past September's thirty-first birthday on the first day of the month.

The detectives had been canvassing the neighborhood. They'd initially placed calls to the residents, seeking to learn more about the Singletons, who'd lived in their house for nearly fifty years, but no one had offered anything. Most said they didn't know them. That they were a cold couple who pretty much kept to themselves. That they had one son, Nathan, Frances's father. Some knew Nathan had died, but no one knew how, except Carol Jenkins, Nathan's aunt.

"You'd think someone would know something," Gretchen said now. She'd rapped on another door and no one had answered.

"What about Nathan?" September asked Carol.

"What about him?"

"Your sister and her husband have been described as cold

and keeping to themselves, and no one seems to remember their son that much."

"Oh, they're all just scared to talk to you." She glared down the row of houses.

"I think it's more of a case that they don't know anything," Gretchen said.

Carol ignored her. "Nathan was a good little boy. Jan and Phillip doted on him, absolutely doted on him. When he and that terrible woman he married—Davinia—died in that small plane crash, they doted on Frances. They took her in and cared for her, more like a daughter than a granddaughter, until she hooked up with *Craig.* Then things weren't good. They weren't good at all."

Gretchen squinted down the street at the twenty-some houses Carol had glared at. "We're going to have to run these people down at work. The Singletons didn't live here fifty years without someone knowing them." She then slid a sidelong look Carol's way. "I don't care if they're scared. You came here today to make introductions and we're still standing out in the sun."

"Yes, of course, but I don't know them that well," she backed off.

September reminded, "You said you know the Myles family."

They all turned to look at the faded yellow, shingle-sided home across the street from the Singletons'. It was why Gretchen had allowed Carol Jenkins to be any part of their investigation.

"I knew Grace Myles, but she's in assisted living now. Early dementia, you know."

"The Myles's son lives there now," Gretchen reminded her.

"Well, I hardly know him. Tynan's Nathan's age, not mine. I'm much more familiar with Grace, but since she's losing her mind . . ."

"Let's go see who's home," Gretchen encouraged.

September and Gretchen started up the cracked sidewalk that led to the equally cracked cement porch, but Carol stayed rooted to the spot. They stopped and looked back at her.

"Shouldn't we call first?" Carol asked.

"We've called and called." Gretchen's smile was more a grimace of forced restraint.

"Do you want to do this or not?" September asked her.

When called on her behavior, Carol straightened up sharply. "Of course I do. I just want the proper protocol to be followed, that's all. The world is certainly short on good behavior, and I refuse to be accused of rudeness, no matter what anyone else does."

Gretchen said, "You're with the police. They'll be looking at us, not you. They're not going to care whether you crossed every fucking *t* and dotted every fucking *i*."

Her face suffused with color. "Well . . . really."

September jumped in. "How about I knock and introduce myself? You can follow along." She shot Gretchen a *really?* look as she walked up the porch steps of the Myles's house and rapped her knuckles on a screen door that didn't look as if it latched properly. She heard a crying baby inside and briefly thought about the child her sister, July, had delivered in June, naming the little girl for the month she was born. This was a Rafferty specialty, and though September and her siblings had all sworn they wouldn't follow suit when they had their own children, July had buckled under when push came to shove and now she had little Junie.

The engagement ring on her left hand winked in the afternoon light, like a cosmic question: *What will you do if and when that day comes?*

Wedding first, she thought just as the door was opened

by a young woman who was juggling a baby in a light green onesie on her hip.

September pulled out her badge and held it up. "Hello, I'm Detective September Rafferty. We've been trying to get in touch with Tynan Myles?"

"Oh God. What's he done now?" the woman asked, making a face.

"Are you related to him?"

"My father-in-law. He's at work. Or maybe not. Maybe he's at a bar. Caleb is about done with him, that's for sure."

"Caleb is his son?" September guessed.

"Yes. My husband." Again, the face.

September indicated the house behind her. "We're here investigating the deaths that occurred at 1233 and are talking to all the residents on the street."

The baby let out a howl, as if he objected to the conversation on principle. Gretchen had moved up to September, her badge out, but Carol hung back.

"I'm Hannah, and this is Greer." The woman jiggled the baby a few more times. September had no clue as to its sex. "You can talk to Caleb when he gets back, but I don't know how he can help you. And Tynan . . . well . . ." she said dubiously.

"Is there a cell number for Tynan?" September asked. She was more interested in speaking to someone of Nathan Singleton's generation than Caleb, who would undoubtedly be closer to Fairy's age.

"God, no. The man lives in a different century. But he'll be here at dinnertime. That never fails."

"Do you know if your husband was acquainted with the Singletons?"

"Sorry." She shrugged.

"All right. We'll come back. Do you mind if I leave a card?"

"Sure." Hannah opened the door and accepted September's

business card, which Greer tried to grab. Hannah made a game of it and Greer finally captured it and shoved it into his or her mouth.

"Oops." Hannah yanked it back, which caused Greer to wail like a siren.

When the door was closed behind them, Gretchen muttered, "Babies . . . gotta love 'em."

Carol said, "You know, she and Caleb are living there for free. Tynan doesn't charge them anything, and he should."

"Thought you didn't know Tynan," Gretchen said.

"Well, yes, but I know the situation. I was friends with Grace before she lost her mind, poor soul."

"So, you're not friends now?"

September would've elbowed Gretchen if she'd been closer.

Carol rallied to the battle. "Friendship's really out of the question when someone doesn't even recognize you, don't you think?"

An hour later September and Gretchen were back at the Laurelton Police Department squad room, September at her desk, Gretchen standing in the center of the room. Detectives George Thompkins and Wes Pelligree were already there, George riding his office chair, his usual position, and Wes across the room, standing in front of his desk. They both looked up as Gretchen and September entered, and George swiveled his heft in his chair and said to Gretchen, "Turning out to be a kinky case?"

She gave him a thin-lipped smile. It was well known that Gretchen got bored with your basic homicide. "Hoping."

Wes, tall, lanky, and black, a secret crush of September's until she'd hooked up with her first love, Jake Westerly, again, strolled over to her desk and joined the conversation. "What'cha got so far?"

"Nobody on that street seems to know anything about the Singletons," September said. "At least that's what they're saying."

"Thought the sister of one of the victims was making introductions," he said.

"Fat lot of good she was." Gretchen sniffed. "Her primary objective is for us to put away her great-niece and the niece's 'filthy hippie' husband."

September said, "We've talked to most of the neighbors, at least the wives. Got a few husbands left to interview, some other family members. We're having to meet them face-to-face or they ignore us."

Gretchen added, "The Singletons didn't play with the other kids in the neighborhood."

"They were in their seventies, climbing toward eighty when they died," September added. "If they had friends on the street, they've all moved away. No one left in their age bracket except Grace Myles, who suffers from dementia, and Mr. Bromward at the far end, where Aurora hits the county highway."

"That about where the county road intersects with High Lake Road?" Wes asked.

"The one that circles Schultz Lake. Yeah," September answered, surprised. "I didn't realize Schultz Lake was so close. Probably a mile as the crow flies from the cul-de-sac at the end of Aurora."

"You hear the decision on Ray Bolchoy?" Wes asked her.

September shook her head. "No. Is the case going to trial?"

"Nope." A slow grin slid across his face. "No evidence. It's either missing, lost, or never was."

"Huh. Good for him," September said.

Gretchen said admiringly, "God, I thought they had him for sure."

"Just wish he woulda got the Carreras while he was at it."
George was dour. "Lucky us, they've moved to our 'hood."

"They've cooled off their acquisitions around Schultz
Lake," Gretchen said.

"Temporary," Wes predicted. "That boating accident
slowed them down."

"What's the name of the guy who died?" Gretchen
queried.

"Bellows," September said, pulling it from her memory.
"They've been pretty quiet since then."

"Calm before the storm," Wes said.

They all thought about the Carrera brothers for a
moment, then George said, "Wes and I just got a double
homicide."

"What?" Gretchen demanded. She hated being left out.
"Who gave it to you? D'Annibal?"

"The lieutenant thought it was too pedestrian for you,"
Wes told her, grinning.

"Bullshit. What is it?"

Wes spread his hands. "Love affair gone bad. Wife
shoots the husband, husband dials nine-one-one as
wife shoots him again, and then shoots herself. Except the
girlfriend was in the apartment about the same time, according to a witness."

"You're right. Too pedestrian. It's either the wife or the
girlfriend," Gretchen said, pretending to yawn.

"You are one messed-up chick." George shook his head
as he swung back to his desk.

"Call me a chick again and I'll pull your tongue out
through your nose."

George seemed about to retort but apparently thought
better of it.

September sat at her desk and pulled out the list of property owners she'd compiled, searching through her own

notations. She'd asked those who would talk to her if they remembered any man in his late teens who was connected to the Singletons, but she'd drawn a blank. She'd also asked Fairy about her grandparents and other neighbors to no avail. No one knew anything about the mysterious extra bones in the basement.

"We've been at this for a couple of months and it's gonna take some more time," she said aloud.

"A lot more time," Gretchen acknowledged from her own desk.

"Well, good luck," Wes said. "When you finally solve it, let's all go to the lodge on Schultz Lake and celebrate."

"Ye of little faith. That lodge is barely started," September said.

"We'll solve it long before the Wrens are done building it," Gretchen stated with assurance.

Wes smiled. "Well, if things heat up, we can always hit Lacey's instead."

Andi ordered the chicken salad sandwich again, and this time she ate the whole thing while Luke drank a glass of iced tea with extra lemon. He'd grown quiet at The Café, after giving her a lopsided grin when they'd driven into the lot and he saw the name of the place. Now he leaned forward on his elbows and gazed at her directly as she picked up her water glass. "You said you wanted personal protection," he reminded her.

"I'm kind of rethinking that."

"You sure?"

Her cell phone bleeped before she could respond, an incoming text. She pulled it from her purse and saw the message was from Carter to both Emma and her: **confer-ence room tomorrow at ten.** She tucked her phone back in her purse and said, "I have a meeting at work tomorrow before the movers arrive. I'll call you afterward. I want to sleep on all this. I'm sorry, I just don't know what I want."

"All right."

She shot him a look, but he was determinedly noncommittal. She paid the bill, and as they rose from the table, Luke added, "Tell me about Wren Development, a little about the business plans. I can figure out what you might need from that."

"You know we're building a lodge at the northwest end. The Wrens own a lot of other property around Schultz Lake, and we've recently acquired land that used to be an overnight area for junior campers. A kids' camp. It's a prime piece at the end of the lake. We're also in negotiations to buy several other properties and just finalized a piece with ten cabins. The Carreras wanted it, but the owner, Mr. Allencore, who has since died, made the deal with us."

"Bet that didn't make the Carreras happy." Luke hit the remote for his truck and unlocked the doors. He would have opened her door for her, but Andi beat him to it. As they both climbed inside, he asked, "Where are you in the building process?"

"The foundation's been poured and framing's started."

He headed back on the road that would take them to his office and her car. "And Brian threatened sabotage this morning."

"That's what it sounded like."

"If that's true, most likely they'll wait until the construction's further along, really make it hurt you. Better make sure you've got good insurance."

"I'm sure that's all in place, but I'll check. Carter'll love that," she admitted with a grimace.

"He doesn't like you checking on him?"

"Not a bit. Since Greg's death, he's the point man. Emma's not around and he thinks of me as the interloper."

"Why isn't Emma around?"

Andi hesitated, but then thought, *what the hell*. Holding back wasn't going to help anyone. "She's less reliable."

"Irresponsible?"

"She drinks."

"Ahh . . . Do the Carreras know that?"

"Probably."

They didn't talk further until he'd pulled in next to her Tucson. Then he leaned an arm on the steering wheel and looked at her. "Okay, I'm going to tell you a few things. You decide what you want to do about them."

"Okay . . ."

"First off, I think you're absolutely right. Brian Carrera threatened you and the lodge project. Just as an FYI, there's no negotiating with the Carreras. They'll find your weaknesses, which includes your sister-in-law's drinking and your pregnancy, and exploit them."

"I told you, they don't know I'm pregnant."

"But they will." He lifted a finger to stop her next objection. "Second, I agree that you need protection. That note was left for you and was likely another threat from them. I don't like the idea of you living in some out-of-the-way cabin—"

"It's not that out of the way."

"—where the security's already been breached. Which leads me to number three: I would step up security at the construction site, and also, I think you do need a bodyguard."

"Like I said, I'll sleep on it."

"You've got my cell number. Call me when you decide, or if anything happens. In the meantime, I'm going to go on the offensive with the Carreras."

"What do you mean?"

"Do you know who Ted Bellows was?"

"Was," she repeated. Then, "Oh. Yes. The guy who died in the boat accident with one of the Carreras."

"After refusing to sell his lake property to them. Bolchoy talked to Bellows's widow, but then she clammed up and wouldn't say anything further. She's scared, but it's been a while. I'm going to make a run at her again."

Andi opened the door, then looked back and met his gaze. "I get the feeling you were just waiting to be unleashed."

His answer was a quicksilver smile. "Maybe," he said.

Chapter Six

Andi arrived at Wren Development at twenty to ten and went to her makeshift office. Greg had occupied the largest corner office, but since his death Carter had taken it over. He'd actually asked Emma and Andi if they thought it would be all right, which was a total surprise. At the time Emma had been shaky, grieving, and hungover, and Andi had been dazed and grieving herself, so they'd both shrugged and said it was fine with them.

Though it wasn't officially hers, because she wasn't officially an employee, Andi had been given Carter's old office. Emma was happy enough with the windowless one next to the break room, apparently, though her husband, Ben, had bitched long and loud about the inequity. Carter had told Ben that Emma could have any damn office she wanted, but she *chose* that one. He'd added meanly that it was next to the break room, where Emma filled up glasses of ice for the bottle she kept in her desk—a lie—but Ben had left in a cold rage. Emma hadn't given a rat's ass one way or the other. Even detached as she'd felt, Andi had asked Carter if there was something they should do to help her, but Carter had thrown up his hands and demanded, "What? Rehab? We tried that once and she got pissed off and checked herself out, and Ben won't lift a finger to help. All he cares about is Wren money."

He wasn't completely wrong about Ben, and Emma ignored Andi and Carter's hints about getting things under control, so the situation remained unresolved.

Andi hadn't seen Emma in a few weeks; she'd been too involved in her move and trying to figure out why she was feeling so enervated. Now, she headed into the conference room early, already wishing the meeting was over. She had things to do, and since meeting with Luke, she felt a bit like a traitor to the Wrens, though there was no rational cause for that she could think of. Carter just had a way of making her feel like an outsider making outsider choices. She knew he wouldn't like Luke being involved even peripherally with the Wren family.

And what do you think of Luke?

Her mouth curved, and immediately she dropped the smile from her lips, disconcerted. *I feel safe*, she told herself. Safer, at any rate. She didn't know if she needed a full-on bodyguard, but Luke knew the Carreras and what they were capable of all too well, and he wanted, maybe even more than she did, to put them away. That was what counted: for her, for the Wrens, and for her baby.

At 9:55 Carter entered the room and sat down at the head of the table, Andi to his right. He pulled back his sleeve and shot a glance at his Rolex. "Well, here's a surprise."

Andi frowned. "You said ten o'clock."

"Yeah, but you kind of stroll into the company whenever you like. I'm surprised you're on time."

"Don't confuse me with Emma."

"I assure you, I'm not."

"I met you at the project and I'm at this meeting now, even though you've made it abundantly clear you'd rather I wasn't invited to the party," Andi answered coolly.

Carter glowered at her. He clearly didn't like her attitude. Before Greg's death she'd been a ghost around the office, and afterward she'd been discombobulated. "You're invited, okay? Greg invited you."

He looked a lot like Greg—same eyes, same hair, same build—but Carter was more devious, a card shark with a surprise ace always up his sleeve. "Do you ever wonder about his death?" she asked suddenly, surprising herself.

"What's to wonder about? He drove off the road at high speed."

"But he wasn't under the influence."

"It was late. Maybe he fell asleep at the wheel."

Andi let that one go. She wasn't exactly sure why she'd brought the subject up. She was certain Carter knew Greg had been with Mimi, but they'd never spoken of it.

Now, he asked, "Where are you going with this?"

"Do you think the Carreras could have been involved?"

"In Greg's accident? No."

"The Carreras are good at accidents."

"Yeah, but to what end? The company goes on without Greg. You're here now. That's all that's changed."

"I disagree. The company's been thrown into a state of flux. All of us have since Greg's death." She shook her head. "We've all been changed."

"I never knew you to be so philosophical, Andi."

"Other things have changed, too."

"Like what?"

She thought about the baby. She had to tell them sometime. She'd told Luke, so maybe she was being too melodramatic about secrecy when it came to Greg's family. They might not like it exactly—adding a new Wren to the nest, so to speak—but Carter would be the child's uncle.

At that moment one of the double doors flew open and Emma Wren Mueller struggled into the room. Her purse slipped from her shoulder to the crook of her elbow and swung onto the back of one of the chairs. "Oops," she said.

Like Carter and Greg, she had light brown hair, shoulder-length and a little uncombed today. Her eyes were dark brown, where her brothers' were blue, and she'd Botoxed her forehead until her painted-on brows barely moved. As she flung herself into the chair opposite Andi's, to Carter's left, Carter's neck turned dark red.

"What?" Emma demanded, looking at her brother. She scrabbled through her purse. "Traffic's gotten ridiculous . . . ridiculous." After a few moments she pulled out a tin of Altoids and popped one into her mouth. The peppermint scent couldn't quite disguise the smell of gin.

"Goddamn it, Em," Carter growled. "The lodge framing's going well, in case you cared, but Dick had to let the framing foreman go because of *drinking on the job*. Now we're bound to get behind, and look at you."

"Dick?" Emma asked, which was Andi's question, too.

"Dick Eggles, our contractor?"

"Oh, Richard," Emma said, nodding several times. "Can't he just hire someone else?"

"That's exactly what he'll have to do." Carter was holding on to his patience with an effort. "But it's one more goddamn delay." He glanced at Andi and said provocatively, "Maybe we should have just sold out to the Carreras."

"C'mon, Carter," Andi said.

At the same time, Emma declared, "Greg would never have allowed that." Then she hiccupped and dug through her purse for another Altoid.

He lifted his hands. "We all know they're crooks. They could do some really bad stuff to us, as Andi was just suggesting, and it's about money, straight up. Money we could use, 'cause whether you two know it or not, we're asset rich and cash poor around here."

Emma frowned at Andi. "You think they'd do something?"

"I don't know. Maybe." Andi wondered if she should have hung on to the note instead of leaving it in Luke's safekeeping.

"She's blaming them for Greg's death," Carter said.

"Not true," Andi jumped in. "I was just worrying aloud."

"Greg was driving too fast," Emma said carefully.

Silence fell around the room for a moment. Andi was sorry she'd brought up the idea. All it did was remind them of those last few months, when Andi hadn't been the only woman in Greg's life.

"You're kidding about the Carreras, right?" Andi asked Carter.

"Am I? This goddamn loan's taking forever. We may need to sell something or we're going to have no money. And I mean none."

"I thought there were reserves," Andi said.

"You want to talk to the accountant, be my guest," he snapped. "I didn't call this meeting because I thought either of you had anything to contribute. I called it because you need to wake the fuck up!"

"We're not selling to the Carreras," Emma stated positively.

"Then let's hear your ideas on making money," Carter demanded. "The lottery? Gold buried in the backyard? A genie in a bottle?"

"Don't be such a dick."

"Emma and I didn't know we were in financial trouble," Andi cut in quickly, worried that Emma might hurl the crystal ashtray in the center of the table at her brother. "But whatever. The Carreras stay out of it."

"Oh, you get to decide?" His blue eyes were cold.

"Brian Carrera threatened me at my club. Threatened all of us."

Emma blinked at Andi as if trying to focus, and Carter demanded, "*Threatened* us? When? What did he say?"

"Yesterday. He said to be sure to tell you both that the Carreras make better friends than enemies, and that accidents happen."

"Oh my God." Emma blinked again.

"Carrera belongs to your club?" Carter asked.

"He was on the treadmill next to me."

"Holy shit," Emma said on another hiccup.

Carter turned on her in a flash of anger. "Pull it together, Emma. I mean it. This is serious, if Andi's telling the truth."

"*If* I'm telling the truth?" Andi could feel her blood pressure spiking, had an image of red liquid shooting up a thermometer. Not good for the baby.

"I just meant—" he began, but Emma ran right over him.

"They're killers. Maybe they haven't been caught, but they killed Ted Bellows. We all know it."

"That was an accident," Carter snapped.

"Another accident?" Emma asked.

Carter turned his angry gaze on Andi. "So, they killed Ted Bellows *and* Greg?"

"All I know is that Brian Carrera threatened me, *us*, and I believe we need to protect ourselves," Andi said. "What kind of security do we have at the lodge? What about ourselves? My cabin was broken into and somebody put a note on one of the beds that's still there. It said, *Little birds need to fly.* And I think the Carreras put it there."

"What?" Carter asked.

"What!" Emma practically shrieked at the same moment.

"Must be a play on our last name. Whatever. I've decided to be proactive. Yesterday I hired Lucas Denton to help investigate the Carreras, pick up where his partner left off, at least legally, and bring them down. He also offered me personal protection."

"Who?" Emma asked, looking dazed.

"That detective?" Carter asked. "The guy who falsified evidence . . . uh, Boucher's . . . partner?"

"Bolchoy. And yes, Luke worked homicide with him at the Portland PD."

"*Luke?*" Carter repeated.

"Yes, Luke," Andi said evenly.

"What kind of personal protection?" he questioned, and Andi resented the insinuation in his tone.

"Any kind I need," she answered.

"God, I need a drink," Emma expelled.

"You're already drunk. And it's barely ten," he railed at her. "Where's Ben? Call him and have him pick you up."

"Fuck you!" Emma shot to her feet, dropping her purse, which spilled its contents all over the floor. She bent down to pick up the items and half fell out of her chair. In a fury she slammed items back into her purse, spitting mad. "You . . . can go to *hell*, you fucking, smirking bastard! *Hell!* Along with the fucking Carrera brothers!"

She flounced out of the room, her exit slightly ruined when she caught the strap of her purse on the door handle. She practically ripped it in two as she yanked it free.

As soon as the door closed behind her, Carter growled, "You should have told me about all this before."

"I've told you now."

He slammed a fist on the table. "No wonder he was smirking, the shit."

"What are you talking about?"

Carter was coldly angry. "The county planner wasn't the only meeting I had yesterday. I met Blake Carrera at Lacey's and we had what I thought was a meeting of the minds. I'm having papers drawn up to sell them the Allen-core cabins as soon as title clears."

"You can't!" Andi flared.

"We need money."

"You didn't even check with me and Emma? You can't do that!"

"Oh, for Christ's sake. I still need both of your signatures. You think I wanted to have this meeting and have to beg and coerce you guys into signing? Jesus H. Christ. I'll tell ya, Emma's not the only one who needs a drink!"

He slammed out after Emma and Andi got up from her chair and stalked to the window, breathing hard. She was infuriated.

Get this out of your head. This isn't helping. Maybe Carter's right and they needed money, but selling to the Carreras? Over her dead body!

She flicked a look out the window and saw a man walking across the front parking lot four stories below. Her heart clutched. It sure as hell looked like one of the Carreras.

Fear wormed through her insides. No . . . no . . . it wasn't . . . was it? No. She watched as the man got into a black sedan and turned out of the lot.

Then she grabbed up her cell phone and punched in Luke's cell number.

". . . barely a slap on the wrist," Iris moaned. "Now there's no record of those forged confessions? Jesus, Luke. If I didn't know better, I'd think you did it for him. How can Bolchoy get off scot-free?"

"He lost his job," Luke reminded her. He was holding the cell phone away from his ear because when she was upset Iris's voice could damn near shatter glass. He heard the beep of an incoming call and said, "I've got another call."

"He said he forged those documents and now they're missing. Who do you think did it? Amberson?"

"Opal would never compromise a case. Doesn't matter if it was Bolchoy or someone else."

"Would she for you?"

"*No.* I gotta go."

"Well, that confession just didn't walk out of the department."

"There was no confession. Bolchoy lied about there being one. Corkland knows that and so do you." Luke hoped that was true.

"There was a forged paper!"

"Come on, Iris. We've been playing this game for months. It's over. Bolchoy's out of the department. No one there wants him back in, and I don't think the union's looking out for him either. Being outside of it all is hell for him."

"Playing what game," she said in a deadly voice.

"None of us have ever believed the Carreras confessed to coercion or whatever else Bolchoy put in that document."

"You admit Bolchoy did it."

"I don't know," he admitted. "But it would be just like him to draw up a fake document, wave it in front of their faces, and tell them he was going to use their forged signatures to convict them."

"That's coercion."

"Whatever it is, it lost him his job. His identity. I'm just glad your boss was smart enough not to take this any further."

"You still think Bolchoy's a badass, yet he's no better than the Carreras," she fumed.

"He's a whole lot better than the Carreras," Luke stated flatly, his temper spiking. He switched over to his other call, but by then they were gone. Realizing it was Andi's number, he felt a jolt of awareness that made him think, *Huh*. He hadn't plugged her into his contacts list yet, but the digits were fresh in his mind. She hadn't left a message, so he called her back, and this time he got her voice mail. "Hey, I'm here," he said. "Sorry I missed your call. I'm going to try to see Bolchoy today. I've got a call in to Peg Bellows, but I haven't heard from her yet. Take care not to move boxes yourself." He paused, then added, "Call me back."

The movers arrived at one and started loading up their truck with Andi's furniture. She thought she'd be happy to begin emptying the house, but she was tired and uneasy after seeing, maybe, one of the Carreras in the Wren Development parking lot. And even if it wasn't either Blake or Brian, Andi recognized how threatened she'd felt.

Though she hadn't lifted anything heavier than her purse, her back and her head ached a bit. She carried a bottle of water around with her as she helped direct which pieces to haul out. The van was going to her storage unit first with most everything but her bed, one small dresser and a nightstand, a love seat and two occasional chairs that shared an ottoman. She was going to have to purchase a smaller table; the dining table she and Greg owned was too large for the cabin.

It took two hours for them to load and head to the storage unit. Andi hadn't called Luke back because she'd felt embarrassed about jumping to conclusions and phoning him with her fears. She didn't want him to think she was half-hysterical, crying wolf at every opportunity. The more she thought about it, the more she was sure she'd let her fears take over.

Don't let your pride make you stupid, though.

"No," she said aloud, picking up her cell and listening to Luke's voice-mail message before returning his call. He answered on the second ring, though he sounded distracted. "How's it going?" he asked.

"Okay. I guess. But . . . oh, damn. Maybe I shouldn't have called. Do I seem kind of panicked? Sorry. It's just that . . . I thought I saw one of the Carreras in the Wren parking lot, but I could be slightly paranoid. Now I'm not so sure."

"You aren't panicked. You have a right to worry."

"So, you haven't heard back from Ted Bellows's widow?"

"Not yet. One of the reasons I want to check with Bolchoy is that he was working with her. I don't know how much help she was. I think there may have been some medical problem. Ray got frustrated, and well, we know the rest of that."

She wanted to ask him if he would come by the house afterward. The desire to have him with her was almost overwhelming. She kept that thought to herself and instead said, "I'll be at the cabin tomorrow, when the movers take over the pieces that belong there. I hope the lock's fixed."

"It is. I went to take a look at it, and it was taken care of."

"You went to the cabin?"

"I said I would. Sorry it took till today."

"I'm just happy it's fixed. What did you think of the place?" she asked tentatively.

"It's great. Nice location on the lake. It's not that far from the Bellows place. They're both on that southwest side."

"Mrs. Bellows still owns the cabin? I thought they were coerced out of it."

"After Ted's death, the Carreras backed off."

"For good?"

"There is no 'for good' with them."

"I suppose that would be too much to hope for."

"I'd say the Carreras are just biding their time. My guess is they've been distracted by your family's recent acquisitions." There was a pause in their conversation, then he asked, "What time're you going to be at the cabin tomorrow? I'll come on by."

"Late afternoon, probably."

"Unless you'd like me to stop by the house tonight?"

Andi realized he was picking up on her nervousness and said, "Tomorrow'll be great. Oh, and I told my brother- and sister-in-law that I'd hired you."

She considered adding that Carter had met with Blake Carrera about selling the Allencore block of ten cabins, but before she could, he asked, "How'd that go over?"

She smiled. "What do you think?"

He chuckled, and she found her smile widening at the sound of his amusement. "I'm looking forward to meeting them both," he said.

"Remember you said that," she warned him, to which he said good-bye, still chuckling.

Chapter Seven

September shoved her cell phone in her pocket, grabbed her coat off the back of her chair, and called to Gretchen as she headed for the squad room door, "Tynan Myles is at Tiny Tim's. Hannah just sent me a message."

Gretchen grabbed her coat as well, camouflaging her gun and holster. "I hope to hell they have air-conditioning," she grumbled, making her way outside.

Gretchen climbed behind the wheel of the department-issue Jeep and backed out of the lot expertly. Strapped into the passenger seat, September rechecked her cell and added, "He's managed to sidestep us too many times for it to be coincidence."

"Eh, he could just be lucky that way. How'd you get the daughter-in-law to tip us off?"

"She's sick of me asking to talk to either Tynan or Caleb. She doesn't want us talking to either of them, apparently, but she chose to give up her father-in-law before her husband."

"Think there's a reason for that?" Gretchen asked, squinting against the sunlight bouncing off bumpers and windshields as she eased into the traffic.

"Other than she doesn't want to deal with it? No. I get the

sense that neither Caleb nor Tynan will be all that excited about being interviewed by the police, and that Hannah thinks they'll get pissed at her for being the liaison."

"It's a little early to hit the bars, or is this Tynan's usual?"

"Hannah acts like he spends a lot more time out of the house than in, but that may be because of Greer."

"Tynan's grandson."

"Or granddaughter. Could you tell?" September asked curiously.

Gretchen gave a thin smile. "Likely one or the other."

Half an hour later, they reached Tiny Tim's, a rambling board-and-batten building stained a reddish-brown color, the windows lit from inside with Corona and Budweiser beer signs in glowing green, yellow, and blue neon. There were some scraggly laurel bushes at the front entry that could have taken over if they weren't so starved for water, their leaves dry and sunburned. September supposed the place would look more inviting in the evening. On a hot Friday afternoon it looked dusty and neglected, and the country western music peeling out was of the sorrowful, wailing sort.

As it turned out, there were a lot of people standing on the rough-hewn wood floor, hovering around the bar and pool tables, starting the weekend early. September had a rough idea of Tynan's age and Hannah had said he worked construction.

There were two fiftyish men sitting at the bar, one in a business suit and one in a pair of jeans and a gray work shirt. The group of pool players were millennials, and there were three other Tynan possibilities scattered around the tables, two with baseball caps atop their silver-haired heads.

September zeroed in on the man at the bar. He was alone, and the other men seemed to be hanging with buddies. She knew next to nothing about Tynan Myles, but something about the way his daughter-in-law talked about him made September feel like he might be a bit antisocial.

"Mr. Myles?" she asked, standing to his right side.

He was hunched over a beer and flicked her a look. "Who wants to know?"

"Laurelton PD," Gretchen answered in a cool voice.

He straightened and swiveled around to give them each a hard look. "My, my. You two sure do credit to the department."

"We've been trying to connect with you," September said.

"Hannah tell you were I was?" He picked up his beer and took a long drink.

"She told you we wanted to talk to you?"

"Little rat fink. I told her to keep her nose outta my business, but here you are." He swept a hand expansively in their direction.

"We just want to talk to you about Phillip and Jan Singleton."

"Who?"

September suspected he knew exactly who she was talking about but would have played along if Gretchen hadn't growled, "Are we gonna play this game? That's what you want to do? That's your choice?"

"Hey, missy. Don't get your knickers in a knot."

September put a shoulder between them, completely aware that to Gretchen, them's was fightin' words. "You knew the Singletons. They lived right across the street from you."

"You're talkin' about the old people who offed themselves?"

"You know exactly who we're talking about," Gretchen said through her teeth.

September hurriedly put in, "That's correct. And Jan

Singleton's brother, Harold Jenkins, died at the house earlier."

"Yeah, he lived there a while. We just didn't see him no more."

This was far more than she'd expected. Encouraged, September swept on before Gretchen could say anything, "That's what we understand. There's an ongoing investigation, but the piece we're concentrating on is the discovery of an approximately eighteen-year-old male's bones. We have no identification on him, so we're talking to anyone who might remember someone of that age around the Singleton home about ten, twelve years ago."

"There's that granddaughter."

"It's a *male*," Gretchen said with forced restraint.

"I heared you all right. That girl ain't no thirty years old or so neither. Just thought she's closer to the dead guy's age than I am, that's for sure."

"Frances didn't live at the house until her grandparents died," September told him.

"Caleb didn't live with me neither, so I guess he's no help, huh?"

"None at all," Gretchen said.

"That's why we're talking to you," September reiterated.

Now that he'd gotten over trying to stay out of their way, Tynan Myles seemed to think it all a great lark that they were talking about his "crazy" neighbors. He launched into a long-winded account of some past Fourth of July when Phillip Singleton had suffered third degree burns on his hands from holding a firecracker too long. "Stupid dumbo," Tynan cackled. "Lucky he didn't lose any fingers. His thumb was like raw meat there for a while. I remember that."

"Did you know Nathan Singleton, their son?"

"Nathan . . . yeah, I knew him." Tynan's mood darkened. "He was in love with that stupid dumbo wife of his, what the hell was her name?"

"Davinia," Gretchen supplied.

"That's right. Davinia. She was screwy as a three-dollar bill, I'll tell ya, but he just wanted her like a drunk wants a drink. Always rubbing her arm whenever they were around, and you just knew he wanted to be rubbing something else. She always looked kinda bored. Never understood why they got married in the first place, except Nathan just wanted her, and maybe she thought he had some money."

"Why was she screwy as a three-dollar bill?" September asked, and Gretchen turned to give her a what-the-hell look. She clearly thought September was going off point, which she was, but she was curious about Tynan's thoughts.

"Well, you know, new boobs, new nose, newfangled diet. Always wantin' more, and Nathan didn't have much. You know that car he drove off the cliff was about a month old. Financial troubles. With her always raggin' on him about the next thing, you can see why he did it."

"You're saying he caused the accident on purpose?" September asked.

"He killed himself and his wife." Gretchen's tone was disbelieving.

Tynan shrugged. "That's what Mom always thought, but that was before she went . . ." He circled his finger beside his ear.

"Your mother. Grace Myles?" September clarified.

"Hannah tell ya she's batty?"

"It's your mother's house you all live in," Gretchen said. "But she's in assisted living."

"House is mine. Smart lawyer got her to sign it over before she went completely nuts. Had to wait a few years before she went into Memory Care so the state wouldn't take it back. She kept wandering off and we'd have to fetch her and drag her home. Finally, we could put her in that place and let the state take care of her. You know how much it costs? Nothin' for us now, thank the good Lord, but woo-wee."

"How well did your mother know the Singletons?" September asked.

"Better'n I did. Lot better."

"Do you think she'd remember them?"

Tynan gave September a long look. "She's batty. Remembers stuff from years ago. Pops out with it. But it don't make a lot of sense. No rhyme or reason, y'know? Just whatever floats across her dumb brain."

"In your expert opinion," Gretchen said sardonically, "do you think it would be worth our while talking to her?"

Her tone wasn't lost on Tynan. He thought about taking offense, actually opened his mouth to snap back, but then thought better of it and clamped his lips shut tight for a few moments before adding, "Go on ahead. She's at Maple Grove Assisted Living."

"Do you know anyone else on the street that was friends with them?" September asked.

"I wasn't around all that much. You could talk to Mr. Bromward. He's been there forever."

"He's at the far end of the cul-de-sac from the Singletons."

"He's got cats," Tynan said, making a face.

"We've met with him," Gretchen said.

"Can you think of anything else about the Singletons?" September tried, realizing they'd about tapped him out.

He stared down at his now-empty mug and shook his head. "Hey, Tim, I'm dry," he called to a bald, overweight man with a Humpty Dumpty look about him. Tim waddled over, picked up the mug, and thrust it under a spigot of Budweiser.

Back in the Jeep, Gretchen shot September a look as she turned out of the lot. "Maple Grove Assisted Living?"

"Do you think it'll do any good?"

"Nope."

"Should we make another run at Bromward? At least he wanted to talk to us."

"Yeah, because he's lonely, and he didn't know anything. And no shit about the cats."

"Lots of cats," September agreed.

"A hundred."

"Twenty," September corrected.

"Twenty'll turn into a hundred real quick unless he gets rid of some of them and gets the others fixed."

September made a face. "Let's go see him. Next week we can talk to Grace Myles."

"An exercise in futility."

"Probably, but we've interviewed most of the people on the street. Tynan was about our last one. A couple more of the husbands, but they're too young and new to the area for me to have much faith in them knowing an elderly couple who kept to themselves."

"What about the Chinese people?"

"What about them?" September responded. "Their daughter says they don't know anything. They haven't been there long enough to matter either. Where we are now is to the previous homeowners. I've talked to a couple. You've talked to a couple."

"I really don't want to see Bromward again," Gretchen admitted on a long-suffering sigh. "I'm allergic to cats."

"No, you're not."

"Okay. Fine. I just don't want to go."

"You'd rather go to Maple Grove Assisted Living?"

"I'd rather go back to Tiny Tim's and drink a beer with Tynan," she said under her breath, "but Aurora Lane and Mr. Bromward's cats it is."

* * *

Ray Bolchoy opened the door to Luke, then settled back in his brown leather La-Z-Boy and to the glass of Jameson he was nursing. Luke sat down on the couch, which could have used a deep clean. Bolchoy, a confirmed bachelor, was an excellent investigator, but a housekeeper? Not so much.

"How's the private side?" Bolchoy asked in his gravelly voice.

"Coming on. Greg Wren's widow just hired me." He told Bolchoy about Andi's encounter with Brian Carrera. He didn't tell his former partner of her pregnancy, but he did relate what she'd said about her brother- and sister-in-law. He finished with, "I'm meeting her tomorrow at the cabin she just bought on Schultz Lake."

His answer to that was a grunt.

Luke added, "Glad the hearing went well."

"Don't have my job back, though."

There was nothing to say to that. They both knew he'd pissed off the department enough over the years for a re-hirement to be unlikely.

Bolchoy lifted his glass toward Luke, silently asking if he wanted a drink. Luke shook his head. "The night before the hearing, Amberson, Yates, DeSantos, and I went out. Iris showed up, too."

He shot Luke a look. "You back with her?"

"No." Luke was firm.

"Bet she isn't pleased about the hearing." He offered up a thin smile. "Corkland wanted me to go down for this."

"He didn't have enough evidence."

"Yeah, but he leans toward the Carreras."

"The DA?"

"He doesn't like going up against 'em. Knows they're dirty, but he's a chickenshit. If I'd managed to actually get something on 'em, he'd be in a real hard place."

"Do they have something on Corkland?"

"Nah. Corkland just has no spine. Iris has more than he does, but she thinks sunshine beams shoot out of the guy's ass. He can do no wrong." He downed the rest of his drink. "But you came here for information on taking down the Carerras."

"I've tried to contact Peg Bellows, but so far she hasn't gotten back to me. Where did she land after everything? She and Ted were friends with the Carreras, or at least they thought so, initially."

"That's what she says," Bolchoy agreed sourly.

Luke knew the story of Ted Bellows's death, but he wanted to refresh his memory before he contacted Bellows's widow. "Ted Bellows died on a fishing trip. The Carreras chartered a boat out of Tillamook Bay that was destroyed by a sudden squall. Coast Guard got to the wreckage and saved the captain and crew member, but one of the Carreras and Ted were on an inflatable, and when that turned up, only Carrera was on board."

"Brian Carrera." He harrumphed and settled himself deeper into his seat. "Bellows's body floated up a day later. Whole thing ruled an accident. The truth is Brian Carrera's an opportunist. My bet is he saw how to get rid of Bellows once and for all. The captain saw them in the inflatable together before his own fishing trawler broke apart. The ones who survived were lucky to be saved."

"Carrera didn't have an explanation of what happened to Bellows?"

"Oh, he said they'd tipped over and the boat was atop them. Brian managed to get the inflatable turned over and inside it, but by then Bellows was gone. Disappeared."

Luke knew Bolchoy had never believed Bellows's death was anything short of homicide, but there had never been any proof. "You told Peg your suspicions."

"She wouldn't believe me . . . at first. But then those documents turned up. The sale of their property with *her* signature, and she didn't sign it. She had to go to court, you know. Actually prove it was a forgery. The Carreras insisted they knew nothing about it. Must've been Ted who put her name on the doc, was their defense. Maybe it was . . . hard to say because he was dead. Carrera brothers skated again, but after that, Peg wasn't quite so fond of them." He slid Luke a glimmering look. "Corkland said that's where I got the idea to forge their confessions."

Luke wanted to ask him if Corkland was right, like he'd always wanted to but had been reluctant to ask. Now Bolchoy was staring him down, almost daring him to, but once the truth was out, there would be no putting it back. Cautiously, Luke said, "Rule number eight: Don't ask questions if you don't want to know the answers."

Bolchoy's mouth settled into a hard smile. "That's rule number six. Don't forget it."

"I haven't."

Bolchoy picked up his drink, though it was empty, then turned the glass in his hands. "At first Peg didn't want to talk to me after Ted's death. She'd had some medical issues. Cancer scare, I think. And anyway, she didn't want to hear my theories about what happened on that inflatable."

"You told her you thought it was a homicide."

"She didn't believe it. She defended those bastards until the document showed up. Even then, though, she shut the door in my face. I tried to contact her, but truthfully, she likes a prettier face."

"What do you mean?"

He laughed shortly. "She liked the Carrera boys. Maybe even better than she liked her husband. I thought about using you back then, but well—" He shrugged. "Things went the way they went, and anyway, the lady wasn't taking my calls. You want to know where she landed? Go see her in person. Knock on her door. She'll take one look at you and you'll be in."

* * *

September walked through the door of the house she shared with her fiancé, a modified 1950s rambler, and dropped her messenger bag atop her grandmother's quilt, which was tossed on the couch. She could smell the barbecue before she entered the kitchen. Jake was on the back patio outside the sliding glass door, which was cracked open a couple of inches. He was tending to a couple of rib eyes he'd flung on the grill as soon as September had texted him that she was on her way home from work.

She lingered a moment in the kitchen while he still didn't know she was there, her gaze skating over his lean form, the strong line of his jaw. She and Jake had been through a lot in the past year; both of them had spent time in a hospital recuperating from various injuries. When he'd asked her to marry him, September had said yes, then had suffered huge doubts about the possibility of wedded bliss . . . or wedded anything, for that matter. Her own family had its share of weirdnesses, and she'd suffered a low-grade panic attack, if there was such a thing, for months on end. But she'd come through that with a kind of what-the-hell's-wrong-with-you moment. Jake Westerly was the only man she wanted and she was damn lucky he felt the same way about her.

So, now they were making plans for a wedding. He didn't care when, where, or how, he just wanted it to happen.

"Hey, Nine," he said when he saw her, a grin catching his lips. Most of the time he still called her by her nickname, the one her twin, August "Auggie" Rafferty had dubbed her with because she'd been born in the ninth month of the year . . . barely. Auggie's birthday was August 31, while September had arrived a few minutes later, just after midnight, hence she was christened September. This was a strange quirk of their father's, started before their births with their brother, March, and sisters July and May. September always wondered what her father would have done if they'd arrived in the same month, but Auggie always figured they'd be August and Augusta. . . . The sad part was, he was probably right.

Jake put down his barbeque tools and bounded back inside, sweeping her into a bear hug that caused September to laugh in surprise.

"You're squeezing me to death!"

"Ah, no. We can't have that." He slowly released her, then laid a big smacker on her. "Got a big account today."

Jake owned an investment business he'd toyed with selling, his desire to make people—rich people—money having waned over the years. He had a half-interest in his father's winery—his brother, Colin, was his partner—and he'd thought about moving into the business more fully. But as soon as he decided to quit the investment world, suddenly everyone wanted him to be their financial adviser. So, he was keeping with it in the meantime, and he'd admitted to September that he had a new attitude since they'd become engaged. "I want to be married to you. Everything else is secondary."

The hell of it was that September didn't feel quite the same. She loved Jake, didn't want anyone else and wanted to be married to him. That was all true. But as far as the job went, she liked being a homicide detective, and after over a year on the job she wasn't quite the newbie she'd been. Not that Jake was asking her to quit, but he did worry about the dangers.

"Are the steaks burning?" she asked.

"Nah. Just a char. I'll leave the salad to you. Pour yourself a glass of wine." He indicated the open bottle of red on the counter as he headed back outside.

"It's salad in a bag," she said.

"Of course." He threw her a grin.

Cooking wasn't exactly her strong suit.

She poured a small amount of a red blend they both liked, looked at the glass, then added in another healthy dose. What the hell? It was Friday and she wasn't working tomorrow, though today had been long. She and Gretchen had changed direction at the last moment and decided to meet with Grace Myles, which hadn't worked. Grace was apparently having a bad day and the detectives were politely, firmly turned away. They'd been on their way to meet with Bromward, but Gretchen had decided she would rather call on the phone than face the man's cats again. Back at the station, she'd phoned the garrulous older man, who'd proceeded to hang on the phone with the just-one-more-thing line long after Gretchen's patience could handle. September's partner had finally just clicked off while Bromward was in midthought, and after spewing a blistering string of swear words, Gretchen had said to September, "Bromward's yours from here on out. I'm not talking to him anymore."

"That's not how it works," September said.

"Yeah, it is."

Now, September grabbed the bag of Caesar salad out of the refrigerator, cut it open, and dumped the hunks of romaine into a bowl. Then she cut open the inner bags of shredded parmesan, croutons, and the dressing. One of the things she loved about Jake was that he could swing from the most gourmet meal to pedestrian fare without comment.

She set the bowl onto the table, scooped up her wineglass, and joined Jake outside. "Gretchen said the skeletons-in-the-closet investigation would be solved in a few days."

"Gretchen says a lot of things that aren't true. You just noticed?"

"Smart-ass." She shook her head. "She dragged me back from vacation last summer because the case was heating up, but it just came to a grinding halt. We don't have a DNA match and no one on Aurora seems to know who belongs to the extra bones. I've gone back through property records to previous homeowners, but no one wants to get back to me."

Jake pulled the steaks off the grill and slid them onto a plate, then picked up his own glass of red. They both walked back inside and sat down at the small kitchen table.

September exhaled heavily and picked up her wineglass. "Gretchen and I connected with Tynan Myles at Tiny Tim's today. He lives at the house catty-corner across the street from the Singletons, where we found the bones. He wasn't a lot of help. His mother, Grace Myles, owned the house before she turned it over to Tynan. She was probably the Singletons' closest friend, according to Carol Jenkins, Jan Singleton's sister. But Grace is in assisted living now and suffers from dementia. We tried to see her, but she wasn't at her best and the powers that be at Maple Grove Assisted Living suggested we come back another time."

"You said the bones are from an eighteen-year-old male?"

"Who would be about thirty now, if he'd lived. Tynan's son, Grace's grandson, is probably closer in age, but he never lived on Aurora. He lived with his mother out of state. And his wife isn't interested in having us talk to him."

"What about the other neighbors?"

"There's a Chinese family in the house directly across from the Singletons. They've been there about five years. They're very polite, but when I ask them questions they just nod and smile. I don't know how much they understand. They have a grown daughter who lives in Los Angeles who I've talked to and who basically interprets. She says they don't know anything, and I believe her. They haven't been there long enough."

"Any other houses?"

"Lots of houses, but no one who really knows the Singletons except the guy on the opposite end of the street. Gretchen had an illuminating conversation with him about pretty much everything but the Singletons, so, now I'm going over the records of people who lived on Aurora before. One house has sold six times."

"Something'll break."

"Yeah. Maybe," September grumbled. "Gretchen's losing interest. Even though she likes the weird ones, she's about ready to jump ship."

Jake touched the rim of his glass to hers. "C'mon. Let's eat. You'll feel better."

Chapter Eight

Saturday morning Luke drove to the Bellows's cabin and was a little surprised to see how well-tended it was. The trees and bushes that lined the lane were trimmed back and there was fresh gravel along the lane that led to the small clearing by the lake, where a newly shingled two-story house had replaced the rustic abode Luke remembered from the pictures Bolchoy had in his file.

Luke parked and stepped out, conscious of the earthy smell of the lake and the light breeze that filtered the heat of the sun. It was late September and there was no discernible change from August. If it hadn't been that he was worried about Andi, it would have been a perfect day.

He sprang up the two steps to the front door, knocked loudly, and waited. Peg Bellows wouldn't answer his phone message, but it might be harder to ignore him on her porch. He noticed the two window boxes with pink, purple, and yellow petunias bobbing their heads in the breeze. She'd put some time, effort, and money into the place, that was for certain. Maybe as a nose-thumbing to the Carreras? It was her property and she wasn't selling.

But Bolchoy had intimated that she'd been swayed by

the good-looking brothers. Maybe she'd had a change of opinion after Ted's death. It sure looked like it.

He knocked again and waited, then moved to the front windows, peering inside. The place was clean and decorated with a more modern feel than the rustic furniture he'd expected. Was he remembering Bolchoy's pictures, or was it merely his own expectation? Either way, this decor smelled like money . . . but if she'd sold out to the Carreras they would've razed the place in preparation for buying more and more land. Like the Wrens, they planned bigger, though the Wrens' lodge was bound to be more family friendly than whatever the Carreras would come up with.

He knocked a third time, pretty sure no one was around. He was turning to leave when he heard the hum of a loud engine approaching. He waited, and a truck appeared pulling a small trailer with landscaping equipment. A man jumped down and looked over at Luke inquiringly.

"Peg Bellows isn't home?" he asked the man.

"Nah."

"I've been calling her and there's been no answer." Luke walked toward him. "You do the landscaping around here?"

"Yep."

"You have a card? I have a friend who bought a cabin just down the way. She could use some help."

He squinted at Luke. "Name's on the truck."

Luke had seen that he was Kessler Landscaping. "Saw that, but there's no phone number. You're Kessler, then?"

"Art Kessler."

"Luke Denton." He stuck out his hand, and the older man hesitated briefly before extending his own.

"I'm looking into Peg's husband's death," Luke told him as Kessler dug in a couple of pockets, apparently searching for a business card. "Did you know Ted?"

"Twenty-five years."

"Ah . . . well, I'm following up. Someone's gotta make sure justice was really served." He knew how pompous he sounded, but he wanted Kessler on his side.

The older man squinted up at the sun. "I gotta get workin'."

"You don't know when Peg'll be back?"

"If you was really workin' for her, you'd know where she was."

"I've reopened the case." Luke wasn't going to back down. "I don't think Ted's death was an accident, and I think the Carrera boys were at fault."

"You a cop?"

"Was. Worked on this case a bit. Now I'm doing it on my own."

"What's your stake in this?"

"I don't like killers escaping justice. That's all."

The older man considered for a moment, then said, "She's away. Won't be back till sometime next month. I'm keeping an eye on the place while she's gone."

"Do you know where?"

His answer was a shrug.

"Okay." Luke nodded. "I'll have to catch her when she's back."

"You really think you can put them boys away?"

"I'm sure as hell gonna give it the old college try," he answered grimly.

"Good luck to you, son." Kessler's lips turned up in what Luke thought might be a smile, but then he headed back to his equipment.

Luke climbed into his own truck and drove back down the lane to the road. Scratch Peg Bellows for now. If he was going to bring the Carreras to justice, he was going to have to go back to the beginning. He should've asked Bolchoy if he'd made copies of the department file on the Carreras, something he was known to do even though it was frowned upon.

He headed back to his office. Saturday was as good a time as any to catch up on reports and filing, and it was a great way to while away the hours until Andi was at her cabin.

The day was long and hot and Andi had banded her hair back and dressed in jeans and a sleeveless blouse. Though she wasn't doing any of the heavy lifting, she was emptying boxes and putting things away. And she felt like shit. Tired and cranky.

She'd asked the movers to haul away the leftover furniture in the cabin as a last request. They'd demurred; not their job. But then she'd given them a substantial cash tip and they'd changed their minds. Now she sank down on the love seat, wishing for an iced tea. Maybe caffeine-free, though she really felt like she could use a dose of some kind of picker-upper. But it was a moot point anyway because she wasn't sure what box held the remains of her pantry and she didn't feel like searching.

What she really felt like doing was getting into bed, but that would mean making up the queen-size in the master bedroom. Again, she wasn't sure where the bedding was.

She picked up her phone and thought about texting Luke to ask when he would be stopping by. A part of her really wanted to see him, and it wasn't because she was looking for a protector, and another part wished she had a day or two to put herself together. Grimacing, she sent another text to Trini, who was being remarkably quiet after practically insisting Andi meet her new guy. This time Andi wrote: Am moved into the cabin. Kinda beat.

She was debating on whether to send Luke a text or

maybe actually calling him—a novel thought in these days of modern communication—when Trini texted back: Bobby and I are spending a night in. Can we see the cabin tomorrow?

Hope she comes by herself, Andi thought wearily, but she wrote back: Perfect.

Then she did text Luke: I'm at the cabin now. Her finger hovered over the Send button, but then she added: Rain check till tomorrow? That would give her some time to feel less discombobulated.

Ten minutes later her phone rang and her heart skipped a beat when she saw it was Luke. *Slow down*, she warned herself, then clicked On. "Hey, there," she said.

"Rain check's fine, but how are you for food?"

"Terrible, actually."

"Maybe I should bring something over . . . or we could go somewhere. What do you feel like?"

"I want to go somewhere," she said, changing her mind. To hell with being tired. "The cabin's still pretty packed up and I'm just in the jeans I've been working in today while they unloaded."

"So nothing fancy."

"Yeah."

"How about Lacey's?"

Andi thought of the burger she'd wanted two days earlier and her mouth watered. "Sounds good."

"I can be at the cabin around five."

"I'll be ready." Her weariness had magically evaporated. *This isn't a date*, she reminded herself sternly, but she was already heading toward the shower.

Lacey's was happening on a Saturday night. The *click* of pool balls could only be heard when there was a break in the thumping music. Several enterprising young women with bare midriffs and Daisy Duke denim shorts were holding bottles of beer and dancing together in the middle of the room. The waitresses looked ready to clobber someone and Luke had to step in front of Andi to keep her from getting pushed by a couple of guys who were standing around the bar stools, telling tales that required a lot of body English.

The decor was a cross between a lake theme and a sports one. There were rainbow trout lacquered to a shiny finish on plaques along the wall alongside dusty pennants from most of the Oregon colleges and a few well-known midwestern universities. Nothing looked as if it had been changed in a couple of decades . . . maybe longer.

None of it mattered, though, because people came for the food. The burgers were great, the French fries hot and greasy, the beer cold. They were shown through a few scattered tables toward the rear of the main room. The bar extended through another archway that led to a second room, where the decibel level seemed even higher. Occasionally there was a roar of noise, as if they were all betting on a game. Maybe they were.

Luke pulled out a wooden captain's chair for Andi at an oak table with a clear, glossy top, the result of layers of some kind of product that made the tables look as if they were encased in plastic. He sat down opposite her and ordered a beer, while Andi asked for a glass of Sprite.

"You okay?" he questioned when the waiter left, the same query he'd hit her with when he'd picked her up.

"I am."

"You're not filling me with confidence," he remarked.

"Okay, I'm a little tired," she confessed. A lot tired, actually. And achy. She worried that she was getting sick, worried what that meant for the baby.

"We don't have to stay."

"No, I'm ready for a burger." This, too, was a lie, even though she'd been practically salivating for one earlier. She'd sort of lost her appetite. She probably shouldn't have come out tonight, but she'd wanted to see him, which was a little crazy. He wasn't interested in her, he was doing a job, and this was no time for her to be interested in anyone.

They placed their burger orders and Luke leaned in close so she could hear him above the noise. "We'll make it quick. Didn't think about it being Saturday. People letting loose, watching football."

Ah. That was what all the yelling was about.

"Carter said he met with Blake Carrera," she told him loudly. "Wants to sell him the Allencore parcel—ten cabins—that Wren Development bought."

"He wants to sell to the Carreras?" Luke asked, disbelieving.

"He said we're asset rich, cash poor, and we're building the lodge so we need funds fast."

"What about a construction loan?"

"That might be in the works, but Greg charged ahead without waiting."

"Can Carter do that?" Luke demanded.

"He needs Emma's and my signatures, so it's not going to happen."

"Attagirl." He smiled at her, and Andi's pulse fluttered.

The front door slammed open and Emma staggered in. For a moment Andi thought she was alone, but then she saw Ben was right behind her, albeit looking around the room rather than at his inebriated wife. His gaze fell on Andi with Luke and he stopped short in total lack of comprehension.

"Oh, geez," she muttered.

"What?"

"Emma just walked in and we've been spotted."

Ben tried to get Emma to head their way, but she was

ordering at the bar and slapped her hand at him, silently telling him to shove off. Ben looked pissed, but he moved away from her and came up to their table.

"'Lo, Andi. Didn't expect to see you here," he greeted her.

"Hi, Ben. This is Luke Denton." She turned to Luke, who thrust out a hand, which Ben shook. "Ben is Emma's husband," she explained. "And Emma's over there at the bar, in the blue dress."

Luke's gaze followed where she pointed. Emma was leaning over the bar, showing a lot of upper thigh. Her curly, blond hair was held back with a thin black headband, but wisps were already springing free. The bartender slid her a clear drink—probably a vodka tonic—and she picked it up carefully and took a short sip, followed by a big gulp. And then she locked eyes with Andi.

For a moment she looked like she wanted to run and hide, but then she sauntered over their way. Andi felt her stomach cramp and she slowly exhaled, telling herself to stop stressing.

"Well, hi, you guys," Emma greeted them, her eyes all over Luke. "Didn't expect to see you here, Andi."

"Ditto." She added another introduction. "Luke Denton, Emma Wren Mueller."

"Oh. You're the one Andi hired," Emma said.

"That's right." Luke nodded.

"If you can get the Carreras put away, more power to you," she said.

"That's certainly the long-term goal," Luke answered.

She accepted that, taking a few more swallows, then turned to Andi. "I guess I left too early. Carter called and told me that he'd met with one of the Carreras and offered up the cottages. Like hell."

"He needs both of our signatures."

"We're not getting in bed with them. Carter knows that."

"Apparently not," Andi disagreed. She took another sip

of her Sprite. Their burgers arrived and she felt her stomach seize. *Oh no.* She swallowed and asked Ben and Emma, "Are you two having dinner?"

"Nah . . ." Emma said with an airy wave.

"Yeah, we are," Ben declared at the same moment.

"Go ahead." Emma shrugged and looked around. Her drink was empty.

"We're both going to eat," Ben argued, but Emma had already gotten up from the table and was heading back to the bar. "Fuck," he said softly between his teeth, then he threw back his chair and stalked after his wife.

"Nope, not a good idea," Luke said, gazing after him.

There followed an argument between Emma and Ben that became louder by the minute. It finished with Ben grabbing her by the elbow and Emma furiously shaking him off. He leaned in and said a few words and then she shouldered her way past him and headed to the ladies' room.

"I think I'll go, too," Andi said, rising from her chair. She swayed on her feet and her head buzzed. *Oh hell no.* She wasn't going to faint again, was she?

Luke reached out a hand and steadied her. "What's going on?"

"I feel a little weird." *And crampy.*

His eyes searched hers, as if he knew she was holding back. "We'll leave when you get back to the table."

"Okay."

Alarmed, Andi followed in Emma's wake. *What was wrong with her?* When she entered the restroom she found Emma swaying on her feet in front of the mirror, glaring at her own reflection. Andi threw her a look.

"He's going to sell us out, y'know," Emma said bitterly. "He's always been a son of a bitch."

"Carter isn't—" She inhaled sharply and bent over as a hard cramp suddenly racked her insides.

"What's wrong?" Emma asked, poised in the act of

reapplying lipstick to her smudged mouth as Andi tried to straighten. Before she could stand up she was overcome by another cramp. Spots danced before her eyes and she put out a hand as she toppled forward. *Oh God no. The baby. No!*

"Andi, you're bleeding!" Emma declared in shock.

Oh, please . . . please, God, no . . .

Andi stared at the drops of red smeared on the tile floor in blank horror. She was seized by a cramp that doubled her up and Emma cried, "You need help! We need help! What's wrong? Oh, God, what's *wrong*?"

"The baby," Andi moaned as a gush of blood followed, and that was all she knew.

Chapter Nine

". . . Em shoulda taken over that company," Ben Mueller was saying, but Luke scarcely heard him.

"Excuse me," he said, standing.

"Something I said?"

"No, I just want to check on Andi and Emma."

"But they're in the restroom . . ."

Luke ignored him and headed toward the front of the bar, drawing a deep breath. Something was wrong with Andi and he didn't feel like hanging out with Emma's husband, who wanted to grouse about damn near everything and didn't offer much to the conversation. He was anxious to get out of there. Anxious to get Andi home.

He heard a loud, wrenching cry from the ladies' room that no one else seemed to notice above the throbbing music and the general din. He was at the door in an instant, hesitating only a moment before throwing it open. What he saw nearly stopped his heart. Andi, out cold on the floor, a spreading stain of blood beneath her, while Emma stood above her, her mouth open in unvoiced horror, her cell phone unheeded in her limp hand.

"Call nine-one-one," Luke ordered.

"I did," she said, holding out the phone. A tinny voice was demanding, "What is the nature of your emergency?"

"Put the phone to your ear!" he commanded. He watched as she lifted it in slow motion, as if it weighed too much. He reached over and took it from her, and she offered no resistance.

"A woman is unconscious in the ladies' room," he said into the phone. "Andi . . . Andrea Wren. She's bleeding."

"She said, 'the baby,'" Emma said, leaning against one of the sinks as if her legs were about to fail.

"Sit down on the floor," he told her, but she straightened and staggered over to one of the stalls.

"She may be miscarrying," he told the operator.

She assured him help was on the way, and he clicked off just as the door opened and two young women stumbled in. Luke blocked their way and they blinked at him uncomprehendingly.

"Use the men's," he told them tautly.

"Huh?" the one with hair too black to be natural said. "What're you doing here?"

He hustled them out and closed the door behind him. "Emergency," he said. One of the bartenders frowned at him and left his post. "Hey, buddy," he started to say, but Luke cut him off.

"Nine-one-one's on the way. There's an unconscious woman on the floor. My friend," he added coldly, as the bartender tried to brush past him. "Man the door. I've got this," he ordered, heading back inside.

"The hell you do. This is my brother's bar!" He pushed Luke out of the way and stepped inside. One look and he spun on his heel, a little paler in the face. "Blood," he said. Luke wanted to throttle him, but the man pulled himself together and took a post at the door.

Luke returned to Andi. Emma was in a stall, talking on

her cell phone, saying, "I don't, Carter. I don't know! The ambulance is on its way, that's all I know!"

"Andi," Luke whispered, getting on his knees. He ripped off his shirt and folded it under her head. His heart was beating so hard he felt like it was moving his skin.

It was mere minutes, though it felt like forever before the EMTs were bringing in their gurney. By this time a small crowd had gathered outside the restroom, and Luke could see a blur of faces trying to look inside when the door was open.

Emma came out of the stall, her makeup ruined. Her eyes were moist. She hiccupped and covered her mouth with her hands. "She's pregnant?" she asked.

"Yes." He hoped she still was, but it didn't look good.

The EMTs carefully loaded her onto the collapsible gurney, then covered her and wheeled her out.

Emma put a hand out to stop him as he followed them out, and he looked back at her impatiently. "Yours?" she asked.

"I've known her less than a week. She said Greg's the father."

She was poleaxed. "Greg?"

He shook her off and followed after the EMTs. They told him they were going to Laurelton General and he headed for his truck. As he peeled out of Lacey's parking lot he saw Ben and Emma's faces in the crowd that had gathered outside to watch the ambulance pull away.

It was all a blur to Andi. She awoke at the hospital emergency room. "My baby," she said, and then slipped away again. It was hours later that she found herself in a private room, an IV in her arm. The room was dimly lit and she sensed it was the middle of the night. No one had to tell her what had happened. She felt the loss already. Miserable, she put her face into her pillow and cried until blessed sleep, and whatever they were giving her, took her away again.

Sunday dawned with gray light, and even though bright sunlight slipped inside, she still felt gray. The baby was gone. A few days of bright joy and hope and now it was gone. She could feel herself distancing herself from the pain, just as she had after Greg's death, only this was worse: deeper, longer, harder. A coma of sorts, Trini told her when Andi surfaced again on late Sunday afternoon.

"There you are," Trini said with relief from the only chair in the room as Andi opened her eyes.

Andi looked around dully. She was in a hospital room with blue and green decor. A blank television stared down at her like an accusing eye. She could see her toes holding up the covers at the end of the bed.

Miscarriage . . .

A wave of sorrow brought tears to her eyes and she closed her lids and fought back a hard cry that wanted to erupt from her soul. She'd barely gotten used to the idea that she was pregnant and now the baby was gone.

"Hey," Trini said. She was beside Andi in an instant, grabbing her hand.

"The baby's gone."

"Um . . . yes, I think so," Trini said soberly after a moment of indecision. "I'm sorry, Andi. I didn't know you were pregnant."

Andi kept her lips tightly closed, afraid if she said anymore she would break down completely.

Trini squeezed her hand. "I know you probably don't want to hear it, but there's something good that came out of this."

Andi just stared blankly ahead.

"It proves you can get pregnant. The last I heard, you said you didn't think it could happen, and it did. Doesn't have to be Greg's baby, you know."

"I don't want to . . . talk about it."

"Just listen then. Soon as you're better, head on down to the local sperm depository and pick yourself out a baby daddy. Pick one with really good genes. Or how about that guy you've been seeing? Luke?"

"No. It's not . . . no . . ." She didn't have the energy to explain.

"I'm just sayin'. He wouldn't leave the hospital even when the staff told him to. He finally took a break about an hour ago to get some sleep, but I bet he's back ASAP. He's like . . . built for sex, and I hope you'll tell me it's just as good as it looks."

"Stop," she said weakly.

"I'm not saying right now, obviously. But later."

"I'm not having sex with Luke," she said with certainty.

"You should. I mean it."

"Don't make me smile, Trini. I feel too miserable."

"Smiling is good. Smiling means you're improving."

"No, I'm too sad." Her voice trailed off, small and loaded with pain.

"What can I do to help?" Trini asked in all seriousness.

"Nothing. Thanks. But nothing."

Trini sighed. "Okay, what if I tell you about my relationship with Bobby? You don't have to talk. You don't even have to listen. Just try not to think too much."

Andi closed her eyes. There was wisdom in that. Let Trini just talk. She could tune out. She needed some kind of distraction or she would be swallowed up by the dark. "Okay."

"He first came to my Pilates class. Did I tell you that he's not my type? I did, didn't I? He looks more like Greg than Tim . . . you remember Tim? My last serious guy . . . relationship . . . whatever you want to call it, that I thought could turn into something more. Not that I necessarily want that, but you know what I mean. Tim had that tattoo that ran down the side of his neck? You told me you thought it looked like Pinocchio's nose, but it was really a flute because he was a musician. Anyway, Bobby's not like Tim at all. He's very corporate, although in a nerdy way. Wears glasses and not cool ones, but I'm working on him. Hard to believe I fell for him, but I have. When you take away all the trappings of nerdom, he's really sexy."

Andi was drifting. The conversation came to her through a watery filter.

As if realizing it, Trini said, "Go ahead and fall back asleep. And relax. I'm just talking here . . . let's see . . . Bobby and I haven't had sex yet. We're still kind of circling each other, y'know? I can't believe I'm going to tell you this, but he wears a hairpiece because he's going bald."

Andi made a strangled sound.

"I *know*! I just know he'd look great if he shaved his head, but as I said, I gotta work on him. Time will tell. You gotta meet him and you'll know what I'm talking about. . . ."

The next time Andi woke up it was night, and she felt like she was weighted down by an invisible blanket. Her chest hurt and she didn't want to move. She kept hoping it was all a nightmare from which she would awaken.

She ran a protective hand over her abdomen. How many days had she known she was pregnant? Four? She wanted to bury her face in her pillow and make it all go away, but she sensed there were others in the room. She opened one eye and saw she was alone. The voices she'd heard were from people in the hall, just outside her door, talking softly.

". . . Greg sure could get 'em pregnant. They just can't hang on to the babies," Emma was saying.

A man's voice answered in a mumble and Andi caught part of it. ". . . lucky for us about Mimi and now this . . . Greg stuck his dick in way too many . . ."

And then Emma again, even softer, "Think she knows?"

"Nah."

Carter, she realized dimly. Talking about Greg's indiscretions. Of course she'd known about Mimi, but not that there had been many more. A sharp stab of pain. Surprising, even so many months after Greg's death.

Or maybe it was just that she felt so low.

Their voices diminished as they moved off. Andi flung an arm over her eyes, willing herself back to sleep.

She awakened with a start to realize it was night. There was someone sitting in the only chair and her heart flipped over until she recognized her psychiatrist, Dr. Knapp.

"What are you doing here?" Andi asked.

"I wanted to see how you're doing."

"How did you know?"

"Your sister-in-law called me."

"Emma?"

"She said she was with you and called nine-one-one. How are you doing?"

Dr. Knapp was a tiny woman in her forties who leaned toward the bohemian look with long hair, flowing skirts, and dangling silver earrings. At her first appointment, Andi hadn't been sure they would be a good match, but she'd come to trust the doctor implicitly. "I didn't know Emma knew about you," she murmured. Carter was the one who'd named her the "guru shrink."

"You know about the baby, I take it," Andi added.

"I heard you just found out. I'm so sorry, Andi."

The doctor's commiseration made Andi's throat go hot, her nose burn with gathering tears. "I'm . . . disappointed."

Dr. Knapp pulled her chair closer to Andi's bed. "This is another big blow. You have a right."

Andi nodded silently, fighting the waterworks.

"Let down," her doctor advised kindly, and Andi bent her head and cried.

PART II

---◆---

MIDDLEGAME

Chapter Ten

The game requires the patience of a saint. Strategizing. One step following another. I have to fight back my increasing desire to be rash. To jump ahead and get going forward faster . . . faster . . . faster.

But that's not the way the game works and it's sweeter for it. That doesn't mean unexpected turns don't infuriate me. Miscarriage . . . ? Gregory Wren got his sweet little bird pregnant? And it wasn't the first time he'd spread his seed, supposedly. Just ask the mistress he was fucking any time he could get away from Andrea . . . Andi . . . the cool, seductive wife. Just thinking about her gets me hard. Before she dies I will fill her with my own seed.

My blood boils with need and rage. Immediately I recognize the danger. Have to wait . . . have to wait . . . This miscarriage has shone a light too brightly on my ultimate quarry.

But there are others who can fulfill my need while the game continues . . . all part of the misdirection.

At seven p.m. Andi lit a candle and put it in the window of her cabin, standing back and staring at the flame. She drew a breath, closed her eyes, and let herself feel the sadness. Today was Pregnancy and Infant Loss Remembrance Day, nearly six weeks since her miscarriage, and each person's candle, lit at seven p.m. in their respective time zone, sent a wave of light around the world in recognition of their loss. Andi had never really participated in global events until this day, but she had to admit this one small act made her feel better.

She'd gone back to work fairly quickly after the miscarriage, but, as she had after Greg's death, she'd mostly walked through the days like an automaton.

Her mother had insisted on flying in from Boston to help her. Andi had weakly protested, but her pleas had fallen on deaf ears. As soon as she arrived, the first thing Diana DeCarolis did was refill Andi's antidepressants, even though she told her mother she still had pills from Dr. Knapp's first prescription. "Then you should be taking them regularly," her mother said flatly, holding up the vial. "If you had been, these would be gone."

She was right, of course, but Andi didn't care to hear it. She'd been doing fine, and it was just as well she'd neglected the pills because she'd been pregnant at the time. She would have been worried sick if the baby had lived because she'd been taking those antidepressants throughout her three-month pregnancy.

She hadn't seen Luke much since the miscarriage, and over the last weeks she'd begun questioning whether she should have hired him in the first place. She'd heard nothing more from the Carreras; none of the Wrens had. And when Andi returned to work, there'd been no more talk from Carter about selling any properties to them. The company's construction loan had finally come through, so they were able to pay their bills and continue building the lodge without the worry of running out of funds. She'd called Luke and given him that information, but she hadn't pulled him off the job as yet. This could be just a lull, and the Carreras would come back swinging. If so, she hoped Luke would find something on them and put them out of the strong-arm business, but she wasn't certain how long their business arrangement should be kept in place.

Meanwhile, her mother took over Andi's move, emptying the boxes, sorting out what was needed and what could go into storage—more, even, than Andi had—then she moved on to what she felt needed to be changed at the cabin itself, namely the nursery furniture and decor. Andi didn't have the energy to stop her, and truthfully, she didn't know what she wanted anyway. With the aid of Andi's brother, Jarrett, Diana brought a double bed out of storage for the spare room, along with various and sundry other items to make the cabin comfortable. She stayed ten days, and by the time she left, Andi was desperate to be alone again. Though she appreciated everything her mother had done for her, a little of Diana went a long way. Organization was her mother's forte, but her drill sergeant ways wore thin fast.

Now, Andi went to the bathroom medicine cabinet and peered inside, seeing the two vials of pills sitting side by side. She'd started taking the new ones but had switched to the originals. What difference did it make?

She was in the kitchen when there was a knock on the door. She started in surprise, then berated herself for being so on edge. Sometimes she wondered if she'd read too much into Brian Carrera's remarks that day on the treadmill. Were they as threatening as she'd believed? Nothing untoward had happened at the lodge, no dead-of-night sabotage. And Carter had since insisted to both Emma and her that he hadn't really been thinking of negotiating with them, which was a bald-faced lie, but whatever. As far as

Andi was concerned, she was glad she didn't have to think about the Carreras for a while. Maybe it was just a honeymoon period, but she was grateful for it anyway.

As she crossed to the door she thought of Luke and her steps quickened. There was no reason to think he would be here. She hadn't seen him in weeks, not since he'd sent Art Kessler to supervise her landscaping, which she'd gratefully appreciated. Between Art and her mother, the cabin was in great shape. She just wished she had a reason to see Luke more.

She checked the peephole and saw that it was her brother on the steps, all six feet three of him. She was surprised and a little disappointed. But had she really expected Luke? The last time they'd talked he'd told her he hadn't been able to meet with Peg Bellows yet, and if he was following any other plan to bring the Carreras to justice, he hadn't let her know.

But what was Jarrett doing here? He'd called her right after she got out of the hospital—after being prompted by her mother, she was pretty sure—to see how she was doing, but that had been their only communication. They'd never been close, and after high school Jarrett had gone into the restaurant/bar business, living late hours and hanging around with somewhat suspect associates, while Andi had taken the college and marriage path.

"Hey, what are you doing here?" she asked as she opened the door.

He sent her a faint smile. "In the neighborhood, sort of. I was at Lacey's and thought I'd stop by."

Lacey's . . . Andi's heart jolted a little. "Not exactly on your beaten path," she remarked. Jarrett lived miles away, on the other side of Portland.

"Yeah, well, thought I'd come by to see you," he said lightly. "You gonna make me stand on the porch all night?"

"Come on in." She opened the door wider and stepped back.

Jarrett crossed the threshold and looked around the cabin with interest. He was tall, dark, and handsome, the total cliché, but he was a hard person to know. But then again, maybe she was, too.

"I saw Trini there," he said.

"At *Lacey's*?"

He half laughed. "I know. Nothing gluten-free and low-salt there."

"What was she doing there?"

"Enjoying the ambience like the rest of us?"

"Well, I never want to go there again."

He gave her a sympathetic look, unusual for him. "Trini seemed to be watching the door for someone, but they didn't show. Maybe another relationship on the edge. She knows how to run through 'em."

Trini'd run through Jarrett once upon a time. That was her normal way, but Jarrett wasn't exactly Mr. Relationship either. Their affair, such as it was, had ended badly, but it was long in the past now.

"You seen her lately?" Jarrett asked casually, too casually in Andi's opinion.

"Not a lot. A few times."

She'd actually only seen Trini twice since her stay at Laurelton General. Once while her mother was here—though the way Diana had kept busying around and interrupting them while Trini was over had cut that visit short—and then another time when Andi had met Trini for lunch. That time her friend had been so distracted and unwilling to talk about herself that Andi had asked, "Who are you and what did you do with Trini?"

She'd jerked as if stung, but then she'd relaxed and managed to dredge up a smile. "That bitch? She's around. Just been busy."

"Lots of classes?"

She shrugged and nodded.

"Still seeing Bobby?" Andi asked. It wasn't like Trini to be so unwilling to talk about herself.

"Actually, he's been like a ghost lately."

"Uh-oh."

"Yeah," she said regretfully. "I think he might be over me . . . us."

"I'm really sorry to hear that."

"Ah, well." She shrugged. "Forget about it. He wasn't my type anyway. Too buttoned-down, didn't I tell you? What am I going to do with a guy like that? I mean, really, over the long haul."

Andi said softly, "You seemed to like him pretty well."

"The sex was great when we finally got to it. And you know, I thought . . . maybe this was just what I need. Maybe I'd been going for the wrong type all along. But it didn't work out, so whatever." She cleared her throat and asked, "What about you? How're you doing, I mean really?"

"Okay. Better. Day by day. Going to work and getting back to my life."

"Any chance you'll be at the gym sometime soon?"

"Yeah, sure." Andi had tried to steer the conversation back to Trini, but her friend hadn't wanted to talk about herself. That was so unlike her usual MO that their lunch conversation had kind of petered out, and they'd parted with promises to get in touch soon, promises yet to be fulfilled.

Now Jarrett stared through the window in the back door, next to the kitchen, to a spot in the middle distance, his gaze running past the willow losing its leaves at the water's edge to fixate somewhere farther on the faintly rippling waters of Schultz Lake. His hair was rakishly long, and he wore jeans and a black leather jacket, the combination making him look slightly dangerous. Her brother was a cool customer who played his cards close to the vest.

"You want something to drink?" Andi asked, heading to the kitchen and opening the refrigerator. She pulled out a pitcher of chilled water.

"I'm not staying. Just wanted to check in on you."

"As you can see, I'm okay."

"Back at work?"

"Yeah, for a while now."

"You know," Jarrett said, still gazing at the water, "he planted willows all around this lake. Schultz did, when he started developing. Had a thing for them, I guess."

Andi shot a look to the partially denuded tree bending down toward the water. The willow branches were knobby whips.

"How are the Wrens?" Jarrett asked neutrally. Andi turned and gave him a sharp look. Jarrett had never said anything against Greg, but Andi had always known he hadn't had much use for him.

"Pretty much the same as always."

"Y'all still having trouble with the Carrera brothers?"

Andi's brows lifted. "You pay attention to our dealings with them?"

"The Carreras get a lot of airplay, and that lodge you're building at the end of the lake keeps coming up."

Andi grunted an assent. She'd seen the lodge on the news as well. It was like time-lapse photography; every time it was shown it was a little closer to final framing.

"One of them was at Lacey's," he said. "Don't know which one."

"What?" Andi's pulse leaped. Jarrett was regarding her intensely, waiting for her reaction.

"One of the Carreras. In fact, Trini was talking to him, or trying to, anyway."

"Trini?"

"She walked right over to him and gave him some shit. You know Trini." Jarrett smiled.

"Oh no. She shouldn't have done that."

"Relax. She was half drunk. Blake or Brian or whoever didn't pay much attention."

"How do you know that? I don't trust the Carreras as far as I can throw 'em. And none of this is like Trini."

"I know. How well does she know them?" he asked.

"She doesn't. She didn't, anyway. I don't get what this is about."

"I guess she was just drunk and flirty."

"She was *flirting* with him? You said she got in his face."

"Yeah, well." He shrugged, as if dismissing the conversation. "It coulda been anything. I didn't talk to her."

Andi sensed he was starting to shut down on her, but now she wanted more information. "She was in a relationship the last I heard, although it wasn't going well," she admitted.

"Must be over now. Or else she's cheatin' on the guy." He hitched his chin toward the window and the darkness beyond. "You oughta get a boat. This'd be a sweet place to keep one, take it out on the water at night."

"Why were you at Lacey's?" Andi asked again. "I mean, seriously."

"Just wanted to make sure you were okay." Another lift of a shoulder, but he was suddenly tense. "I stopped in at the bar. Don't make a federal case out of it." He moved toward the door.

"Wait! I didn't mean to piss you off. It's just you've never gone there before, at least to my knowledge, and I get the feeling you're holding back."

His expression shifted, his lips flattening. "I knew Trini'd be there, okay?" he finally spat out. "I texted with her and that's where she was going."

"You planned to meet her?"

"I just wanted to talk to her. But like I said, I think she went there to find somebody."

"Bobby?"

"Who's Bobby?" he asked.

"The guy she was seeing. The relationship that's maybe over now."

"Well, she gave the impression that she was there to meet other guys. Her eyes were on the door until Carrera walked in."

"And then she got in his face?"

"I was talking to her and she just lost the conversation as soon as he came in. She went right over to him."

"What'd she say?"

"Like how great the lodge you're building was and how happy she was that some properties were going to stay intact. A kids' camp, or something?"

"I didn't know she knew so much about it."

"I think she said something about you and a treadmill?"

"Oh God." Andi paced across the room. "What the hell is she doing?"

He dismissed her. "I wouldn't worry about it. He just blew it off."

"She wasn't waiting for him, was she?"

"Nah. She kept looking at the door, so she was waiting for someone, but I don't think it was him."

"Was she still there when you left?" Andi asked.

"Uh-uh. She took off. By herself," he added when he saw the question forming on Andi's lips. "She was picked up by Uber."

"Oh. Good."

Jarrett headed back toward the front door and Andi said, "You're not leaving, are you?"

"I should probably get going."

"What did you want to talk to Trini about?"

His answer was another shrug. "Nothing that matters." He gave her a quick smile, then he was out the door and striding toward his Land Rover. Through the front window she watched him reverse in a tight circle and head back toward her green canopy of firs, evergreens that didn't lose their needles. His vehicle disappeared beneath the trees like a magician's trick.

As soon as his taillights flashed out, she grabbed up her cell and texted Trini: **You were at Lacey's and saw one of the Carreras?**

Her answering text came back a bit slowly. **Who did you talk to?**

Jarrett said he stopped by.

Yeah, I saw him.

He said you saw one of the Carreras, Andi texted rapidly.

Brian. I gave him hell for scaring you.

Don't rile them up. Please.

K. I gotta go. Call you later.

Not trying to be a bitch. I'm just worried.

No need. I'm good.

Next week at the gym?

There was no further response, and Andi stood for a moment locked in indecision. She gave up texting and put a call through, but Trini didn't answer, which was also kind of her way. She half wanted to go over to Trini's apartment right now, but she knew she wouldn't appreciate it. But Trini didn't really know the Carrera brothers, and Jarrett was looking at the situation through his own filter, thinking she was being flirty even while she'd confronted Brian.

She gazed at the flickering candle. She didn't want to stay home tonight. She'd had enough nights "in." If that was a signal that she was moving on with her life, all to the good.

She went to her medicine cabinet, shook out one of the antidepressants, and took it with a sip of water from the glass she'd left on the counter. If these were the reason she was better, she didn't want to mess with success.

Back in the living room, she picked up her cell phone again and ran her thumb lightly over the keys, thinking. What if she called Luke? What would she say? *I'm tired of being alone and I could use some company*? God, that was dumb. Almost as bad as pretending you're nervous and want that bodyguard after all. *Oh yes. That idea's been circling your mind, hasn't it?*

"No."

Andi made a face. Maybe she should go over to Trini's and bang on her door. It was sad how few friends she had. She supposed she could call Emma . . . well, no. They weren't friends, and at this time of night Emma could be more than a few drinks ahead of her.

Instead, Andi went to the bedroom and changed into pajamas even though it was early. She thought about looking for something to eat, but she wasn't hungry. She decided to pour herself a glass of white wine, get into bed, and turn on the television, which she did, and then she flipped unseeingly through the channels.

She tried to remember how she'd spent her time before Greg's death. They'd rarely watched the same programs, and sitting down to a meal had become a rarity. She'd spent a lot of time alone then, too, though it hadn't felt as lonely as this did. He wasn't home much at all those last few weeks, maybe months. If it hadn't been for that one night when they'd both dropped their defenses and made love, Andi would have basically said she was single.

And then there was the day when Mimi Quade was shepherded into the Wren Development offices by her brother, Scott, who explained that his much younger sister, barely out of her teens, was pregnant with Gregory Wren's child. Andi had been at the office that day and witness to this debacle because Greg had asked her to bring him his glasses, which he'd left on the kitchen counter. Andi had stared at Mimi, whose eyes were only on Greg. Greg's face had turned a brick red. He'd ordered Scott and Mimi from his office. Carter, who'd allowed them in, had looked stunned and quickly ushered them out, with Scott shouting that he and his sister demanded a DNA test. The thought of Mimi's pregnancy had crushed Andi and she'd left Greg and wouldn't listen to his denials, though they were long and hard. He'd railed that she didn't trust him, and it was true, she didn't. If she'd known she was pregnant herself, she might have tried harder, but in those heated moments she'd just locked him out of their bedroom, and Greg had pounded on the door, yelling that he would prove the truth to her.

And then his vehicle had careened off the road and he'd died of his injuries. Andi had gone from depressed and angry to totally numb. She'd sleepwalked through those weeks until learning of her own pregnancy.

She woke up slowly, confused about where she was. The television and lights were still on, and it took a few moments before she recognized her own bedroom. Glancing at the clock, she was surprised to see it was two a.m. For a moment she was frightened. Had she just fallen asleep? It felt a lot like her other episodes. Blackouts, Carter had insisted. But those had just been a few minutes.

She got out of bed and went to the kitchen for a glass of water. Swallowing the water, she realized every time she thought about Mimi Quade's pregnancy, she seemed to shut down, if not physically, then mentally.

Maybe it was time to confront Mimi to ask what had really gone down between her husband and the young woman. Was she even pregnant? Greg had insisted it was all a hoax perpetrated by Scott Quade, and it was true that since Greg's death she'd heard nothing from either Mimi or Scott. Andi had pushed it all out of her mind. She'd had other things to think about.

But if Mimi is truly pregnant with Greg's baby, how are you going to feel about that now?

Andi shook her head, headed back to the bedroom, and crawled back into bed. The idea made her feel like she was under a heavy weight. Firmly, she thrust her own grief to the back of her mind. If Greg truly were having a child, the Wrens needed to step up and acknowledge that fact. That was the bottom line. Even if it meant working things out with the odious Scott Quade and his sister, Greg's ex-lover.

Chapter Eleven

Luke walked over to his coffeemaker and poured himself another cup. He kept a pot going all day when he was in the office and generally managed to make it to the bottom before quitting time, which tended to vary dramatically, depending how many cases he was working on. He also had a bottle of rum stored in a bottom desk drawer, but he was a beer man, so he only brought it out to share with the occasional client.

The coffeemaker had shut down hours before, so Luke placed his cup in the microwave and zapped it for two minutes. It came out hot as Hades. He carefully took a sip, trying to avoid burning off the top layer of his taste buds, but he couldn't abide coffee unless it was blistering. Something about a one-time ex-girlfriend who'd poured him a cup and said, "Lukewarm. Made for you, sweet thing." She, of course, was long gone. Anyone who called him *sweet thing* and/or made a play on words of his name would be long gone. Luke's motto was get real or get out. He'd bent that rule with Iris to unwelcome results.

His cell phone rang. He checked the caller ID. Speak of the devil . . .

He almost didn't answer the call, but that was the

chicken's way out. Hitting the Answer button, he said, "Hello, Iris."

"Well, you don't have to take that tone," she replied. "I'm calling to give you some good news."

"Yeah? What's that?"

"Corkland isn't pursuing Bolchoy any longer. Not enough evidence, and well, the Carrera brothers haven't been screaming for your old partner's head. Guess we're all just getting along."

"Kinda figured as much, after the hearing."

"Just thought you'd like to know once and for all."

"Thanks," he said. Actually, it was a relief, though Bolchoy would still give his right arm to be back with the force.

"Want to catch a drink tonight for a belated celebration?" she asked lightly.

He'd been ducking her calls the past weeks. The last thing he wanted was to start something up again with her. When his thoughts turned to women, they went to Andi Wren. Their relationship was a nonstarter in the romance department, but she'd affected Luke more than any other woman in recent history. Whatever happened there—good, bad, or indifferent—he knew he wasn't going to backslide with Iris just because it was convenient.

"I don't think it would be a good idea," he said.

"Now what does that mean?"

"I've got a lot to do, and I don't know when I'll be free." *Bock, bock, bock, you chicken. Just tell her!* "Iris, I—"

"What the hell, Luke," she cut him off angrily.

"I want us to be over." There.

"I just asked for a drink. God." She was fuming.

"Yeah, well. No. I'm out."

"Fine. Be a bastard."

The *click* in his ear sounded final and he hoped that was truly the case. With Iris, it was hard to say.

His cell rang in his hand and he gazed at it with a certain

amount of trepidation. The number was familiar, but it took him a moment. Helena. She'd made the colossal mistake of attempting to kidnap Emily. Just what he'd told her *not* to do under any circumstances. But no, Helena had driven with her to Los Angeles, ostensibly to save her from being taken by Carlos back to Colombia. But it had turned out that Carlos was just part of the picture. There was another man in LA Helena had taken up with. He was a Hollywood producer—*uh-huh, tell me another one*—who was on the verge of putting together a blockbuster film, and it seemed Helena had dreams of being an actress.

But Carlos had learned where his wife was and had dutifully gone down there and picked up both Emily and Helena. He'd brought his wife back, kicking and screaming, apparently. Luke had learned of the fiasco from Carlos himself, who'd come into Luke's office and calmly asked Luke if he was having an affair with his wife. Luke had told him no, that he was in a business arrangement with Helena. Carlos had put two and two together and said quietly, "So, she is sleeping with someone else again," and left Luke mildly alarmed. He'd phoned Helena and told her Carlos had been to see him, but she wasn't interested in talking to him. She believed he'd been the one to sic Carlos on her and the producer, though Luke had had nothing to do with it, and wasn't interested in listening to reason. She'd snapped, "I'm not paying you," before she ended the call, just in case he'd had ideas about going after her for the two hundred dollars she still owed him. Luke had let her off the hook. Sometimes it was in everyone's best interest to just walk away. So, now she was phoning him . . . ?

"Luke Denton," he answered.

"You bastard! You told him where I was again!" Helena shrieked.

Called a bastard twice in the space of a few minutes.

Luke generally considered himself an affable kind of guy and was immediately annoyed. "Told who? Carlos? I had no idea where you went."

"He hired you. He told me he went to see you. And now he's pressing charges, you fucking asshole. I'll have your license for this!"

"One: He didn't hire me. Two: If he had, he would have been afforded the same confidentiality I gave you, so if I had known where—"

"He had me *arrested*. He was just waiting for a reason to get me out of the picture and you gave it to him!"

"Nope."

"What am I going to do?" she wailed. "You've got to help me. You owe it to me!"

"Take a breath, Helena. And put your listening ears on. Carlos did not hire me. He asked me if I was your lover and I said no. He'd already brought you back from LA. That whole idea that Carlos was going to kidnap your daughter? That was a story you gave me. You tried to use me to prove you had a reason to take her first."

"How do you know this? It's not true!"

"I know people in law enforcement and the DA's office. You wanted a credible ally. That's why you hired me in the first place."

Silence. He could hear her rapid breathing. She was quick to anger, quick to blame, quick to fight. Iris was cut from the same cloth, which said something about him that he wasn't sure he liked. Maybe that was why Andi had affected him so much. She was calm. She was an observer. She had yet to blame him for something beyond his control, and that in itself was worth its weight in gold.

"I'll find a way to make you pay," she threatened.

"Helena, Carlos is a good guy. You can't make him out

to be a Colombian gangster and expect everyone to believe you just because you say it's true."

"You're all the same!" she spat, and then she clicked off as well. This time he feared the finality he hoped for was a distant dream.

He was back at his laptop, writing up the final report for Helena even if he never gave it to her, when his cell phone rang again. This time he recognized the number immediately because he'd been calling it every week for the past six weeks. "Luke Denton," he answered.

"Mr. Denton, it's Peg Bellows."

Her voice held a modicum of reluctance, something he often encountered when people knew they were returning the call of a private investigator.

"Hello, Mrs. Bellows. Thank you for calling me back." He kept his voice neutral. Now that he finally had her on the phone he didn't want to scare her by sounding too eager.

"I've been unavailable."

"Sorry about all the messages. I'm in the middle of an investigation and am trying to interview people who've had dealings with the Carrera brothers."

"You don't have to be shy about it, Detective," she said dryly. "I know who you are. You want to put the Carreras away."

Remembering Bolchoy's warning that she'd been attracted to the brothers in the beginning, he said carefully, "I know you talked to my partner, Ray Bolchoy, after your husband's death."

"Do I think Brian Carrera killed him? You bet. Is there something I want to do about it? No. I just want to be left alone. I don't want any further involvement."

"I understand, but—"

"Do you? Understand? I doubt it. I put my trust in them

and Ted died because of it. Sometimes I can't even . . . speak . . ." she said, her voice tightening. "The enormity of it all, and it's my fault."

"I don't think that's entirely true," Luke said softly.

"You're wrong. It *is* entirely true. I urged Ted to go on the boating trip, and I knew Brian was going to put the pressure on to sell. I hate this cabin. I wanted to sell. I begged Ted to listen to them. They were offering a good price."

Luke was getting a different picture than he'd been told. "But Ted didn't want to."

"He suffered from nostalgia. His grandfather built the original cabin and, after a fire, his father rebuilt it into what it is today. Ted wouldn't touch a nail to renovate, so I did, since it's the place I'll most likely die."

Anger, he thought. Very likely forged from guilt. "Would it be possible to talk to you in person? I promise I'll be as quick as I can."

There was a long pause. He really thought she would refuse him. It hung in the air like a dark threat. "I saw you on the news," she finally said. "When you were interviewed at your partner's hearing."

On the steps outside. He hadn't been the warmest interview. "I was worried about Bolchoy's chances."

"I applauded you. Pauline Kirby is an overbearing bitch."

"Ah . . ." He cleared his throat, fighting a smile. Maybe Bolchoy had been right. She'd seen him and taken his side against the shark reporter.

"I suppose you can come to the cabin," she said doubtfully.

"If you would prefer to meet somewhere else . . . ?"

"No. I'm not going anywhere, so if you want to stop by today, just give me a time."

He looked at the clock. Noon straight up. "Two o'clock?" he suggested.

"You know the address?"

"Yes."

"Then I'll see you at two, Mr. Denton. And it's Peg," she added.

"And I'm Luke," he said.

"Luke," she answered carefully, as if trying it out.

He clicked off, thought about it a second, then reached for the phone to put a call through to Andi. He hesitated with his thumb over her number on his favorites list. It would be better to wait until after his full interview with Peg. He was rushing. Eager to let her know he was making progress on his mission to bring the Carreras to justice. But was he? He had no idea really what Peg Bellows could offer him.

He warred with himself for a few minutes, then grabbed his jacket and headed out into a crisp October afternoon. He would get lunch and go over the case notes he'd written out for himself, part of which were the questions he wanted to ask Ted Bellows's widow. Preparation. The type of writing he was best at.

She'd been broken after the fate that had befallen her and had retreated from the world. She was proud and alone and refused to be coddled, even when coddling would have fulfilled his own desire to play the hero. He wanted to protect her, wanted to be the one to make her safe, wanted to shine in her eyes. . . .

"Total crap," he said aloud as he climbed into his truck. Picking up his cell, he punched in his brother's number. Dallas didn't answer, so he left a voice message, "Just so we're clear. I'm not writing any goddamn book."

September walked out of the squad room and through the door to Laurelton PD's reception area. She passed by Guy

Urlacher, who slid her a look as she exited the front doors. Guy was a stickler for protocol and had intimidated September with his strict rules when she'd first been promoted to detective. He never intimidated Gretchen, however, who did as she pleased and told Guy he could do many colorful things to his body should he really demand she sign in and out every time she entered or left the building. Over the last year September had become inured to his stiff and small ways and had adopted some of Gretchen's chutzpah. Now there was a silent, cold war brewing between them, but at least he'd stopped sliding the clipboard her way and demanding her signature.

She was alone and intent on interviewing Grace Myles, Tynan Myles's mother, at Maple Grove Assisted Living. Weeks had passed since she'd planned to contact the elderly woman to see what, if anything, she could glean from her memory, weeks when she and Gretchen had been drawn into other cases, both of which were Wes and George's, but for one reason or another on which they'd needed extra help. Gretchen had actually gotten a pot thrown at her by the infuriated husband whose wife and girlfriend had been cheating on him. She'd deflected the missile but not the hot soup it contained and she'd ended up with a scalded arm.

September had helped unravel what had truly gone down among the three of them along with Wes, Gretchen, and George who, true to form, had spent most of his time in the squad room rather than doing legwork. She and Gretchen had helped be Wes's "partner" while George rode his swivel chair. Lieutenant D'Annibal had seen what was happening, but so far nothing had changed, and because no big cases had come along, the relationships within the squad room were status quo . . . except that Wes's feelings about his partner had taken a slide down the scale. He'd moved from mildly annoyed to pissed off to out-and-out angry with George.

They were all on edge, actually. Talk of cutbacks had reached the department, and being the newbie, September knew her job would be axed first. She honestly didn't know what she would do, if that were to happen. She was as attached to her job as if she were already a lifer. And she knew, even though she'd been a media darling for a while, that it wouldn't cut any ice if and when jobs were cut.

So, Gretchen was with Wes, interviewing several eye-witnesses to a knifing outside a sports club in downtown Laurelton, while George was working the phones and following up on the background of the prime suspect. September hadn't been needed on the case, so she'd gone back to the list of Aurora Lane residents she'd compiled, anyone who'd lived in the houses over the last thirty years. It was discouraging how little people remembered or knew about the Singletons and/or the eighteen-year-old male whose bones had been found in their basement. She'd worked the phones and walked Aurora Lane and generally bothered people to the point where none of them wanted to talk to her or anyone from the Laurelton PD any longer. Gretchen had tried her own brand of bullying with even less productive results. More interviews with Fairy and Craig had seemed to only confuse them, so for all intents and purposes, she was back at square one.

Today, after another unproductive conversation with the Lius' daughter, Anna, whose Chinese, non-English-speaking parents had lived across the street from the Singletons and whose patience with September was paper thin, she'd decided to make another run at Grace Myles. She'd been to see the older woman twice and had been rebuffed by the administrator who ran the facility both times with what September now thought might be excuses. She'd sensed that Tynan, for all his expansive talk about allowing his mother to be interviewed, had asked that she be left alone, and the place had complied. September had been nice about it. She truly didn't believe Grace had any information for her. But she was at loose ends and pissed off and cranky, and so today she'd thought, *to hell with it* and had headed out to take a final stab at it. Gretchen was busy, so she didn't have her partner with her, and maybe that was a saving grace as well; subtlety wasn't Gretchen's strong suit.

Maple Grove Assisted Living was a two-story, aluminum-sided building painted a pinkish beige. The second floor boasted green shutters on the windows, though the color had faded and showed patches of white, and several hinges were loose or broken, making them lopsided. The effect wasn't exactly in keeping with their motto, The Closest Thing to Home. If September had been asked to move in she would have run the other way.

This time she passed through and, noticing the sign-in sheet wasn't being closely manned at the moment, sailed down one of the corridors, checking the nameplates on the doors. Several older women were deliberately pushing walkers down the hallways and one gent followed her with his eyes and finally called out, "Hey, good-lookin'. Come back here."

Grace Myles's residence was up a flight of stairs and toward the end of a corridor, which suited September just fine. The room wasn't on the way to anywhere else, so therefore might be less traffic outside her door. Good. September didn't want to talk to the battle-ax of an administrator if she didn't have to. She gave a soft, perfunctory knock, then tried the handle, which opened beneath her palm.

September peeked into the bedroom. No sign of Grace, but the bathroom door was closed. Stymied, she waited a few minutes, then knocked on that door, too. "Grace? Do you need any help?"

"Go 'way!" was the feisty reply.

"I'm not with the staff here," September said, shooting a look over her shoulder. She'd closed the door to the room behind her, but that was no guarantee someone might not enter behind her.

"I'd like to talk to you," September called loudly.

"Sit down, then. Don't take my chair."

That was as good an invitation as she was going to get. September looked around and settled herself on the small love seat that was hugged up against a La-Z-Boy with a green-and-gold afghan draped over the back. It took another ten minutes before Grace appeared, and when she did, she walked without the aid of a wheelchair or walker and chose the La-Z-Boy. "Who are you?" she asked.

"I'm September Rafferty. I'm a police officer. I came to visit you before and—"

"Braden Rafferty?" she interrupted sharply.

September gave her a long look. The two times she'd interviewed Grace before, she hadn't made that connection. "My father's name is Braden Rafferty. I'm one of his daughters."

"You're rich."

September gave a slow nod. "My father is," she corrected. She was a little surprised Grace Myles knew of Braden Rafferty, but he and Rosamund knew how to get their names in the paper, and if you were paying attention to the Portland *Who's Who*, their names would certainly be there. "I'm a police officer, Mrs. Myles," she repeated.

One hand flew to her chest and she cried, "Oh my. What happened?"

"Nothing. I'm here about a different matter. Do you remember meeting me before?"

"You gonna arrest someone? Not me! Not me!"

"No. No, not you. I'm just looking for information about

the Singletons. Do you remember them? Jan and Phillip Singleton?"

"Harry?"

"Yes, Jan's brother's name was Harold," September said, encouraged.

"He was a randy one," she said, giving September a knowing look.

"You knew Harold?"

"Not *that* way," she said with an outraged sniff.

"I meant you were acquainted with him?"

"He was sweet on me, but I was loyal. You don't cheat. Uh-uh." She wagged her finger in front of September's face. "You don't cheat."

This was more than September had hoped for. On her previous trips to see Grace, the older woman hadn't been able to remember the Singletons at all. "The Singletons had a son, Nathan, who died in an automobile accident," September reminded her.

"Oh yes." She nodded gravely.

"I'm trying to identify a man who's been deceased for about a decade. He may have known Nathan, and he would be in between Nathan and Frances's ages, I believe. Maybe a friend . . . ? He's someone who's likely connected to the Singleton family."

"You mean Tommy."

"Tommy?" September repeated.

"He mowed their yard."

Grace seemed so clear and on target today that September had to remind herself she suffered from dementia. "Was Tommy around eighteen?"

Grace chortled and clapped her hands together. "Oh, heavens. You gotta be kidding. He was a *kid*."

"Okay. How many years ago was this?"

"I don't know. You ask a lot of questions."

"I do ask a lot of questions." September smiled. "I was

talking to your son, Tynan, and your grandson, Caleb, and his wife, Hannah."

"Oh, *her* . . ."

September soldiered on. "The man I'm trying to identify would have been about eighteen when he died. He may have known the Singletons or been connected to them in some way. He would be about thirty now."

"Talk, talk, talk." She flapped a hand at September.

Realizing she'd probably gotten everything she could from Grace, she nevertheless asked, "What do you remember about the Singletons?"

"Oh, them. Stuck-up. No good. Snotty, snotty." She sniffed. "And that son of theirs . . . a no-goodnik through and through. Yes, ma'am."

"Nathan?"

"Uh-huh. And his wife . . ."

"Davinia."

"Who?" She frowned and shook her head. "The blond one. Always had all the jewelry. La-di-da. I hated her."

"You could be describing Davinia, Nathan's wife?" September heard voices outside Grace's door and readied herself in case someone was coming to find out who Grace's visitor was.

"Naughty, naughty," she singsonged, nodding sagely.

"Why do you say that?"

Grace pressed a finger to her lips and looked around surreptitiously, as if afraid someone would overhear. "You know they were having intercourse."

"Who?"

"Davinia," she hissed. "And that *boy*."

"That boy?"

The voices outside the door grew louder and September heard keys rattle. She braced herself, but another door opened and slammed shut, and she guessed whoever was there wasn't coming to Grace's room.

"Yes, ma'am. The one she was mmm-mmm-mmm-ing with," Grace clarified.

"Davinia was having an affair? Do you remember with whom? His name? The boy?"

She drew back and eyed her up and down. "What do you want him for?" she asked suspiciously.

"I'm trying to identify a . . . body . . . a male who died when he was about eighteen. He would be thirty now."

"He died?"

"Yes. He could maybe be Davinia's lover?" she tried.

"Go ask the blond bitch. She's a cheater. You shouldn't cheat. Never, never."

"If you mean Davinia, she died in the automobile accident with Nathan."

"She cheated. Everybody knew it."

"Did Nathan know it?"

"Oh sure."

"Do you remember who she cheated with?"

"That boy," she said, as if September were the densest person on record.

They were stuck in a loop. "Who is that boy?" September asked a trifle wearily. "Tommy?"

"No, he grew up and got fat. Big blubbery blubberhead. That's what my grandson says."

"Your grandson, Caleb?"

"Caleb . . . no. Not him. The other one."

"What's the name of your other grandson?"

She reared back and her face grew red. She suddenly shrieked, "He's dead! He died from those drugs! *Don't talk to me about him*!"

And with that she reached back and yanked a cord attached to the wall. Realizing she was calling for help, September scooted for the door. She didn't want to be there when the cavalry arrived. "Thank you, Grace," she murmured, letting herself out.

"Bitch," Grace snapped as the door closed behind September.

As she slipped into the hallway, she could hear muffled howl after howl coming from Grace's room. September heard brisk footsteps heading her way. She prepared herself to meet with the administrator, but two young aides paid no attention to her as they headed at a leisurely pace to Grace's room.

Chapter Twelve

Andi pushed through the front door of Wren Development and made her way to the elevator, her head full of unresolved issues. Telling herself she needed to confront Mimi Quade and her unborn child was one thing, doing it quite another. She'd picked up the phone half a dozen times only to put it back down. She'd even thought about calling Luke, but though she'd told him about Greg's affair during one of their conversations, she'd brushed over the details and didn't want to go into them any further now.

Instead, she'd decided to talk to Carter about the situation. Like Greg, Carter firmly believed Mimi was faking it, but Andi wasn't so sure.

Her phone rang when she was in the elevator and she was surprised to see the call was from Trini. She answered and said quickly, "I'm in the elevator, so if I lose you, call me back."

"Are you at work?"

"Yeah, I'm coming in a little late today."

"Well, I won't keep you, but I just wanted to say, things are better."

Andi heard the lightness in her voice. "Oh?"

"With Bobby. I was really bummed. I just didn't want to

talk about it. All these years, y'know? Of being the dumper, instead of the dumpee . . . Well, it really sucks to be on the other end."

"It sure does." Andi smiled.

"But we're seeing each other again, so maybe, *maybe*, fingers crossed, I can finally have you meet him this weekend."

"Good. Yeah. Let's do that," Andi said with a little more enthusiasm than she really felt. She and Trini had drifted apart some, and she wanted their relationship back on track, but to do that she thought they might need to see each other alone.

"Okay, listen, I gotta go. But I'll call you, okay?"

"Sure. Sure. Just glad to know you're all right."

"Oh, of course I am."

"Well, don't confront the Carrera brothers. That's all I'm saying. They're dangerous."

"Okay . . . noted," she said, sounding slightly abashed. "I'd had a little more to drink than I should have, and I'm not a drinker."

"I know you're not. That's what worried me."

"I probably said some things I shouldn't have, but Carrera didn't pay much attention to me anyway, as far as I can remember."

"What were you doing at Lacey's anyway?"

"Oh . . . I don't know. I just was missing Bobby and I . . . well, it doesn't matter now. We're back together and everything they say about makeup sex is true." She laughed. "So I'll call you, and we'll get together. Now go to work. Make some more Wren dough."

"Aye aye."

The conversation buoyed Andi's spirits and she was in a better frame of mind when she walked into Carter's office. He was standing by the window, looking over the wetlands behind the building, talking on his cell. Seeing

Andi, he wrapped up with, "I'll call you back," then clicked off. "You look well," he observed.

"I just talked to Trini and I hadn't spoken to her for a while. My friend from college," she clarified, in case he'd forgotten.

"The one who didn't come to your wedding."

So he hadn't forgotten. "Exactly. Have you ever met her?"

"Don't think so."

"She's been going through a tough time, but things have improved." She took a breath. "I have something I want to talk to you about."

"Fire away."

"I've been thinking about Mimi and the baby."

He made a sound between a snort and a groan. "There is no baby."

"I know that's what you and Greg thought, but I've never been convinced. So I'm going to call her, connect with her. Find out how she's doing, and if you're right and she's been faking, then we'll know. And if she's pregnant, we need to reach out to her."

"*If* she's pregnant and *if* it's Greg's. Two big ifs."

"Well, we need to find out, then."

"Why? Mimi Quade and her brother Scott are con artists. Greg was an idiot for getting involved with her. Sorry, Andi. It's true."

"I'm not arguing with you, but I need to know once and for all, and so do you. The child would be your niece or nephew."

"I have no interest in any bastard child of Greg's."

"Carter, come on."

"Andi, I've got other things to think about. Like the finances. I know you and Emma have just given up, but I have to worry about these things."

"The construction loan went through. What are you talking about?"

"Cost overruns. Unexpected problems. Do you know how fucking expensive it is to build a lodge? Don't even answer. I know you don't."

"I've got a pretty good idea," Andi said.

"We've got other expenses on top of the loan. It's all tapping us out and we've got a long way to go yet."

"So we're in financial trouble again?"

"Not again. The same problems." He made a face. "And don't worry about it. I'm handling it."

"I am going to worry about it. We're in this together. All of us. It's been a hard summer and fall . . . losing Greg, the miscarriage . . . but the lodge is coming along, and things are getting better."

"Are they?"

"Yes."

"If you're stirring up things with the Quades, I'm not so sure."

"I just want the truth. The total story. And to learn that, I need to see Mimi."

"Fine. I've got some appointments to keep. More red tape with the county," he said with a wave of his hand, telling her it was the same old rigmarole. "Tomorrow, let's meet at the lodge. I want to go over some things with you and Emma."

"Have you contacted Emma?"

"You mean because she never shows up for work? Not .yet, but I will."

"I could call her," Andi offered.

"No, I'll do it."

Carter was good at complaining he was doing all the work but less so at delegating true responsibility, so she was pleased he was attempting to include both her and Emma. Oftentimes he had a tendency to think his way was the only way, no matter if there was evidence to the contrary.

He'd placed his cell phone on his desk, but now he swept it up again. "I'll move a few things around and let's meet at nine."

"Great. Anything else you need before then?"

"Aren't you meeting with Mimi?"

"Yes, but that's not going to take up all my time."

"There's nothing specific, so do whatever you usually do." He flipped a hand toward her office, as if her value as a company member was practically worthless. It burned her, but she didn't want to fight with her brother-in-law.

As she turned to leave, he said, "Let me know how it turns out."

"Sure," she answered shortly.

As Andi was leaving his office she got another call. Luke. Her pulse quickened in spite of herself. Taking a deep breath, she answered, "Hi, there," as she headed into the hallway, closing Carter's office door behind her.

"Hi. Been a while since we talked."

Gooseflesh rose on her arms at his warm tone. She could feel her cheeks heat and she shook her head at her own susceptibility. It was ridiculous. They were business associates and barely that. As soon as the Carrera problem was put to bed, her relationship with Luke would likely be over. Maybe they would be friends, but maybe not.

"I've finally got an appointment with Peg Bellows."

"Great. When?"

"Two o'clock this afternoon."

"She called you?"

"Yep. I've been checking with some of the other families who were pressured by the Carreras, but they say the same thing you do: everything's quieted down. Maybe it's the calm before the storm; I don't know. But ever since that night at Lacey's, nothing much has come out of their camp.

Peg's been MIA, but maybe she can shed some light on the situation."

"Good. It's kind of strange how little we've heard from the Carreras."

"I know. How are you feeling about the protection thing?"

"I can't believe they've just given up."

"Oh, they haven't. Not for good anyway."

"But they don't seem to be focused on me as much right now. I'm wondering if I misread the threat in that note."

"No, no. That note was meant to scare you."

"Well, then, it worked." Andi took a breath and added, "I wanted to tell you that I've made a kind of decision. Remember Mimi Quade? We talked about her a little."

"The woman your husband was seeing?" he responded carefully.

"That's the one. Just before Greg died, Mimi and her brother, Scott, came to the office and broke the news about her pregnancy to Greg. Carter, Emma, and I were there, too. It was a scene. Mimi was crying and Scott demanded a DNA test, and then, before anything got resolved, Greg died."

"You think there's a connection?"

"Oh no. It was an accident. But he was driving away from seeing her when it happened. We had all pushed the 'Mimi problem' away. Nobody knew what to do. I'm not proud of that, but Greg and I weren't getting along as well as we could at the time. . . . Anyway, now I want to know what happened. How she's doing. If she's pregnant with Greg's baby, I need to know. I just had a talk with Carter about it again."

"What did he say?" Luke asked curiously.

"He's never believed she's really pregnant. Thinks her brother put her up to it. I don't know. But if there is a child, and it's Greg's, then he or she is a Wren. I just need to know, and so does Carter . . . and Emma."

"Sounds like you're putting things in order."

"A little late, but yeah. We need to."

The elevator doors suddenly slid open and Emma and Ben burst out as if they were being chased by wild animals. "Looks like I gotta," she said.

"I'll let you know what Peg says."

"Good. Thanks. Maybe . . . why don't you stop by the cabin afterward and fill me in?" she asked.

"See you then," he agreed.

"Where's Carter?" Emma demanded as Andi ended her call.

"In his office." She inclined her head toward the door to the room she'd just left.

"What are you doing here?" Ben asked.

"I work here." *I could ask you the same thing,* she thought. Ben seemed to consider himself a fourth partner.

"You've been here all day?" Emma looked chagrined. Andi had to think hard to remember the last time Emma had come to the office.

Andi moved past both of them toward the elevator. "I just talked to Carter about Mimi Quade. I'm going to contact her to find out if she's pregnant with Greg's child."

"You are?" Emma stared at Andi with consternation. "Are you okay with that?"

"Well, yeah. We have to be. Scott said she was pregnant with Greg's baby and wanted a DNA test. I say let's find out."

Andi pressed the Down button and luckily, the elevator car was still on their floor. As she stepped inside, she added, "Talk to Carter. There's a meeting scheduled at the lodge tomorrow. I'm planning to be there and Carter thinks you should be, too."

The elevator doors whispered closed and Andi let out a pent-up breath. *No time like the present,* she thought. She pulled up the contact list on her phone and punched in the number Greg had given her for Mimi months earlier in a show of good faith about his commitment to their marriage. "Ask her anything," he'd said. "It's over." Of course, she hadn't made the call. Hadn't believed she ever would, until now.

Scott Quade sat at the kitchen table inside the apartment he was currently sharing with his sister. He'd had to move in with her after the incident with the landlord at his last place. Could he help it if his date had gotten completely wasted and walked out of his unit naked? It wasn't any kind of reason to kick him out, but hell, he was behind on the rent anyway, and it was kind of understood that if he just left, the skinflint bastard who ran the place wouldn't come after him for October's rent. The security fee, which was only about half the month's rent anyway, would be used instead, and there would be no cleaning fee returned. Scott had made certain of that.

Now he was accessing the neighbor's unsecured Wi-Fi from his grinder of a laptop. It was embarrassing that he had such an ancient piece of equipment, that he couldn't afford a tablet. He was damn lucky to have a smartphone, although he was behind on that bill as well. He'd always crowed about being a master of the get-rich-quick scheme, but the shitty truth was none of his ideas had panned out yet.

Mimi was gasping on the phone, her eyes practically bugging out. Scott threw her a dark look. He was really over her histrionics, though this time there seemed to be something else going on. The girl was damn near hyperventilating.

What? he mouthed to her, but she turned away to look out the teensy, dirt-smeared window above the sink, her cell phone at her ear.

"Uh-huh . . . okay, yeah . . . uh-huh . . ." was all she was saying, but she looked about to faint. "Okay, then."

"What?" Scott asked again as Mimi dropped the phone on the counter with a clatter.

"OMG! You know who that was? Andrea Wren! Greg's *wife*!"

"She fucking called you?" Scott stared at his dim-bulb sister.

"Yes! What does she want? OMG," she muttered again and began chewing on her thumbnail like a pit bull on a bone.

Scott held himself back from yanking her hand from her mouth. He also hated the way she verbalized texting short-cuts, but she was his meal ticket. She might not realize that fact, but he sure did. "Well, good. It's about time they got back to us. That fucking Carter's been refusing my calls. Goddamn Wrens."

"Don't say that. You know how much I loved Greg."

Scott's black mood slipped into further decline. "They screwed you over, Meems. All of 'em, not just Greg. And now you're goddamn Ebola."

"What do you mean?"

"You're the plague, ding dong. The fucking plague."

"But I'm not pregnant anymore," she said in that little baby voice that made his teeth hurt.

"I. Know. That."

It pissed Scott off to no end that Mimi had been out playing volleyball on the beach last summer and jiggled the damn thing free. Oh, he'd heard that it just happened that way sometimes, women miscarried all the time, but he didn't believe it. If she'd taken care of herself, they'd still be sitting pretty. A little bun in the oven, the only heir to the family fortune. He'd wanted to crow with laughter when they'd gone into those expensive offices and let the Wrens know that Gregory stick-up-his-butt Wren had screwed his sister senseless and would now pay the price. Woo-wee! Scott had been on cloud nine. Couldn't wait to twist the knife and cut out a hunk of that Wren dough for himself. Oh, he knew the Wrens. Had damn near grown up with Carter and Greg . . . well, at least during the summers, when the Wrens visited their lake place. He knew how rich they were. He'd seen them from afar and had speculated on their money even when he was a kid. Scott knew the value of a dollar, yessirree.

He'd planned to find a way to be just like the Wrens, though some of his moneymaking plans hadn't quite worked out. Like that alfalfa farm . . . shoulda been a gold mine, but his own shitty luck had held out and he'd lost every dime he owned on that venture. He'd been toying with becoming a marijuana grower. Hell, they were making bank in Washington, and now Oregon was about a year behind and he could get in while the getting was good. But meanwhile, dear little Mimi had been growing into a woman. A real woman at that. With her long legs and perky tits—a little small, perhaps, but they stood up nice—Mimi had stepped across Greg and Carter's paths . . . with only the smallest push from Scott.

Carter hadn't shown much interest, but Greg's eyes had followed little sis in a way that had made Scott chortle. He'd arranged for Meems to be in the same building with Wren Development, telling her to pretend she was visiting one of the law firms. And then Greg had headed out to lunch and she'd literally run into him, the oldest trick in the book, just dumb, little old Meems accidentally falling into his arms, spilling the contents of her purse. One thing led to another and they were meeting for a drink or two. Happy hour spilled into happy evenings together, during which Greg had admitted his marriage was all but dead. He'd been ripe for the picking and it hadn't taken long at all for Mimi to wangle him into the sack and then *ka bam!* Bonanza! A new Wren in the nest!

He'd hustled her down to the Wren offices and it had been perfect. Just perfect. The best day of his life. They'd all been there: Carter and Emma and Greg and *Andrea* Wren, the poor, misunderstood, cheated-on wife. It was such a coup! Andrea had been weirdly contained: no hysterics, although her face had drained of color. All the drama was from Meems, who was crying, swearing she loved Greg, the stunned idiot, and making a damn fool out of herself, which was all the better. Neither Carter nor Greg acted like they even remembered Scott, though he knew they did. As far as they were concerned, Scott was just dog shit on the soles of their shoes they'd scraped off years earlier.

In that one moment, Scott had been triumphant. *Bet you don't forget me now*, he'd thought smugly, even while he'd been jealous of the man for being married to such a sophisticated beauty. How had he given that up to *shtup* Meems? Libido was a bitch sometimes, he guessed, though he, Scott, would never let a woman's vagina get between him and his goals.

But then, Jesus, the guy *died*. Just like that. One moment Scott was in the catbird seat. The next he was scrambling around to keep the remaining Wrens aware that they had a new heir on the way. Scott had tried to contact Carter almost immediately, but he never got past the receptionist, who kept coolly putting him off. Cunt. Who the hell did she think she was? No minimum wager was going to keep him from getting to Carter and Emma and the ice queen widow.

And then . . . the fucking volleyball game during which Mimi lost the baby. He'd nearly lost his mind. What? *What?* Unbelievable. Mimi had still been weepy over Greg's death and had gone to the beach with friends to feel better. Scott had warned her to be careful, but had she listened? God no. When did Meems ever listen? The only saving grace was that the Wrens didn't know the baby was gone. So, okay, the big score was no more thanks to stupid Meems, but there had still been time to devise a way to get a slice of Wren cash. Maybe they'd like to pay for an "abortion," say. He doubted any of them was going to want to share with Greg's bastard. He'd been just getting ready to make the first move on his new plan, a tearful Meems saying she couldn't keep the baby and a late-term abortion was sooo expensive and dangerous, and probably not even legal, but there were ways . . .

But he didn't want Andrea Wren to be the one to make the first overture to Mimi. How had that happened? Fucking A. He was pretty sure she'd nix the idea of an abortion at this late date. She'd just had a miscarriage herself, hadn't she? God. Maybe she would want to keep the baby! That was no good. No good at all.

He needed to deal with Carter or Emma, the true Wrens. They would be more likely to fork over the dough. If he played it right, he might be able to squeeze ten thousand out of them, right? A promise of discretion might go a long way. Or . . . maybe even twenty, if Mimi could be any kind of actress and pretend she was seesawing over losing her precious unborn child.

Andrea Wren, though . . . she had to hate Meems and, by association, him. She couldn't get in the way now. Scott wasn't going to let it happen.

"Well, what did you say to her?" he demanded. He wished he'd been paying closer attention, but he always closed his ears to Mimi's babbling. A sane person could only stand so much. Every time she was on the phone with friends he wanted to yank the cell from her hand and throw it across the room.

"I told her I was busy, but then she said she would stop by Nailed It tomorrow to see me, so I told her to come over now."

"Come over *here*? Now?" Scott swooped up his laptop and leaped to his feet. "Goddamn it, Meems! You're such a fucking pushover. Go get dressed. And put that baby bump on. Jesus, you should be showing a lot by now. Goddamn it!"

"I can't lie to her, Scott," she burbled, her big blue eyes filling with tears.

Scott counted to three and forced a smile. "You have to. Or call her back and get out of it."

"But then she'll come to see me at work! I can't do her nails. I can't!"

"Well, I can't be here."

"What am I gonna do?" Her wail had turned into a shriek.

Scott set the laptop back down on the table, counted to ten, then went to his sister, placing his hands on her shoulders and looking deeply into her dewy eyes. "Listen to me. The Wrens owe you, you know that. Greg loved you and they killed him." She started to shake her head, but he went on harshly, "They killed him. You know they did. They'd just found out about you and they thought you were in the car and they pushed his car off the road." This was the lie he'd told her so often he almost believed it himself. Almost.

"It was a single-car accident," she insisted, saying the words by rote, as if they were in some foreign language. She could mimic the sound, but she had no idea what the words meant.

"Fucking A, Mimi. That's what they want you to believe. They probably came at him in another car and Greg swerved to avoid them. It only looks like a single-car accident. It could have been his wife who went after him after she found out he was screwing around. She doesn't want to share her part of their fortune with somebody else's brat."

"I don't think—" she began, but he cut her off.

"True, Meems. True! You *don't* think. Not enough."

"No . . ."

"Yes!" he insisted, his fingers digging into her shoulders.

"Greg said he and his wife had drifted apart from each other. He called her Andi. They couldn't have children. I thought he'd be so thrilled when I told him I was pregnant, but—"

"Never mind." Scott didn't want to hear that *again*. He was sick of Mimi bemoaning how the news of her pregnancy seemed to send Greg back into his wife's arms. Counterintuitive, but then, who knew what guilt would make people do? Scott knew Wren's car slipping over the embankment was just an unfortunate accident, but that wasn't going to help him now. Mimi had to feel some righteous indignation if she was going to play this right. And she needed to play it right.

"Sweetie," he went on in a conciliatory tone, "if we don't get some money soon, we're gonna be out on our asses. Fucking rent's skyrocketing, especially around the goddamn lake."

"We could move back to Laurelton," she said hopefully.

"This is where we grew up," he reminded her tightly. "We're not getting run out by the people with all the money. Gentrification. Goddamn it! We belong here, too."

She tried to think. He could practically see the wheels trying to turn in her mind, though they were slipping a few cogs.

"Maybe," she said, "it was those brothers who ran Greg

off the road. Those twins." Her mouth wobbled and more tears filled her eyes.

He had to give her credit for that one. She could almost be right about the Carreras. "That's not what happened," he said. He had to keep her on track. "Now listen to me. Andrea Wren's going to be here soon, so I've gotta leave."

"No!" She gazed at him in fear.

"You need to do this alone."

"Oh, Scott. I can't!"

"Yes, you can." He steered her upstairs to the bedroom. She tried to dig her boot heels into the carpet, but he was stronger and Mimi was always one to give in. "Put on a loose blouse. Where is that damn bun-in-the-oven thing? Get it out and put it on."

"It's in the bottom drawer," she said dispiritedly. She stared at the blue chest of drawers with the white knobs. Mimi'd had it since they were kids and was fond of it, had planned to use it for the baby, whereas Scott had thrown all measure of their earlier life with their single mom away. Depressing stuff.

He yanked open the drawer and dug through some T-shirts before he found the baby bump. It wasn't that large. He'd bought it for her as soon as she'd miscarried, already thinking ahead. She should be showing a lot more by now, he thought. Still, it would probably do the trick. He handed it to Mimi, who reluctantly took off her T-shirt and fastened it around her middle. She put the T-shirt back on and Scott was happy with how it looked. She could be the kind of woman who didn't show a lot. "You're wearing this to work, aren't you? We talked about this, Meems."

"I wear it," she said, her lower lip thrust out in protest.

"Good. Don't let Greg's wife get too near," he warned.

"I can't do this."

"Yeah. You can. You have to. Now listen . . . you need to

let her know that you really want this child, even if abortion would be the better choice. You got that?"

"I would never have an abortion!"

"Mimi, we're playacting here. Use your fucking head for once. Jesus. This is important."

"I know we need money!"

"That's right. That's exactly right. We need money. And you don't like Greg's wife. She's a rich bitch. You know that's true."

"They met at college. She has an MBJ."

"MBA," he corrected.

"Oh yeah. Masters of business and . . ."

"Administration. Meems, please . . ." He despaired of her. "Come on." He grabbed her hand and led her down to the kitchen. "After you let her in, go back and sit in this chair. Keep the table as a barrier, you understand? You don't want her to look too closely at you, and you definitely don't want her to touch you."

"Uh-huh."

"Make some coffee. Oh, shit, you'd probably be drinking decaf. . . ." He looked around the kitchen.

"I drink decaf tea," she said, slipping from his grasp. Opening a cupboard, she collected two mugs and set them on the counter. Then she lifted the lid on the cookie jar that sat next to the toaster and pulled out two tea bags. "I just fill the mugs with water and zap them in the microwave."

"Good enough. Make sure she doesn't stay long."

"What does she want? Why is she coming?" She started chewing on her thumb again.

"Stop that. It has to be about the baby."

She dropped her hand. "What if she wants to touch my stomach? People do that, y'know. I like to do it. It's good luck."

"Just sit at the table. Got that? Just sit at the table and keep her away from you."

"After I give her a cup of tea."

"Yes."

"I wish she wasn't coming."

You and me both, he thought, but he said, "Yeah, well, maybe this is a good thing. They've all ignored you for months. Maybe this'll get the ball rolling."

Mimi swiped at another round of tears. "I wish I still had the baby for real."

"You fixed that for all of us. But get over it. We have work to do."

Chapter Thirteen

Andi drove into the parking lot of Brightside Apartments, Mimi's address, which was on the north side of the lake and about half a mile from the water. In those weeks after she'd first learned of Greg's relationship with Mimi Quade, she'd been half crazed with anger and a wild possessiveness. She'd found herself following him from work, and it hadn't taken long before he drove to a large complex designed with rows of town houses. It wasn't one of her finest moments by a long shot, but when Andi had learned Mimi's address, she'd filed the information away for future use, just in case she needed it. Later Greg had told her about going to see Mimi himself. He'd let her know it was over. He insisted Mimi wasn't pregnant and the affair was really over before it had begun. Andi hadn't fully believed him, though she'd wanted to, but she wasn't convinced Greg had been faithful even before Mimi. There were rumors . . .

But at the time she'd pretended to believe Greg. It was easier than fighting. Later, though, she'd found out where Mimi worked and she went to the nail salon and observed Mimi as she gave a manicure to an older woman who requested a glittery diamondlike gem be affixed to every one of her nails. Andi got a pedicure from another woman and wore fake glasses, her hair bound in a scarf in case Mimi chanced to look her way. She figured if she was found out, too damn bad; she'd take the heat. But the scattered girl with the big eyes who'd gazed at Greg so adoringly in their offices had been too involved with her work that day to notice.

Greg had been true to his word about ending it with Mimi, however. As soon as Mimi and her brother announced her pregnancy, the affair was over. From Greg's point of view, a quick transgression was turning into something more complicated that didn't fit with his plans. He told Andi the only woman he'd ever really loved was her, that he'd failed her and that he wanted to make it up to her. Andi hadn't believed him, but the words had soothed her wounded heart, and somewhere in the next few weeks she'd forgiven him enough to sleep with him again. All of that was a blur. Lost time. Blackouts. The fog of misery. Call it what you will, at the time Andi had felt like she was going through the motions of someone else's life.

Then she'd gotten the 9-1-1 call: her husband was being life-flighted to Emanuel Medical Center in northeast Portland. Reality was a bucket of ice water poured over her head. She'd driven to the hospital in a controlled panic, but by the time she got there, Greg was already gone.

Now, thinking back, she had only snapshot memories of seeing Carter and Emma and Ben there, though she could smell Emma, who'd been blindly drunk and reeked of booze. Through it all, Andi had forced herself to stay focused. She needed to ask the right questions. She needed to keep moving forward, make decisions. At one point, Carter had pulled her aside and hugged her, his heart beating fast and hard. She'd noted it from a distance as he rarely touched her. Ben, taking a cue from his brother-in-law, had then hugged her, too, though more stiffly, until Andi eased away. Emma hadn't been able to do anything but stumble around and cry.

After Greg's death, Andi had barely thought of Mimi. She'd been diminished by the loss of Andi's husband. Both Emma and Carter had believed Greg that Mimi's baby, if it even existed, wasn't his, so they wanted nothing more to do with the Quades.

A couple of weeks after Greg's death, Carter told Andi, "I did some research on wonderful Mimi and her brother. Scott Quade's an extortionist. He's looking for a quick score, and in this instance Greg played right into his hands. I'd be surprised if the bitch is really pregnant at all, but even if she is, the chances of it being Greg's are slim to none."

Emma had agreed with her brother, but had added, "Oh, Scott's always been around," she said. "He's one of the lake rats."

"Lake rats?" Andi queried.

"No money. Old cabins. Scruffy and poor. Schultz Lake was full of 'em. Not so much anymore. Scott's just trying to make a score."

"Maybe you knew him. I never did," Carter corrected her.

"You had your share of lake friends. I caught you with Melanie."

"We were kids," he'd dismissed, sounding long-suffering.

Andi had let the issue go. Her own mental health demanded it, and there wasn't a lot she could do about it anyway. Carter had relieved her of acting in any way by telling her, "If she's really pregnant, and if it's Greg's, we'll figure out what to do soon enough," so none of them had approached Mimi or Scott about the issue again. Then time passed and Andi was pregnant, then she miscarried. . . . Now she wanted to know the truth from Mimi about Greg and the baby.

She had butterflies in her stomach as she remote locked her Tucson and headed toward Mimi's town house. She reached the front door and knocked, noting the deferred maintenance in the faded and scarred black paint on the door and the dry, scraggly bushes flanking an exposed aggregate sidewalk riddled with cracks. Glancing around, she saw that the town houses were in total decline. Even so, with the greater Portland area's blistering rental rate climb, she knew the rent wouldn't be cheap.

It took a while for Mimi to answer, but when she did, Andi's eyes were immediately drawn to the very prominent baby bump sticking out from Mimi's middle. The sight of it made Andi's ears buzz. Pregnant . . . Mimi really was pregnant.

Mimi stared at her for a moment, then suddenly broke into tears. "I miss him so much!"

Her wail brought Andi slowly back to the present. She sensed she should say she missed him, too, but the words stuck in her throat and Mimi rushed in with, "You probably hate me. I'm so sorry. I . . . I loved him!" She was gulping hard and shaking with emotion.

"Yeah, well, um . . . he was a good man." Was he? Andi wasn't sure about that.

But Mimi, her blue eyes full of naked pain, said on a hiccup, "He was. He really was. I can't believe he's gone. I just can't believe it."

She looked at Andi, clearly waiting for her to explain why she was on her doorstep. "I just wanted to . . . see how you were," Andi said.

"Would you . . . you want to come in and have a cup of decaf tea?"

"I think maybe I should go." She gestured toward the evidence of Mimi's pregnancy. "I just was thinking about everything and . . . we really haven't really given you any support."

"Oh, it's okay." Her mouth worked as she fought for control.

"No, it's not. If you're . . ." She stopped herself and said instead, "We were surprised when you and your brother showed up at the offices and announced—"

"Please come in. I'll get you some tea."

She left the door wide open and hurried toward the back of the town house. Andi stood on the porch a moment longer, reluctant to enter, already wishing she hadn't come. Exhaling a pent-up breath, she followed in Mimi's wake.

"Is chamomile okay?" Mimi asked as Andi stood by the small kitchen table at the end of the U-shaped kitchen.

"Sure." Andi had harbored a lot of bad thoughts about Greg's lover, but faced with this pregnant woman child, those feelings started to slip away. Mimi was too open and gullible to despise, though Andi could sense she might grow impatient with her very easily.

"Could we talk about Greg a little?" Mimi asked. "I'm . . . I'm just . . . I know he is . . . was your husband and all, but . . ."

Mimi was holding two mugs and suddenly her hands started trembling so violently that hot tea splashed onto the backs of them. Andi jumped forward to help as Mimi dropped one mug, shrieked, then burst into a fresh flood of tears.

"No, leave it," Andi said when Mimi bent down to address the mess. "Sit down." She led her toward a chair.

"I'm so sorry. I'm so sorry."

"Just take a breath." Once Mimi was seated, Andi grabbed a paper towel and picked up the mug, which had stayed remarkably intact except for a broken handle. She threw the mug into a trash bin under the kitchen sink, then grabbed more paper towels and mopped up the rest of the tea. Throughout, Mimi apologized profusely. When Andi was finished, she tried to hand Andi the still unbroken mug in her hand with its half-full contents, but Andi refused.

"You keep it. I really can't stay long anyway," Andi said. "We need to work this out, but I need to talk to Carter and Emma, Greg's brother and sister, and remind them about the baby."

Mimi looked down at her stomach. "They've forgotten?"

"A lot's happened," Andi said. "We really didn't know where things stood with you after Greg died. When are you due, by the way? I think you told us, but I really can't remember. I was . . . processing."

"Oh, um . . ." She looked away. "I don't know if I'm keeping it."

"You're putting the baby up for adoption?" Andi's mind grappled with the thought.

"I don't know. I don't think so." She gulped down some tea. "I wish Scott were here. He always knows what to do."

"Is Scott not around?" Andi questioned.

She thought that over hard. "He's at work."

"He still lives around here?"

"He never wants to leave the lake," she said, almost in a whisper.

Andi automatically looked past her and through the window that looked over the back parking lot. Schultz Lake was somewhere beyond, but the view was blocked by more apartments. "What's Scott do?"

"You mean like a job? Um . . . lots of things."

Andi wondered if that meant he was between jobs. "Is he . . . helping you with the baby?"

"Kind of. He wants to talk to Carter, but the receptionist won't put him through."

"Did he leave a message with Jill?"

"I don't know. I guess. That's just what he said."

Carter hadn't let Andi know he'd been contacted by

Scott Quade, but then, Carter didn't believe Mimi was carrying Greg's baby. However, the way Mimi felt about Greg made it hard for Andi to believe the child was anyone's but his. "I'll tell Carter to talk to Scott."

"Okay," she choked out.

"I promise we're not going to ignore Greg's child any longer," Andi told her.

She flapped a hand at Andi, too overcome to say anything more.

Andi said a few more words of encouragement, aware how ironic it was that she was the one comforting Greg's paramour. She let herself out the door, almost feeling bad about leaving Mimi. She put a call in to Carter, who didn't pick up his phone, and left him a message about Mimi's pregnancy, saying they could talk about it further the next day.

She didn't notice the car that eased from a parking spot down the block and followed after her.

The Bellows's cabin was much like he'd remembered it from his first visit, but the flowers beside the porch had all withered and died. The rest of the landscaping was trimmed and tended, courtesy of Art Kessler undoubtedly. But Peg had said she was at the cabin, so Luke bent his head to a soft but persistent rain and hurried to the front door. He knocked loudly, the sound harsh and foreign in the bucolic setting. He could see through the cabin to the other side, where the gray waters of Schultz Lake were dimpling with the rain.

No answer.

Luke checked his watch and saw it was two minutes past two. He was right on time. He grew impatient, wondering if she'd stood him up. What the hell was that about? Bolchoy had intimated that she'd found the Carrera brothers attractive and that he should expect the same, but Peg had cooled off on them. At least that was the impression he'd gotten on the phone.

He heard a noise inside the house and peered through the window once more. Peg Bellows was moving toward the door slowly. She wore a bathrobe and a scarf was tied around her head.

Some kind of cancer . . .

Luke had a sinking feeling. He'd pushed and pushed and now realized she was ill. When the door opened he half expected her skin to be gray or sallow, but her cheeks were flushed pink.

"Luke, right?" she greeted him with an ironic smile.

"That's right. How're you doing?"

"You mean the breast cancer?" She shrugged lightly. "It's a battle I'm losing."

"I'm sorry."

She shook her head and sighed, then waved him inside. "Come in. Take a seat. You want some coffee? I've got a pot brewing."

"Sure. Would you like some help?" He felt embarrassed that he'd pushed her into playing hostess.

"I've got it. You want cream or sugar?"

"Black's fine."

Luke saw one particular chair arranged directly in front of the television and bypassed it for a white, leather chair angled to one side. He perched on the edge, wondering if he should ignore her command and follow her into the kitchen.

But she returned a few moments later with two mugs of coffee. "My vice is loads of cream and sugar. I figure, what does it matter now? I struggled with weight all my life and now I just keep losing pounds. Be careful what you wish for, huh?"

"Thank you," he said, accepting his coffee. "Let me just say, I'm sorry I left you so many messages."

"Don't back down now. You want the Carreras and so do I. Let's work together."

"Okay."

She settled herself in the chair in front of the television. As she sat down, one skinny white leg escaped the robe, but she tucked it back in quickly. "They killed my husband."

"I'd like to prove that."

"But there's no hard evidence. It's just a theory proposed by a grieving widow. Make that a guilt-stricken grieving widow because well, she had an affair with one of them and her husband found out."

This was more information than Luke had expected, but he sensed that Peg was racing against time and was bound and determined to make things right, or as right as they could be, no matter at what cost to herself. "Which one?" he asked, and she barked out a short laugh.

"That's the question? Not did your husband know? Did you tell him? Or did he go to a watery grave thinking you were still the starry-eyed ingénue from forty years earlier?" Before he could answer, she said, "Blake Carrera. The sexy one with the scar. Brian's good, too, but Blake's the really dangerous one. He's the predator."

Little birds need to fly . . .

"Can you give me an example?" Luke asked.

"Whenever Ted was away, or engaged by something that took his attention, Blake was always touching me. He was careful at first, I realize now. Testing the situation. He was funny, too. Clever. I found myself thinking about him a lot, and I looked forward to any time they would be coming by to talk about selling the cabin. At first I was against selling, like Ted. I thought, if they want it so badly, we should hang on to it. But I've never really liked the place, and then Ted kept stringing them along and stringing them along, and one night he was with Brian at some bar and Blake came by and . . ." She drew a slow breath and exhaled it carefully. "We just fell on each other like we were the last people on earth. Or at least that's how it was for me. And then he was like a drug. I couldn't have enough of him. And that's when he started pulling back. Just a little, then a little more. You know how it goes." She looked at the blank eye of the television, but he could sense she was seeing something else. "Then they went out on that boat. Not Blake. Brian and Ted. And then Ted was gone, and you know what my first thought was? Now I'm free."

Luke didn't say anything. She was on a roll, and he sensed she'd been waiting to unburden herself.

"The breast cancer came back with a vengeance after Ted's death. Maybe it was karma. I don't know. I've been away to 'cancer camp.'"

"Cancer camp?"

"That's just what I call it. Living with my sister. Chemo and radiation." She shot him a sideways look. "Fun times."

"I really would like to put them away," Luke said.

"I'm not above manufacturing evidence," she said, "but then, I'm dying and I don't care. Your old partner . . ."

"Bolchoy," Luke offered.

"He would take the risks, but I'm guessing you walk the line more."

"I want them behind bars, not me."

She smiled and it lit up her face. Then she immediately grew sober. "I want both of the Carreras to pay for taking Ted's life. I owe him that." Her eyes grew moist, but her expression was set and angry. "So, whatever I can do to help you, just let me know."

"Let's go over their tactics. How they first approached you and Ted. What they offered."

"They were insistent right from the start. They wanted our property more than the others, at least that's the way it seemed. They were undone that the Wrens were building the lodge, that it had been approved. That really pissed them off. Made them see red and more determined than ever."

"Might be just the way they do business, from what I understand."

"They're cruel. Blake is anyway. They want it all. More than just the deal. I think they wanted to cut Ted's balls off. Steal his wife, his home, his life. It's like a game to them, and I fell for all of it." She gazed back at the blank television. "Just promise me you'll make them pay."

"I'll certainly give it my best shot."

"I want to see Blake Carrera dead," she stated flatly.

Luke understood the sentiment. "All right. Tell me all about how you met the Carreras, what your first dealings were with them, when you determined you weren't going to sell to them. Things like that."

She nodded and got up from her chair, heading toward the kitchen. "This is going to take a while, and if that's the case, I'm going to add some rum to my coffee. Let me know if you need a shot yourself."

"I think I'm okay."

"Suit yourself."

Waiting for Luke to contact her after his meeting with Peg Bellows was torture, and it gave Andi way too much time to review her meeting with Mimi. She texted Carter as soon as she was home, because he still hadn't gotten back to her, and she added Emma to the string as well. Both of them got back to her almost immediately.

Emma: Shit what r we spose to do about that?
Carter: Is it Greg's?

Don't know yet, she texted back to both of them. She was just delivering the information, not analyzing it. Let them stew on it a while, and then maybe they could all work out how they wanted to deal with the baby's impending birth. As far as she was concerned, the child was a Wren until proved otherwise.

It was half past four when Andi heard Luke's truck rattling up her long drive. She glanced out the window in time to see him sweep into view from beneath the canopy of fir boughs. Her heart beat light and fast. It had been a long time since she'd seen him. Too long, she thought.

At that same moment she heard a text come in on her phone, which she'd left on the table by the door, where she always dropped her keys. She glanced at the screen and saw the message was from Trini: **Bobby coming by Friday. I'm asking him if we can get together Saturday. Work 4 u?**

Saturday was two days away. Andi didn't have plans for either Friday or Saturday. **Sure,** she wrote back, dreading the meeting a little. It would be different if she had a date herself, she supposed, and idly wondered if Luke was busy.

Like you're really going to ask him to go with you to meet your friend and her boyfriend. Then she thought: *If you hire him as a bodyguard, you'll see him all the time.*

"I worry about you, Andi. I really do," she murmured aloud as she, with a glance at the window, watched Luke's long legs stride across her small yard and up the steps to the front door. He rapped once and she crossed the room in an instant.

He looked . . . good. She imagined what that hard chest would feel like pressed up against her and felt a jolt of awareness even though he hadn't touched her in any way.

"Hey," he greeted her with a big smile.

"Hey yourself." She held the door wide. "Come on in."

"Been awhile," he said as he entered her small cabin and looked around. "Looks nice."

Andi followed his gaze to the furniture arrangement, a few items of artwork that included an impressionistic painting of sunflowers she'd done herself and hung over the fireplace. "I've been making it mine."

"How're you doing?"

"Fine. Really. I'm fine." He looked at her closely, as if checking the veracity of her statement and she shook her head and said, "I don't know if I thanked you enough for calling in the cavalry at Lacey's that night."

"You thanked me over and over. Trust me. I'm just glad you're okay."

"Yeah, well, bad things happen and we get past them." She half laughed. "I wish that were true of the Carrera brothers."

"One way or another, we'll get past them."

"You promise?" She lifted her brows.

His flashing smile made her heart squeeze a bit. "Gonna do my damnedest."

This was a dangerous conversation. She purposely changed it by asking, "Would you like something to drink? I've got coffee, tea, water, and I think there's a diet cola rattling around somewhere. Or beer, wine . . . a martini?"

"You having anything?" he asked curiously.

Andi's thoughts returned to Mimi and her baby bump. "I sure am. Red wine and a lot of it."

"Ah. You met with—"

"Mimi Quade. About six months along maybe?" she added brightly.

"I think I'll take some of that red wine, too." Then, "I'm sorry."

"It's not like I didn't know she was pregnant." Andi walked toward the kitchen. "It was just kind of hard, seeing her."

"I can imagine."

"What did Peg Bellows have to say?" she asked, deliberately changing the subject again as she pulled a bottle of cabernet from her tiny, black wrought-iron wine rack.

"Well, there's no love lost over the Carreras there anymore."

Andi opened a drawer and took out the corkscrew, but her mind was stuck on the image of Mimi's baby bump. It was like she couldn't see anything else all of a sudden. She sensed herself sinking into despair and was surprised that it had come up on her so fast when she'd thought she was past it.

Luke went on, "The brothers worked both Peg and Ted, coming off as friends, benign investors who would buy their house for a maximum price. They'd done the same thing with the Bellows's neighbors. A little different scenario, but all with the same goal."

Andi stood perfectly still. Loss had her in its tight embrace, squeezing the breath from her. Unaware, Luke said, "It's the same tale I hear whenever the Carreras are involved."

She tried to speak but couldn't find the words. Her nose burned and she sensed tears building. She clutched the corkscrew with a death grip.

"What's wrong?" he asked, coming nearer until he was right beside her as she faced the counter. "Something happen?"

She shook her head.

"Here, let me do that." He took the corkscrew from her now unresisting hand. Tears filled her eyes. She was embarrassed, but there was nothing she could do. Luke shot concerned looks at her as he uncorked the bottle. To her consternation, he reached forward and caught a tear with the tip of his finger. "Hey, it's okay," he said softly, and that opened the floodgates.

"I'm fine." Her voice shook.

"I know." He reached forward and folded her into the strength of his arms. She could smell the earthy, masculine scent of him and she wanted to cuddle into him and weep. Instead she stood like a stiff rod and squeezed her eyes closed, trying to stem the flow. "I don't want to cry."

"I know."

"Doesn't do any good and it makes you look like hell." She choked out a miserable little laugh.

"I don't think you could ever look like hell."

"Don't be nice to me."

He tightened his grip. "Okay, I'll treat you bad."

That made her laugh for real and she pulled back, but his arms wouldn't completely release her. "I'm so sorry," she said shakily. "I'm fine. Really I am. It just came over me."

"It's okay."

"I want to hear more about what Peg said. I really do."

He hesitated a moment, then admitted, "She said she wants to see Blake Carrera dead."

"Dead?" Andi swiped at her tears, turned away from his scrutiny, and he finally, somewhat reluctantly, released her.

"They had an affair. It ended badly, and Ted died."

"I thought it was Brian on the boat with him."

"It was, but where there's one Carrera brother, there's another. You sure you're okay?"

"No, but I'm trying. Okay?"

He nodded and she managed a thin smile before opening an upper cupboard and pulling out two crystal stemmed wineglasses.

"That's a little fancy for me," Luke said. "I could break that. How about a small tumbler?"

"No. Sorry. If you break it, you break it. But I need a little bit of . . . ceremony and beauty."

"Like that, huh?"

"Yes, like that," she said, pouring them each a glass. The red liquid shone like blood under the lights. "You want to walk out to the lake?" she asked.

"Sure."

They carried their wineglasses as Andi led the way out the back door. The rain had ceased and the afternoon was easing into a soft evening, with the smell of damp earth rising upward. A capricious breeze teased the willow branches. Luke picked up a denuded branch and curved it into a circle. "Art Kessler still doing your yard?" he asked.

"Yeah, I like Art."

"Good."

"What else did Peg say?"

"She said after the Carreras cultivated a friendship with them, they began to pressure them to sell, slowly at first but then with more push. The brothers had a vision for the south end of the lake, and the Bellows's cabin was the linchpin of their plan. If the Bellowses sold, then other property owners would fall like dominoes, and the Carreras would control the south end of the lake."

"Greg worried about that," she murmured.

"With good reason. The Carreras have bought and sold tons of property all over the Northwest, but it sounds like they were really on this one. Meanwhile, your family was doing the same thing on the north end."

"We weren't pressuring homeowners. Mr. Allencore sold us his ten cabins before he died, and the junior camp was something Greg worked on for a long time."

"The lodge was approved. Peg said the Carreras were undone about that. That's the word she used. Undone."

"You think that's why they gave me the bird message? To scare me off?"

"Yeah, but why just you? Why didn't Emma get one, or even Carter? I'm still trying to figure that one out."

"Did Peg say anything else?"

"Just that the Carreras thought they could beat you to the punch and control more properties because they had connections within the county. They're planning on stopping the lodge any way they can."

"It's too late. Carter has connections, too. And Greg had connections."

"Yeah, I think the brothers made a mistake there. They thought they could gum up the lodge works through the county, but whoever's in their pocket wasn't able to stop your construction."

"I don't get why it's such a fight. The lake's big."

"I keep telling you: the Carreras don't like to share."

"What is that?" Andi asked, gesturing to the ring Luke had made out of the willow branch.

"Art. Can't you tell?" He grinned.

Andi gazed at him in amusement. It was way too easy being with him. "I'm embarrassed about falling apart."

"Forget about it."

"I'll try." She took a couple of steps closer to the broken-down dock that had once afforded access to the water. "Carter keeps meeting with different people in the county."

"Then maybe he's the one who foiled the Carreras' plans. After Ted Bellows's death, the tide turned away from them politically. The county balked on issuing them building permits. The homeowners stopped trusting them. A few of the Bellows's neighbors did sell, but most held firm, although one of them told me the Carreras had upped their offer to a price that was hard to resist."

"Recently? So, there is some action with them?" Andi had hoped they'd closed up shop and moved away from Schultz Lake, even though she knew that was unlikely.

"The owner didn't say when, but he admitted he didn't sell out of respect to Ted and Peg."

"Which means it's probably only a matter of time."

Luke took a swallow from the crystal wineglass. Andi focused on his hands, thinking how strong they looked. "Does Peg want Brian dead, too?"

"Maybe." He started to say something, thought about it, shook his head. Finally he said, "She's been gone because she's been having cancer treatment. Chemo. Radiation. She's been living with her sister."

"Oh no."

"The cancer recurred after Ted's death and she's living with a lot of guilt and regret." He shook his head. "She probably wants 'em both dead."

Just as Luke finished his glass of wine the rain returned in a soft drizzle. They walked back to the cabin together. "I'd better go," Luke said. "I'll let you know if and when I learn something more about the brothers."

"Okay."

He handed her the willow ring and they both smiled. Then she walked him to the door.

"Keep in touch," she said lightly, feeling like having him on retainer was more of an indulgence than a need. But it was her money to spend.

"Will do," he answered, then he ducked his head against the rain as he headed for his truck.

Chapter Fourteen

Friday morning Gretchen, full of nervous energy, swiveled back and forth in her desk chair. She'd been waiting for Wes to come into the squad room, but so far he was MIA. They'd finished their reporting on the homicide stabbing, and Lieutenant D'Annibal had suggested they work with their original partners again. Cutbacks were still a worry, and D'Annibal had called George into his office and drawn the blinds on the glass wall that separated it from the squad room. Whatever was said between them, George had come out looking grim. Though he was currently seated at his desk, his eyes on his computer screen, he hadn't been interested in joking around.

September tried not to let the thought of the cutbacks gnaw at her guts. She was the most recent hire and the youngest detective. Her brother had moved semipermanently to the Portland PD, and it had looked like he might be coming back to the Laurelton PD, but now things had changed. Money was tight all over, but Portland had both larger staff needs and more fluid job opportunities. Laurelton was a lot smaller, and people who took jobs with the police department had a tendency to stick around.

September glanced over at the back of George's head.

She liked him. She didn't want him to lose his job. But if it came to a showdown between them about who was the more industrious employee, she would win hands down. However, should the issue turn on office politics, she really didn't know which way the dominoes would fall. George had friends in odd places.

"So where are we with the Aurora Lane crowd?" Gretchen asked.

September had tried to tell her about her meeting with Grace Myles two days earlier, but she had listened with only half an ear. Now, however, she was paying attention. George's heart-to-heart with D'Annibal had raised antennae all around the squad room.

With an effort, September forwent making a smart remark about Gretchen's lack of interest to date and answered, "I've interviewed every current homeowner and called the numbers I have for previous owners. Nobody seems to know anything. I'm just updating my report."

"The other day you were hot for whatever the Alzheimer's victim had to say," Gretchen said.

"You actually heard what I was talking about? I couldn't tell."

Gretchen pretended to stifle a yawn. "So what did Grace Myles say?"

"She intimated that Nathan Singleton's wife, Davinia, was having an affair with someone younger than she was. I was thinking about asking Tynan about it. Maybe this could be our vic."

"Or maybe not."

"Or maybe not," September agreed. "Maybe the affair's the reason Nathan drove off the road and killed them both. Tynan didn't go into that when we interviewed him, but there's a reason the man did what he did."

"That means Davinia was having an affair with an eighteen-year-old."

"Maybe younger," September said. "Davinia died thirteen years ago and forensics has determined the eighteen-year-old male would be about thirty now, if he'd lived. So he died twelve years ago, and Davinia's been gone thirteen."

"Meaning Mr. Bones could have been seventeen."

"Like you said, he might not even be the lover. If there was a lover. All speculation."

"We don't even know if it's a murder," Gretchen pointed out.

September nodded. This was why Gretchen wasn't all that interested in the case. Mystery bones in the basement were weird, but not weird enough to intrigue her unless there was foul play involved. In this case, the cause of death had been indeterminable.

"I'd sure like to know why someone buried the body and then dug it up again and put the bones in the Singletons' basement."

"No DNA from the bones."

September shook her head. "Not that the crime lab has been able to recover."

"You said Grace mentioned a name, but that you thought he was too young."

She was slightly surprised Gretchen remembered. "Tommy. Grace said Tommy used to mow lawns. She acted like she was a kid, but it's hard to know what time frame she was thinking of. Any way around it, Grace's account could be terribly flawed."

"Bound to be," her partner agreed.

"I called Mr. Bromward and left a message on his phone, asking if he remembered Tommy. He's hasn't called me back, so I'm thinking about just stopping in. He's one of the few not sick of answering questions."

"The guy with the cats."

"The guy with the cats who's really hard of hearing,"

September reminded. "Probably why he isn't answering his phone."

Gretchen grunted an assent. "Maybe Tommy mowed his lawn, too."

"That's what I'm hoping."

"What about the Asian neighbors?"

"The Lius' daughter, Anna, has become less and less interested in helping. She's tired of interpreting. Says her parents don't know anything. Pretty much everyone I've interviewed is fed up with my questions."

"I'll talk to her," Gretchen said, setting her jaw.

As glad as September was to have her partner back on the case, she knew Gretchen's take-no-prisoners approach could backfire. It had before. "I've also got a call into Elias Mamet. His house is the rental two doors down from the Singletons'. He's been promising me a full list of his renters over the last twenty years, but he hasn't come through."

"Give me the number."

"I will. But . . ."

"What?"

"Try not to piss him off. He's brusque and impatient and I've worked hard to get him on my side."

"You don't think I have the finesse to deal with him?"

September looked into Gretchen's blue cat's eyes and answered truthfully. "No, I don't."

"Then I won't threaten him with jail if he doesn't produce the list by Monday."

"Good idea," September replied dryly. "I mentioned Tommy to him and he didn't remember him, but . . ." She flipped through her notebook. "He said I should talk to the Hasseldorns, who moved away about ten years ago. Randall Hasseldorn's retired, but his wife, Kitsy, is a real estate agent with Sirocco Realty. Mamet acted like Kitsy knew all."

"Great. Let's start with her," Gretchen said.

"After Bromward."

"Hell no."

"You just don't want to revisit all the cats."

"You got that right."

"Too bad," September said, unlocking her desk drawer and reaching for her messenger bag. She used to keep it in a locker in the break room, but she was in and out of the station so often, she liked it closer at hand.

Gretchen looked like she was going to argue the point about Bromward, but then her gaze strayed to George and her expression grew thoughtful. With a shrug, she led the way out of the squad room, saying, "Fine. I'll drive."

Andi arrived at the lodge fifteen minutes before the scheduled meeting. She could smell the clean scent of fresh lumber and realized they were adding wings that jutted away from the main building at forty-five-degree angles to both ends of the central structure. A lot more money, she thought.

The echo of hammers reached her as she walked across chunky gravel toward the lodge, stepping carefully around pieces of wood, stacks of shingles, various piles of building supplies, workers' trucks, and vans. There was a make-shift ramp made out of two-by-six boards that led to an open six-foot-wide gap that was the lodge doorway at this point in the construction. She headed up the sloping planks, glad yesterday's rain had stopped; she suspected the wood could be slick.

Inside, the foyer's soaring roof, still just rough framed, rose up two stories. The hammering was sporadic: rhythmic for a while, then not, then ceasing altogether, then starting up again. The muffled whine of a saw sounded from down a hallway. She wasn't sure where Carter planned to meet, so she stayed just inside the door, aware the lodge was still in the beginning stages. Maybe it would be ready for business by next summer . . . maybe.

She heard a car approach and looked back through the front door opening. It was Carter's BMW. She watched him climb out and remote lock his car as he walked toward her. He hurried lithely up the planks. "You're already here," he said.

"Well, yeah."

"I guess I'm used to Emma, the perpetual no-show."

His eyes were bright with some inner excitement and Andi asked, "What?"

"What? What do you mean?"

"You've got something on your mind, so . . . what is it?"

"Oh, I'll wait till Emma gets here."

"If she gets here," Andi reminded him. "You just said she's a perpetual no-show."

"We'll just wait for a little while, then. What do you think of the place?" He gazed up at the ceiling and around, a slight smile playing on his lips. He was like a proud papa, Andi realized.

"It's coming along. I see the wings are going on. I thought that was going to be our second phase."

"It was. But you know how it goes . . . it's cheaper to get the work done now, while all the subcontractors are here."

"Will our loan cover it all?"

"Not all of it," he admitted. "We have to get some creative financing, but I've got it handled."

"You're making me nervous, Carter."

"No need to be." His smile was indulgent, as if she were a bright but pesky child, and it set Andi's radar on high alert.

"What are you planning, Carter?"

"We have Allencore's ten cabins and the junior camp."

"Which we're keeping as a camp," she reminded him.

"Possibly," he said, moving toward the front opening so he could see Emma arrive.

"It was agreed that we would keep the kids' camp."

"I know. But it's between our lodge and the Allencore cabins. We can make it part of the plan and then that whole northeast side can be part of the resort."

"We have the northwest side."

"It's just not that much property. We're going to be fighting boundaries. Well, unless we get people to sell to us."

"Why don't we strong-arm them? That's what the Carreras would do," Andi suggested.

"You really go to the worse-case scenario," he said, his voice a tsk-tsk. "What's wrong with making an offer? They can refuse it. But let's face it: We've got property on the east side of the lodge. Let's make use of it, and then we can ask people to sell on the west side, and if they do, great, and if they don't, we're still expanding."

"We've barely got going. Let's not change our plans yet."

"We do have to make some adjustments," he admitted. "Financially speaking. The two wings have tapped out our loan."

"Then we should have waited." She was becoming annoyed and slightly alarmed. Carter loved to forget that she and Emma had voting rights. "Didn't we just get out of financial trouble?"

"We're not going back into financial trouble. I have a plan. I told you."

"Well, let's hear it."

"Soon."

After that, silence fell between them. Carter never failed to get under her skin. He was just too sure of himself, and she wasn't convinced he made good choices.

"I got a call from Scott Quade," he said after a time.

Andi's brows lifted in surprise. Now he deigned to tell

her? It would have been nice to be informed. "What did he say?"

"He wants money. Same as always. He's angling for a settlement. Said he'd get his sister to abort and we could—"

"Hell no. She's six months! At least I think. There's no abortion."

"I know what you just went through, Andi. I know how you feel."

"You don't have a clue!"

"But don't let your personal feelings—"

"No, Carter. End of subject. Mimi wants Greg's baby. She won't go for it, and it's way too late anyway."

Andi's clipped tone brought Carter's lips into a thin line. "I'm just telling you what he said. It's all part of a goddamn scam, if you ask me. Quade's behind the whole thing and Mimi's a pawn. I don't know what their game is yet, but I'll find out eventually."

"No abortion," she stated tautly.

He waved a hand at her, annoyed. They both heard tires crunch on the rough gravel and Andi moved closer to him to look out the doorway to the approaching vehicle. A black Cadillac Escalade was pulling up beside Andi's Tucson. "That's not Emma," she said.

Carter slid her his cat-and-cream smile. "No."

Andi watched one good-looking, dark-haired man climb from the cab, while another got out of the passenger side at the same moment. Two identical bookends. "Oh . . . God . . . shit." *The Carrera brothers in the flesh.* She turned toward Carter in numb shock. "What are they doing here?" she squeaked out, only to see the sheepish look on his face. "What have you done?"

"I just invited them to have a talk with us. Emma should be here. Goddamn her. This is important."

"You son of a bitch."

Carter flushed a dark red. "Careful with the name-calling, Andi."

"Emma will never go for this and neither will I." She scrambled inside her purse with one hand, damn near hyperventilating. Her fingers closed on her cell phone and she yanked it out.

"Who're you calling?" he demanded.

"Luke Denton. It looks like I need protection."

Luke swept up his cell phone from where he'd left it in his cup holder, risking a ticket when he saw it was Andi. He was driving to his office and a meeting with Dallas. His brother had asked him to do some work for him, which was kind of a surprise. Dallas was a defense attorney, but to date he hadn't seemed to believe his younger brother was really going to stay being a private investigator. He'd nudged Luke to write after he'd quit the department, but he hadn't hired him as a PI until Luke had flat out told him the writing gig was a no-go.

"Hey, there," he greeted her warmly.

"I'm at the lodge with Carter," she clipped out. "The Carrera brothers just drove up. Carter invited them to a meeting."

Luke went cold. "I'll be right there."

"Good. I see Emma's just driving up." Then, "Hurry," and she was gone.

Luke made an illegal U-turn and headed toward Schultz Lake and the Wrens' lodge. He brought up Dallas's number on his cell and put it on speaker so he wouldn't have to hold the phone to his ear.

"I'm on my way," Dallas answered, but Luke cut him off.

"Change of plans. Gonna have to reschedule."

"I'm halfway to your office."

"This is important, Dal."

"Okay," he said, clearly mystified. "Call me."

"Will do."

Andi stood her ground, though she felt like running as the two brothers approached. One was dressed in a black crew-neck shirt with a black leather jacket and slacks and the other wore jeans, a light gray sweater, and a gray jacket. She couldn't tell them apart and her heart was pounding so hard it made it difficult to think. She wanted to kill Carter.

Emma's car pulled in at that moment, but it was Ben who climbed out of the driver's seat. For once Andi was glad to see him. He saw the brothers and started walking rapidly their way. There was no sign of Emma.

"We meet again," the one in jeans greeted her with a smarmy smile. Brian, she realized. She dragged her gaze from him to the man in black and saw the scar near his left temple. It was faint now, but still a telltale mark to be able to use to tell them apart, and it looked like it must have been quite a doozy of an injury.

Carter said, "I was just telling Andi about our plans for expansion."

"*Our* plans?" Andi's voice was brittle. "Who are *we*?"

Brian said easily, "I told you we'd be better friends than enemies. Your brother-in-law agrees."

"My brother-in-law doesn't have complete say-so." Andi could feel her insides quiver, but she was bound and determined not to let it show on the outside.

"That's why we're meeting today," Carter said pleasantly, but Andi could tell he was totally infuriated. As Ben clomped up the planks, Carter asked, "Where's Emma?"

"She couldn't make it."

"Couldn't make it," Carter repeated. Andi could tell he was holding himself back with an effort.

"She's not feeling well."

Read that to mean she's drunk or hungover.

Carter flushed, getting the message loud and clear as well. "Then she's just nullified her vote," he said, swinging his attention back to the brothers. "Yes, we're doing business with you. We need the money, and we're all interested in developing the lake."

"And we have very different views on how that should be done." Andi stared at Carter in disbelief. They hadn't signed anything. There was no way she and Emma would agree and he knew it.

Blake Carrera spoke up. "Is there a problem?" he asked Andi.

"More than one," she answered.

He turned to Carter. "You said you could handle the women."

"We haven't had a formal meeting yet," Carter side-stepped.

"Emma should be okay soon," Ben put in, a trifle anxiously.

Andi took exception to Blake Carrera's condescending tone and comment. She decided to try something, though it took all her courage. "This little bird is involved in all Wren Development business," she stated firmly.

She waited, but neither brother reacted to her words.

Then Blake said, "Well, *little bird*, maybe you should start making some decisions that will actually help your company."

"We've got some time," Brian put in, clearly trying to cool off his hard-nosed brother. "We're starting our business relationship today."

"There is no business relationship." Andi was clear on that.

"We want to help you keep your project moving," Brian kept going. "Time's money, and we're here to help."

Andi snorted, but her insides were quivering with fear. *Oh sure.* She wanted to steal a look at the time on her cell phone, find out how long it had been since she'd spoken to Luke, but she refrained. All her attention needed to be on the Carreras. "We're not ready to make any commitment to a partnership of any kind. I'm sorry if you were misinformed."

Blake's cold eyes met Andi's. "We weren't misinformed, *little bird.*"

Her heart flipped painfully. "As I said, I'm sorry."

"I think that's our cue to leave," Brian said. He looked at Andi with regret, and she worried about what was going through his mind. What did he have to feel badly about?

Carter stated flatly, "I'll be calling you, sooner rather than later."

Blake said something to his brother as they were walking off that Andi couldn't catch. "What did he say?" she asked Carter.

It was Ben who answered. "I don't think you want to know."

"Tell me," Andi snapped.

"I believe he called you a cunt," Carter said.

As the Carreras backed out of the entrance to the lodge, Luke's battered truck pulled in. He sat idling for a moment, and Andi could almost read his indecision. She stepped into the front of the opening to the lodge and waved at him. After a moment he got out, his long legs eating up the distance between them, the entry planks making hollow sounds as he ran up them.

"You okay? You want me to go after them?" He ignored Carter and Ben, his eyes on Andi.

It was her undoing. She could be strong for a while, but in the face of someone who was concerned for her, her emotions jumped to the surface. "No, I'm fine. There's no need to go after them. Like I said, they were invited."

"It's not your business," Carter said to Luke before he could say anything.

"It's family business," Ben put in quickly.

"You're family?" Luke asked him.

"Ben is Emma's husband," Andi said. "Emma's . . . out sick."

Ben's face turned red, but he didn't contradict her. It was Carter who'd had enough tiptoeing around. "I don't know what your deal is with Andi, but I do know this is outside your job description. You want to play bodyguard or whatever, go ahead. The Wrens will work things out as a corporation."

Andi said tightly, "Did you forget about the note I got, Carter? And the threat Brian made to me at the gym?"

"I've never known you to overreact, Andi." A muscle in Carter's jaw worked.

"She didn't overreact," Luke said, his tone firm. "I'm here because she called me, because she feels threatened by a couple of thugs named Carrera."

"Emma's not going to like this," Ben said.

"Well, next time fucking sober her up and get her to the meeting." Carter shouldered past Luke and down the planks. Ben blinked a couple of times, then left as well, albeit without the fury radiating from Greg's brother.

Andi started shaking visibly. "Reaction," she said, embarrassed thinking of Carter's cutting remark. "Or overreaction."

"Hey, none of that." Luke put an arm around her. "You have a right to be upset." He glanced at the parking area. "Do you want to leave your car? I can drive you."

"No." She shook her head and let out a long breath. "I don't want to leave my car. But can you come to the cabin?

I want to go home, but I want to work out our arrangement. I want a bodyguard."

"I'll follow you. Drive safe."

"I need to stop by the office first," she realized. "Pick up the mail. Sort through a few things?"

"I'm right behind you," he said.

Chapter Fifteen

Sirocco Realty's Laurelton offices were inside a Georgian-style brick building that took up an entire block in what served as Laurelton's city center: a cross street on the highway through town that led back to Highway 26. There was no municipal architectural planning. The city had just built up around the main road in a hodgepodge fashion where sidewalks rimmed parking lots.

September walked beside Gretchen but took the lead when they entered the offices and were met with the receptionist whose name tag read Tracy. Gretchen had refused to see Mr. Bromward first, and though her high-handedness irked September, she hadn't really felt like dealing with the old man and the cats much either. "After lunch," Gretchen had said, and September had agreed.

"May I help you?" Tracy said perkily. She had short, dark hair and an elfin look that was accentuated by her green sweater and slacks.

"We're here to meet Kitsy Hasseldorn. I called earlier; Detective Rafferty," September clarified. "I left a message and Mrs. Hasseldorn called me back and said she would be in the office after eleven."

Tracy stared at September as if she hadn't understood the message. "Detective?" she finally said.

"That's right."

"Oh, uh. I don't know if Kitsy's in. I didn't see her."

At that moment another woman walked out from the inner offices. "She's here," she assured the receptionist. "I just saw her." She smiled briefly at September and Gretchen.

"Musta been when I was on break," Tracy said. "I'll call her desk." She seemed boggled by Gretchen and September. "Kitsy? Oh, hey, there's a detective here to see you, and another woman."

"Also a detective," Gretchen said.

"Yeah, okay." Tracy hung up the phone. "You can go right back. It's down that hall, the last office on the right."

"Thank you," September said.

"Not the brightest lamp in the room," Gretchen remarked when they were out of earshot.

Kitsy Hasseldorn's office was adorned with Halloween decorations, one being a full-sized plastic skeleton standing in the corner. Gretchen walked over to get a closer look as Kitsy, all five foot three of her, stood up and shook hands with September.

"Police detectives," she said, smiling uncertainly. "And you want to know about Tommy Burkey? That's what the message was?"

"That's right. Burkey's Tommy's last name?"

"If he's the one you mean."

"He apparently mowed lawns for some of the residents on Aurora Lane."

"That's Tommy Burkey all right. He did yard work when he was a kid," Kitsy said. "What do you want him for?"

"We're investigating the death of an unidentified male whose bones were found in the Singletons' basement," Gretchen said, giving up her perusal of the skeleton to take the other club chair across from Kitsy. September had seated herself in one already.

"Oh, yeah. I saw that on the news. And the Singletons poisoned each other?"

"That's the way it looks," September said.

She shook her head. "Sounds just like them."

"You knew them." September made it a statement.

"Not really. We only lived in the neighborhood a couple of years, but they were memorable. They were always sniping at each other . . . whenever they got out of their cars, if they were both outside, one of them getting the mail and the other on the porch. . . . They were always yelling. Always." She frowned, little lines appearing between her eyebrows as she remembered. "I suppose I shouldn't speak ill of the dead, but they weren't nice people, that's for sure."

"We're trying to determine if Tommy Burkey's bones could be the ones in the basement," Gretchen explained.

Her face clouded over. "I suppose . . . it's just that . . ."

"What?" Gretchen prodded impatiently.

"Tommy was just kind of a goof, y'know? He mowed our lawn a few times, but he did a terrible job. He just didn't pay attention to detail. Randall went back to taking care of it. It was just easier. I've always just pictured Tommy off somewhere, still being goofy."

"How old was Tommy when he mowed your lawn?" September questioned.

"About eleven, probably."

"And how long ago was that?"

"Thirteen years, give or take."

That didn't jibe with what September knew to be the age of the unidentified bones. "Do you recall any other boy from that time period? He would have been about eighteen. Maybe he knew the Singletons?"

"There were those renters," she said reluctantly. "They had a son, but I hardly saw him. He was a drug addict."

"And he was about eighteen at that time?" September asked.

"About."

"Did he know the Singletons?" Gretchen pressed.

"Yes . . . I think so . . ." Kitsy was taking more and more time answering. "I don't recall their last name, something like 'shoe,' I think."

"I can check with their landlord," September said.

Gretchen put in, "How well did this kid know the Singletons? Did he know Davinia Singleton?"

Kitsy pressed her lips together, clearly reluctant to speak. "Yes."

"When he was in high school?" Gretchen fished around.

"Well, he wasn't an adult when it started," Kitsy said. "Almost, maybe. But he wasn't eighteen for sure."

"*It*?" September asked.

Kitsy reacted in surprise. "Oh, I'm sorry. I thought you were talking about the affair."

"That's exactly what we're talking about," Gretchen jumped in. "Davinia's affair with a much younger man, who sounds like he could have been a minor."

"Well, I can't say for sure." Kitsy backed right down. "That was the rumor, of course. And there were drugs involved, which is really why he got involved with Davinia; because she had the money, you know. That's what my husband, Randall, always thought anyway. But then Nathan ran the car off the road and killed them both, and that ended it."

"What happened to him—the kid—after that?"

Kitsy considered. "Oh, I don't know." Again her eyebrows puckered. "It kind of seems like the boy was gone first. I'd have to ask Randall. He's better at dates than I am. I think he ran off or something, but I'm pretty sure it was before Nate drove the car off the cliff. The Singletons sure wanted everyone to think it was an accident, but we had our doubts."

"You can't recall his name?" September asked again. She'd pulled out her notebook and was writing down Kitsy's comments.

"I just said I don't know," she said a little impatiently. "We just called him the druggie, y'know? He was always with other scruffy-looking guys. I heard one of 'em had money, but you sure couldn't tell by looking at 'em. They were all the same, like their faded baggy jeans and hoodies were some kind of uniform."

"Any of these other guys live on Aurora Lane?" Gretchen asked.

"I don't think so. You could ask the Myleses. You know them?"

"We've met," September said.

"Grace used to know everyone, but she's got some dementia now." Kitsy said it carefully, as if even mentioning the word would make the disease visit upon her.

"I interviewed Grace," September admitted.

"At that assisted living place?" Kitsy was surprised.

"She's the one who remembered Tommy."

"Ah." Kitsy shook her head. "My mother had dementia before she died. Terrible."

September nodded, then tried to ease her back to the subject at hand. "Anything else you can remember about the 'druggie' kid?"

She grimaced. "Don't say that came from me. We just didn't know his name, so we had to call him something. But if you find Tommy Burkey, he might know what happened to him."

"They were friends?" September asked, surprised because of the age difference.

"The kid was quite a bit older than Tommy," Kitsy said.

"Maybe six years or so? But I saw them together a few times, sometimes with some of those other scruffy kids, too. Tommy's mother let him run wild. She paid no attention to who he was hanging with. It's a wonder he was as nice as he was, but then he was . . . a little bit mentally challenged, almost like he had dementia himself sometimes."

September remembered the Burkey name from the list of previous Aurora Lane owners she'd compiled. The Burkeys had never returned her calls. "Which house did the Burkeys live in?" September asked.

"They were next to the Myles', and the rental house with the druggie kid was a couple doors down from the Singletons, toward the main road. All those houses on that side have land that borders that old farm, which is acres and acres."

September knew the area well now. "And part of the farmland ends up at Schultz Lake."

"That's right."

"The druggie's house was on the same side of the street as the Singletons and Mr. Bromward?" Gretchen asked.

She nodded.

They asked her some more questions about the residents of Aurora Lane, but Kitsy Hasseldorn was tapped out. "I'm sorry I couldn't be more help," she said as she followed them out. Tracy, the receptionist, was on the phone as they approached, but upon seeing Kitsy, she hung up and sat straighter in her chair, her smile as fake as her breasts.

Andi was furious with Carter. Now that reaction had set in, she wanted to kill him. How could he just call up the Carreras? He *knew* how she felt. If Luke hadn't come and supported her, she didn't know what she'd have done.

She climbed out of her car at the office and waited for Luke to park and get out, too. She knew that half of her just wanted him to be around, but the other half sought safety and protection. That was what she told herself anyway, and it didn't matter in any case because he was here and she was glad.

She was shivering when he reached her.

"You okay?" he asked, looking down at her in a way that made her stomach flutter.

"I'm more mad than scared now."

"I'm going to want the blow-by-blow of what happened once we get to the cabin."

"I'll just be a minute."

"I'm coming in with you."

She gave a short laugh but didn't argue as she entered the building. They walked across the glossy black tile of the entry foyer to the two elevators that led to the upper floors.

"What's Carter's game?" he asked.

"He's focused on getting more financing for the company at any cost. He expanded too soon, all in the name of saving money in the long run. He's not wrong, he's just . . . he always takes the easy way. That's what Greg used to say, and it's proven to be true."

The elevator dinged for the floor of Wren Development. Andi unlocked the main office door and found a pile of mail left on the edge of their part-time receptionist's desk. She swept it up as she unlocked her office door and headed straight to the credenza, where her phone charger was still plugged in, its cord a neat coil.

Luke came in after her. "This is your office?"

"Yeah. Now." She put the charger in her purse. "We should be in something less expensive, but we have a lease that isn't up for another year and a half. It wasn't a problem until we started building the lodge. I think it's all going to be great in the end, but it may have been too big a project in scope."

"You're building a hotel."

"A large hotel," Andi agreed. "I think we have the resources to do it, but Carter's put us out on a limb. Greg was more conservative, and so am I."

"Where does Emma stand on all this?"

"Mostly she agreed with Greg, and now with me, but now she's less reliable than ever. We need some checks and balances." She looked up at him. "Thanks for coming to my rescue."

He smiled. "I haven't done anything yet."

"Yes, you have." She plucked a white envelope addressed to her from the pile of notices and junk mail. No return address. A feeling of déjà vu and dread stole over her.

"What?" Luke asked, seeing her face.

Andi opened her top desk drawer and pulled out a letter opener. She slit open the top of the envelope and carefully drew out the hard note card within. At the same moment she read *It's too bad when little birds have to die*, they heard the elevator bell ding. Luke was beside Andi in a moment, reading the note.

"This came through the mail?" he demanded tersely.

"Yes."

She was still holding the card, albeit in shaking hands, when they heard a male voice ask, "Carter?"

Luke was out Andi's door in an instant and looked toward the reception area. Andi could see him but not their visitor. "Can I help you?" he asked.

"I'm looking for Carter Wren." Then, more curiously, "Who are you?"

Andi lay the note carefully on her desk, went to the door, and peered out. Scott Quade stood by Jill's desk, frowning at Luke. As soon as he saw Andi, he said, "Oh, it's you. I called Carter and he said he would be here, but I can talk to you."

"Is Mimi all right?" she asked, hearing how tight her voice was. Luke reached a hand back to her, touching her arm in support.

"You saw her. Did she look all right?" he demanded belligerently.

"What do you want?" Luke was terse.

"Luke, this is Scott Quade," Andi introduced belatedly.

"Mimi's brother," Luke said, never taking his eyes off Scott.

"Well, great. I still don't know who you are," Scott said. "But you sure act like you have some authority around here."

"Luke's a private investigator," Andi said as the elevator began to hum, called by someone on another floor.

Scott blinked in surprise. "You work for the company?"

"What did you want to talk about?" Andi asked, her voice sounding as if it were coming from a long way away. She was trying to act normally, but she could hardly think straight. Her mind was still on the note and what it meant. She wanted to throw herself into Luke's arms and never let go.

"Mimi. Her condition. She can't have this baby and all of you know it."

"Don't even mention abortion," Andi said coldly.

"It would be a lot less expensive than taking care of Greg's kid."

The elevator stopped and the doors opened. Carter stepped out and stopped short in surprise. "Quade," he greeted Scott tautly.

"Well, let's hope you're in the mood to save money," Scott said.

"No abortion." Andi was shaking, and she felt Luke's arm steal around her, his palm at the small of her back. She had no idea what Carter would say.

"Are we talking abortion?" he demanded.

"Not according to your sister-in-law," Scott stated, flushing.

"Well, it's not going to happen." Carter was firm. "Where's Mimi? You said you'd bring her."

"She didn't want to come. You people scare her."

"Maybe you didn't bring her because she's not pregnant."

"Ask her." He pointed to Andi. "She went and intimidated her and now all Mimi can do is cry!"

"That's not true," Andi sputtered.

Carter said, "All you want is money. Well, you came to the wrong place. When Mimi delivers, get that DNA test you were screaming about last time you were here. If it's Greg's, we'll deal with it then."

Scott opened his mouth and closed it again. "You don't know what I want," he growled, and then he headed back to the elevator, slamming the button with his palm. It had been called away and so he had to stand in fury, staring at the door, waiting.

Luke said calmly, "The Exit sign for the stairs is to your left and down the hall."

Scott whipped around and stared at Luke, then at Carter. "You can't intimidate me anymore."

The elevator opened once more and Emma stood inside, next to Ben. Her hair was disheveled and her face pale. She said, "Oh God, Quade. Is this why you wanted me here?"

"You were supposed to be at the lodge," Carter snapped. To Scott, he said, "You're the one trying to intimidate my family."

Scott angrily brushed past Emma and Ben as they exited the elevator car and stabbed the button several times. "I'll bring Mimi next time," he declared.

The doors closed on him, but Carter didn't wait. He headed toward his office without another word.

"Carter?" Emma asked, following after him, confused.

Ben grabbed her arm and dragged her after him, saying, "I picked her up at home. Figured she needed to be here."

Andi looked at Emma's unfocused stare and turned to Luke. "I'm done here."

He said, "Where's the note?"

"On my desk."

He walked over and picked it up carefully by the edges and slipped it into his pocket. Then he came back to Andi and put his hand to the small of her back again. "I'm following you home and making sure you're safe and secure."

"Okay," she said softly.

Alvin Bromward had more cats than September remembered. She counted five in sight and suspected there might be a whole lot more. From the smell of the apartment, she guessed there was a litter box somewhere nearby that needed cleaning.

Gretchen stood beside her, her face screwed up in distaste. Her partner could easily hide her feelings behind a professional façade when she chose to, but this was not the occasion.

"Sit down." Alvin waved at them with a liver-spotted hand. He was seated in a wheelchair with a blanket over his legs. His hair was gray and greased to his head, patches of pink scalp showing through the wisps.

They'd already been through this routine. Like last time, there wasn't a seat available that wasn't rife with cat fur. "Thank you," September said, "but we prefer to stand, if you don't mind."

"Oh, push Tigger out of the way," he said, making shooing motions to the huge orange tabby that was lounging on its back on the couch, softly snoring. The little beast didn't care one iota that strangers were in the house.

Gretchen suddenly sneezed and shot September a baleful look.

September had already explained that they'd met with Kitsy Hasseldorn, and now she asked for the second time, "Do you remember Tommy Burkey?"

"Sure," he said. "A brat. Treated my cats bad, I can tell you. Caught him throwing rocks at 'em and threw one back at him. Hit him in the arm. He howled like a banshee and ran home to his mommy."

"You threw a rock at a child?" Gretchen asked.

He swatted the air in her direction. "He weren't no child. He was hangin' with those smokers. One of 'em threw a rock through my window, just to let me know they were watchin'. Lookin' out for Tommy, who wasn't too bright, you know."

"Did he mow your lawn for you?" September asked.

"No. He didn't do nothin' for me. And those boys . . . those smokers. They were bad news." His mouth worked and he added in a rasp, "They left Little Lillian in my mailbox for me to find. Skinned her, they did. I called you people, but nobody did nothin'."

September recoiled. "Lillian was one of your cats . . . ?"

"Yep."

"And they skinned her?"

Gretchen grimaced, this time from the image, September believed.

"Sure did," Bromward said, his jaw working. "I was careful after that, but they moved on."

"Tommy Burkey was one of them?" September asked.

"Mmm . . . no . . . not really." He made a face. "They just kinda tolerated him, I think. The older boys. He was a freckle-faced goon who was too stupid to know they used him for their enjoyment. Kinda like a mascot, you know? He was throwin' rocks to impress them. Didn't realize it when I threw the rock at him. Thought he'd thought it up all on his own, but it was them older boys."

"Do you have a name for any of those older boys?"

"One was the renter's boy. Gimme a minute. I'll think of it."

They waited patiently, or at least September did. Gretchen kept shifting her weight from one foot to the other.

"Those renters were the ones with the RV. They took off in it after their kid disappeared. The mom was pretty tore up. The dad . . . his name was Pauly, I think. He was a piece of work, too. Never worked, far as I could tell. The mom was a cashier down at the Shop and Save grocery."

"Did they have any other children?"

"Just the drug addict. He was a decent enough sort. It was really that friend of his that was so . . . what's the word you use these days? Hmmm. Entitled. That's it. He was entitled. Wouldn't surprise me if'n he wasn't the one to kill Little Lillian."

September paraphrased, "You're saying that Tommy hung out with a couple of older boys, seeking acceptance, but that the older boys were really the ones making the bad choices."

"Tart it up all you like, it boils down to the older boys goading Tommy, but the really bad stuff, yeah. That was them."

"Would you call them scruffy?" Gretchen asked.

"Sure. Looked like every other boy does then and now. Ripped jeans. T-shirts. Facial hair, if they can grow it."

"Do you remember Davinia Singleton?" Gretchen questioned further.

"Oh-ho. Now I know where you're goin'." His smile was sly. "Shoulda asked me the last time you were here. Yeah, she was a hot pants for the young ones. Ripped out Nathan's heart, but nobody thought he had the gumption to kill her and him. That's when Jan and Phil went around the bend. After the 'accident.' Weren't no accident, but then, people'll try to make things seem better than they are. They raised that little girl all right, though."

"Frances," September put in.

"Yep." He nodded sharply. "After she was all grown up and out of the house, I think that's what did 'em in. They looked around at each other and thought, *I don't like you.* That's my guess anyway."

"As I said before, we're trying to identify a set of bones that belongs to an eighteen-year-old male that was found in the basement of the Singletons' home," September said.

The old man scowled. "You think it's Davinia's lover, the marijuana smoker?"

"Marijuana. You're talking about the RV owners' son?" September asked. Everyone called him a drug addict, and she'd just assumed they meant he'd used something stronger.

"I know it's legal now, but it weren't then. He was smokin' all the time. Smelled like a skunk."

"With another friend and Tommy?"

He shrugged. "And some others. Now wait a minute. . . ." He pinched his nose. "Maybe the druggie was that other kid."

"Which other kid?" Gretchen asked, sounding annoyed.

"The one with the horse. That wasn't the same time, though, was it?" He screwed up his face in thought.

"From what I can tell, the Burkeys left about eleven years ago," September prompted. "Can you remember any name, of either the druggie kid or the one with the horse?"

"Or their parents?" Gretchen put in.

"One of 'em was kind of a common name, it seems. Escapes me for the moment. That's the problem with old age. It'll come back to you when you don't need it no more."

"You can call me," September said, pulling out a business card and handing it to him. "That's my cell number on the bottom. If you think of any names, just let me know."

"Any time? Day or night?"

She smiled. "I might not answer in the middle of the night, but yeah."

"Can you think of anyone else who could fit the age description of the person we're looking for?" Gretchen asked, edging toward the door. "An eighteen-year-old male, give or take a year."

"I'll think on it. . . . There were a whole bunch of littler kids on the street at that time. They're all growed up now, too."

"Call me," September encouraged.

As they turned to leave, Tigger suddenly awoke and stretched, then jumped to the back of the couch, tail switching, watching them depart with sleepy gold eyes. As soon as the door was closed behind them, Gretchen sneezed again.

"Are you allergic?" September asked.

"Probably." She was dour. "I never want to go back there again. If he doesn't call you, we need to move on to other sources."

"At least he gave us something. He didn't say much of anything the first time we contacted him. He's getting to know us."

"Great." Gretchen looked at the face of her cell phone. "It's lunchtime. Let's get something to eat and head back to the station. Wes might be back by now."

September nodded as Gretchen quickened her footsteps. Obviously, she was over this whole investigation.

* * *

Time to ramp up. Push the game. Maybe tonight I'll take another little bird. I've strung her along long enough. She's not the endgame. Far from it. The endgame's still a few moves ahead.

But this one will do in the meantime . . . and it will further boggle them. They'll look for connections that aren't there. A little misdirection to keep them from the truth.

Yes . . . tonight.

The pressure's built and I need a release.

Little bird . . . I'm coming for you. . . .

Chapter Sixteen

Andi followed Luke around her cabin as he checked each room and made certain there was no one lying in wait for her. "It's intimidation," he said as he checked out her bathroom and opened her closet door. "Whoever it is had to break in, so they don't have access. They sent you a note through the mail, so they're careful. They don't contact you electronically, where there could be a trace. There may be fingerprints, but I'm guessing that's unlikely. I'll check into it. The letter was postmarked in Portland, and I'll check that, too. But I don't think it'll help us much. Anyone from anywhere could drop it into a box."

"Why are they doing this?" Andi whispered, biting her lip. "Why me?"

"Your association with the Wrens? The bird thing suggests something to do with your name."

"The Carreras don't like us, no matter if Carter's trying to make nice. They'll burn us in the end." She exhaled heavily. "But I don't get why I'm the target."

"Maybe you're just the way in. I don't know. I need to have a powwow with the brothers Carrera."

"Can we wait on that?" Andi asked. "I just . . . don't want to poke the hornet's nest yet."

He looked at her, and whatever he saw on her face—fear, anxiety, desperation—caused him to nod in reluctant agreement. They walked back to the living room. "I've got some work to do, but I'll be back later."

She spread her hands. "I need to start paying you. With everything that's happened, we never really got to that."

"Don't worry. We'll figure it out. I want to get the Carreras as much or more than you do, so I'm looking at this more as a partnership. That work for you?"

"Yes." She liked the sound of that.

"Okay, so I'll go finish up some of my own stuff, then I'll do some digging into Scott and Mimi Quade, too. When you add up people who feel wronged by the Wrens, they're high on the list."

"Okay."

He came directly to her and put his hands on her shoulders, looking down at her. "I don't want you to be scared."

"I don't want to be either."

"So, if it seems like the thing to do, I'm going to bunk on your couch tonight."

Andi shot a glance over to her sofa, which didn't look like it would come close to fitting his lanky frame.

He saw her glance and added, "Maybe I'll bring a sleeping bag."

"Good thinking."

He gave her shoulders a quick squeeze and said, "See ya later."

Long after he left, she felt the comforting imprint of his fingers.

Out of her last Pilates class of the day, Trini jumped into her Mini and drove straight to the grocery store. She shopped like she was a sweepstakes winner, throwing items into her cart. She swiped her credit card and wiggled the toes on her right foot anxiously. She glanced at her Fitbit to see the time. She was late, as always. It was a cosmic wonder that she couldn't get anywhere on time. She tried. She really did, but her own biorhythms seemed to be on a separate plane, and well, hell, who cared anyway?

Four thirty. Well, that wasn't too bad. Bobby was coming over at five. A little early for him, but he'd told her tonight was something special and she had no idea what that meant, but it could be anything. Good, bad, indifferent. She was really hoping for good. Great. Maybe a weekend away, just the two of them. A spa vacation in the desert, or hell, admit it, wouldn't it just be marvelous to go somewhere far, far away? Some place stunningly exotic? Like those resort rooms on stilts over cerulean water in Bora Bora. Oh God.

She juggled the grocery bags and nearly dropped one on the way to her car. She did drop her keys but managed to pick them up. Who was she kidding? she thought, as she switched on the ignition. Bobby wasn't the type for trips to another corner of the world. He was too careful. His idea of a vacation would probably be to the Oregon beaches, or maybe the mountains. Somewhere closer, more intimate. Maybe not sooo extravagant. And that was just fine with her. He was so imperfect, he was perfect.

She pulled into her assigned spot at the apartment complex, then hauled out the bags and carried them up the flight of stairs to her door. She had to crush the bags against the wall to free up one hand and thread the key in the lock. She thought of Bobby making love to her. It had been nearly a week and it was too long. Last time had been a wild ride on her bed that had her screaming so much he'd slapped a hand over her mouth. Jesus. Just thinking about him made her wet. Lord, she had it bad!

She'd decided to make dinner for him, so last night she'd gone to the little market down the way and checked on their poultry products. Nothing had grabbed her, so she'd put off buying what she needed till today, stopping at a supermarket instead. She'd decided on a vegan meal and hoped Bobby would like it as well. She wasn't completely that way, but she definitely leaned away from meat. Last night, as she was about to leave the little market empty-handed, one of the owners had tried to talk her into the prawns, singing their praises. He'd swept a hand toward the seafood case and there they were, displayed in a pretty row, all plump and pink and lying innocently on a bed of ice, the little killers.

"No, thanks," Trini had told him. She'd debated on going into her allergies, and Bobby's, but she hadn't really had the time, and anyway, would he really care? The man was just trying to make some conversation, hoping for a sale, doing his job. He didn't really want her whole story, and really, did anyone?

So today she'd purchased flour tortillas, planning to make cheddar and cotija cheese enchiladas with verde salsa and pico de gallo. She didn't think Bobby would squawk too hard about the vegan angle. She'd throw a salad together and make her own dressing with a south of the border flair. He really preferred eating in to going out to restaurants anyway, and though Trini didn't think of herself as much of a cook, she was certainly learning.

It took her a while to set up and get the meal rolling, and then the oven didn't seem to want to come up to temperature. When it finally did, she shoved the pan of enchiladas inside and slammed the door, then cleaned up the mess of bowls and pans, although she kind of did a half-assed job. She was hot and sweating when she was finished. Glancing at the oven clock, she saw it was closing in on six. Where the hell was Bobby?

An hour and a half later, when he still hadn't shown, she was full-blown pissed. How dare he stand her up? And how dare she care? He wasn't even her type, she reminded herself as she slammed her way out of the apartment and walked in a huff to the nearest neighborhood restaurant, a tiny place with a U-shaped bar adorned with twinkling white lights. As she entered, a bell tinkled overhead, announcing her arrival. There was a smattering of customers. Though the ambience was nice, the food was pedestrian, and most people came for a drink and then moved on.

She took a place at the bar, a black cloud of anger hanging over her. To hell with it. She was over abstaining from alcohol. "A mojito," she said. "Not one of the fancy ones with added mango or pomegranate or any of that shit. Just the usual lime and mint."

"You got it," the bartender said. He slid her a look while she tried to remember his name. "Haven't seen you in a while," he said.

"Been busy." Actually, after that debacle at Lacey's, she'd stayed away from alcohol entirely. It wasn't good for your body anyway. After a night drinking, she could smell the alcohol-laced sweat when she worked out, and it only added to her embarrassment. What had she been thinking that night? She'd just been so low, and she'd had a momentary blip of really, really bad judgment.

The front bell tinkled, announcing a newcomer. Trini looked over as a matter of course and then froze as she recognized Jarrett Sellers.

He looked around, spotted her, and eased over to the bar, leaning his elbows on the polished surface. "Hey there," he said.

"I'm not going to believe you just happened to walk in here."

He hung his head like a bad boy. "Okay, I followed you."

"Why?"

He lifted his head and said to the bartender, "Jack and Coke." Then he turned back to Trini and said, "I was driving by your place and saw you walking down the street. When I saw you turn into the bar, I decided to join you."

"Why were you driving by my place?"

"I kind of thought we left on bad terms at Lacey's." He waited a moment, and when she didn't respond, he said, "Okay, you're going to make me say it? I wanted to talk to you. I wanted to see you."

Trini relaxed a little. "No, you don't. We're no good for each other, Jarrett. We can't even be friends."

"That's not true."

"It is true."

"This is what I like about you, Trini. You always keep everything hidden. Always play coy. Never speak your mind."

She smiled in spite of herself. At least he was pulling her out of her bad mood. "Okay, maybe we can be very distant friends, but that's as far as it goes."

Jarrett's drink came and Trini sucked down her mojito and ordered another. He had a second as well, but when the bartender offered her a third, she declined.

"I've got dinner made at home," she said, getting to her feet. She tried to pay, but Jarrett wouldn't let her.

"Is that an invitation?"

"No. God, you're pushy." She squinted at him. Jarrett had a nice smile. She'd forgotten that. Why, she wondered, had it not worked with him? Apart from the fact that they really couldn't get along.

She thought back to their last meeting at Lacey's. She'd been in a kind of altered state at the time, sick at heart over how things were going with Bobby, and Jarrett had asked all those questions and she'd just wanted him to go away. He'd damn near ruined her game, and all she could think about was Bobby . . . *Bobby* . . . though that wasn't his real name. And the bad hair and glasses? A fake. She'd fallen for it at first, before she'd really cared. He'd been a novelty and she'd been amused. But then he'd become a crush and now . . . now he was a drug she couldn't live without.

But she wanted the deception to be over now. No more games. Since they'd been back together she'd tried to get him to come clean about the disguise, but he'd pretended not to know what she was talking about. And then he'd also been so distracted, and really, all she wanted was for him to screw her brains out, and he'd done that beautifully.

But he'd left her tonight . . . and here was Jarrett.

". . . one more for the road?" he asked.

"Okay, sure."

Why not? she figured.

He brought her the drink, its green contents glowing beneath the lights above her head. She sank back down on the stool. She wished she wanted to be with Jarrett. She almost begged herself to give him a second chance. She needed to get over Bobby and stop being such a rat woman, but all she wanted was to have him in her bed. The true definition of a rat woman.

You've got it bad, girl. Really, really bad.

She drank down half her drink, then asked, "Do you ever wish you didn't have a conscience? That you could do whatever you want and damn the torpedoes? No consequences. Just live your life any way you want."

"Yes," Jarrett said.

Trini gave him a long look. She remembered making love with him. It had been good for a while, but then they'd started fighting, and they just couldn't stand each other as time wore on.

"I want to go home with you," he said in a husky voice.

She laughed. She couldn't help it. All she could think about was Bobby . . . inside her . . . breathing hard . . . pounding into her. The thought shot a jolt of desire up her vagina to her core. Damn, it felt good. "You can come over and have dinner," she said, "but that's all." She reached in her purse, but he said, "I've got this."

Actually, she'd been about to pull out her phone, intending to text Bobby to tell him she was *busy*. But then she recalled the last time she'd texted. She'd been a little pissed 'cause he'd been late then, too. It had made her climb the walls, like an addict needing a fix. He'd done it on purpose, she was sure. Later, he'd told her that something had come up and reminded her not to text him. She'd accused him of having a secret wife or something. A big hardy har har that had her chuckling but made him go coldly silent. For a moment she'd worried that truly was his secret, but he'd responded with a warning he'd given her once before: "I'll text. You respond."

Caveman stuff. Nothing she could normally stand.

"Why?" she muttered to herself. *Why do you put up with this shit?*

"We're good," Jarrett told the bartender as he threw some bills down on the counter. The bartender thanked him for the tip, then Jarrett put his hand at her elbow and steered her toward the door.

"This isn't going to work," she told him as they walked up the street. A blast of surprisingly cold wind, more suitable for December than October, hit them, and Trini huddled close to Jarrett to keep warm. He put his arm around her until she was snuggled against his chest.

"Don't be such a pessimist."

"It didn't work before; it's not going to now."

"All I'm trying to do is get a free meal."

"Bullshit. And I'm not going to sleep with you."

"What did you make for dinner?"

They were at the steps to her apartment and she stumbled on the first one. Jarrett caught her arm and she pulled it away, smiling at him from several steps up. "It's vegan. You'll love it."

"Blech."

"I lead a healthy lifestyle. I really do. I wouldn't drink, but I can't help it. My man drives me to it."

That caught him up. "Your man?"

"My man," she repeated with a nod.

They entered her apartment and she flipped on the lights. She saw the two plates set at the table and a wave of misery welled up from her gut. *Oh Bobby.* And then there was anger. Fury. Maybe she *would* sleep with Jarrett.

"Is this the guy Andi told me about?" Jarrett asked. He perched on the wooden arm of her couch as Trini put the enchiladas onto plates and zapped the first one in the microwave.

"Yep."

"So, he drives you to drink. That's why you're not with him tonight?"

"Right again."

"Is it wrong of me to hope it doesn't work out?"

She wagged her finger at him. Another mojito or two and she wouldn't care so much, but she did care. Why? God knew.

"Here." She pulled out the heated plate and slid it across the black granite counter that showed every freaking mark. She grabbed up a fork, a knife, and a napkin, and Jarrett seated himself at the kitchen bar.

"This is good," he said after a moment, a touch of surprise in his voice.

"I know. I have skills now." Jarrett smiled at her in that way that used to melt her heart. "Don't say it," she said.

"What? I'm just eating."

"You were going to tell me how wonderful I am. I saw it on your face."

"You're an egotist."

"Uh-uh. I just know you." She'd heated up a second

plate and the microwave dinged, but she didn't jump to answer the call.

"Your food's ready," Jarrett observed, pointing his fork at the microwave.

"I'm going to be honest with you, Jarrett. I was stood up tonight and I'm pissed. So that's why we're here, because I feel low and you're making me feel better. But you have to leave after you finish eating, and then I'm probably going straight to bed . . . alone."

He bent his head to his meal and didn't say anything until he was finished. Trini had lost her appetite completely. She just felt sad.

Jarrett had taken off his coat and put it on the back of one of her kitchen bar stools, but now he swept it up and put it on. "Thank you," he said seriously.

"You're welcome."

"If I came by again, would you see me, just as a friend?"

"I don't think it works that way for us, but yes. I'll give it a try."

She walked him to the door and he hesitated, his hand on the knob. "I just miss hanging out with you," he said.

Music to her ears . . . someone who actually liked her. But it wasn't enough. Not the way she was feeling.

He stepped onto the landing outside her door. "Good night," she told him.

"A kiss good-bye," he said.

"No." She half laughed. "Just go!"

He reluctantly moved to the stairs. "I'll be back."

She shook her head and closed the door. She returned to the microwave, wondering if she should try heating her enchiladas again, but she still didn't have an appetite. *God, Bobby. What you've done to me!*

That was when she saw Jarrett's wallet sitting on the couch. Swooping it up, she headed for her door. He wouldn't have left it there on purpose, would he? *Geez, Trini, you are an egotist!*

She opened her door and stepped onto the landing and was inhaling to take a breath and yell after him when something slammed her against the wall and she damn near saw stars.

"Who the fuck was that?" Bobby snarled.

She opened her eyes. "Bobby," she said, filled with relief. "Ow. You hurt me."

"Sorry." His voice was terse. He pulled back from her and stood tensely, his hands tucked in the pockets of a black leather jacket that looked great on him. His body was so taut. You didn't notice at first. He didn't emphasize his physique, but the man was all rock-hard muscles under this nerd exterior. She loved it.

"I forgive you, but man, my head hurts. That was Jarrett Sellers. He's the brother of my friend Andi, who you're meeting tomorrow."

"What was he doing here? He asked you to kiss him."

"Actually, I was showing him to the door. We used to date, but it was a long time ago. I wanted to give him this." She held out the wallet.

"He looked like he wanted to jump you."

She smiled. It warmed her heart that he sounded a teensy bit jealous. Her gaze roamed over all of him and she saw he had an erection.

"Yeah, look what you did to me," he said, his voice softening.

She suddenly wanted to stroke his cock and throw him down on the walkway by the stairs that led to her unit. She wanted the whole world to know he was hers. And if that meant getting arrested for making love in public, well, she'd happily go to jail. She knew it was crazy, but it was wonderful! She couldn't get enough of him.

He seemed to sense she was about to hug him and

swarm her body over his because he sidestepped. She was immediately hurt, but then he plucked the wallet from her, grabbed her hand, and said in a rough voice, "Let's get inside before I freeze my nuts off."

"It's not that cold." She turned back to the door, which had closed behind her. Suddenly he was behind her, pushing against her butt, one hand slipping to the front of her jeans and jamming down inside. "Bobby," she whispered, half scandalized, half thrilled.

"Missed you," he growled, rubbing between her legs. It was a little hard, a little painful, but she didn't want to complain.

"God, I want to do it right here," she said, reaching to unbutton her pants and give him better access. "Right on the landing."

He laughed silently in her ear. "It is that cold. But you're hot. I'm gonna fuck you crazy."

"I already am crazy. This is crazy."

"Get in there."

They practically fell through the door, and as soon as they crossed the threshold he tossed the wallet onto the console table, kicked the door shut, and pushed her toward the couch. His forcefulness stole her breath. Then he literally threw her on the couch and jumped on her, ripping at her clothes so hard that she protested faintly. She'd paid a lot for this blouse and he was ruining it.

"I'll buy you a new one," he said. "This one's mine."

"Bobby . . ."

He slammed a hand down on her mouth. "Don't say anything. Don't fucking say anything."

She nodded mutely. She knew when she talked too much it ruined it for him. "I'm sorry," she said around his fingers.

"And don't fucking apologize!"

He slid a condom on his rock-hard cock and she ran a hand over the rubbery outside, wishing she could feel his flesh. She'd told him over and over that she was on the Pill, that he didn't need one, but he'd been burned once by some gal who'd sworn she was taking birth control pills, then oops, she had a pregnancy scare that luckily had turned out to be false.

Now, he swept her hand away and rubbed the tip of the condom between her legs, seeking entry. She was shifting to accommodate him when he slammed into her, hard. Luckily, she was ready for him or he could have ripped something. Then he started pounding away like a battering ram, his breathing rapid and hot in her ear. She tried not to tense up. The first time was always like this, just for him. But the crown of her head began hitting painfully against the wooden arm of the couch, again and again. She tried to slow him down a little, wanted him to recognize that he was hurting her, but he was on a mission for his own pleasure and wasn't interested in any of her signals. In the end she just went with it. The second time was always better than the first because that was when he gave her a chance to reach an orgasm. Not that she wasn't crazy wet for him all the time, but when he was so brutal . . . no, that wasn't the right word . . . when he was so *focused*, it was kind of difficult for her to actually enjoy herself to the limit.

Then it was over. She felt him exhale, replete, and she wrapped her arms around him tighter and wished he was pumping his sperm inside her instead of into the condom. Immediately her eyes flew open. Had she just thought that? God, no. That wasn't her! She didn't want a baby.

But if it was his baby?

She immediately thought of Andi, and how unfair it had been for her, losing Greg's baby.

It was just as well Bobby was so careful because she didn't trust herself with him. If for some reason she ended up pregnant, it would crush Andi. Trini had always avowed that she would never have children, whereas it seemed kids were all Andi had ever wished for.

Bobby pulled out of her and sat up on the couch. Trini was disappointed because it seemed like he didn't intend to go for a second round. She put a hand to her head and gingerly touched the sore spot at the crown. She didn't mean to. She didn't want to emphasize that he'd hurt her because he might get angry and leave her, but man, her head throbbed.

"What's wrong?" he asked.

"Guess I've just got to get a new couch without wooden arms," she said lightly.

"You're complaining?"

"I just don't want to be knocked out before I can enjoy myself," she said with an edge.

For a moment his lips tightened, like he was really pissed, but then his expression changed, became more indulgent. "Okay. I'll be more careful next time," he said, kissing her lightly.

This was the Bobby she loved. She threw her arms around him and buried her face in his neck, smelling him, wanting him. But he gently pulled away from her and reached for his clothes.

"I came to tell you I can't stay," he said regretfully. "I wanted to see you in person."

"What happened?"

"Nothing you need to worry about."

"Are you sure?" Disappointed, Trini started redressing as well. What was it about him that made her serotonin go into overdrive? When he was around, her brain seemed flooded with the stuff that made you feel so damn good.

"Yep."

"I made enchiladas," she coaxed. "I just heated one in the microwave, but I've got more."

"Ahh . . . no . . ." He smiled at her. "I can't stay. I thought we'd just have . . . appetizers," he said meaningfully.

"Want to go again?" she said, ready to rip off her clothes.

"Maybe. If we're quick. First, I brought us some energy bars."

"Energy bars? Now?" She laughed. "Come on, Bobby. I've got dinner ready."

"This is a new kind. They're really great. I tried one before I came and decided you've got to try one."

"How about after dinner? I've got the fixings for a salad, too. I just haven't put it together yet."

"I told you, I don't have time." He got to his feet abruptly.

"You're not leaving right now, are you?" She heard the desperate tone in her voice and could have kicked herself.

"Can't stay."

"Wait, wait. I'll try one."

"No, you don't want to, so forget it."

"Bobby!"

"Gotta go, sweetheart. I'll see you in a week or two."

"A week or two? What are you talking about? Stay for a minute. I'll have one of the energy bars."

"God, Trini, I'm not trying to force you. I just like them and wanted you to like them, too."

"I get it. Okay. Hand it over." She held out a hand and wriggled her fingers.

Somewhat reluctantly, he reached into the pocket of his coat and pulled out one energy bar in bright blue foil and another in magenta. He ignored her outstretched hand and held them in front of her so she could see the front of each bar. The brand was called Cricket Boost. "Which one do you want?"

She dropped her hand. "This isn't like marijuana or something? Some kind of edible you're joking about?"

He laughed. "I wouldn't do that to you."

"I'm not against it. I'm just saying."

"No, it's just what it says, an energy bar."

She squinted at the label on the blue bar, which read: Cricket Boost. All Day Energy That Keeps You Singing! Black silhouettes of a bird trilling away, a cricket rubbing his legs together, and a frog croaking covered the top of the wrapper. She saw the blue one was made of oats and macadamia nuts and honey; the magenta one contained walnuts, dried cherries, and blueberries.

"I guess I'll take the magenta one."

He completely relaxed. "I figured. The blue one's good, too, though." He ripped open the magenta bar and placed it into her palm, then started unwrapping the blue bar for himself. "I thought of you because of the bird."

Trini smiled. "My friend Andi's last name is a bird, too. Her married name anyway."

He grunted in acknowledgment as he bit into his bar. Trini remembered she'd told him all about Andi being a Wren, so she added a bit lamely, "It was just so funny when she married into the Wren family and I was already a Finch."

"Trinidad Finch," he said.

Trini took a bite and Bobby sat back down beside her on the couch. While she chewed, he leaned forward and rubbed his thumb over her lips. "You're so kissable," he whispered.

"My mouth's full," she mumbled.

"Well, swallow it and kiss me."

She did, and he gave her a quick peck on the lips, then pulled back and thrust his own energy bar toward her mouth. "Take a bite of mine."

"You think maybe we could retire to the bedroom for a while after this? A quickie before dinner?" she asked as she bit into his bar.

"Maybe we'll make it a longie," he said suggestively. "One more bite."

"I've hardly swallowed this one."

"One more."

She obediently bit off a chunk of her bar with the blueberries while Bobby bit into his. An uncomfortable heat had started to fill her up inside and she found herself swallowing hard, her throat feeling as if it were constricting. "Uh-oh," she said on a strangled gulp.

"What's wrong?"

"Something . . . in it." She was suddenly struggling for air, her windpipe closing. She knew immediately she was in the beginning of an allergic reaction. A bad one. "EpiPen," she gasped.

He was frozen in the act of biting into his bar. "What?"

"Epi . . ." She couldn't get anything more out. Her lungs felt on fire. She couldn't breathe!

"EpiPen? Why? What? From the *energy bar*? No way. Look at me, I'm fine."

She signaled frantically toward the bathroom. "Med . . . med . . . cabinet!"

"Are you faking?"

"No!"

She was frantically clutching her throat. She couldn't breathe at all! "Help . . . help . . ."

He got to his feet and looked down at her. Her hands were clawing at her throat. She gazed up at him in mute horror, sliding her eyes toward the hallway. When he just stood there, she tried to scramble up from the couch. He suddenly pushed her back down, pinning her in place. She flailed about, struggling to pull air through a windpipe that was all but closed.

"Trinidad Finch," he said, saying her name as if he were tasting it.

He let go of her to take off his pants. She clambered wildly to her feet, but as soon as she was upright, he pushed her back down, hard. Her head slammed into the wooden arm again, the one Jarrett had sat on less than an hour earlier.

"Oops." He laughed.

Then he was stripping off her pants as she raked the skin at her throat, her fingernails gouging her own flesh. He crushed down on her with his full weight. She begged him with her eyes, but the smile on his face was filled with cruel enjoyment.

Then he was inside her again, laughing and laughing, as he rhythmically thrust into her ever harder, watching her face, smiling coldly as her lungs felt ready to burst and her world receded to a black dot.

"Good-bye, little bird," he whispered.

She tried to scream one last time, but it was no use. She could do nothing but stare into the eyes of her killer.

At the moment of her death, she saw him throw back his head as he climaxed with the wild howl of a conqueror.

Chapter Seventeen

Andi woke up feeling sluggish. She'd fallen into a comalike sleep after leaving Luke to sort out his sleeping arrangements on the couch or the floor. He'd assured her he was fine, and she'd reluctantly headed to bed, hurrying through the bathroom so he could use it whenever he needed to. She'd thought she would toss and turn, thinking about him in the next room, but it turned out to be one of those nights when she felt like she was drugged.

She threw on a robe and peeked outside the bedroom door. She had a direct view to the living room, where Luke's sleeping bag was rolled up and set on the couch. He was nowhere to be seen, but then she heard him in the kitchen, opening cupboards quietly.

She headed into the bathroom, checked her hair, made a face at herself without any makeup, and tried to force herself to go out to see him as she was. No dice. She quickly brushed her teeth, put on some eye shadow and mascara, and took a moment to conceal the circles beneath her eyes. Then she walked toward the kitchen.

Luke was in jeans but was shirtless. She saw the whorls of light brown hair on his chest and the sculpted muscles. The man was in great shape. She had a moment of comparing him to Greg and was mad at herself. Greg had been Greg. He'd had good points and bad, like everyone, and he was part of her history.

He was making a cup of coffee from her Keurig machine, brown liquid pouring into the cup he'd placed beneath the machine's spigot. Hearing her approach, he looked up. "Good morning," he said. "Thought I'd rustle up some coffee."

"There's cream in the refrigerator. Sugar bowl's up there." She pointed to a cupboard.

"Black's fine."

Luke had returned to her cabin the evening before with Asian food from the restaurant where they'd first had lunch together. "Figured we could use some food," he'd said, and they'd sat at her table and shared the same dishes they'd ordered before and a few more as well.

Of course, once she was away from the threat of the Carreras she'd started having second thoughts about having him stay over. She'd said as much, but he'd swept her protests aside. "I'll feel better," he insisted, and that had decided it for the moment.

"Want a cup?" he asked, sweeping a hand toward the rack of small cups of coffee, flavored, decaffeinated, and regular. "I can make you anything you want. How about hazelnut? Or vanilla?"

"Regular," she said, smiling.

"Coming right up." He pulled another mug from the cupboard above the machine, removed his steaming cup, then put hers in its place and pressed the button. Immediately coffee began to pour into it. "Cream? Sugar?" he asked.

"A little cream."

He pivoted to her refrigerator and found the half and half. By the time he got back to the machine her mug was nearly filled. Taking the mug from the Keurig, he lifted a questioning eyebrow as he began pouring a slow stream of cream into it.

"Perfect," she said, and he lifted the spout, put the carton back in the refrigerator, and picked up his own cup.

They stared at each other. Then both began to talk at once.

"You don't have to stay—" she began.

"I want to ask you something—" he said.

"Okay, you go first," Andi told him, motioning toward him with her mug.

"I've been thinking. Psychologically, the 'little bird' cards aren't like the Carreras. It could be them," he added quickly, apparently feeling she was about to protest, "but, like I said before, the brothers are generally more confrontational. I'd like to go at them hammer and tongs, but it wouldn't be smart."

She nodded in agreement.

"The Carreras are dangerous, and I don't like that your brother-in-law is trying to do business with them, but one thing about it: As long as they're working out a deal, I don't think they'll risk hurting you. They're already under a microscope and that would bring the authorities down on them like a tsunami."

"Okay."

"But I want to keep staying with you. Someone out there is threatening you, purposely scaring you, and I want to know who it is before you stay another night here alone. Maybe it's the Carreras, maybe it isn't, but either way, that's what I'd like to do. With your permission."

"Absolutely. I just don't want you to feel like you're wasting your time."

"It's my time to waste."

"I know, but you know what I mean."

"I'll work up the paperwork for our partnership today. I

have work to do for my brother." He gulped some coffee. "What are your plans?"

"It's Saturday, so I'm not going into the office."

He frowned. "You just plan to be around the cabin?"

"Would you rather I was somewhere else?"

"You're kind of isolated out here."

"I'll go into Laurelton. Shop or something. Just gotta shake the cobwebs out of my head."

"Stop by my office. I'll be there later."

"Okay. You can use the shower first," she invited.

"No, go ahead. I'll call Dallas." He reached toward the counter where his cell phone lay.

"Dallas is your brother?"

"A defense attorney." He grinned suddenly. "We didn't see eye to eye when I was on the force. I thought a lot of his clients were dirtbags. People he was just trying to get off. Meanwhile, he kept trying to get me to quit. I kept saying I didn't know what I'd do. He thought I should be a writer. Then I did quit, and he really pushed it after that. But now he wants to hire me as an investigator." He shook his head. "Life's circular sometimes."

"Yes, it is."

Andi headed to the shower. It was strange to have no plans. Normally she would just stay home, but Luke's comments about her isolation had resonated and she didn't want to be anywhere without other people around.

Trini, she thought. Andi didn't think she gave classes on Saturdays, so she might as well drop by to see if they were still on for tonight.

Tracy Farmgren stopped by the Sirocco Realty offices and smiled at the girl with the big eyes at the reception desk. It was *her* desk. She was the receptionist and this girl—Heidi—the daughter of one of the principal brokers, was a growing problem. First just weekends and then a few more days here and there . . . Tracy had been through the same thing before and this time she was staking her claim before things got out of hand.

God. Her name was Heidi and she actually wore her hair in two braids. It was enough to make you puke.

"Hi," Tracy greeted her with a big smile. "I forgot something in my desk."

"Oh. Okay." Heidi zoomed the rolling chair back and sat back and waited, which really pissed Tracy off.

"Um, would you mind getting me a cup of coffee?" Tracy asked. "I might be just a few minutes. . . ."

"Sure," she said somewhat reluctantly, then finally got her butt out of the chair and moseyed away.

What a nightmare. Tracy opened the bottom drawer and pulled out the small locked case within. It held duplicate keys to some of the homes, mostly expensive ones, that Tracy liked to walk through and pretend were hers when she knew the owners weren't home. No one had noticed when she'd sneaked the keys away and had the duplicates made. She'd only done it a time or two.

Of course, that's where she'd met *him*. Handsome, lots of money, dressed well. He caught her coming out of one of them and getting into her car, and he knew she was lying when she said she lived there because he knew the actual owners. She'd been sick at heart. She'd begged him not to tell. What she did was harmless. She just liked pretending. Was it so wrong?

She'd expected him to turn her in, but instead he told her that her secret was safe with him. But he would call her in a day or two and ask her to do something for him. Just a little thing. No big deal.

She'd lived in utter fear those seventy-two hours. Three days, not two. What was he going to ask? She had a feeling it was going to be big, no matter what he said, and she would have to confess to the principals and lose her job. Then he showed up at her work and asked her to lunch. She sat across from him at a bistro while he persuaded her there was no reason to worry. They were friends, he assured her. But the way he'd looked at her, she'd been pretty sure his little ask might be a few times in the sack with him.

She could do that.

So she had a few drinks, just a couple of vodka martinis, and let herself loosen up. He told her he was an investor. Just moved out from New York a few years earlier. He didn't ask her for anything that day, but she knew it was coming. When a few weeks went by and all they did was have lunch in some out-of-the-way places, she started to think she was wrong. In her fondest dreams she wondered if he really just wanted to date her.

And so she dated him. The lunches . . . a couple of dinners, a few drinks, and finally he came over to her place and they went to bed together. Truthfully, Tracy wasn't all that fond of sex. Kinda messy and sort of stupid. Half the time she wanted to clap her hand over her mouth to stop from giggling. But she managed to play the part and do a lot of moaning and breathing hard, and all in all, it was okay. She did really like him. He had a way of listening to every word she said that made her feel important.

And then came the day he asked her for the key to the cabin on Schultz Lake.

"That's what you wanted?" she asked, disappointed.

"And you," he assured her. "But don't worry. I'll bring the key back," he promised.

"But we sold the cabin. The new owner's going to move in soon."

"I'll only use it for a couple of hours. That's all."

Tracy could practically feel her blood freeze. "Don't make a copy, whatever you do."

He held up two fingers. "Scout's honor."

She'd given him the key, and true to his word, he'd brought it back that same day. She'd wanted to ask him what he needed it for, but something about him suggested that would be a bad idea. So she'd gone on as if nothing had happened. She'd replaced the copy she'd made of that key in her little box.

After that they kind of drifted apart, however, which hurt her feelings. She called him a few times, but he let her know very clearly that he would call her, not the other way around. He'd asked her to dinner on a couple of other occasions, but he'd had to cancel before the plans were hatched, and he stopped coming over for sex.

She'd just been lamenting her boring life when those police detectives had shown up and wanted to talk to Kitsy, who'd had the listing for the cabin. Edie Tindel had been the buyer's agent, and Tracy had lived in fear that the detectives would want to talk to her, too, but she didn't know if they had. Edie could tell them about the break-in, which, Tracy worried, had something to do with the key, though she didn't know what.

Scared, she'd called him after the detectives left. He'd flipped out, but she'd said it wasn't her fault. There was no way they could know about the extra key. No way. But saying it seemed to remind him of that fact, and he asked her to meet him and bring the key.

So now they had another date. But it was all over the fucking key.

She took the little case in its entirety and left before stupid Heidi could return with the coffee. Let her drink it, the bitch. Tracy hated coffee.

Luke drove to Mimi Quade's address and parked down the block, where he could watch the unit without being noticed. He'd done some research on Scott Quade and it looked like the man was currently in between addresses, so it stood to reason he might be bunking with his sister. If not, he would see what he could learn about Mimi and the baby. He called his brother as he was waiting, and Dallas picked up on the fourth ring.

"Thought you weren't going to answer," Luke greeted him. He could hear sounds in the background, music and someone asking if they were ready to order.

"I'm in a meeting with a client," Dallas answered.

"Having an early lunch?"

"Coffee."

He could tell by Dallas's careful answers that he couldn't talk, which was fine. "I'm watching a place, so I'll be here a while. What time did you want to meet?"

"I'll call you."

"Okay."

He hung up and let his mind wander back to Andi Wren, a wandering that was becoming more and more frequent. The last thing he wanted was a romantic entanglement. He'd been trying to extricate himself from Iris for months and had determined he was bad at breakups. And every new relationship had a breakup waiting for it; Taylor Swift sure had that one right.

But . . . he liked Andi. Her quiet ways. Her ability to understand her own motivations. Her strength in times of terrible loss. She'd been tousled and fuzzy this morning in a thoroughly charming way.

Were the Carreras behind the scare tactics? Brian Carrera had sought her out at her club and threatened her, so it seemed likely. Or was there someone else hiding in the shadows with their own agenda?

The thought brought gooseflesh rising on his skin. A warning. A whisper. He scoffed at all things clairvoyant, but he trusted his own instincts, and the message he was picking up was that he'd missed something. What? He did a quick recap in his mind of the people surrounding Andi and chronicled the events that had taken place both before and after they'd first met.

One: Scott and Mimi Quade came to the Wren Development offices and announce her pregnancy.

Two: Gregory Wren skids off the road to his death in a one-car accident.

Three: Andi learns she's pregnant.

Four: Brian Carerra threatens her at her club.

Five: Andi comes to see Luke at his office.

No, that wasn't quite right. Five was that Andi's cabin was broken into and the note was left on her bed. Six was when she came to his office.

Seven: Andi miscarries.

Eight: A period of inactivity from the Carreras, but in the background Carter Wren is working to form a financial partnership with them.

Nine: Andi goes to see Mimi Quade and determines Mimi is pregnant.

Ten: Scott Quade comes to the Wren Development offices again and wants . . .

Money, Luke determined. His leverage was Wren guilt over philandering Gregory and his baby.

As he considered this, a vehicle left the parking lot of Mimi's apartment complex and began to turn north on the main street in front of the building, the same direction in which Luke's car was facing. Luke's binoculars were already in hand and he lifted them to his eyes in time to determine that the man behind the wheel was Scott Quade. He switched on the engine and was about to follow when a second car came out of the lot. This time it was Mimi behind the wheel. Luke had seen pictures of her on the web site for Nailed It!

He chose to follow her instead and eased in behind her. It was eleven o'clock and traffic was fairly light. She drove directly to Nailed It! and pulled into the lot. Luke turned into the one-level business complex as well and drove past her just as she was climbing out of her car, juggling a Starbucks cup, her purse, and a bag that likely held items she used for work. Her baby bump was clear and he shook his head at Scott's intimation of an abortion, when suddenly her work bag banged against her stomach and she dropped it with a *thud* to adjust the bulk in front.

It was a quick move, accompanied by a surreptitious look around to see if anyone noticed. Her eye found Luke's car, but it passed over him as he drove away. Then she gathered up her items and headed into the salon.

Luke parked at the far end of the lot, looking back. A fake baby bump. Scott and Mimi Quade were pulling an extortion racket. That was why there was all the talk about paying for an abortion. There was no baby.

His mind whirled. But there had been, he concluded, and it had been Gregory Wren's because Scott had originally demanded a DNA test. Neither Greg nor Carter had wanted to believe Mimi was pregnant. Then Greg had died and Carter had refused to deal with Scott, so he and Mimi had faded into the background.

She must have miscarried, Luke concluded. Otherwise Scott would have been in their faces about the baby regardless. He wasn't the kind of personality to just let things go, especially if there was money to be made. Luke had picked that up in just one meeting with the man, and it hadn't taken any kind of mental leap.

Could Scott Quade, after losing one ploy, have embarked on another? Scaring Andi Wren with his little bird messages? To what end?

Luke drummed his fingers on the steering wheel. He couldn't see how that would turn into a moneymaking scheme, and unless there was another, darker side to Scott

Quade, he would bet his own last dollar that money was the man's prime motivation.

You don't have enough information yet to draw any conclusions.

But it was something to know Mimi Quade was faking her pregnancy.

He picked up his cell phone to call Andi.

Tracy was standing outside her apartment, waiting. She'd driven back home and placed her call. "I've got it," she'd said, hearing how miffed she sounded. She was still in a bad mood from seeing Heidi sitting in her chair.

"Meet me outside. I'll pick you up in a few minutes."

"I'm at home," she told him, though he'd already hung up on her, so obviously he already had that information.

Now she saw a blue Buick sedan pull up to the curb. She peered inside the passenger window as it rolled down.

"What's this car?" she asked.

"It's my other one. Get in."

His high-handedness kind of pissed her off, but she complied, and he raced away with more speed than she'd expected. "Where's the fire?" she asked.

"I want to take you somewhere."

"This is new," she said, not bothering to hide the pout in her voice. Their relationship to date, if that's what it was, had been a quick meal here and there, nothing fancy, nothing expensive, almost like he thought he was obligated to be nice to her.

"Where's the key?" he asked, as they headed west on Highway 26, away from Laurelton.

"I've got it in my little lockbox." She patted her purse, which sat on her lap. She knew he wanted her to open it up, but she didn't feel like it. Let him beg her for it. She liked the idea of that.

They didn't talk for several miles and she finally said, "You're not taking me all the way to the beach, are you?"

"What if I am?"

"Don't be a dick. I'm not going." Actually, she had nothing to do and the idea of heading out on a lark appealed to her, but for reasons she didn't fully understand, she didn't want him to know that . . . yet.

"What're you gonna do?" he asked, amused. "How're you gonna stop me?"

"I don't know. I'll think of something." He was jollying her out of her bad mood and it was working, and that kind of pissed her off, but it also made her smile.

"So, those policemen who showed up at Sirocco. Who were they? Do you remember their names?"

He was a little too casual and Tracy's radar antennae rose up. "No. They were two women . . . one of 'em had reddish-brown hair, like it was streaked, but it was natural, I'm pretty sure. The other had kinky, dark hair."

He was frowning. "Women?"

"Yeah, women. Both of 'em."

"Was one of 'em black?"

"No . . . maybe sorta. She looked more Hispanic, maybe? I don't know. She didn't talk as much."

"The auburn-haired one was the one talking?"

"Auburn-haired?"

"Reddish-brown? You don't know auburn?" He shot her a pitying look, which brought back her bad mood in a rush.

"Well, excuse me for living."

They were on the outskirts of Quarry, Oregon, which was kind of a podunk town, with one main street and a lot of little rural shacks. Tracy had once dated a guy from there and after meeting his family had thought, *no way*. They were all hicks. To her consternation, he took the turn off to nowheresville.

She groaned. "What're we doing here?"

"Seeing the sights."

"There are no sights to see in Quarry," she grumbled. "Take me home, for the love of God."

He drove down the main street. Small town USA in spades. Tracy leaned her head against the window and looked out. All she could really see was Heidi's big blue eyes and her butt slapped onto *her* chair.

"You've caused me some trouble," he said conversationally.

"Huh?"

"You said the policewomen were there to see an agent about the cabin."

"Yeah, Kitsy."

"Who?" That seemed to surprise him. "I thought Edie Tindel was the agent."

"She was the buyer's agent. Kitsy had the listing. But I don't think they were there about the cabin. They were detectives, not policewomen. It was something else."

They'd passed through town and were on the road that led toward the old quarry, the landmark the town was named for. She'd learned way more than anyone should know about the place from her ex-boyfriend, who'd taken her to the plateau above the quarry for a make-out session because it was some kind of lover's lane. Figured.

"What was it?" His voice was cold.

"I don't know. Kitsy doesn't confide in me. I just overheard her talking to some other agents. Something about the street she used to live on."

"What's Kitsy's real name?"

"I don't know. She goes by Kitsy. What is this, the third degree?"

"What's her last name?" he asked with extreme patience.

"Hasseldorn."

"Shit."

The word expelled through his lips like a bullet. Tracy

gave him a sideways look, wondering what the hell was going on with him. "You know her?"

He suddenly jerked the car down a rutted lane that was overgrown and scattered with small tree limbs. Tracy put her hand on the dashboard to brace herself. He made it about a quarter of a mile, then was stopped by a downed tree, its bole about two feet wide.

"You want to go to lover's lane, it's the quarry," she said sarcastically. "And it's thataway." She jerked a thumb to indicate the way they'd come.

He suddenly reached over and grabbed her by the hair. She slapped at his hand instinctively. "What the fuck?"

"Who did you tell about the key?"

"No one. God. What do you take me for?"

"The police detectives."

"No!"

"This Kitsy Hasseldorn?" He shook her head hard. It felt like her hair might rip out at the roots.

"Goddamn you!" she snarled.

He slapped her. So hard it would have snapped her head if he hadn't been hanging on to it by her hair. She opened her mouth to scream and he slapped her again. Then he was slamming her head into the dashboard. Pain exploded in her head and he slammed her head again and again, until she was crying and ready to pass out.

"What? What?" she burbled.

"We don't even have time to fuck," he raged, slamming her head again. "I don't have time for this. You understand? I've got it all worked out and you're not going to fuck it up!"

"I'm sorry. I'm sorry," she apologized between sobs. She didn't know what she was apologizing for, but she knew it was what he wanted to hear.

"Sorry," he spat. He slammed her head again, and this time she passed out and knew no more.

* * *

He looked down at her in disgust. What a fucking bitch. And he had hours before it was dark. Damn. She was ruining his game! Yes, there were unexpected twists and turns to the game, but this was too much. What about those detectives? And Mrs. Hasseldorn?

Tracy had to be done with once and for all or she would talk. That was all there was to it. When they found her body at the bottom of the quarry, maybe they would think her death had something to do with that ex-boyfriend from that loser family she'd told him about.

Just as long as there was no blowback on him.

Mrs. Hasseldorn. He remembered her and her exacting husband. He knew just which house they'd lived in on Aurora Lane. He'd heard they'd moved to Schultz Lake, but he knew every family who lived on the water and knew that to be a lie. Maybe they'd planned to once, but it hadn't come to be.

He put on gloves and reached into her purse, pulling out Tracy's lockbox. Searching around, he found her keys and the tiny one that opened the box. Inside were more keys. He wasn't sure which one went to the cabin, so he took them all, half impressed at how many she'd made for herself. It was almost too bad she was such a waste of space because he recognized that she was a little criminal in the making, something he could appreciate.

But today was her last day on earth. So sad. Not part of his particular game, and there was no time to suck the enjoyment out of this particular death. This one was just about expediency.

With that, he pulled the gloves out of his appropriately named glove box, slipped them on, and choked the life out of her.

* * *

Andi sat outside Trini's apartment, blown away by Luke's information. She couldn't make herself move. The news she'd just heard about Mimi had stunned her. Not pregnant. *Not.* Wearing a fake baby bump.

She'd been fooled. Andi had bought into Mimi's story, hook, line, and sinker.

Luke had called her and given her the information. He'd apologized that he couldn't give it to her in person, but he had some appointments. She's been totally okay with hearing it over the phone. What was there to say anyway?

"Carter was right," she said aloud, still disbelieving.

And Greg. He'd sworn she wasn't pregnant, although Luke had suggested she might have been once, and that may have given Scott the idea to shake down the Wrens. Maybe she had been pregnant but had miscarried? But something had changed because Scott had stopped asking for DNA and wanted money for an abortion.

An abortion. Red-hot rage shot through Andi as she thought about Mimi sobbing her eyes out, all the while wearing a fake baby bump. Damn her. Damn *them*! She ached inside when she thought of what she'd lost, and though Mimi had possibly been pregnant in the beginning, the whole charade had been performed for her benefit.

And it hurt. A lot.

Andi thought it over some more, then climbed out of her car and paced around the parking lot a bit, before charging up the stairs to Trini's door. She banged on it angrily, letting out her fury.

No answer.

But Trini was here. She had to be. Andi had spied Trini's Mini in its designated spot. Parking was hell around here and sometimes Trini Ubered her way to work just to keep poachers away.

Andi frowned. Maybe she had a class now and wasn't home. Oh God, no. Right now Andi needed a friend. Someone she could confide in. Someone to cry and scream and rage to.

She pounded on the door again, this time so hard her fist hurt. "Come on, come on," she said under her breath, willing her friend to answer the damned door.

Could Scott Quade be behind the notes? Were they more his style than the Carreras? But why, *why*? Why her?

"Trini?" Andi called loudly and hit the door again. "It's me!" Under her breath, she said, "God, I hope you're home. Please be home."

She'd already tried texting and calling her friend's cell phone, but there'd been no answer. No surprise. Trini often ignored her phone for hours.

"Damn it all!" Frustrated, Andi walked to the end of the wooden landing and looked over the rail. Trini's apartment had windows facing west and they were covered with miniblinds that were slanted downward but were partially open, offering tantalizing tiny slits of views inside, but it was hard to make out anything. Leaning over the railing, Andi squinted, peering inside Trini's living room, but she couldn't get a full picture. It almost looked like someone was sleeping on the couch . . . or maybe that was wishful thinking on her part.

Once more she pounded on the door.

Once more no one answered.

She thought about her friend and remembered she kept a spare key in a magnetic box inside the wheel of her car. If she went searching around her car, would people wonder what the hell she was up to? Probably.

She dialed her friend's number again. Trini's cell went straight to voice mail. "Call me, Trini," she said. Hung up, then exhaled heavily and sent yet another text: I'm here. At your house!

Still nothing.

"Oooh." She almost threw her phone in frustration. She so needed to talk to someone. Maybe she should just call Luke back, ask to meet him. She knew he was working, but she didn't know what that entailed. Was it an all-day thing, or could he knock off early? If he even wanted to, she reminded herself. She was going to see him tonight one way or another, so maybe she should just wait for that.

After a few moments of pacing in front of Trini's door, she called Trini's workplace and asked if she had a class.

"Finch?" the guy who'd answered the phone asked. "She blew off two classes already today," he said, sounding pissed.

"She did?"

"Uh-huh. She's got another one at four, but I've been calling her and there's been no response. None."

"I'm a friend of hers. This isn't like her." At least not when it came to her job.

"No, it isn't," he agreed, but he wasn't happy about it. "We're scrambling around here, trying to get people to cover for her and . . . oh hell, look, if you find her, she'd better be dead, cuz that's the only excuse I want to hear why she couldn't call in." He clicked off.

Now Andi was nonplussed. Trini had blown off two classes and maybe wasn't going to make a third? That just didn't compute. Trini was flaky about certain things, but she took her classes very seriously.

She tried to peer through the window again. Was that a person on the couch? Possibly Trini? She wished there was a light on; it was a dark afternoon and the interior of the apartment was darker still.

She gave up and texted Luke.

> My friend Trini missed her classes. Not her usual
> MO. Kinda weird. I'm at her apartment. Car's here
> but she's not.

Maybe she was with Bobby, Andi thought. Trini was seeing him last night and they were supposed to all meet up tonight. Could Bobby talk her into missing her classes, though? Without a heads-up to the club?

A whisper of fear lifted the hairs on Andi's arms. She didn't like the way the guy at the club had said *she'd better be dead*, even though he'd been joking.

"Finch," he'd said, identifying her to Andi.

Andi stood stock-still. It hadn't occurred to her during this whole little bird thing that Trini had a last name that was a bird. Trini and Andi had laughed themselves silly when Trini learned that Greg had asked Andi to marry him.

"Jesus, I never thought we'd both be *birds*," Trini had said, shaking her head first, then breaking out laughing.

"Birds of a feather stick together," Andi had responded, and they'd shared a rare moment of hilarity, even though Trini hadn't really wanted Andi to marry Greg.

It's too bad when little birds have to die . . .

Andi clenched her teeth. What if something had happened to Trini? Was that too far-fetched to consider? It was crazy. Pointless. But the fear that was filling her veins with ice was very real.

Luke texted back: Where's the apartment?

Andi checked the address and texted it back to him, adding: I know where a key is.

He responded with: I can be there in thirty minutes?

She knew he was asking if her concern warranted him joining her. She thought about it a minute, then answered: Yes, come.

She stood outside another ten minutes, then went down to Trini's car. Luckily, she was dressed in jeans as she knelt on the pavement near the front passenger wheel well and ran her hand around inside. She failed to find the magnetic box, so she moved to the rear wheel and reached forward, searching blindly. She was about to give up when her fingers connected with something. She struggled a bit trying to break the magnetic grip, but suddenly it broke free.

Feeling like a sneak thief, she curled her fingers around the tiny box and ran back to Trini's front door. Her fingers were shaking as she slid open the tiny metal door to reveal two keys: one to Trini's car, the other to her apartment. Andi plucked the apartment key out and shut the metal receptacle again, pocketing it for the moment. She checked the time on her phone. Luke still had ten minutes.

Maybe she was borrowing trouble. Influenced by her own problems. The Carreras or Scott Quade would have no reason to hurt Trini. Yes, she'd gotten in Brian or Blake's face at Lacey's, but from both Trini and Jarrett's accounts, it hadn't been that serious of a confrontation.

Just do it. Open the damned door!

Apprehension skidded down her spine.

Setting her jaw, she threaded the key in the lock, aware that her pulse was escalating. With a click, the door unlocked and she slowly pushed it open.

Trini was sitting up, slumped over on the couch, her eyes open, her tongue out. She seemed to be staring at Andi, her expression frozen in a look of horror, her clothes ripped and hanging off her.

One look and Andi knew her friend was dead.

A wave of heat swept over her, followed by icy cold. She drew in a huge gasp of air, squeezed her eyes closed, and screamed for all she was worth.

PART III

———◆———

ENDGAME

Chapter Eighteen

Have to get my mind back on the game. Forget the female detectives. Forget Tracy and her sour attitude. Go back to Trinidad Finch . . . just thinking of her puts a smile on my face. All of them will be running around, trying to make sense of her death. Have you figured it out yet, little bird? Let me give you a hint: It's all about misdirection. Do you see that my moves are merely smoke and mirrors? No, you're too afraid. Too confused. You're frightened that I'll find you and crush you, and I will. Just not yet. I've got more gambits planned . . . just wait. . . .

Luke heard the terrified scream as he was locking his truck.

His heart froze. *Andi!*

He whipped from the numbered spot he'd poached, the one next to her car and took off at a dead run. His hair stood up on end, every one of his muscles tightened. Why the hell hadn't he brought his damned gun? Heart pounding, he reached the stairs and took the steps two at a time. "Andi!" he yelled, heading straight for the open door.

Jesus God, he hoped she was okay and kicked himself for not staying closer to her. "Andi!"

Through the door he plunged.

Andi was standing in the center of the room, her back to him, her arms out for balance, but weaving on her feet like she was about to topple. He grabbed her and she shrieked again.

"It's Luke," he said. "Luke. I'm sorry. It's Luke."

She turned in his arms, her eyes stretched wide. "She's dead . . . I think Trini's dead. Oh God . . . no."

Holding her close, he gazed past her to the small woman slumped on the couch.

"She's dead?" she asked, trembling, but the tone of her voice convinced him that she already knew what was so patently obvious. One look at the body and he was fairly certain Andi was right. The woman slumped on the over-stuffed cushions was staring fixedly ahead, her skin and lips the ashy gray of death. He suspected Trini had been dead for a number of hours. That meant her death had probably happened the day before, or possibly earlier, but there was no scent of rot yet, so sooner rather than later. She was slumped sideways and there was a bit of purple-colored foil next to her left hand. "Yes, I think so." He double-checked, releasing Andi for a second to bend over Trini and touch the cool flesh of her neck. No sign of a pulse.

"Oh God . . . oh God . . . my God . . ." Andi, quivering from head to toe, was staring at her friend.

Luke steered her back toward the door. "Let's go outside and I'll call nine-one-one."

He managed to get them both outside the door and re-alized several people were in the parking lot, looking up at them. "Somebody screamed," one of them, a man in his thirties wearing a Blazers cap, said.

"Yeah, it's all right," Luke assured him. He didn't need any lookie loos at this juncture. He reached into his pocket with one hand for his phone, holding Andi close, her face pressed to his chest with the other.

"Y'sure?" an older man wearing a driver's cap asked. "Sounded like holy terror. Gave me the willies."

Luke didn't respond, just turned his back on them and placed the call.

"Nine-one-one, what is the nature of your emergency?"

"I believe a young woman is dead inside her apartment," Luke said quietly into the receiver.

Two hours later Andi still stood outside Trini's unit. She hadn't gone inside as the police first and then a crime tech crew arrived and began going over Trini's small abode.

Trini's dead. The words failed to compute inside Andi's brain, even though she'd understood that truth as soon as she'd looked at her friend. She knew it was real yet still felt like she might wake up from a horrible dream.

A uniformed officer had asked her questions, which she'd heard herself answer, but it was as if she were having an out-of-body experience. Then an overweight detective arrived. Luke handled most of what they wanted, answering as best he could, but there were a few queries for Andi personally, like where she found the key, why she felt it was necessary to enter her friend's place, what was the nature of her relationship with the deceased.

No one was saying how she died, or even if a crime had been committed, but Andi had heard someone mention anaphylactic shock. That stirred her enough to tell them that Trini was deathly allergic to shellfish.

"But she's always really, really careful," Andi had managed to choke out.

She'd initially clung to Luke like a burr, only releasing him when one of the crime tech team recognized him. She was a woman in her fifties with short, dark hair and a thin smile. "Denton," she said.

"Hi, Marjorie." Luke's response was warm.

"When're you coming back to the force?" she asked.

"Don't think it's gonna happen," Luke said, to which she shook her head, as if he'd made a poor choice.

Toward the end of the two hours Andi had dared a peek inside the apartment and was relieved to see that Trini's body had been zipped into a body bag. There was fingerprint dust everywhere, and some kind of foil wrapper had been tweezered into a clear plastic bag that Marjorie was showing to Luke. In another plastic bag was a man's wallet.

"What is that?" she asked Luke.

"The wrapper for some kind of energy bar," Luke said. "The foil's a perfect medium for fingerprints, but there aren't any on it at all."

"Trini's would be on it if she'd unwrapped it."

"Exactly. Maybe it was wiped clean, but then why would it be left at all?"

"What do you think it means?"

He shook his head.

Marjorie had consulted with one of the other techs, who was working on a laptop. "Denton," she called, waving him over. Andi followed, keeping her eyes averted from the black bag that held her friend.

"This particular energy bar is made with cricket flour. See the cricket on the label? If we had more of the wrapper, we would see the warning."

"What warning?" Luke asked.

"Crickets are in the same family as shellfish."

Luke looked from the computer screen to Andi, who

was still processing. "Oh my God," she said, tears springing to her eyes. "You're saying it was a mistake? She ate something basically with *shellfish* in it?"

"The warning's pretty large," Marjorie said, turning the computer screen for Andi to see it. On the back of the foil-wrapped bar, the one currently on the screen, was a large black circle with a slash through it over the words *cricket flour*. Below it was a warning that crickets were in the shellfish family.

The heavyset detective who'd asked Andi all the questions was in a conversation with one of the other techs about the wallet. He looked up and noticed Marjorie exchanging information with them and a frown creased his face. Seeing him start their way, Luke recognized trouble. "Thanks, Marjorie," he said, pulling Andi to one side.

"You need to wait outside," the detective told him, his uncompromising gaze encompassing Andi as well. He then shot a warning look at Marjorie, who ignored him.

Luke shepherded Andi back onto the deck outside the apartment. He checked to make sure they were out of earshot, then said, "If she was as careful as you say, it's a little surprising she didn't see it. It's pretty obvious."

"She would have seen it, wouldn't she? She would have seen it."

"Don't know how she wouldn't have noticed it," Luke admitted. "I wonder whose wallet they have." He glanced back toward the detective, who was standing just inside, gazing their way. "That detective . . . Thompkins. He's with the Laurelton PD, but I don't know him."

"How could Trini miss it?" Andi asked. "I don't understand."

"She would have seen it. Unless . . ."

"What?"

"Unless she was handed the bar, unwrapped."

"Somebody gave it to her? And she just didn't know?" Andi whispered. Her gaze traveled back to the open doorway and the detective. "But the wrapper was near her hand."

"Part of it. The foil would show some kind of print or mark, but it's been wiped clean. It was just sitting beside her left hand, and it was just the piece with a bit of the warning. So where's the rest of the wrapper?"

He was talking to himself more than to her.

"What are you saying?" Andi asked, her voice barely audible.

"I don't know yet. The wrapper . . ."

Luke didn't like the idea that was formulating in his brain, that someone had deliberately fed Trini the bar and then left the foil on the couch for the authorities to find, a kind of gloating, a *See what I've done!* meant to show how smart he or she was.

"Who knew she was allergic to shellfish?" he asked.

"I don't know. Lots of people. She didn't keep it a secret. She wanted people to know, just in case she missed something, so someone else might come to her rescue."

"What about this boyfriend?" Luke asked.

"He's allergic, too. She told me that." Andi shuddered and wrapped her arms around herself. "She was meeting him last night. I was supposed to finally meet him tonight. You think that's his wallet?"

"He's allergic to shellfish, too?"

"That's what she said."

"The police are going to want to talk to him. We need to, too."

"The detective, Thompkins, already asked me about Bobby. If it's his wallet, they know more about him than I do. He came to one of her classes and he was buttoned-down, not her type at all, and I think he wore glasses and maybe a hairpiece, but like I said, I never met him."

"She was a Pilates instructor."

"Yes."

"Okay. Look, I'm going to take you home, and then I'm going to try to talk with Thompkins some more. They may rule this an accident, but I want to be sure."

"Luke . . ."

He looked at her.

"My friend Trini . . . her full name is Trinidad Finch."

"Okay." He was anxious to talk to the detective.

She didn't say anything else but was looking at him hard. Luke ran her friend's name through his mind and felt a zing of surprise, followed by the chill of realization. "Her last name is a bird, too."

"Do you think . . . I mean, am I crazy to think there's a connection? That last note . . ."

"But she's not involved with Wren Development." He heard himself and added, "If that's what this is about."

"'It's too bad when little birds have to die,'" Andi quoted, her voice shaking.

"Let's go back to your place. I'll talk to him after they've cleared the scene."

"All right."

September stretched her arms over her head. She was tired of paperwork and tired of the runaround on Aurora Lane. It was Saturday and she wasn't supposed to be working, but Jake was busy with a rich client who'd sprung for a working weekend at a hotel and spa in Oregon's wine country, not far from his own family's vineyard, and though September had been invited to join them, she'd met the wealthy client before and had deemed him an obnoxious waste of space, so she'd declined. "Traitor," Jake had told her, and she'd kissed him and told him to have a good time, if he could.

She'd then started the day curled up on the couch with a cup of coffee watching television shows mindless enough to make her realize she couldn't remember when the morning news program turned into an Infomercial. She was inside her own head, thinking about Jake and his weekend, their engagement, but even those thoughts were eclipsed by the one really occupying her mind: the bones found in the Singletons' basement.

So she'd gotten dressed and headed to the station. She wouldn't be able to clock the overtime and she didn't much care. George and Wes were working on call today and September and Gretchen were on for Sunday. If the detectives weren't needed, they would stay home. If they were, that's when the overtime kicked in. As a rule, most of Laurelton's crimes could be handled by police officers. The cases that required detectives weren't plentiful, which was why the department cutbacks were a worry. September had been lucky to be involved in several big cases over the last year and a half, and she and her fellow detectives had certainly had their share of work-related injuries that sidelined them for a while—the memory of a man stabbing at her caused her to inadvertently rub the scar near her shoulder—so the work level had been consistent. But now they were in a lull that, although great for the public good, wasn't so great for her career.

She'd called the number for the Burkeys from Elias Mamet's list as soon as she'd left the interview with Kitsy Hasseldorn. No answer. She'd called again a few hours later and the same thing: no answer. The Burkeys weren't getting back to her and she could find no separate listing for Thomas Burkey.

After that she'd phoned the landlord again, but Mamet was as unhelpful as ever. Though his rental house was only a few doors from the Singletons' and had been for years, he swore he didn't know much about them. He also didn't remember anything about a tenant with an RV, and he brushed aside the horse by saying that a number of tenants had a horse or two. It was one of the draws of his rental.

Mamet's records were as lousy as his attitude, but September had managed to winnow the long list he'd given her down to four names that could possibly belong to the family of the kid with the addiction problem. She'd called Mamet again later, trying to jog his memory on the four names, but his responses had devolved to gruff yes and no answers, except for his assurance that he didn't really like police officers of any kind.

Now she was going over the four names of families who had rented the Mamet place. None of them were anything that sounded like *shoe*, as Kitsy had recalled, and only a couple of them had answered her calls or returned them. Of the two who had, most had some recollection of Tommy Burkey, but the kid with the addiction problem rang no bells, most likely because she hadn't connected with the boy's family yet. The whole process was like moving through molasses, slow, slow, slow, but that was the nature of police work.

After their talk with Kitsy Hasseldorn, September and Gretchen had been called to a domestic disturbance that ended in death. The wife had hit the husband with a frying pan filled with chicken Marengo, which had burned him and sent him to the hospital. What had killed him was the heart attack that followed this altercation, and the wife was so distraught and disbelieving, it was pretty clear she hadn't meant to kill him. The case was now in the hands of the DA, who could decide whether to pursue it further. Afterward, it was time to go home, but September had wanted to pick up where she'd left off on the Aurora Lane case today, on the weekend, and here she was.

She put in one more call to the Burkeys, preparing herself for yet another voice message when, to her surprise, the line was answered by a suspicious male, who asked, "Who is this?"

"I'm Detective September Rafferty," she began, but he cut her off.

"You've been leaving messages."

"Yes, I have. Is this . . ." She'd been going to say Douglas, Mr. Burkey's name, but changed her mind and asked, "Tommy?"

His intake of air told her a lot. "What do you want?"

"Like I said, I'm just looking for information about a boy who lived on Aurora Lane who—"

"You gonna arrest him for drugs?"

September trod carefully. "Well, no. I just want to talk to him."

"Why don't you call his mom and dad?"

"I don't know their names, Tommy. What's your friend's name?"

"He's not my friend. He wasn't nice to me."

"What do you call him?"

"Laser."

"Laser? Is that his first name or last name?"

"It's just his name. He's got laser eyes, y'know?" There was the sound of a sharp female voice and Tommy took on an aggrieved note as he said, "I was just talking to her! She wants to know about Laser!"

"Hang up," the woman ordered.

"Well, geez!" Tommy said, at the same moment September cried, "No, wait!"

The phone cut out.

"Damn it," she murmured, but she was elated she'd at least gotten some information.

She glanced down the list of four names: the Kirkendalls, Wrights, Pattens, and Brannigans. She'd called them all to no avail, so she phoned the Myleses again. Hannah answered while a baby babbled loudly. The conversation was

short. Of course, Hannah Myles was too new to the family
and Aurora Lane to offer up any information, and her husband and father-in-law weren't available.

"Story of my life," September said after hanging up.
Frustrated, she tapped her fingers on the phone, feeling as
if she were running around in circles, getting no-damned-
where. She considered chasing down Tynan again, but she
felt he'd told her everything he was going to.

"Damn, damn, and double damn." She leaned back in
her chair and her thoughts turned back to Grace. The older
woman's recollections couldn't be trusted, but there were
kernels of information there that came out that were almost
easier to decipher than the roadblocks the other Myleses
seemed to want to erect.

And Maple Grove Assisted Living wasn't all that far
away.

What would it hurt to try to talk to the old woman again?

Grabbing her coat from the back of her chair, she
headed out. This time she'd just flash her badge and bully
her way in to see Grace, even if it brought the staff and all
the other Myleses down on her. To hell with it. She was sick
of pussyfooting around. She wanted answers.

Andi hit the remote on her single-car garage and drove
inside. The trembling had stopped, but the disbelief and
horror remained. She sat for a moment behind the wheel
and watched in the rearview mirror as Luke's truck pulled
to the side of the drive behind her.

Climbing out of the car was difficult; she felt like she'd
aged a year in the last few hours. It didn't seem strange
when Luke joined her in the garage and walked her to the
front door. He inserted the key and pushed the door open,
holding it so she could enter first.

Once they were inside she walked into the kitchen and

then stared around, completely forgetting what she'd gone there for.

"You want to sit down?" Luke suggested, following after her. He stood by the table, clearly concerned. He'd tried to drive her home, but she hadn't wanted to be stuck without her car. She could tell he was worried that she was going to fall apart completely.

"I have antidepressants," she said. "I should take them regularly, but . . ."

"Are they in the bathroom? Medicine cabinet?" At her nod, he went to get them without her asking.

He returned with the two vials of pills. "They look the same."

"They are the same. Dr. Knapp prescribed them both, but some were prescribed earlier and then the others after my miscarriage. Dr. Knapp wanted me to keep taking them, and I should. I don't know why I don't, except . . . I'm drug sensitive." She gave him a quick look. "I've lost time . . . had blackouts . . . so I don't always want to take them."

"You've had blackouts from the pills?"

"I don't know."

"Do you want one now?" he asked dubiously.

She shrugged. She wanted something. She just didn't know what it was.

He held up the two bottles and extended one to her. "These pills look a little bigger."

"Are they? They were both prescribed by Dr. Knapp." Andi's head hurt. She didn't want to have this conversation. She just wanted to lie down and pretend nothing had happened.

Luke took off the caps of both vials and shook a few tablets into his palm. It was true. The white tablets all looked like aspirin, but the ones from the first vial were slightly larger than the ones from the second one. He squinted at both of the labels.

"Same prescription. Same pharmacy," Luke said.

She shook her head.

He gave it up and put the tablets and vials on the table, then came over to her. Resting his hands lightly on her shoulders, he steered her to a chair. "You want water? Coffee? Tea?"

"Tea would be great, actually. I've got some for the Keurig."

He made her a cup and brought it to her. Her cell phone rang, muffled inside her purse, which she'd dropped on the table. She looked at it without much interest, then sighed and reached for it. When she plucked out her phone and saw it was Carter, she grimaced. "I haven't had a chance to tell him about Mimi and Scott yet. God. It seems so unimportant now."

"Want me to talk to him?"

She nodded and Luke answered the phone. "This is Luke Denton."

"Where's Andi?" Carter demanded. She could hear his tinny voice clearly.

"She's right here. She's had a shock. Her friend Trini was found dead in her apartment this morning."

There was a moment of silence, then "Dead! What do you mean dead? You don't mean . . . dead-dead . . . ?" he asked in shock.

"That's exactly what I mean." Luke spent a few moments bringing Carter up to speed.

Carter responded, sounding poleaxed, "Okay . . . okay. Well . . . I still need to talk to her."

Andi reached out a hand when it looked like Luke was going to fob him off. She knew Carter. It would be easiest to just find out what he wanted. "Hi, Carter," she answered.

"Andi, I'm sorry. It's unbelievable. I hardly know what to say. . . . Do the police know anything? Was it foul play?"

"We don't know anything yet. Just tell me what you need."

He cleared his throat. "You're not going to like to hear this. The Carreras are meeting with our lawyer on Monday. They're bringing a five-million-dollar check."

"Five mil—" She couldn't finish. "Goddamn it, Carter. It's not going to happen! They can bring us a hundred million. I don't care! Do you get that? Do you? I'm so sick of this!"

Luke was on the balls of his feet. "What?"

"I've talked to Emma and—" Carter began calmly.

"No. No, you haven't. She would never agree," Andi practically shouted into the phone.

"I was going to say, she feels like you do. But she at least said she'd come to the meeting. I didn't know about your friend, but you and I need to be there, too."

"No. *No.*"

"If Greg were alive, he would be there."

"Greg didn't trust the Carreras either. You know that."

"Listen to me, Andi. Greg would want to make sure the company wasn't in financial trouble. This is our grandfather's company. One my dad continued, and now it's up to us." His voice had taken on an edge. "I don't want to fight you, but Andi, this is important Wren business, and let's face it, you're really not a Wren."

"Tell that to the Carreras," she choked out. "They're the ones sending me 'little bird' notes."

"I don't know what that's about, but it's not the Carreras."

"I gotta go," she said.

"Andi—"

"Oh, wait. There's something you need to know. Luke saw that Mimi's baby bump is a fake. So you were right about that. But you're not right about the Carreras!"

She clicked off and dropped the phone on the table, then put her head in her hands, fighting off sobs.

Luke dropped down in front of her and said soberly, "I'm going to connect with Detective Thompkins, but it's also high time I confronted the brothers."

She lifted a tear-streaked face to him. "Please don't. I appreciate it. But not now."

"You came to me because of them."

"I don't want you to go anywhere."

"I don't have to leave right this minute," he said, though he looked like that was exactly what he wanted to do.

"I don't know if you heard. I have a meeting on Monday with Carter, Emma, and the Carreras."

"I heard enough."

"Come to the meeting with me on Monday," she said abruptly. "You can confront them there. I told Carter I wouldn't go, but I have to. Be there with me."

"I feel like the momentum's now," he tried to argue, rising to his full height.

She shook her head, gazing up at him, mutely pleading.

"I want to find the Carreras and lay our cards on the table," he explained.

"What cards?"

"That we know about their coercion, that they're responsible for Ted Bellows's death, that they're not going to take the lodge away from the Wrens."

Andi got to her feet, facing him. She grabbed his left hand. "Don't go."

Luke's jaw worked. "I can't stand the way they're forcing themselves on you and your sister- and brother-in-law. I want to know if they had anything to do with your friend's death. I want to stop them."

"Yes . . . but wait." She held hard to his hand.

"Andi . . ."

They looked at each other for a long, tense moment. Slowly, Andi placed her hands on either side of his face.

Then she leaned in and kissed him, feeling the warmth of his lips against hers.

She pulled back slowly. She could see how his eyes had darkened.

"I'm pretty sure this is a bad idea," he said.

"I just want to feel something good."

"I stay away from clients."

"I stay away from everyone," she admitted. "Greg was the anomaly, and now he's gone."

"My last relationship ended ugly. Still ending."

She finally heard that. "You're still getting over it?" She closed her eyes and exhaled. "Oh God. I'm sorry."

"I'm over it. Was never really in it," he admitted. "I'm just . . ."

"I'm going to be embarrassed tomorrow." She took a step backward, needing space, when his arm reached for her and he dragged her back to him. Her breasts were a hairbreadth from his chest. She had to angle her face upward to meet his hungry gaze.

His hands ran up her arms to her shoulders, his grip tight. She could feel he was struggling, but then, with a sigh, his lips captured hers again. Her hands were limp at her sides as his mouth ravaged hers. She sighed in complete abandonment, her knees trembling. She wanted to make love to him until they were both exhausted.

He suddenly swept her up and carried her to the bedroom, standing her on her feet beside the bed, silently looking at her, questioning her. She could practically see the words *are you sure?* hanging in the air between them.

"Yes," she said.

Then she was unbuttoning her blouse, her fingers uncoordinated with emotion, and he swept them away and took care of the duty himself. She was out of her blouse and bra before she could think, and then he was taking off his own shirt, pulling it over his head, and she was running her hands over his hard chest, her fingers drifting to the waistband of his pants.

He unbuttoned her pants and drew down the zipper, sliding the fabric smoothly down her legs. She unsnapped his fly and did the same, hungry for his body atop her, inside her.

He drew a strangled breath as he looked at her and she could tell he was going to say something, maybe another warning or denial.

She shook her head and slipped off the wisp of her underwear and, after the briefest hesitation, he drew down his boxers. They took a moment looking at each other's bodies, and Andi could feel desire sweep through her, awakening her deadened nerves.

"If—" he started to say. She put a finger to his lips.

"Make love to me."

That's all it took. With a muscular twist, he drove them both onto the bed and she was on her back and he was atop her, his mouth everywhere. Andi clutched the bedcovers, closed her eyes, and groaned. She couldn't wait. *Couldn't wait.* "Please," she whispered, then Luke was stretched out above her, his knee wedging between her legs. She drew her legs apart and he slid between them easily, like they'd rehearsed their movements a thousand times before.

And then he was inside her and they were rocking in rhythm together. She had a moment of thinking of Trini and a sob collected in her throat, but the friction against her skin, the hardness inside her that probed her core, the desire firing her blood smashed those thoughts until there was only this, only him, only a reaching for pleasure. She heard herself, the breathy "Oh, oh, oh!" that accompanied the rising feeling of pure need. When she burst into climax, she cried out, and his answering groan of release followed almost immediately.

Afterward they lay in silence for several moments, except for the rapid beatings of their hearts, their twin raspy breathing.

When he lifted his head and looked at her, his blue eyes were sated but also filled with questions.

"Don't spoil this moment," she whispered. "I swear to God, Luke. Don't."

He half smiled and shook his head. "I have to. I didn't use a condom. I didn't even think about it. Maybe for the first time in my life."

She closed her eyes, feeling tears well out of nowhere. "It's all right. Nothing will happen." *I can't get pregnant. What happened with Greg was most likely a one-time thing. And then I miscarried.*

Whether he believed her she didn't know. But he didn't pursue the subject and instead began kissing the line of her jaw, and soon enough they were making love again, this time excruciatingly slowly, in a way that drove all coherent thoughts out of her head.

Chapter Nineteen

It was five p.m. by the time September entered Maple Grove Assisted Living. She practically had her hand on her badge, ready to flash it at anyone she met, but the reception room and dining hall were empty, as were the halls. Saturday, she realized. Probably a skeleton crew on staff.

She made it to Grace's room undisturbed and knocked on her door. "Grace?" she called. The television was blaring loudly, so September tried the handle, which turned beneath her palm. She eased the door open. "Grace?" she called again, louder, though the woman was seated on the sofa. She realized then that she was fast asleep.

Shutting the door behind her, September stepped across the room and switched off the television. The sudden silence practically screamed, yet Grace slept on. Worried, September walked over to her and checked her breathing. In that moment Grace woke up and yelped in fear.

September immediately stepped back, holding up her hands. "I didn't mean to scare you, Grace. I'm September. Do you remember me? I came to see you a few days ago."

She squinted at her. "Sure, I know you."

September wondered. "I'm the detective who was asking

you about Aurora Lane. I had a couple more questions. There was a family who drove an RV? Maybe had horses."

Grace harrumphed. "Lots of 'em had horses. Hoity-toity, puttin' on airs. But those ones—they didn't have horses. White trash. That's what they were."

"Um . . . the RV people?"

"Uh-huh."

"Do you remember their names?"

"Kim and Shithead." She made a burbling sound that September took as a laugh. "That's what I called him 'cause he was so mean. Got expelled by that other shithead, the landlord . . ."

"Mr. Mamet?"

"Sure enough."

"He evicted them?" September asked.

"Yeah, they didn't pay. Shame, shame, shame. So Elias kicked their butts right out of there."

"Did they have a son?"

She screwed up her face, thinking hard, then said brightly, "My grandson!"

"You're not talking about Caleb?"

She flapped a hand at September. "'Course not. Okay. He had money and he was a flirt." She slid a sly look September's way. "I just called him my grandson."

"Was he Kim's son?"

"Wha'cha talkin' about?" She glared at September. "He was the horsey one!"

"The family that had horses?" September asked, trying to follow.

"*No*! You don't listen! He came from over there." She waved an arm out the window, and September wondered if she was thinking she was at Aurora Lane again.

Grace proved her right when she said, "By the lake. Hoity-toity. Y'know?"

"Your grandson—you called him your grandson—came from the Schultz Lake area?"

"He rode horses there." She closed her eyes and heaved a deep sigh. "There were horses around and they rode them across the fields."

"Was there someone whose name sounded like *shoe*?"

"No."

"Or Laser?"

She blinked, clearly lost. "Who are you again?"

"Detective Rafferty. September Rafferty."

"You ask too many questions."

September smiled. "You might be right."

"You ask too many questions! That's what you did before!" Her face started to turn red. "Get out. Get out of my room!"

September debated asking her a few more, but an explosion was imminent, if it wasn't already happening. Badge or no badge, she wanted to sidestep dealing with the staff or the Myleses if she could.

"Thank you, Grace," she said.

"Get out!"

She hurriedly did as she was told, practically racewalking back down the hall. At least she had enough to ask Elias Mamet some further questions about his tenants. And she wasn't going to let him put her off.

Andi turned over in bed and into Luke's arms. She felt sad and needy and deeply scared but undeniably safer with Luke around . . . and well, better now.

"Do you know what time it is?" he asked.

He was leaning on one elbow, watching her face. She smiled faintly. "Seven?"

"Five thirty."

"You sound like you're getting ready to leave." She

couldn't keep the disappointment from her voice. "You're after the Carreras."

"No, you've convinced me. I'll wait till Monday for them. Now I want to catch up with Thompkins, if I can. Maybe I can call Marjorie. Get some more information."

"But you plan to come back tonight."

"Yes, but I'd like you to go with me. I don't want you here alone. It's too isolated. It might be better if I tackle Thompkins alone, but I can take you to my office or my apartment, but my office is closer to Laurelton PD."

"As much as I'd like to see your apartment, I'll opt for the office." Feeling his gaze following her as she climbed out of bed, she turned back. "Do I have time for a shower?"

"I need one, too. Maybe we could—"

"Share water? Save the environment?"

He flashed a grin at her and threw back the covers with gusto.

September was talking fast into her cell phone. "Mr. Mamet, if you could just take a moment to search your records. I would like the name of the people who owned an RV but leased your rental house from you. Or they purchased the RV before they left your rental. I understand you may have evicted them?"

She held her breath as she pulled into the station. Mamet had answered her call, but he never stayed on the line long. He was retired and she'd been to his home once, but it was about two hours south of Laurelton, and that time he'd practically thrust the list of renters at her and slammed the door in her face.

"RVers," he said.

"That's right. RVers. They could possibly be named Kirkendall, Wright, Patten, or Brannigan." She had the four renters' names she was focused on down pat.

"Kirkendall," he spat. And then, "Or Patten. One of 'em."

"I know I've asked you this. But did any of them own a horse, or horses?"

"Look, ma'am," he said in a warning tone. He never would call her detective. "I already told you, they brought horses in, took horses out, never paid me a dime. That land stretched back to the creek and there's a gate, then you can go all the way to Schultz Lake on Flinders' farmland. You know the Flinders? Owned everything around here, and that big piece of land is just waiting for some greedy developer to chop it up."

This was more information than she'd gotten in all her phone calls to him. He seemed to like to gripe, so maybe that was a way of cracking open his resistance. "Do you remember the names of any of those horsey people?" She inflicted just a touch of sarcasm on *horsey*.

He jumped in eagerly this time. "One of 'em, the missus, was a horse nut for sure." He snorted. "Husband was a beer drinker. Watched lots of sports. Big Raiders fan. He was a plumber, but mostly he was out of work. By choice, 'cause he didn't much like work, that's for sure. But the missus had her nose in the air. Thought she was all that and more, but she wasn't nothin' much. He knew it and made faces about her behind her back."

Lovely couple, September thought as she climbed from her Jeep and headed for the department's front doors. "Did they have a teenaged son?"

"How the hell should I know?" he groused. "They lied to me about the horses. Probably lied about kids, too. All of 'em."

"Were these horsey people any of the four names I gave you?"

He sighed heavily, as if she'd really put her out. "All of 'em coulda had horses. Probably did. Nobody was honest. That's the trouble with renters. Maybe it was the Brannigans who snuck in an old piece of dog meat for a while. Had little kids that liked to ride. Thing was so wide you couldn't get a saddle cinched around it." He wheezed out a short laugh.

"And the Brannigans aren't the RV people?"

"Nope, those were . . . the Kirkendalls . . . or the Pattens. I told you."

"Yes, thanks. But the horsey people could be the Brannigans, or any of the other three families?"

"That's what I'm tellin' ya." He was annoyed.

She pushed through the glass double doors and saw that Guy wasn't at the reception desk. Hallelujah. It was Saturday, and a young woman named Claudia was at his post, so September wouldn't be subjected to all Guy's rigmarole. "Do you remember anything about the Wrights?" she asked Mamet. "The other name on the list?"

"Nope." He was shutting down.

"Why did you evict the RVers?"

"Didn't much like 'em."

That didn't sound like legal grounds for eviction, but maybe he just hadn't renewed their lease. Before she could formulate another question, he put in, "Now I've told you all I'm gonna tell you. You have more questions you keep 'em to yourself. And I don't care if you're the police, the Pope, or God, I'm through talkin'. You got that, missy?"

"Loud and clear," September responded.

Her answer was a click in her ear.

Claudia buzzed September right through with a quick nod of recognition. Thank God for small favors.

September set her messenger bag down at her desk and pulled her notebook out of it. She shrugged out of her coat and draped it over the back of her chair, then sat down and wrote down her conversations with Tommy, Grace, and Elias Mamet, as close to her recollection as she could come. Then she looked up the phone numbers and addresses for the four names she'd zeroed in on. The Pattens' current

phone number and address were in Hood River, about an
hour and a half from Laurelton in good traffic. The Wrights
had moved to Tacoma, south of Seattle, and the Brannigans
now lived in Portland, on the east side of the river. They
were the closest, except for the Kirkendalls, who were still
in the Laurelton area but apparently had no phone. Or none
that September could discover. But she had their address,
so it was just a matter of catching them at home.

No time like the present, she decided. She was stuffing
her notebook back in her bag and was about to leave the
near-empty squad room when her cell phone buzzed. Seeing
it was Wes Pelligree, September answered with a smile.
"Okay, detective, you caught me. I'm working. For free, so
don't tell anyone."

"I just got a call to come in, but I'm with my mother,
who's taken a turn for the worse."

"Oh, Wes, I'm sorry." Wes's mother had been in the hospital for several weeks with an internal infection that
wouldn't clear up.

"George is on another case, but dispatch called me. The
Sheriff's Department found a body in the Quarry quarry.
Her ID was with her. She's Tracy Farmgren, twenty-five,
and it looks like she was dumped there. She lived in Laurelton, so we're going to be working with Winslow."

Quarry, Oregon, was serviced by the Winslow County
Sheriff's Department. "You want me to call them?"

"Yes. Thanks. The deputy's name is Barb Gillette." He
gave September the number.

"I hope your mother's going to be all right."

"Me too."

September phoned the Sheriff's Department and was put
through to Detective Gillette. When she explained who she
was, Gillette said, "The body's at the morgue and it looks
like it was thrown over the lip of the quarry. We're working
the ridge above, hoping someone saw the doer. It's kind

of a lover's lane, but so far we've drawn blanks. We're also short-staffed, so we thought maybe you guys could check with her place of work? It's in Laurelton."

"Be glad to."

"She was a receptionist at Sirocco Realty on Third and Londale."

September had been writing down the name in her notebook but now froze in mid pen stroke.

Gillette went on, "Tracy worked there about two years. I spoke with one of the principal brokers, Kitsy Hasseldorn, who's at the office today. That's Kitsy with an *s*, not Kitty. She's the one who'll be expecting you." There was a pause. "You got that?" she asked a bit impatiently, when September didn't immediately say anything.

"I recently met Kitsy Hasseldorn."

"You did?"

"Not related to this." At least it didn't seem to be . . . "What's the cause of death?"

"Strangulation. Killer wore gloves. Okay, then, call me back after the interview."

September's mind was whirling. It was an odd coincidence that she'd just seen Tracy and now the girl was dead. Killed.

She put a call in to Gretchen, who didn't pick up, so she didn't leave a message. Her partner was known for late nights when she wasn't on duty, so she'd probably turned her cell off.

Sliding her jacket off her chair again, September headed for the door. What the hell. She'd check things out by herself.

And it looked like she might be getting that overtime after all.

* * *

Luke said a quick good-bye to Andi at his office and drove to the Laurelton Police Department, about a mile away. He'd already called them and asked for Detective George Thompkins but had been informed the detective would call him back. Maybe Thompkins was still on-site. Or maybe he was screening his calls. Whatever the case, Luke wanted to talk to him sooner rather than later.

He smiled at the young female officer manning the desk as he let himself into the station.

"I'm Luke Denton. Here to see Detective Thompkins."

She gave him the once-over but made no move to buzz him through to the squad room. Luke considered trying to charm her. It sometimes worked, but her dark, suspicious eyes told him it would be a no-go here. She had that everyone's-guilty-until-proven-innocent attitude that came with inexperience. He was forced to cool his heels and wait.

But waiting brought back images of how he and Andi had spent the afternoon, and as pleasurable as that had been, he didn't want to think about it too much. It felt like a problem in the making. Not that he wasn't interested. God no. But it was too soon after the debacle that had been his relationship with Iris.

As if her radar were attuned to him and she knew what he was up to, his cell phone dinged, and he looked down to see Iris was texting him. She wanted to meet him.

He shook his head. Getting involved with her had been a mistake from the get-go. He'd known it but had let himself fall into a relationship that, if he was completely honest with himself, was more about her working for the district attorney's office and his need to clear his ex-partner than any real feeling on his part for her.

You knew better, he thought with a grimace.

Thinking of lawyers reminded him of his delay in calling his brother back. A lot had happened in a very few hours, he consoled himself. Dallas would understand. Still, he texted his brother: Wrapped up in a lot of unexpected stuff. Okay to check in next week?

A few minutes later Dallas wrote back: OK. Call when you can.

And then his cell rang and he saw it was Andi.

"Hey," he started, but her panicked voice cut him off.

"I just got a call from Jarrett. It was his wallet at Trini's! He went back to her apartment to get it and saw the police and left!"

"Your brother," Luke clarified.

"She knows him. They dated."

He stepped back outside and lowered his voice. "He didn't talk to the police?"

"No. Oh God. That was his wallet. What does it mean?"

"Did he have an explanation?"

"I didn't really talk to him. He was stunned and shocked, and then he just got off the phone. What should I do? I can't just sit here!"

Luke saw headlights from an approaching vehicle, then a black Jeep with the Laurelton Police Department stenciled on it appeared. "Wait for me. I'll be there soon. I think Detective Thompkins just arrived."

"Do they think it's a homicide? Do they think . . . Jarrett's involved?"

"Andi, hang tight. Let me get some information."

"I wish I'd come with you."

"It's better that you didn't. Where is Jarrett now?"

"I don't know." She sounded about to break down and he could hardly blame her.

He was right about it being Thompkins. He saw his bulk move from the driver's seat and then he was walking toward Luke. "Give me ten minutes. I'll call back." He clicked off and waited for the detective, who wheezed from the effort of walking.

"What are you doing here?" Thompkins asked him with a weary frown.

"I wanted to talk to you about Trini Finch's death."

"I got nothin' to say."

"I know the wallet you found belongs to Jarrett Sellers and that he dated Trini once upon a time."

That earned Luke a long stare, then he said, "Marjorie said you're ex-Portland PD."

"I am. Quit over the Bolchoy case."

He grunted, then motioned Luke to precede him inside. This time the girl at the desk hit the buzzer without hesitation. Luke followed Thompkins down a short hallway that opened into the squad room, which was about thirty feet square and held a number of desks. An attractive woman in plainclothes was just slipping on her coat and Luke realized he knew her. Rafferty. Named for one of the months like her brother, Detective August "Auggie" Rafferty. "Detective Rafferty?" Luke asked.

She was preoccupied, but he caught her attention. "Yes?"

Thompkins said, "He's ex-Portland PD."

Luke added, "I've worked with your brother. I'm Luke Denton." He thrust out his hand.

She studied him. Her eyes were a warm hazel and her hair had the faintest of red in its shoulder-length brown tresses. He realized he'd seen her on television, interviewed by Pauline Kirby.

"You were Ray Bolchoy's partner," she said, accepting his handshake. "September Rafferty."

"Look, I'm about to get out of here," Thompkins said, throwing himself into a desk chair that shrieked under his weight. He motioned Luke to a chair at the end of his desk. "You wanna talk to me, now's the time."

September asked, "Is this about a case?"

Thompkins frowned at her. "What're you doing here?"

"Don't worry. I'm on my own time." She returned her attention to Luke, who decided to lay his cards on the table.

"You got a minute or two?" he asked.

She shook her head. "I'm on my way to an interview."

"What interview?" Thompkins asked.

"Winslow Sheriff's Department asked for our help on one of their cases. Wes can't be here and I already was. What were you on?"

"Five minutes," Luke cut in before he could answer. "Let me tell you why I'm here." Both Thompkins and Rafferty looked about to protest, but Luke launched into the story of his working relationship with Andi, her friendship with Trinidad Finch, and, most importantly, that she was Jarrett Sellers's sister. "I want to know more about the cricket flour," he finished.

"So do I," September said regretfully, "but I'm already late. I'll check in with you later," she said to Thompkins.

"You want this case?" he said, halfway belligerent. "It's yours. They're going to fire me anyway."

"We're all in the same boat," she muttered as she headed for the door.

"What have you got on the victim?" Luke asked Thompkins when they were alone.

He regarded Luke speculatively for a while, checked the time, then seemed to shrug mentally. "Coulda been a mistake. She ate the bar and didn't look at the label 'til it was too late."

"What about Jarrett Sellers?"

"Well, if it's a homicide, he'd be our number one suspect."

"When are you going to know if it's a homicide?"

"When we know." He pressed his lips together, then exhaled heavily. "I have a call in to Sellers that he hasn't returned. If I thought it was urgent, I'd be chasing him down."

"Have you checked her cell phone?"

"Haven't found it yet," he admitted, and then went a step further, saying, "and the wallet was clear of fingerprints."

"No fingerprints? Sellers's prints would be on it."

"Yep."

Luke thought about it. "Maybe someone touched it who didn't want their fingerprints found at the scene, like the foil."

"And then left it there for us to find, just in case we decide it's a homicide?" Thompkins finished the thought.

"Something like that. The piece of foil wrapper left by her hand seemed staged to me. If she ate the bar and left part of the wrapper, where's the rest of it?"

"Not in the trash," Thompkins admitted.

"There are just too many little details that don't quite fit with an accident."

"If it's a homicide—and I'm not saying it is—the doer should have taken the whole wrapper and not touched the wallet."

Luke said slowly, "He wants us to know. Not completely, but sort of. He's crowing about what he did."

Thompkins snorted. "So he's a psycho?"

"Not necessarily."

"What's his motive? And where does Sellers fit in?"

Luke shook his head. They were both good questions, but he wasn't any closer to an answer than he had been earlier. "Sellers might just have been opportunity," Luke suggested.

It's too bad when little birds have to die.

He considered mentioning the threat to the detective but decided to wait. Luke wasn't sure which way Thompkins was going to jump on this, and he had some ideas of his own. "She had a boyfriend other than Sellers," Luke told him. "I asked Andi about him, but she's never met him."

"That's Andrea Wren, the friend of the victim and sister of Sellers?"

"Yes."

Thompkins shrugged. "I gotta wrap this up for tonight, Detective."

Luke felt a certain nostalgia upon hearing Thompkins mistakenly call him detective. He took his cue to leave and headed outside, driving back to his office with thoughts circling his brain.

Instead of pulling into the back lot he drove toward the front of the building and, as he turned the corner, felt a cold jolt of alarm upon seeing a dark-haired man standing outside his office door, rapping sharply on the panels.

Chapter Twenty

Luke whipped into a parking spot and was out of the car in three seconds flat. "What do you want?" he demanded as he stalked toward the door. He got his second jolt when he realized it was Carlos Garcia, Helena's husband.

"Carlos."

"You have my wife in there?" Carlos asked flatly. He looked calm, but for the first time Luke saw the cold implacability that Helena had alluded to.

"Hell no. I haven't seen Helena since I've seen you," Luke said.

"You lying to me?"

"Carlos." Luke stared at him.

"Who's in there?" he asked suspiciously.

"A friend."

"A woman?"

"Yes, a woman friend," Luke said, starting to get angry.

Carlos lifted his hands, conceding the point. "Helena has taken Emily again."

"Carlos, you know I'm not involved in this. Now move out of the way. You've probably scared her to death."

Luke shouldered his way past Carlos and into his office.

Andi was sitting at his desk in the near dark, her cell phone in her hand. "Luke," she said.

"Don't worry. Carlos thought you were someone else."

Carlos stepped into the room behind Luke, who whipped around to glare at him. He held up his hands again. "I am leaving. If you need anything," he told Luke as he handed him a card, "you call me."

"I don't need a landscaper, but thanks."

"You might need something else sometime." He shot Luke a knowing glance, then took off.

Luke locked the door after he was gone, then turned back to Andi.

"That sounded kind of ominous," she said, rising to her feet. She practically stumbled into Luke's arms.

"I think I may have underestimated Carlos," Luke admitted.

"What did Thompkins say? Jarrett hasn't called back. Everything's so out of control."

Luke brought her up to speed, finishing with, "Thompkins is leaning toward her death being an accident, but I'm leaning the other way."

"Bobby?"

"I didn't tell the detective about the bird messages. I maybe should have, but I wanted him engaged in this and I'm not sure how much he is. I met another detective I'd like to contact again. She might be more helpful."

September arrived at Sirocco Realty twenty minutes later than she'd expected. She pushed through the front door to find three sober female employees, Kitsy and two others, one closer to Kitsy's age whose coat was slung over her arm as if she were on her way out, and another in her early twenties. The one in her twenties sat in the reception desk chair, wide-eyed and pale, braids falling to her shoulders.

The other woman was drawn and tense, and Kitsy held a tissue in one hand, her eyes red.

"Detective," Kitsy said in relief upon seeing her. "I'm sorry. I can't remember your name."

"Rafferty."

"That's right, Rafferty. That's right." She looked helplessly at the other two women, who were staring at September.

"I'm Edie," the older woman introduced herself. Her eyes were dark with sadness. "When Kitsy told me about Tracy, I . . . I knew I wanted to talk to you."

"And this is Heidi Sorenson," Kitsy said, motioning to the girl in the chair. "She's our part-time receptionist. Works mostly weekends."

"Hi," Heidi said dully.

"I'm sorry about Tracy," September began. "I was asked by the Winslow Sheriff's Department to meet with you and—"

"Who could do this?" Edie broke in, unable to hold back her horror. "Why?"

Kitsy said, "None of us knew Tracy all that well outside of work."

"She was here yesterday," Heidi said, squeezing out huge tears. "She came in for a few minutes. I got her a cup of coffee, but she didn't drink it."

"She came by to pick something up, apparently," Kitsy explained. "It wasn't a workday for her."

"Pick something up?" September questioned.

"In the desk. Bottom drawer." Heidi pointed. "It was partly open and the box was gone."

"What box?" Edie asked.

"I don't know. But it was there before she came. . . ." More tears followed and ran down Heidi's cheeks. "And then it was gone when she was gone."

Kitsy looked at Edie, who shook her head. September gazed from one to the other. "Something you want to tell me?"

Kitsy kept right on looking at Edie, as if daring her to speak up. Finally, Edie said, "I told Kitsy I suspected Tracy was letting herself into some of our listings without our knowledge. She didn't have an electronic key so she couldn't access the lockboxes."

"She wasn't a realtor," Kitsy explained.

Edie went on, "But she was inside a couple of homes. One, the seller called me and was really upset. She'd come home and there was Tracy, who acted like she was there on Sirocco business, but she wasn't."

"What was she doing?"

"We don't know." Edie pressed her lips together and shook her head, then said, "I was worried she was stealing, or planning to steal."

"Tracy wouldn't do that!" Heidi burst out.

Kitsy said, "Of course not, dear," but over Heidi's head her silent gaze said, *Well, yes, maybe she would.*

"Nothing was ever reported stolen," September guessed.

"No," Edie admitted. "I just hope we don't have somebody six months from now realizing their diamond earrings are missing."

"What do you think was in the box?" September asked.

No one said anything for a moment, but then Heidi finally spoke up reluctantly. "Keys."

"Keys? To homes?" September asked.

Heidi confessed, "I picked up the box and shook it once." Her breath caught on a sob.

"Oh God." Edie looked dazed. "What was she doing?"

"Do you think . . . could this have anything to do with what happened to her?" Kitsy asked, her voice turning into a squeak.

"We're just beginning the investigation," September said.

She asked a number of further questions about Tracy,

but as Kitsy had already said, they knew nothing of her social or personal life outside the office. Finally, September recognized she'd exhausted them as a source of information and put her notebook away.

Kitsy drew a breath and then asked, "This isn't connected to the bones you're trying to identify, is it?"

"What bones?" Edie asked as she shrugged into her coat.

Heidi sat in silent horror.

"No, that's a separate case," September answered Kitsy. She followed Edie toward the door, Kitsy trailing a few steps behind.

"How are you doing on that one?" Kitsy asked. There was no real interest in her tone. She was just making conversation.

But she'd given September an opening. As Edie held the door open for her, September said, "I've whittled down the rental to four names of people who could've lived there, on Aurora, during the window of time I'm investigating. Kirkendall, Wright, Patten, and Brannigan."

"Patten," Kitsy said immediately. "Like the shoe. Patent leather."

"Patten," September repeated.

"Lance Patten," she said. "That's his name. And the parents were Joan and . . . hmmm. Escapes me. They had a horse."

Lance Patten. Finally, a name! September felt that tiny little zing, the one that sizzled through her brain whenever she realized she'd made a connection, an inroad into a sticky investigation.

Staring at the floor, Kitsy went on, "The kid rode it sometimes, but that was before he went off the rails, I think." She was frowning, remembering, but she looked up and met September's gaze. "Does that help?"

"Yes," September assured her.

Kitsy sent her an uncertain smile. "I, um, I hope we can keep Sirocco's name out of this. We don't need any bad publicity. I mean, I'm so, so sorry about Tracy, but . . ."

"Too late. That reporter talked about Tracy on the news," Heidi spoke up. She'd finally roused herself from the chair and had pulled her purse out of a drawer. "I saw it in the break room."

"When will we know something about Tracy?" Edie asked. She was still holding the door.

"As soon as we have some information," September said.

Luke took Andi to dinner at a steak house that had been in the area for sixty years. It still served baked potatoes in foil, though the iceberg salad wedge with blue cheese dressing was a new addition. Andi had no appetite whatsoever, so she just chased lettuce leaves around on her plate.

"Eat something," Luke told her.

"I can't. I feel tied up inside."

"You still need to eat something or you're gonna crash."

She knew he was right. What she really wanted was one of her antidepressants. She hadn't taken one earlier when they were talking about them, and she needed to get back to evening herself out. The pills were supposed to help. "Jarrett said he'd call back and he hasn't."

"He's supposed to call Thompkins, too."

"He's not hiding or anything, is he?" Andi asked, worried sick.

"What did he say to you?"

"Nothing. He was freaked that she was gone." She gazed at him unhappily. "I can't even say the word. *Dead.* There. I said it."

He reached across the table and captured one of her cold hands. "Give yourself some time. Come on, I'll take you home."

"What if . . . I mean . . . what was Jarrett doing there?"

"Call him," Luke suggested. "See if he'll pick up. Ask him yourself."

Uncertainly, she reached in her purse for her cell phone. He was right. What was she afraid of?

When she pulled out the phone she saw she'd missed a text from Emma: **Carter told me about Mimi! WTF! Scott's an asshole!!!!** Andi made a strangled sound. "I guess he didn't tell her about Trini."

"Who?"

Rather than explain, she turned the phone so he could read the text. "It's from Emma," she said. "It seems so stupid and trivial now. I was thinking Scott could be behind the bird messages, but I don't think he is really. And even if he is, I don't care."

She put in another call to Jarrett, but once again he didn't answer; her call went straight to voice mail. She didn't bother leaving another message.

Luke paid the bill and put his arm around Andi as they headed to his truck. He drove her home through a dark night filled with fits of wind-driven rain. The cabin's front light welcomed them. The place really did feel like home.

Once inside, Andi took off her coat and went straight to her bedroom. The willow circle Luke had made was lying on her dresser and she picked it up and brought it back to the living room, where Luke had dropped to the couch and was looking at his phone.

He glanced up. "You okay?" His gaze fell to the willow ring and he looked kind of sheepish. When she went into the kitchen, he asked, "What are you doing?"

"Hanging this up."

"Come on." He laughed. "You don't have to."

She brought out a hammer and nail and opened the front door. Setting the willow branches on the ground, she hammered in the nail, then hung the wreath on her door.

"A talisman against evil spirits," she said.

For an answer he came to her and wrapped his arms around her, kissing the top of her head. "I'm not gonna let anything happen to you."

"I know." Her gaze fell on the vials still sitting on her table. She briefly thought about starting the antidepressants again, but having Luke around was better, and the urge she'd felt in the restaurant, the need for the pills as some kind of hopeful balm, had eased. "It's early, but I want to go to bed."

"Okay."

When he didn't follow after her, Andi looked back. "Coming?"

"No more couch for me?"

"Not unless that's what you want."

His answer was to bound after her. "I didn't pick up any condoms."

She switched on the bedroom light. "It's not likely to matter. My pregnancy was an anomaly." She started unbuttoning her blouse, but he swept her hands away.

"I'll get some tomorrow," he said huskily, pulling her body to his and tilting up her chin.

Andi already felt like melting wax in his hands. "I just want to forget everything."

He kissed her gently, then with more urgency.

After that there was no more talking.

Poor, poor little bird. So distraught over your friend. You don't see me here in the shadows, but I see the light in the bedroom beneath your shade. Are you sleeping alone? Not a chance. You're all set to bed your knight in shining armor. Do you know about his other women? Maybe I should tell you . . . leave you another note. Y'see, I've been doing my research on the ex-cop. He's got some honeys in the wings. There's the hot one from the district attorney's office and the even hotter one with the red hair . . . supposedly a client, but there's no way he's kept his dick out of that much woman.

Yes . . . a little note about ex-detective Denton. Maybe I'll leave it in that god-awful wreath of sticks on your door. Willow branches . . . someday soon I'll tell you a story about them.

But first I'm going to let you in on all the little secrets your lover's not telling you.

I can hardly wait. Hurting is an important part of the game.

Chapter Twenty-One

Luke and Andi spent Sunday in bed. They slept, made love, talked about the Carreras and Trini, and Scott and Mimi, then made love again, slept some more, and talked some more. Andi had enough fresh vegetables to make a salad and some frozen hamburger that Luke thawed and they threw together a pasta dish out of a jar of marinara sauce and some bow tie pasta. "Butterfly spaghetti," he called it, and Andi just let it all happen.

She could still scarcely process Trini's death. And she was worried sick about Jarrett, who still hadn't returned any of her calls.

As the day wore on, Luke outlined what he wanted to do over the coming week. Monday was the meeting with the Carreras; then he wanted to meet with Detectives Rafferty and Thompkins again and apprise them of the little bird messages.

"I also want to do some checking up on my own about the boyfriend, Bobby. Trini met him through one of her classes," Andi told him.

"At the gym where she worked?"

"Um. That's what she said. She said he was buttoned-down, like Greg. Not her type at all."

"But she fell for him."

"Yeah, big-time. So out of character. She knew it." There was something else that was bothering her. "Oh, and she said he wore a toupee and glasses. Again, not Trini's usual type. She was all for the rock-hard gym rat; y'know, most of her exes could have been male models. So it was all weird. I don't think she thought anything about him at first, but then she was smitten."

"Smitten. I like that word."

He smiled at her and she managed a smile back. She almost felt guilty finding joy in anything with her friend gone. "Trini kept saying how crazy it was. He pulled back for a while and she thought it was over and was kind of crushed, then recently they were back on."

"And he said he was allergic to shellfish as well?"

"That's what she said."

"We need to know more about him."

"Maybe at the gym where she held her classes?"

He nodded. "My thought exactly. We'll go there first thing tomorrow morning, before the meeting with the Carreras," he said.

Andi inwardly shivered, but said, "Okay." She wasn't looking forward to that meeting at all.

September clicked off her cell phone and threw it on the couch in disgust.

"Still no response?" Jake asked her. He brought a bowl of popcorn for them to share as he sank down beside her on the couch.

September took a handful and munched away, scarcely tasting it. "Face-to-face is always better, but I've suddenly got lots to do. Tomorrow I'm meeting with the Winslow Sheriff's Department, and George has that other case I told you about."

"Cricket flour," Jake said, nodding. "Who knew?"

"Not Trinidad Finch, apparently."

"And this ex-cop wants to meet with you about that case?"

"Denton. He didn't say that exactly, but George was being pissy. Practically threw that case at me, too, although he really doesn't want me to have it. What he wants is someone else to work it, so that he can sit at his desk and do research. I should have him make these calls and just do the legwork."

"Leave it till tomorrow," Jake suggested.

She mowed her way through more popcorn, unable to turn her brain off. "I think I'll go visit the Pattens first thing tomorrow."

"They're the ones in Hood River?"

She nodded. "Kitsy said their son's name is Lance and Tommy Burkey said his friend's name was Laser, but maybe that's a nickname Lance used. I've tried calling the Burkeys, too, but no one's picking up my calls there anymore either." With a wry smile, she added, "I guess I'm persona non grata."

"You're a cop. Get used to it."

"I have." She took another handful of popcorn, her fingers scraping the bottom of the bowl.

"What about the RV people?"

September slid him a look. "You've been paying attention."

"You've been making calls all day and swearing in between them about the RVers, and the Patent Leathers, and two Wrights make a wrong. . . ."

September choked on some popcorn and motioned for Jake to hand her his water bottle, which was on the table beside him. Once he gave it to her, she drank lustily, then cleared her throat, slapping at his arm with the back of her hand. "You made me laugh and I sucked in a kernel. I didn't say any of that stuff!"

He lifted a brow at her faux outrage.

Rolling her eyes, she admitted, "Okay, maybe I did."

"Well, I'm just glad you threw your phone down for a while."

"Me too."

She handed him back his bottle, then leaned her head on his shoulder and eyed the engagement ring on her finger. "I'll give it up for a while."

"Good."

Ten minutes later her cell rang. Jake groaned, and even September was slow to reach for her phone. "I'm taking the rest of the day off." She looked at the screen and didn't recognize the number, though she thought it was slightly familiar. "After this call," she said, then clicked on and said, "Hello."

"Is this Detective Rafferty?" a woman asked.

"Yes, it is. Who's this?"

"It's Annaloo."

September blinked, aware that the woman on the other end of the line thought that would mean something to her. Then her brain sharpened. Anna Liu. The daughter of the Asian couple who lived across the street from the Singletons. September had ceased calling her after her frosty voice had told her enough times that her parents didn't know anything about the bones in the Singletons' basement.

"Hello, Miss Liu," she said, straightening up in her position on the couch.

"I know I've said over and over that my parents knew nothing about the Singletons, which is still the truth. But recently I've learned that they remembered something about a teenage boy who knew them."

"A teenager who knew the Singletons?" September clarified.

"Yes."

"What did they remember?" She could feel her pulse start to race.

"That he . . . was cheeky. Impertinent. Flirtatious. Maybe a little entitled."

September thought about Davinia Singleton's supposed affair with a teen. "Did they think he was flirtatious with one of the Singletons in particular?"

"I took it to mean that was his overall attitude. They didn't mention anyone's name."

"Did he live on Aurora Lane?"

"They didn't say."

"Or that he may have had an addiction problem?"

"I just told you all they said. I thought I'd pass it along." She was starting to sound impatient again.

"Thank you. I appreciate it. If you have a chance, would you ask your parents if they remember the Patten family? They rented from Mr. Mamet, just down the street. The Pattens had a son named Lance, and they had a horse Lance used to ride in the fields behind their house."

"I'll ask them," she said dubiously.

September hung up and Jake looked at her. "Well?" he asked.

"I need to talk to Lance Patten, so I'm going to Hood River tomorrow to drop in on his parents."

The sound of an approaching vehicle caught Andi's attention. She was standing in the kitchen in her bathrobe, pouring a glass of red wine for both herself and Luke, who was in his boxers and nothing else when she heard the engine. She glanced at the clock and saw it was nearly nine p.m.

"Late visitors," Luke observed, walking toward the bedroom, where he'd left his clothes.

Andi followed after him but heard a car door slam and then hurried steps to her front door. The imperious rapping caught her breath, but then she heard, "Andi, it's me! Open the door."

Jarrett.

She quickly hurried to the front door to turn the lock and allow him entry. "God, Jarrett, I've been calling and calling you!"

"I know." His face was white as chalk. "I had to talk to that detective." He strode inside and sank onto the couch. "What a nightmare." He shoved stiff fingers through his hair before another thought struck him. "Whose truck is that? The one parked outside."

"It's a friend's. Luke Denton."

"Where is he?" Peering around, he eyed the sleeping bag rolled up on the couch beside him.

"Right here," Luke said, entering the room. He was dressed, but his feet were bare. Jarrett barely seemed to notice.

"What did you say to the detective?" Andi asked. "Jarrett, were you with Trini on Friday night?"

"God, Andi, I'm just sick." He dropped his head into his hands. "Yeah, I was there. I met her at a bar down the street. I met her purposely, and I walked home with her. She was making dinner. . . ." He broke off and swallowed hard. "Oh Jesus. I would never hurt her." When he lifted his eyes they were swimming with tears, his fists balled. "Never! You gotta believe me. I didn't realize I'd left my wallet till yesterday afternoon. I tried texting her, calling

her, but . . . she didn't answer." His voice cracked and he
threw his head backward, staring at the ceiling.

"Andi said Trini was meeting her boyfriend Friday,"
Luke said.

Jarrett said, "He stood her up. But maybe he came back
later. I don't know." His face twisted at the thought. "That's
what I told the detective."

"What did he ask you?" Luke questioned.

Jarret finally seemed to focus on Luke. Andi could tell
he was wondering what the deal was, so she explained,
"Luke's an investigator. I hired him to help me with the
Carreras."

Jarrett's eyes slid toward the bedroom, but what he said
was, "He asked me if I'd bought her an energy bar. I said,
'No, I bought her a drink.' Energy bar? What did he mean?"

Andi started to say something, but Luke caught her eye
and shook his head. She felt a flash of anger, aware that
Luke wasn't completely trusting Jarrett's story. But she
clamped her mouth shut.

Luke asked, "Is Thompkins looking at it as a homicide?"

"He wouldn't give me my wallet back. Does that answer
your question?"

Luke shrugged and shook his head.

Jarrett looked at Andi, and his white face finally flushed
with color. "Who was this boyfriend anyway? She said he
drove her to drink."

"She called him Bobby," Andi said. "She met him in one
of her classes."

"Well, my money's on him," Jarrett said, his jaw tightening. "And if I find out he had anything to do with this,"
he added with a cold calm, "I'll kill the bastard myself."

Jarrett stayed for another hour, but he was inconsolable
and had trouble tracking any conversation. Andi ached for

him, and Trini, but somehow knowing Jarrett cared as much as he did made the situation more bearable. When he left, he was still awash in misery. After she closed the door behind him, she turned to Luke and said, "He didn't have anything to do with Trini's death."

"I just didn't want to give anything away."

"He's still in love with her."

He nodded but didn't seem totally convinced.

"Trust me, I know my brother," Andi insisted. "He's closed off and careful, but he's no actor. He loved her."

"Okay." Luke half smiled.

"You believe me?"

"I believe somebody wiped his wallet clean of fingerprints, which seems to indicate another player. And from what you've said about her, I don't think Trini just missed the information about cricket flour in the energy bar. I think it's a homicide." His expression grew dark. "And I think we'd better start looking for Bobby."

I've let circumstances affect the game and I've had to take care of loose ends. But it's time to ramp up. I have momentum and I won't let others get in my way any longer. There is one final piece to my puzzle and it's taking place tonight. While I wait for my next little bird, I'll compose my note to Andi about her lover in my head.

I look down the rails of the tracks at my feet, imagining how the night will develop. I get hard just thinking about it.

Time to fade back and wait for the train.

So many little birds . . .

The Portland MAX station was damn near empty at this late hour. Christine Brandewaite waited impatiently for the eastbound train that would take her to Gresham. She really wanted a cigarette but she'd run out at work and wasn't supposed to smoke on the job anyway, though she did sometimes, locking herself in her office at Nachatz Trucking, which was sometimes sniggered at as No Chance Trucking, and well, their reputation for delivery kinda proved that right. It was Sunday night, but she worked weekends mostly, and no one paid too much attention to her.

Christine shivered, but it wasn't a shiver of cold. It was anticipation. She probably shouldn't smoke now anyway, before she saw Robert. OMG the man did things to her that were scarcely legal!

She laughed silently to herself. She'd spent way too many hours searching dating web sites with no success. Losers. Fucking losers, every one. But then Robert had asked to be her friend on Facebook, and she'd thought *who the hell is this guy?* but she'd seen his picture . . . okay, it wasn't strictly his, but that was part of the joke, wasn't it? And anyway, he'd turned out even better, so no harm, no foul. And well, she was closing in on forty, and that fucking bastard Gerald had told her she looked like a gristly, dried-up sixty-year-old . . . Heaven Sent Matchmaking, my ass . . . so it had been *so nice* to have someone like Robert appear.

The light-rail car rattled into the station and Christine climbed on. Hardly a soul on board. She'd had to damn near stay till eleven to get all the work done. Work she'd put off because she just couldn't keep her mind on it. Woo-wee! She'd had her share of partners, but Robert had simply screwed her brains out, making her forget them all.

There was a heavyset woman a few seats up, sweating in a cotton twinset even though the temperature was cool. She turned and looked soberly at Christine. Christine almost stuck her tongue out at her, she felt that sassy. She managed to contain herself but not the shit-eating grin she couldn't control. She thought about Robert's tongue, and his probing fingers, and the way he'd slammed into her that had gotten her screaming so loudly that he'd covered her mouth with his hand and held it until she could scarcely breathe. She'd been gasping when he finally released her, and then they were both laughing.

"Shhh," he said, licking her earlobe a few moments later. He'd been ready to go again and Christine had been right with him.

She was still sore and that had been days ago. She'd been thinking of him constantly. E-mailing him because, well, the sad part was he was married and he couldn't receive phone calls or texts. He was getting a divorce, though, and yes, she knew they *all* said that, but Robert was sincere. And such a damn good lay!

She looked out the window. The lights of the city flashed by, interspersed with lengths of darkness. She lived way out of town. She was lucky Robert was willing to come all the way to see her. Sometimes she wondered what he saw in her, but then she practically slapped herself. She was still an attractive woman, with a lot to offer a man. She wasn't beautiful by magazine standards, sure, but really, how many people were? And she had a thin body, not an ounce of fat on her, and maybe that allowed for a few more wrinkles, but gristle? That was just rude. And untrue.

The heavyset woman got off three stops before Christine and then she was alone. By the time the train deposited her on the platform she was in a fever of need and then had a moment of terror when she saw the man in the dark hoodie standing beside her car until he said, "Psst," and she realized it was Robert.

"What're you doing here?" she asked, relieved and delighted.

"Thought I'd meet you. I came on an earlier train. We can go in your car."

"Pull that thing back so I can see you," she said, reaching up to yank the cowl from his face.

He caught her hand and kissed it. "C'mon, get in. I've got a surprise for you."

Christine happily climbed behind the wheel and Robert got in the passenger side. She wanted to touch him and couldn't help running her hand across his broad shoulders.

"Where're we going?" she asked.

"Marine Drive."

"What for?"

Marine Drive ran alongside the Columbia River, and at this time of night, given where they were, nothing would be open and there would be only long stretches of unlit road.

"If I told you, it wouldn't be a surprise."

"Should I—"

"Shhh," he said, and then he put his hand between her legs and started massaging her in a way that made her go all wet and limp.

"I can't drive!" she panted.

His soft laughter drove her mad. "Yes, you can. Be careful. Don't want to go off the road too soon."

"Too soon?"

"We'll be parking," he said, rubbing harder.

It was all she could do to keep the car at a decent speed as they headed east on the two-lane highway. Luckily he left her alone until they reached a dark stretch of highway.

"Over there," he whispered in her ear, his breath suddenly coming hard and fast.

"Robert . . ."

"C'mon, turn the wheel."

As she bumped onto the narrow shoulder, she saw the dark water of the Columbia River gliding by down below the slight cliff they were parked on.

"I—" Her words ended in something between a grunt and a shriek as he suddenly tased her. A crackle of light and

an electric smell filled the car. She couldn't move. Was
locked in pain like she'd never known. She tried to talk,
couldn't, and then he tased her again. Dimly she heard his
laughter.

And then he was out of the car and on her side, opening
the driver's door and pulling her to the stubbly hard ground.
Her head banged hard, but that didn't stop him. He dragged
her across the ground by her feet and all she was filled with
was disbelief and confusion, too frozen to do anything
about it as he rolled her down the steep slope, where she
got hung up on a snag, dazed, her feet in the cold water.

She came to enough to see the stars above, a billion
lights flung into a black sky. Then he was on her. Yanking
off her jeans and panties, unzipping his trousers, his prick
already encased in a condom. Then he was thrusting inside
her and yelling, "Oh, oh, oh!" in a way she'd never heard
before, then groaning in ecstasy at the pinnacle of desire.
She realized dimly that he'd been playacting till now. He
hadn't cared about her. He'd been waiting for this moment
all along. He'd been an illusion.

"Lovely," he said and kissed her softly on the lips. "Little
bird," he whispered, then tased her once more and rolled
her into the water. She sank beneath the surface but bobbed
up in time to see him climbing back up the bank to her car.
The interior light flashed on and she saw he was by the
driver's side door. He was pushing her car toward the edge,
she realized, getting rid of the evidence. Then she heard the
vehicle's fast descent to the water, the wrench and scrape of
metal on rocks and branches, the splash as her Jetta dived
into the river.

She couldn't breathe, was choking on water.

Suddenly she heard a loud engine from the road. Oh
God. Rescue! A motorcycle maybe?

She tried to scream, to do anything. A moment later she
realized the motorcycle was Robert's. He'd hidden it at this

particular site, knowing what he was going to do to her. But why? *Why?* Why her? Was it something on her Facebook page? But there was nothing there! Why Christine Tern Brandewaite? She was nobody. Nobody! So why had he picked her? *Why . . . why . . . ww . . . hhh . . . yyy . . . !*

She struggled hard, but her throat filled with water. She couldn't breathe. Couldn't think. She gurgled fluid, her lungs filling. Her eyes closed and she lost consciousness. Unaware, her head lolled on her shoulders and she sank back beneath the flowing water.

Chapter Twenty-Two

Early Monday morning September took off for Hood River. The drive along the shores of the Columbia was longer than expected due to a delay on I-84, but September arrived at the Pattens' home only five minutes late.

She'd called ahead to make certain Lance's parents would be home and the wife, Raquel, had been a bit baffled by the call but had assured her that, now retired, they would be tending to their farm, ten acres just outside Hood River. Raquel's directions and the GPS route were spot-on, and as September wound her way along a rutted gravel lane guarded by fir trees, she caught glimpses of a snowcapped Mount Hood piercing a thin layer of clouds. Not a bad place to retire, she thought, and a huge step up from the rental they'd lived in during their years in Laurelton.

An older SUV peeked from an open garage that was separate from the main house, an A-frame built sometime in the late seventies. September pulled to a stop beside it, scooped up her messenger bag, and headed toward a sagging front porch. A few outbuildings were scattered around the fields where a couple of goats scampered and a clutch of brightly feathered chickens pecked at the ground, clucking softly as she passed. Farther off, three horses grazed, and September was reminded of the one Lance had supposedly ridden in the fields behind the rental house.

Before she reached the first step the screen door opened with a clatter. A man and a woman, both somewhere in their sixties, greeted her together. A small dog, a spotted terrier of some kind, dashed out, jumping up on her despite the woman's shouts of, "Down, Precious! You get down!" She finally scooped up the excited dog and whispered into one pointed ear, "Troublemaker!" then she set her back down and shooed her inside. The dog launched itself at the screen door, so Mrs. Patten took the time to yank the heavy door shut. "Sorry," she apologized as the dog's barks became muffled and frustrated. "You must be Detective Rafferty." She dusted her hands on worn jeans and managed a worried smile.

"Yes, I am. Thanks for seeing me on such short notice," she said, showing her ID.

"What's it about?" the man asked.

The woman jumped in. "I'm Raquel and this is Maury."

They shook hands all around, though Maury was more reluctant than his wife. September was about to respond, but Maury cut her off. "Something about our boy? Don't suppose you found him." He was a tall man with a buzz cut of gray hair and a trimmed beard that didn't hide his jowls. His jeans were belted below a stomach covered by a T-shirt that had seen better days, and though he was supposedly retired, his whole demeanor suggested he was too busy to be bothered with any interruptions, even—or maybe especially—the police.

"Is it Lance?" Raquel asked anxiously. Behind rimless glasses, her eyes swam with worry. "Do you have news about him after . . . after all this time?"

There was no way to sugarcoat this. "We've located some bones in a house on Aurora Lane and we're trying to identify them. All we know is that the body was of a male, approximately eighteen years old."

Raquel grabbed her husband's meaty hand to squeeze it. "Lance? Oh God." She dropped into a once orange plastic chair.

"What house?" Maury asked.

"The Singletons'," September answered. "At the north end of the lane toward the lake."

"Think I saw something about that on the news." He swallowed hard, but his face set in a scowl.

"We're trying to ID the body," September said.

"Boy was always trouble," Maury stated flatly.

His wife protested, "But he had a good heart."

Snorting his disagreement, Maury lowered himself into the chair next to his wife's and waved September onto a stool placed against the porch railing. His jaw worked as he let Raquel cling to one hand. "What is it you want to know? It's been a long time."

"He would be thirty-two now," Raquel whispered.

"You don't know what happened to him?"

"No," Raquel whispered hoarsely. "We haven't seen him since before he graduated from high school." Her throat clogged, but she managed to get hold of herself.

Maury's crusty exterior melted a little as he patted his wife's knee. "He just up and disappeared when we were living in Laurelton in that rental. The one that skinflint Mamet owned."

His wife sent him a disapproving look.

"Well, he was. A type A-one bastard in my book." Ignoring his wife, Maury, whom September had expected to be the silent one, started talking. "The truth is, our kid got caught up in the wrong crowd. First drinking, then marijuana, and then God knows what else. We had lots of fights about it and he took off a couple of times but always came back." He let out a long breath and said a little more quietly, "And then he just didn't." With a look toward the mountain, Maury added, "The kid just couldn't, or wouldn't, get his act together. Never figured out which it was. Maybe a little of both."

Raquel was shaking her head, gray ponytail sliding across her shoulders. "We looked for him. Called all his friends, the hospitals, the police . . . anyone we could think of. He didn't have a cell phone back then, but we had a family computer, such as it was."

"Hand-me-down clunker from my brother," Maury interjected.

"But," Raquel went on, "nothing . . . not a word. Ever."

"Do you know if he went by a nickname?" September asked.

Raquel shot her a look. "A nickname? No? Maury, here, called him 'Son,' but that was about it."

"What about Laser?" September asked as a breeze kicked up, touching the back of her neck.

Maury shook his head but said, "That crowd he ran around with had all sorts of names, or handles, or whatever you want to call it, for each other. Some not so nice, if you know what I mean."

"Would you happen to have anything of his that might help me either to ID the body or eliminate Lance as the victim?"

Raquel shuddered at the idea.

"You mean like for a sample of his DNA?" Maury asked. "Like they do in all those cop shows? What, a toothbrush or a hairbrush?"

September nodded. "Or a lock of his hair, maybe a first tooth from when he lost them?"

Raquel threw her husband a dark glance. "We've got nothing of Lance's."

"I thought it best when we moved here to start clean,"

Maury said. "We're retired and this is a new phase of our lives, so . . ."

"So we threw away everything. Gave what we could to charity, then tossed the rest." Raquel slipped her hand away from her husband's as a goat bleated. "*His* idea."

"I already admitted that," he said flatly. Obviously this was not the first time they'd had this discussion, a sore point in their marriage.

"What about the name of your dentist, in case I need to compare his records to the victim?"

Raquel said, "Dr. Emerson saw him. He had a practice on Main Street back then . . . but I think maybe Lance's last appointment was before he got his permanent teeth. We, um, we didn't have a lot of extra money back then, y'know, before I inherited this place." She rubbed her hands together between her knees. "I'm sorry."

"She blames me for that, too," Maury said.

September changed the course of the conversation, asking about Lance's relationship with Tommy Burkey and/or Davinia Singleton, but neither of them had much to say on either subject. She asked more about his drug use and they reluctantly talked about it a little but were clearly uncomfortable.

"I understand you had horses on Aurora Lane," September said, purposely changing to a more neutral topic.

"A horse. Lance rode him some," Maury said. "Now we have room for a few more."

They looked up at her expectantly, waiting for the next question, but September was about finished. "Did you know any of the other people who rented the house before or after you?" she asked.

"The Kirkendalls lived there before us," Raquel said. "Kim and . . . oh, what was her husband's name? He was a real piece of work."

"Leland," Maury supplied. "Son of a bitch parked his RV on the front lawn. Made horrible ruts. Remember?"

Raquel said, "'Course I do. Couldn't plant anything there for years."

"And you think that loser Mamet would fix it? Hell no. Even though he evicted them for not paying their rent on time."

"Well, they had a reason," Raquel said and Maury nodded, as if the Kirkendalls' troubles were common knowledge.

"And that was?"

Raquel said, "Their daughter, of course."

"What happened?" September asked.

"She died. That's the real reason we got the place," she said. "Their lives fell apart. They stopped paying rent. They stopped doing anything, as I heard it. The mother, Kim, couldn't stand living there after Wendy was gone."

"She was killed," Maury said bluntly. "Drowned . . ."

"No, strangled," Raquel said. "And dropped in the lake. Happened right before we moved in."

September felt her skin break out in gooseflesh. Something niggled at the edge of her consciousness. Almost a memory. "I think I recall her death."

"Yeah, it was all over the news," Maury said. "Anything else we can help you with? We'll look for anything of Lance's that might help, though there's not much here."

Raquel said to September, "But if you do find out those—bones—are my son . . ."

"You'll be the first to know," September assured her.

She drove back to the office, ignoring the speed limit. The discussion of Wendy Kirkendall had built an urgency inside her. She went straight to her desk, glad George was engrossed in his computer and Gretchen, though September saw her jacket on the back of her chair, was away from her desk. She sat down and accessed her computer terminal. One quick search and Wendy Kirkendall's name popped up. Now September remembered. It had been on the news when September was in high school herself. Wendy's body had been found floating in Schultz Lake, but she'd died of asphyxiation, the result of a willow branch tied around her young neck.

"I'll drive," Luke said, snagging his keys from his pocket as Andi rounded the corner from her bedroom. She'd been dreading this meeting with Carter and the Carrera brothers all night, but she'd told herself not to be intimidated; she could get through it. With everything she had to deal with lately, including Trini's death and the suspicion that she might have been murdered by Jarrett, Andi figured dealing with the twin thugs would be a piece of cake. Especially because Luke would be with her.

"I think I can handle it." She found her own set of keys. "I feel like I've been an invalid, and I'm over that."

"I like it."

She walked past him to the front door, unlocked it, and stepped into the cool morning air. She breathed deeply, smelling the scents of fir and pine and the earthy odors coming off the lake behind the house.

God, she loved it here.

And she loved being here with Luke.

Don't go there, she reminded herself as she fantasized for half a second about a future with him, here, so close to the lake that she could watch herons, ducks, and osprey fly over.

A jacket tossed over his shoulder, Luke followed her onto the porch and yanked the door shut. "What's that?" he asked in a tight voice.

"What?"

He was staring at the willow wreath she'd hung on the door, his willow wreath. Her heart clutched as she saw him gingerly pluck a white card from the ring of sticks.

"Another note?" he asked, and her heart went cold. All the happiness she'd felt seconds earlier, the fantasies, had shriveled.

Carefully, just touching the edges, he turned the card over.

Little birds should be careful who they choose as a mate. Tsk, tsk. There is no such thing as faithfulness. You should know where he's also been putting his pecker. Be careful. Seabirds can die, too.

"Shit," Luke muttered under his breath.

Andi started quaking deep inside. "What is this? Why are they doing this?"

"To scare you," he said grimly.

She shook her head.

"Our note writer is threatened by me," he observed. "Not sure what he means about being faithless. Maybe he thinks our relationship has gone on longer than it has."

"All this about birds. Trini and me . . . and now seabirds?"

"Some kind of clue," Luke said. "Goddammit. He's a coward."

"It's getting personal and he's pissing me off." That was true. The shivering inside her body, the fear, was morphing into anger. She was furious about Trini's death, about her brother's involvement, about creeping around and trying to terrorize her and now . . . *now* bringing Luke into his sick, twisted game.

"We have to find him," Luke said grimly.

"You got that right."

"He either came last night or very early this morning." He stared at the ground. "If he drove, there might be tracks . . .

but I don't see any." His gaze ran over the area around the cabin, the ground under the windows. "No footprints visible."

Andi checked her watch and hesitated. "Maybe we should call the police," she said, then thought about their treatment of her brother. "But right now, we're late."

"Give me a sec. I'll be right back. Give me your house key, then start the car."

She didn't argue, just gave him the key, then headed to her Tucson and slipped behind the wheel. She'd barely switched on the ignition when she saw Luke appear on the porch again. He took a second to lock the house, then, with his jacket and a small plastic bag holding the card, jogged to her SUV and climbed inside. "Let's go," he said, and before he snapped on his seat belt, he gave her a quick peck on the cheek.

"What was that for?"

"Not letting the bastard's attack on me get to you."

"Oh, it got to me. Just not the way he intended."

Luke flashed her a smile as he clicked his belt into place. "Hit it. We don't want to keep the Carrera brothers waiting."

"Wouldn't dream of it," she said and did a quick one-eighty before ramming the SUV into drive.

They were only a few minutes tardy by the time they reached the Wren Development offices. It wasn't surprising that Carter was waiting for them, but the fact that Emma, more sober than Andi had seen her in weeks, was also waiting was a little unexpected. Dressed in a black dress, coat, and heels, her makeup perfect, her eyes only slightly bloodshot, she looked ready to do battle. Of course, the ever-dutiful Ben was at her side.

Carter took one look at Luke and his features tightened. "This is a meeting for the members of the business only." He wagged a finger at both Ben and Luke. "You two can wait outside. Maybe you can go get coffee or," to Luke, "a beer. It must be five o'clock somewhere."

"Luke's staying," Andi snapped, tired of Carter's high-handedness.

Emma stood her ground as well. "Ben, too. We're a team."

Carter immediately began spouting off reasons and rules, all of which Andi ignored. She cut him off with, "I assume we're meeting in the conference room? Then let's get started." She led the way, Luke one step behind her. Emma's high heels clicked sharp and fast. Carter had no choice but to follow them in.

Andi took her usual chair, the one Greg had generally occupied. Carter appeared to want to start making a scene but thought better of it. As the majority shareholder, Andi had the right to direct the meeting and sit anywhere she damn well pleased. She was just thankful that Carter had the sense and decency to acquiesce instead of going for schoolboy tactics and tantrums.

But he'd called this meeting, so he was today's director. "Okay," he said, pulling a sheaf of papers from his brief-case. "Everything I'm proposing is digital, sent to your computers, but here are hard copies of my plan." He shot Luke and Ben each disparaging looks that caused Ben to redden but began a slow smile across Luke's lips. Ben might be bullied and cowed by Carter, but Luke Denton was another story.

Perfect, Andi thought as she caught the pages Carter slid across the polished mahogany. "Where are the Carerras?"

"Yeah, where are they?" Emma asked, staring down Carter. She hadn't bothered looking at the proposal; in fact she seemed edgy, as if something was on her mind.

"They'll be here soon. I gave us a half an hour before they get here so we could have all our ducks in a row. We need to be on the same page when they arrive."

Emma said tightly, "That'll be a trick."

Carter met her stony gaze. "This is serious."

"Everything is with you," she responded. She grabbed up the papers and started leafing through them. "Let's see what you have planned. Oh great. The Carreras' names are all over this." She dropped the pages on the table.

Sensing fireworks were about to explode, Andi tried to ameliorate. "I'll look through the papers, but I haven't changed my mind about the Carreras."

"This is what's best for the company," Carter insisted.

"Best for the company?" Emma repeated, her voice rising. "What's wrong with you, Carter? You know better. Or you should. Greg never would have gone for this."

"Greg's gone," Carter said. "And we have to make some hard choices."

"Greg's gone because they killed him," Emma stated flatly.

"Wait a minute," Andi said.

Luke leaned forward in his chair. "Why do you say that?"

"Are you insane?" Carter threw back at her. "Of course they didn't—"

"You think that 'accident' just happened?" Emma practically shouted. "Because Greg was tired, or had a little too much to drink, or got confused or something? He'd driven that road a thousand times. No way would he have just missed the curve."

"Emma," Ben said, reaching for her arm, but she yanked it away.

"This is between me and my brother! He's looked at Greg's death as a *gift*."

Carter blanched. "That is not true."

"Honey, maybe you should calm down," Ben said. "This is upsetting and maybe you had a little drink before you came here and—"

"I've never been more sober in my life."

Silence followed. Everyone stared at her. Finally, Emma said, "Those thugs . . . murdered our brother. Somehow they forced him off the road, and by God, I am not—*we* are not—doing business with them. Not on this project, not on any project." She was shaking by this time, her face red, her fists clenched in conviction.

Luke asked, "How do you know this?"

"She doesn't," Carter shot back angrily. "She's grasping at straws. What the hell's wrong with you, Emma? Is your brain pickled from all the booze?"

Emma's eyes widened in hurt, and Ben jumped in. "Hey now, we don't need to go there."

"Sure we do." Carter wasn't having any of Ben's arguments. "Emma, we're kin. You and me. We're together on this. We need the Carreras to preserve the company."

"You've thought I would side with you from the beginning, but I can't. Think about it, Carter. About how it all came down."

"How am I supposed to keep us afloat? We don't have the money!"

Emma turned to Andi. "We're not doing business with them."

"We're not," Andi agreed.

Carter tried to interrupt, but Emma overtalked him. "That bastard Blake called me last night."

Ben's head whipped around. "What?"

"He scared the shit out of me," Emma said.

"Did he threaten you?" Luke asked.

"He just made it clear we needed to do business with them." She glared at Carter. "So you figure something else out because I'd rather die than deal with those bastards." She scraped her chair back and started for the door. Ben scrambled to follow.

Carter entreated, "Wait, Em. You can't just walk out."

"Like hell." She stormed out the door and Ben, looking backward, threw them all an apologetic look as he trailed after her. Their footsteps faded and Andi heard the elevator *ding* before the car collected them.

"Are you fucking kidding me?" Carter threw back his head and closed his eyes for a second, as if he could conjure up a different ending to his conversation with Emma. "Sober, my eye. Takes somebody drunk to act like that."

"I agree with her," Andi said.

"You believe the Carreras were behind Greg's accident? Oh, come on, Andi. You're better than that." The elevator dinged again before Andi could retort, and Carter muttered, "Oh great. They're here. Now what? What will we tell them?" He was suddenly desperate. "We have to sign with them, Andi. It's imperative."

She shook her head. What really had been said between Blake and Emma? She thought again of the note she'd received in the willow wreath this morning, so much subtler than whatever had occurred between Blake and Emma. No, the coy notes had much more finesse, a secret little smug quality that wasn't the Carrera brothers' style. She remembered her meeting on the treadmills with Brian. An upfront and in-your-face kind of intimidation.

Hearing a double set of footsteps in the hallway, Andi braced herself for the inevitable showdown. Carter drew a breath and Luke grew very still as they all turned to the door.

Scott and Mimi Quade appeared in the conference room doorway.

"What the hell?" Carter said.

"We need to settle this," Scott stated coldly, his gaze taking in Andi and Luke. He frowned, clearly not liking what he saw. Mimi seemed to curl in upon herself. Her baby bump was still in evidence. Scott threw out his chest and declared to Carter, "We've got a problem. Your problem."

Mimi whimpered and Scott grabbed her arm, as if willing some starch into her spine.

"There is no problem," Luke said before Carter could really get going. "Because there is no pregnancy."

Scott stayed focused on Carter. "Mimi's having Greg's baby," he insisted.

"Luke found you out," Carter said calmly.

Scott blinked, but went on, "Your brother knocked up my sister."

Luke said, "Why don't we ask Mimi?"

They all looked at Mimi, who started shaking as if an earthquake had hit.

She broke down in sobs. Yanking her hand away, she backed up and blubbered, "I loved him so much. None of you care. He was everything to me."

"Everything but the father of your child," Carter said in disgust.

Andi ached for Mimi. She should be furious with her, but she just felt sorry for her. "Mimi," she began.

"I was pregnant," Mimi cried. "I wanted that baby so much. But I lost it." Mimi had started hiccupping then, nearly hyperventilating.

"See what you've done!" Scott raged, his face beet red. He turned to his sister. "It'll be okay, sweetheart. We'll take these bastards to court. They'll have to take care of you."

"But . . . but I just want Greg."

"You've lost, Quade," Carter said with a certain amount of satisfaction. "Now, take your *pregnant* sister out of here. We have business to do."

"You Wrens are going to make things right," Scott declared. "I know things about you people." His eyes glittered as he took in the lot of them. "All of you. You're no saints.

This is no goddamned ivory tower. And Greg, that lying bastard. He was as bad as the rest of you."

"Get out," Carter said through his teeth, but Scott didn't back down. "You know he didn't just drive off a cliff, don't you? That was no accident up there on the ridge."

Andi stared at him. First Emma, now Scott.

Carter walked around the edge of the table. "We've already heard the theories."

Beside Andi, Luke rose to his feet.

"You all have blood on your hands." Scott grabbed a blubbering Mimi by the arm and marched her toward the door. As he passed out of the room, he snarled, "You goddamned Wrens. Always thinking you own the world. I haven't forgotten, you know!"

A few minutes later they heard the elevator bell ding once more, and then Mimi's sobs grew more distant.

"What was that all about?" Andi asked.

"Extortion." Carter straightened his tie and looked at Luke. "Thank you for finding out she was faking it."

"She miscarried," Luke corrected him.

Carter threw him a dark look. "Then she faked it."

"She did love Greg," Andi said.

"Yeah, let's all feel bad for poor Mimi," Carter snapped. "Where the fuck are the Carreras?"

Carter's words were still floating in the air when the elevator bell sounded again. Andi stiffened her spine, and two minutes later Blake Carrera strode through the door. Carter, already on his feet, strode the distance between them and stuck out his hand, a welcoming smile on his face.

"Sorry I'm late," Blake said without any emotion.

"And your brother?"

"Ran into car trouble. Can't make it. No problem. I can handle everything." His eyes skimmed across the table to Andi and Luke, then back to Carter. "Where's your sister?"

"She had to leave. Something came up."

One dark eyebrow cocked and Blake's scar became more visible. "What?"

"Personal stuff. Come on in, sit down." Carter was pulling out a chair for him.

"Don't bother," Andi said. Despite her innate fear of the man, she screwed up her courage. "Nothing's changed. Emma and I aren't going to sign any papers today or any other day. We've decided it would be in Wren's best interests to forge ahead on our own."

Carrera regarded her silently as Carter started to bluster, but Andi went on, "No amount of coercing or bribing or threatening is going to change our minds. You can't intimidate me or Emma. She told us you called her and tried to strong-arm her some way."

"What are you talking about?" he asked, his eyes cold.

"We're not doing business with you," Andi assured him with a lot more confidence than she felt.

"Andi," Carter warned, "we should listen to what Mr. Carrera has to say."

"He'll be wasting his breath. And my time." Despite the fact that her heart was pounding with trepidation and her hands were clammy, she rained a cool smile on the big man. "Maybe you should go help your brother."

Blake turned back to Carter. "I thought you said you'd take care of this. Of her."

"I will."

"Gentlemen, I think we're done here. You heard Mrs. Wren," Luke said.

Carter looked at him. "Who's running this meeting, Denton?"

Luke didn't respond, didn't need to. He and Carrera had locked eyes and the air in the room crackled with words unsaid. Andi threw Luke a worried look, but he held Carrera's gaze.

Blake said, "I heard you were hooking up with Greg Wren's widow. And I thought *Nah, not Denton, not the guy who was all on the side of might and right when it came to his ex-partner, Bolchoy*. But look at you now, huh? You've finally figured out who the winning team is. Comforting a rich widow is a smart move. I admire that." He smirked, and Luke's fingers curled into fists.

"You know where the door is," Luke said, his lips barely moving.

"Wait a minute now." Carter stepped between the two men.

Panicked that an actual fight might break out, Andi jumped to her feet and took hold of Luke's hand. "Let's go."

"Stop!" Carter ordered. "You can't just walk out of here." He turned to Blake. "I'll talk to Emma. I said I would, didn't I? She'll come around."

"He's lying to you," Andi told Blake as she tugged Luke after her and headed for the door. "My sister-in-law and I are in total agreement. No deal. We've told Carter. Said it over and over."

Luke reluctantly followed her into the hall.

Blake called after them, "We're busy, y'know. Me and Brian. And we can't keep wasting time over this with you Wrens. If you want a battle, okay, you've got one. Meanwhile, I've got other things to do. You're not the only fish in the sea," he added loudly as Andi stabbed the button for the elevator. "Or should I say *little birds*?"

Her head whipped around at that one, but Luke stayed calm.

"Did you hear what he said?" she whispered as the elevator doors closed behind them.

"Every word."

"Should we have asked him about the card? About Trini?"

He slid her a glance as they exited the elevator, crossed the building foyer, and headed outside into a brisk wind

that was whipping leaves in a furious eddy in the center of
the parking lot.

At her Tucson he said, "I want to wait on that."

She climbed behind the wheel and started the engine.
"Do you think the Carerras are behind Trini's murder? Why
would they kill her? Because she's a *bird*?"

"That just doesn't hang together," he admitted. "There's
always a financial purpose to what they do. Their aim is
money, first, last, and always."

"Well, then, what's all the *little bird* stuff?" She could
hear her voice rising and her hands were clenched on the
wheel. She had to force herself to relax.

"I don't know."

"I made the mistake of calling myself a little bird to them
before so . . . maybe they're just trying to make fun of me,
turn my words around, find a new way to psych me out."

"Maybe I should have driven," he said as Andi's wheels
touched gravel.

"Sorry. I'm fine."

She drove with concentration the rest of the way back,
but once they were in the cabin, she accused him, "You
don't think the Carerras are behind the notes."

"Do you?" He'd crossed the room to switch on the television. The midday news was just starting.

It took her awhile to answer, but then she said, "No. But
I don't know what that means. Who else has a grudge
against me?"

"Quade's certainly got it in for the Wrens."

Andi shook her head, but then she remembered the
threat he'd hurled on his way out. That he knew something
about the Wrens. Emma had referred to him as a lake rat,
someone who hung around with the wealthy lake crowd,
feeding off the crumbs left to him.

Luke stripped off his jacket and tossed it onto the couch next to his bedroll.

Andi tried to calm down, to get a grip on herself. She was home. Safe. With Luke. She flopped onto the couch and inhaled the aroma of this morning's coffee, which still lingered in the air. It mingled with the faint smell of smoke from a fire built days before and should have provided her comfort. But not today, not after the bedlam that had been the meeting at the office. Running her fingers through her hair, she tried to sort it all out. Of course that was impossible.

Luke pulled the latest plastic-encased note from his pocket and eyed it.

On the television, Pauline Kirby's face appeared. The local reporter was outside, standing near a huge river, the sky as leaden as the gray depths of the water.

Luke said, "I want to talk to the police. Detective Rafferty, not Thompkins. I've dealt with his type a lot of times. They don't like being pushed and they become intractable. Until it's his idea that Trini's death was a homicide, he'll drag his feet. And I don't know if he'll get there in time. We need some momentum on this case. If the bird messages involve Trini, we gotta move. Find out who's doing this before something else happens."

"Something to me, you mean."

"Just because I don't think the Carreras are behind the notes doesn't mean I'm forgetting about them. Blake scared Emma. He thought he could get her to do what he wanted, but she ran from him. I want to know why she's so damned sure the Carreras were behind your husband's death. Is that just fear talking, or did Blake say or do something that convinced her the Carreras are killers?"

"Do you think Scott's behind the notes?"

"Or Mimi, because they're directed at you."

Andi shook her head slowly. "I don't think she's faking how undone she is. It's too calculating."

He nodded but said, "I just don't want to be blindsided."

Andi flicked a glance at the television, where Pauline stood near the water's edge . . . some lake?

"It's the timing of everything that bothers me. At the time of Greg's accident, Wren Development had been okayed on the lodge, and that pissed off the Carreras. We already know they wanted the land. So maybe they decided to retaliate."

On the television Pauline was droning on, her hair caught by a strong wind. "What do you mean? By killing Greg?"

"Greg's death threw you all into chaos. Everyone involved was upset. If Carter hadn't kept pushing, the project might have failed because Emma has her own problems and you were lost in grief."

"I was a walking zombie," she admitted.

"That's the kind of thing the Carreras do," Luke said grimly.

"So what happened to Trini? I'll never believe she just didn't read the label on that energy bar."

Luke's attention was on the TV, where a body bag was being loaded into an ambulance. Pauline was staring directly into the camera's eye, saying, ". . . Police refuse to ID the woman until next of kin is notified, but we've learned that a woman from the Gresham area is missing. Christine Tern Brandewaite. She goes by the name Christine Tern. She worked late last night but didn't show up this morning."

"We need to find the boyfriend," Luke said, his eyes glued to the screen. She realized he wasn't really listening to Andi anymore.

"What is it?" Andi asked, but Luke didn't answer, so she tuned into the program to see what had riveted his attention.

A bird wheeled over Pauline Kirby's ravaged hair, crying out. "This is a possible homicide because we have confirmed the victim was tased several times," Pauline was saying. "She may have been unconscious or unable to save herself when she went into the water. If anyone has any information on Christine Tern, please call the police or our station."

"Tern . . ." Luke said, shaking his head as if to remove dust.

"You know her?" Andi said, her heart somersaulting uncomfortably.

"I don't know how she spells it, but a tern is a seabird."

"Oh God." Andi stared at the television.

"It makes no sense," Luke said. Then he was in motion.

"What are you doing?"

"I'm calling Detective Rafferty."

Chapter Twenty-Three

"Where've you been?" Gretchen asked September as soon as she returned to the squad room.

"I was in Hood River, following up on the Pattens. The renters whose son had the addiction problem."

"I know who they are, but what about the body in the quarry?" Gretchen demanded. "George said you were working on that one."

September shot a look at George. He was riding his chair, still engrossed in whatever he saw on his computer screen. "It's the Sheriff's Department's case. I just followed up for them at Sirocco Realty."

"Where you and I went last weekend," she pointed out. "The body at the bottom of the quarry is their receptionist."

"We were working an entirely different case."

"Were we?"

"Yes. And I tried calling you yesterday," September said, knowing where this was going. "I was just helping out the Sheriff's Department." She brought Gretchen up to speed, telling her about Tracy's hidden box of what they believed to be keys, and how realtor Edie Tindel believed Tracy had been using the keys to gain access to clients' houses. She finished with, "But that one's out of our hands. You want to talk new cases, George is the man to talk to."

"I told you you could have that case," George reminded her coolly over his shoulder.

"Yeah, and I'm making traction on the Aurora Lane case," September snapped back.

Gretchen ignored September and turned to George. "What's your case?" she asked him, which really pissed September off.

"You want to tell her, Nine? Be my guest." George wouldn't look away from his screen.

September tamped down the smart response that sprang to her lips with an effort. The cutbacks and threatened job security had ruined all their attitudes. Instead she succinctly told Gretchen about the death of Trinidad Finch, which appeared to be from anaphylactic shock after eating an energy bar made out of cricket flour.

"Cricket flour?" The disgusted look on Gretchen's face was comical.

September added, "Crickets are part of the shellfish family and she was apparently highly allergic to shellfish."

"Evidence isn't conclusive that it was a homicide," George put in.

"Well, what do you think?" Gretchen asked September.

It was rare that her bullheaded partner took the time to really pick her brain, so September considered her answer carefully. "Do you know Luke Denton? Detective Ray Bolchoy's ex-partner?"

"I've heard the name. Saw him interviewed by Pauline Kirby once."

"Nine's our media darling," George said. "A few times on television and now Kirby asks for her. They're BFFs."

"You got a problem, George, just spit it the hell out," September said.

He jerked as if surprised and finally dragged his eyes

away from the computer. "Somebody's damn touchy today," he muttered

Gretchen groaned. "Somebody just tell me what's going on."

"When the ME says the Finch case is a homicide, it's a homicide," George declared, drawing his line in the sand.

September turned her shoulder to George and said to Gretchen, "Denton was on scene at the victim's apartment: Trinidad Finch. He's the one who reported her death to nine-one-one. He's working for the Wrens of Wren Development . . . have I got that right, George?"

"So far."

"Anyway, one of the Wrens was a friend of the victim."

"Andrea Wren," George put in helpfully.

"She tried to reach Finch and failed," September continued, "so she went to her apartment and found her. George can tell you more."

"There isn't any more until forensics come back," George said.

"What are you doing now?" Gretchen asked September, who'd started writing on her computer's word-processing program.

"Transcribing notes." She glanced down at her open notebook. "I'm working up a time line for Lance Patten. He disappeared right after his senior year of high school."

"The druggie?" she clarified.

"Yeah, I asked his parents about his drug use. They didn't want to classify him as an addict, but they're his parents, so they may be putting a positive spin on it. He used marijuana and occasionally harder drugs. He was friends with Tommy Burkey, who called him Laser. Still don't know why exactly, but I'm pretty sure Laser and Lance are the same person. Maury Patten said Lance hung with a group of friends who may have used that nickname. Lance sometimes rode their horse over to Schultz Lake and had friends over there. I also asked about Davinia Singleton, but both parents played deaf, dumb, and blind." September shrugged. "They don't want to hear anything bad about their son."

"You should have taken me with you," Gretchen said.

September nodded rather than argue that Gretchen would have tried to talk her out of the trip because the case didn't interest her. "There's something else," September added.

"What?"

"The family that left in the RV were the Kirkendalls. They rented Mamet's house directly before the Pattens. They had a daughter, Wendy, who was strangled and dumped in Schultz Lake. That crime's never been solved."

Gretchen frowned. "Something familiar about that."

"I thought so, too, so I looked it up. Wendy Kirkendall was strangled with a willow branch."

"That's right! That's what it was." Gretchen narrowed her sharp blue eyes. "Is there some connection between Lance and Wendy?"

"I don't think they knew each other. She was gone before the Pattens moved in. But I do think the bones are Lance's, and if that's the case, then there are two crimes connected to Aurora Lane within a short period of time. And that's not counting Nathan Singleton's *accident*, which is on the books as a murder/suicide."

"Lance must've been the one screwing Davinia Singleton. The parents just don't want to say so."

September nodded but just said, "Maybe."

"You don't think she was satisfying her cougar's itch?"

"The affair seems real, but Anna Liu referred to the boy involved as flirtatious, cheeky, entitled. . . . That just doesn't sound like my picture of Lance. He used drugs. He befriended Tommy Burkey, who was much younger and on the mentally slow side. I've never heard he had a car.

He rode a family horse in the fields behind their house. It doesn't seem to add up to the same guy."

Gretchen thought that over. "The real estate woman mentioned that the druggie hung around with other scruffy boys."

"Kitsy."

"Yeah, Kitsy. She said one of 'em supposedly had money, but that they all dressed alike in baggy jeans and hoodies."

September nodded. "We need to learn more about Lance Patten's buddies. And Wendy Kirkendall's murder."

She shot a look at George, who was their heavy hitter on research, mainly because he didn't like to do fieldwork. His phone had rung while September and Gretchen were talking and he was engaged in a conversation that was mostly listening on his end. She heard the terms "game player" and "chess" and grew curious. Gretchen, too, paused, and both of them listened in unabashedly.

Finally, George hung up and gave them a baleful look. "I'm working," he said, as if they'd criticized him.

Gretchen raised her palms in surrender.

George pursed his lips. "That was one of the regulars from Trinidad Finch's Pilates classes. She said a few months back a new guy joined who clearly had a thing for our vic. He didn't talk much, but he did mention that he was a game player. This gal asked him what he meant, and he said he played chess, among other things. He was flirty and she kinda thought he was cute, though he wore a toupee. . . ." He shrugged. "Some women don't care, I guess."

"Did he make a pass at Finch?" Gretchen asked.

"Maybe. They got together somehow. Apparently the hormones were raging."

"What's his name?" September asked.

"I checked with the club. He's listed as Robert Fisher.

He's probably the boyfriend who was supposed to see her that night. Jarrett Sellers said she was stood up, so maybe that's when he made his play. Andrea Wren, who just happens to be Sellers's sister, mentioned Finch was seeing someone she called Bobby."

"The name Robert fits. We have an address?" Gretchen asked.

"Only a fake one," George said.

"Well, that's suspicious." September thought foul play was definitely in the picture. "We have a photo of this guy?"

"Uh-uh." George shook his head.

"What about cameras at the club?" September pressed.

"There's an outside one. I'm getting a copy of the last month's video." He sounded less than excited and September didn't really blame him. Going through hours of security tape was tedious work.

"So you're leaning toward homicide now," Gretchen said.

George nodded slowly.

"All right, well, we've got our own to solve Mr. Bones's," Gretchen said.

September's brows raised. She was pleased her partner finally appeared to be back on their case.

Gretchen went on, "We need to find some thirtysome-things who used to be part of a scruffy band that hung out at Aurora Lane when they were teens."

September grabbed up her bag and jacket again. "Sounds like they really hung out at Schultz Lake."

"Where are we going?"

"To talk to the Kirkendalls. They live in Laurelton. No phone, so we're just going to drop in."

"I'll drive," Gretchen said.

They were climbing into the department-issued Jeep

when September's cell rang. The number looked familiar, but she couldn't place it. "Rafferty," she answered.

"Detective, it's Luke Denton."

"Hello, Mr. Denton," she said, hiding her surprise as she shot Gretchen a meaningful look. Her partner registered with a nod that she understood the message. "If this is about the cricket poisoning, Detective Thompkins is still the investigating officer on—"

"That one's a homicide," he cut her off. "Gut instinct and a few other things tell me that. But I've got some other things to say."

"Okay."

"Andi's been receiving threatening notes. That's why she hired me."

"Andrea Wren's been receiving threatening notes," she repeated for Gretchen's benefit.

"Yes."

"And you think this has some bearing on Ms. Finch's death."

"Maybe. Or they're separate issues that share a big co-incidence."

"I'm not following you."

"Andi and Trinidad both have last names that are birds. They're Ms. Wren and Ms. Finch, respectively. The notes are a play on their names. The first one was left in Andi's cabin, on her bed. It said *Little birds need to fly.* The second one was at her office and said, *It's too bad when little birds have to die.* That note came the day Trinidad Finch was killed."

September was scrabbling for her notebook as Gretchen pulled out of the parking lot. "Say that again." Denton repeated himself and September scratched out the phrases. "You think the second note was meant for Ms. Finch?"

"Maybe. It sure seems that way. And then Andi got a

third note today, left on her front door." He cleared his throat and said in a faintly ironic voice, "I believe it was referencing me. *Little birds should be careful who they choose as a mate. Tsk, tsk. There is no such thing as faithfulness. You should know where he's also been putting his pecker. Be careful. Seabirds can die, too.*"

September was writing furiously. After a few moments, she questioned, "Seabirds . . . ?"

"I don't know what that means, but I have a theory, . . ." She heard a woman's voice in the background and Denton corrected himself. "We have a theory."

"What is it?"

Gretchen glanced at what September had written, then shot her a look, questions in her eyes. September switched to speakerphone.

"This is going to sound flat-out crazy, but on the news today, Pauline Kirby was reporting on the woman they pulled out of the Columbia River this morning. She'd been tased. Looks like a homicide. Her name is possibly Christine Tern Brandewaite, who's been missing since last night or this morning. Police aren't saying yet."

"You want us to follow up on that?"

"Yes."

"And this crazy theory?"

"According to the news report, a lot of people knew the missing woman as Christine Tern. I looked up her case further and saw *tern* was spelled with an *e*. And terns are seabirds."

September started. "You think the note about seabirds was referencing Christine Tern? Is there a connection between Ms. Wren and Christine Tern?"

"No. None. Except that their last names are birds. Detective, I believe that body pulled out of the Columbia is Christine Tern and that she was killed, like Trinidad Finch."

"I'd like to see these notes," September said.

Gretchen murmured, "You're gonna have to fight George over that case."

"But Detective Thompkins is still the lead investigator on the Finch case," September was forced to say.

"He doesn't think it's a homicide," Denton stated flatly.

"He's leaning more that way."

"I know how it'll work, Detective Rafferty. He'll dismiss the whole damn thing."

"You don't know that."

"I don't have time to convince him, and that's fine. I'm investigating this on my own. I just wanted you to know."

And he was gone.

"Damn," September said.

Gretchen gave her a sideways look. "You've got ex-Portland PD working George's case. That'll make his day."

"I'd better tell him." She put a call through to him, and when he answered, she asked, "Would you look up cases where someone with a last name that could be a bird have been killed?"

"What?" George snorted.

"Bird names. Like Finch and Starling and Robin."

"Why?"

"Just do it," Gretchen called loudly. "It's for your case."

"You want me to look up homicides where the victim's last name is a bird?" he reiterated.

"That's exactly what I want. But there's something you should know," September started.

"And we'll tell you all about it later," Gretchen yelled, signaling for September to hang up the phone. After she did, Gretchen said, "Let Denton do his worst. At least he's in the field, and that's more than we can say for George."

* * *

"What did she say?" Andi asked. She was curled up beside Luke on her couch.

"Just what I expected them to say. It's a wild theory, but what the hell. At least they know."

"You didn't mention the Carreras or Scott Quade."

"That'll be my next report."

"What do we do now?"

That stopped him for a moment. Andi looked from him to the bedroom door and back again.

"Now that is a great idea," he said.

The Kirkendalls lived on one side of a duplex on a street with homes crammed up next to one another and patchy yards. Their RV was parked in their driveway and, based on the splotches of rust, looked to be the same one they'd owned years earlier. It was currently being pummeled by a harsh rain that seemed to come out of nowhere.

Gretchen and September huddled at the front door beneath a small overhang that listed to one side but kept them reasonably dry from the squall. A small woman with sad eyes answered the door.

"Yes?"

"Mrs. Kirkendall, I'm Detective Rafferty and this is Detective Sandler." They both pulled out their identification as the woman's hand flew to her chest.

"You've found out who killed Wendy!"

"Unfortunately, no," September said. "I'm sorry. We're working on a case that involves a family on Aurora Lane. May we come in to talk to you?"

"We only lived there a short time. I don't know what I can tell you." She reluctantly held the door open wider.

"I tried to call you, but I couldn't find a phone number," September apologized.

"Oh, Leland doesn't much like cell phones. So many charges. We use disposal ones."

"Leland's your husband?"

"If you can call him that." She sniffed, and September remembered Grace Myles had referred to him as Shithead.

September said, "I spoke to the Pattens this morning, the people who rented from Mr. Mamet after you did."

Kim Kirkendall flushed. "That landlord was a butt. He kicked us out. Leland was a bit late on the payment, I admit, but after Wendy died, we didn't know what to do. And he didn't care at all!"

September nodded sympathetically, but Gretchen, ever impatient, asked, "Do you know about the bones discovered in the Singletons' basement?"

"Saw it on the news. Very, very creepy. I didn't know those people. Leland didn't like them."

"Some of the bones are from an eighteen-year-old male who would be about thirty-two now," Gretchen added. "We're trying to identify them. A working theory is that they might be the Pattens' son, Lance."

She shook her head. "I don't know him."

"Is Leland at work?" September asked.

"He used to be a plumber a long, long time ago. Now he's a bum, if you want the truth. If you need him, he's probably at Tiny Tim's."

"Can you tell us about Wendy?" September asked.

Her sad eyes gazed at September for a long moment. September wasn't sure she was going to answer, but then she said, "Wendy was a good girl. She didn't deserve what happened to her."

"No," September agreed. Gretchen moved restlessly, but September gave her a hard look.

"I always thought it was those kids that did it. You know, those spoiled brats with lots of money."

Gretchen asked, "What kids?"

"The ones at the summer camp. Parents sent 'em there to get 'em out of their hair, that's what Leland said. Otherwise they'd just be hanging around, getting into trouble. Well, they got into plenty at that camp, too. Even the counselors."

"Wendy hung out with people from the camp?" September asked.

"Oh yeah. Thought they were so la-di-da. Think she was sweet on one of 'em, but she wouldn't tell me about him. Leland woulda had a fit. I told the cops about 'em back when they found her. Oh, they looked around. Knocked on some doors. But they thought it was a serial killer, y'know. There was another girl killed around the same time, but she was in Portland. I don't know. I think it was one of them campers."

September tried to quiz her more about Aurora Lane, but she had nothing to add. She had no recollection of Davinia or Nathan Singleton, which was entirely possible because if Lance was involved, the suspected affair would have occurred after the Kirkendalls left Aurora Lane.

"You can't remember any name from the campers?" September questioned again, just before they left, but she just shook her head.

"You think one of 'em did it, too?"

"That's what I'm trying to find out."

They left Mrs. Kirkendall on her porch, watching them with her sad eyes. In the Jeep, September said, "It all comes back to Schultz Lake."

"You're thinking Wendy's death is tied to Mr. Bones's," Gretchen said.

"Wendy and Lance both lived on Aurora Lane, and they both mingled with the Schultz Lake crowd. If Lance is Mr. Bones, then it's a pretty big coincidence that two teenagers died in a narrow space of time on one short street."

"I think you're right." Gretchen started up the vehicle.

"I know the summer camp she meant. It's closed down and either Wren Development or the Carrera brothers are planning to build on the site."

September thought that over. Lots of threads of cases were floating around that could tie together. She just couldn't see it yet. "Must be time to talk to somebody who worked at that camp."

"Let's get a list."

Andi lay beside Luke, her head resting against his chest. His cell phone buzzed from inside his pants pocket and he had to fumble around to retrieve it. "It's Peg Bellows," he said in surprise. "I called her so many times, I know the number."

At that moment Andi's phone rang, its tone muffled from within her purse, which she'd set on the bedroom dresser. "They've found us," she said, climbing out of bed to retrieve it. She would have left it, but Luke was already on his phone, so what the hell?

"Hi, Peg," Luke greeted as Andi pulled out her own phone. Seeing it was Carter calling, she made a face and thought about not taking the call. She wanted to cocoon herself inside the cabin with Luke and let all the bad stuff stay outside.

But he would probably just call back.

"Hi, Carter," she answered. Luke had stepped away from her, standing naked, his muscled back to her, listening hard to whatever Peg was saying.

"Andi!" Carter said, his voice tight. "God. Emma fell down a flight of stairs!"

"What? Oh no. Is she all right? Where'd it happen?" She almost asked, *Which bar?*

"At the office. It was this morning. She and Ben came

in separate cars and he waited for her at home, but she never showed. He finally found her in the office stairwell. She's in the hospital."

"Oh my God!"

"I thought she might be drunk when I first heard, but she was sober."

"Is she all right? Where is she now?"

"Laurelton General."

"Oh, Carter. Oh no." Andi could scarcely think.

"Jesus. I mean . . . fuck . . ." He sounded totally undone. "Andi, she's unconscious. They don't know if she's going to make it."

Chapter Twenty-Four

Laurelton General had been designed on a steep hill with its west side at the bottom of the slope. Entering on the west side brought you to floor one, but the main entry was on the south side and at the top of the hill, which was why above the door a sign announced in big block letters: FLOOR THREE.

Andi pushed through the main floor's double glass doors, hurried up to the front desk, and explained that she was Emma Wren Mueller's sister-in-law. She was referred to a doctor on the fifth floor and counted in her head to calm herself as she and Luke took the elevator up.

Terrible thoughts circled her mind. Thoughts of the Carreras and how Emma had defied Blake, not once but twice. Hadn't Brian warned her about the Carreras being better friends than enemies?

"What did Peg Bellows want?" she asked.

"She put a call in to Blake Carrera. Wants to have it out with him."

Andi had asked the question more to make conversation than because she had any interest at this point, but now her head whipped around. "Did you tell her about the meeting with him today?"

"I just told her it would be better to stay away from him."

"Do you think she'll listen?"

"No. She said she was inviting him over. But then you were talking to Carter, and with Emma's fall, I told her I'd call her back."

"He's dangerous. They both are."

Andi was heading toward the medical hub when she saw Ben pacing outside one of the rooms. He saw Luke and her at the same moment and charged toward them. "They did this. You know they did this."

"How is she?" Andi asked. "Is this her room?"

He nodded, but then turned to Luke as Andi headed into Room 511. "Carter's on his way. He talked to some of the other people in the building. Someone in a hoodie was hanging around the offices. A girl from one of the other businesses saw a guy wearing a hoodie hanging around the building and she reported him to her boss. He was gone when they looked for him, but maybe he'd already pushed Emma down the stairs."

"Wait a minute—" Luke started.

Andi said at the same time, "I thought it was an accident. I thought she tripped or something."

"She was sober today, Andi," he shot back.

"I know she was. I saw her."

Andi pushed open the door to Emma's room. The space was dimly lit and the afternoon gloom deepened all the corners. Emma lay on a bed, unconscious, strapped to monitors that recorded her respiration and heartbeat.

Ben was beside her in an instant, placing himself between Andi and the bed, as if he didn't trust anyone to be near her. "She should be in ICU," he muttered.

"Why isn't she?" Andi asked. Luke had walked in and was standing beside her.

"They upgraded her," Ben said, his mouth tight. He clearly thought it was a mistake.

"That's a good sign, then," Andi said.

"Someone tried to kill her," Ben said, glaring at Luke as if it were his fault.

Luke asked, "Maybe we should have this discussion outside her room."

"Good idea." Ben waited for them both to leave first.

Once they were in the hallway, Luke asked, "Why are you so certain it wasn't an accident?"

"Because of those notes!" He turned to Andi. "Little birds have to die or something? She's a Wren!"

Luke and Andi shared a glance. Ben's thinking was along the same lines as theirs. "I got a third note today," Andi admitted.

Ben swept in a breath, shocked. "Oh God. What did it say?"

"It was to me, not Emma."

"It was mostly a warning against me," Luke told him.

"I'm telling you, this was no accident. Someone pushed her. The guy in the hoodie."

Andi remembered the day she'd seen a man walking outside the offices, the fear she'd felt. She wanted to deny Ben straight out, but she had doubts herself.

"Have you talked to the police?" Luke asked.

"No. I'm waiting for Carter. He'll know what to do."

And with that he sent them each a look, as if they were not to be trusted, and headed back into Emma's room. After a moment Andi followed after him. Though it was clear Ben didn't want her, she wanted to be there for Emma.

September and Gretchen entered the squad room together. Seeing them, George actually rose from his chair and handed September several sheets of paper.

"What's this?" Gretchen asked suspiciously.

"You asked for the research," he said, regarding Gretchen coolly.

"Don't be such an asshole, George," Gretchen responded. "Cutbacks. What the fuck. We're all on the same side."

September scanned the pages and muttered, "Holy God."

"What?" Gretchen moved closer to her.

September read, "'The body of a woman washed ashore in Puget Sound in late August. The victim has been identified as Belinda Meadowlark of Friday Harbor, Washington. She was on the last ferry to Orcas Island when she presumably fell overboard. Her death has been ruled an accident.'"

"So this is about my case," George pointed out.

"Yes, your case," Gretchen snapped.

"Was it an accident?" September said aloud, more to herself than anyone else, but George took it as if the question were made for him.

"As it's *my* case, I dug a little deeper. Meadowlark has an estranged sister who lives in the Seattle area and tries to keep in contact with her. Last summer they had a fight over the care of their father. The sister felt she was doing all the work. She wanted Meadowlark to move to Seattle to help out. Meadowlark then drops the bomb that she has a serious boyfriend, which apparently is a first. Sister doesn't believe it and Meadowlark throws out the name *Rob Fisher.*"

"Well, there's the connection," Gretchen said. "Same name as Finch's boyfriend." She smiled faintly. "My kind of weird."

George relaxed a bit. "Yeah, it is," he admitted. "I made some calls to Meadowlark's coworkers and friends. No one ever met Rob. Consensus is that she made him up."

"Be a lot better if she had," September said. "Did you check to see if he was on the same ferry?"

"Yes, ma'am. He was. Didn't even try to hide his name."

They all looked at one another, thinking. "He's playing

with us," September finally said. "He's a serial killer who targets women with the last name of birds and he's daring us to find him."

"Most serial killers use the same method," Gretchen pointed out. "Plays into their fantasy."

"I know," she agreed. "Water's involved in Meadowlark's death . . . possibly Tern's."

"I'll find out if the victim is truly Christine Tern," Gretchen said, heading for her desk.

George frowned. "What victim?"

"The one pulled out of the Columbia," Gretchen threw over her shoulder.

"But Finch's death was entirely different," September said, reaching for her cell phone.

"Who're you calling?" George asked.

"Luke Denton. He's the one who postulated our doer is targeting victims by their 'bird' names."

Luke signaled Andi to walk back into the hall with him, away from Ben and the still unconscious Emma. "I gotta call Peg Bellows back. Let her know what's happened to Emma. Impress upon her that the Carreras are dangerous."

"You really think they pushed her?"

"It's more their style than obscure, threatening notes. What I want is for Peg to remember they killed her husband. To be cautious. I might leave and go see her, if that's what it takes."

She nodded. "I'll stay here with Emma. If I need a ride, I'll Uber it, or maybe catch one with Ben."

"Don't go back to the cabin without me." He thought a moment and then pulled out his keys, taking one off the ring. "This is my apartment. If you go anywhere, go there. You know the address?"

"Yep, but I'm sticking around here for a while."

"I'll come back to the hospital. This is just a precaution."

Luke's cell rang. He pulled it out and looked at the screen, wasn't sure of the caller. "Denton," he answered.

"This is September Rafferty. I have some information for you."

"Christine Tern?"

"Working on that information now. But I thought you should know we've discovered another woman with the last name of a bird, Belinda Meadowlark, who died last summer after falling overboard from a Washington State ferry. She told people she had a boyfriend named Rob Fisher. Robert Fisher is also the name of a man in Trinidad Finch's Pilates class, one she became romantically involved with."

Luke stood stock-still. It was his theory, his and Andi's, but hearing it from the detective's lips brought it to reality.

"What is it?" Andi asked him.

"I'd like to talk to Ms. Wren," Detective Rafferty said into his ear.

"She's right here, standing beside me."

"I'd like us to all meet in person. Possibly tonight, or tomorrow?"

"Tomorrow's probably better, but I'll let Andi decide."

Luke handed her his cell phone and Andi answered cautiously. He listened with half an ear to her side of the conversation, his mind running ahead, as Rafferty told Andi much the same information, and then Andi explained the next day would be better as she was at the hospital with her sister-in-law, who'd had a fall. They set a time and exchanged cell numbers before Andi clicked off and handed Luke back his phone.

"Oh my God," Andi said, looking stunned. "He's really out there. Killing women with last names that are birds."

"I know."

"Bobby killed Trini."

Luke nodded slowly. "Bobby, Rob, Robert . . . all the

names he uses are derivatives of Robert. And his chosen last name of Fisher." Luke shook his head. "It's gotta be a fake name. An alternate identity. He wouldn't use his own."

"But why? What's he after?" Andi asked, her eyes huge as they looked up at him.

He gathered her face in his hands and kissed her on the lips. "I don't know yet. But I'm going to find out."

Gretchen slammed down the receiver on her desk phone. "Yep. It was Christine Tern's body they fished out of the Columbia."

George said, "Where the hell's Wes?"

"He's with his mother," September said.

"I know that. But he should be here." George grabbed up his own cell and put through a call.

Gretchen said, "We're here to help, George. Mr. Bones isn't going anywhere."

She was at her computer. "There are a lot of Robert Fishers around the area."

"I agree it's an alias." September was on her computer as well. She'd wanted to meet with Denton and Andrea Wren tonight, but there really was no need. They were all up to speed, and as George kept saying over and over again, it was his case. She was already stepping on his toes.

"I'm sure it's an alias," Gretchen rejoined. "But I might as well make a list."

September checked Google for local camps and scrolled through the lists that popped up. "The North Shore Junior Camp, now defunct, was located on Schultz Lake. It still has a web site with the administrator's name: Ronald Dumonte."

George had gotten through to Wes and when he hung up his expression was grim. "Sorry, man," he said. "No, we're good here." He hung up and said, "Looks like Wes's mom's not gonna make it."

"Oh no," September said.

"He'll call us later. He wanted to come, but he can't," George admitted.

Gretchen looked up soberly. "That's too bad. I always want to work when things are hell."

It was the most emotion September had ever seen from Gretchen. She thought about Wes and her heart ached. She'd lost her own mother years earlier.

Gretchen shook her head, as if physically shaking off the moment. "There was a chess champion in the seventies named Bobby Fisher. Think that means anything?"

September looked at the clock as she put in a call to Ronald Dumonte. Five twenty. She had his home phone, but he could possibly be at work. When the call was answered, it was a woman on the line. September introduced herself and the woman asked her to wait a moment, then Ronald Dumonte was on the other end of the line.

"I'm calling about North Shore Junior Camp," September told him after she'd introduced herself.

Dumonte sighed heavily. "Make room for development. Bulldoze the past. Leave no trace of the good that came before."

"Um, yes," September said. "I take it you're against Wren Development's resort plan."

"I fought with everything I had to stop that monstrosity, but the county planners didn't listen. It's all about money, Detective Rafferty. It always is. Sometimes we just hope farsighted thinkers prevail, but it so rarely happens."

"You ran the camp in its last years," September said, easing the conversation back to what she wanted to talk about.

"That I did. Retired afterward."

"I understand that many of the wealthy and part-time residents around Schultz Lake sent their children to the camp."

"Yes." He sighed. "We wanted it to be available to everyone, but it was expensive compared to other camps, so we had a predominance of elitist's children."

Elitists . . . September had tapped into Dumonte's prejudice. She decided to use that knowledge. "Can you name some of the elitists?"

"The same ones who are still there." He rattled off a number of names and ended with, "And, of course, the Wrens. Henry Wren attended our camp when he was young, and he sent all three of his children there. I was administrator when the three of them were there." His tone was carefully controlled, but he clearly wasn't impressed with Gregory, Carter, and Emma Wren.

"Do you recall a boy named Lance Patten? I doubt he was a camper, but he may have hung out with some of them."

"I'm sorry. I don't know the name."

"Or Wendy Kirkendall?" September tried.

He swept in a breath. "The girl who was strangled and then dumped in the lake? Certainly not. It was a terrible tragedy, but it didn't affect our camp!"

September asked him a few more questions, but he became less and less interested in talking. Finally, he said reluctantly, "I suggest you call the Wrens. There was an incident with a young man over animal cruelty."

September straightened in her chair. Mr. Bromward had complained about severe cruelty to his cats.

"Henry Wren was very opposed to his children associating with the young man."

"Who was this young man?"

"Not from the camp. He was . . . he rode a horse and mixed in with the others."

"Lance Patten," September repeated sharply.

"Oh." Dumonte collected himself. "Yes, maybe. I'm sorry. I didn't think that was the name. It doesn't sound quite right. They called him something else."

"Laser?"

He inhaled sharply. "Yes, that's it."

"Thank you, Mr. Dumonte." September couldn't wait to get off the phone. George and Gretchen were still discussing Robert Fisher, but Gretchen looked over at her.

"Something?" she asked.

"Animal cruelty from a guy named Laser." She was checking the clock and punching in the number for Wren Development. If she couldn't raise Carter Wren, she would call Andi back. Maybe Emma would be awake.

"This is Detective September Rafferty," she told the receptionist. "I would like to speak with Carter Wren, please."

She half-expected to be put off, but soon a male voice answered briskly, "Carter Wren."

"Mr. Wren, I'm Detective September Rafferty. I'm researching a cold case from about thirteen years ago and I'm hoping you can help me."

"Okay," he said, mystified.

"A young man named Lance Patten disappeared from his home on Aurora Lane. He used to ride a horse from his home toward Schultz Lake—"

"I know Lance," Carter interrupted. "Or knew him. He used to come to North Shore, the old summer camp my father sent us to. Has he turned up?"

"We think so."

"Is he all right?" Carter asked, keying off her cautious tone.

Deciding it was best to lay all her cards on the table, September told him about the cache of bones found at the Singletons' home. "We believe one set of human bones belongs to Lance Patten."

"Holy . . . God . . ."

"If you could tell us anything about him that might help us discover what happened to him . . ."

"You know, my brother Greg knew him better than I did," Carter said slowly. "And Emma . . . Lance was, well, he smoked dope. We all did," he confessed. "But I think he influenced Emma the most."

"Did you ever feel he was cruel to animals?"

"God, no. He loved that horse."

"I understand your sister is in the hospital."

"Yes," he said, surprised. "How did you know?"

"I spoke with your sister-in-law on another matter."

He was taken aback. "She told you about the bird messages?"

"Yes. So, you've discussed the notes."

"Well, we all are Wrens," Carter said. "Although whoever's sending them seems to be targeting Andi."

September didn't tell him that the notes were taking the investigation outside of just the Wren family. "Would it be possible for me and my partner to talk with you this evening? We could come by your office."

"I was heading to the hospital . . ." He thought about it a moment. "But sure. I'll just have to get going pretty soon."

"I understand."

"Lance was . . . a good guy but messed up. It's too bad you can't talk to Greg. He was the one who really knew Lance well."

Luke pulled up to Peg Bellows's and felt his blood freeze. The vehicle parked in front was the same as the one he'd watched leave Wren Development. He knew it was one of the Carreras' without being told.

"Goddammit," he whispered to himself as he stepped

from the truck. He had his Glock in the glove box. He generally didn't wear a gun anymore, since he'd quit being a cop, but now he reached back inside to retrieve it. This whole setup just didn't feel right.

Cautiously, bent down, he hurried to the front door. Hearing normal voices inside, he debated what to do.

One of the Carreras was saying, ". . . can't be held responsible for what happened to Ted. He was my friend. We were all friends."

Brian, Luke figured.

Then Peg's voice, "He should never have gone on that boat."

"Brian's sorry about the whole thing, Peg," Blake said. "But it wasn't his fault. You know that."

"Do I?" she asked, but she actually sounded like she was being swayed.

That was enough for Luke. He pounded his fist on the door. "Peg, it's Luke Denton!"

"Shit," one of the brothers said.

"Let him in," Peg said calmly.

"We don't need—"

"Please open the door, Blake," Peg ordered.

A few moments later the door swung inward. Blake Carrera stepped backward, allowing Luke entry, his gaze hard. "What are you doing here, Denton?" he growled.

"Keeping the lines even," Luke said. He moved toward Peg, who was standing by the dining area in a pink bathrobe. Her cabin was the reverse of Andi's, but otherwise just the same. The Carreras were planted in the living room, looking for all the world as if they planned to stay. "What's going on here?"

"She invited us over," Brian said.

"Everything's fine, Luke," Peg said, but her face was pale. From the disease or from fear, Luke couldn't tell.

"Think I'll stick around just the same," Luke drawled. "You know Emma's in the hospital."

"What?" Peg asked.

"She fell down a flight of stairs."

Blake tipped up his hand in a drinking motion as Brian said, faintly smiling, "Clumsy of her."

Fury fired through Luke's blood. "Some people think she was pushed."

Beside him, Peg gasped.

"Ah, c'mon, Peg. This guy's just yanking all our chains," Blake said. His smile didn't quite reach his eyes.

"Did you push her?" she asked.

Luke glanced at her, arrested by her calm tone. She was looking at Blake.

He pointed both hands at his chest in a who-me? gesture.

Brian said, "She's a drinker, Peg. Don't listen to Denton. His partner tried to frame us and he damn well should be going to prison for it, but you know, you can't fight the cops."

"Did you push her?" she asked Blake again.

"Hell no." Blake's brows slammed together. "Fuck it, Brian. We're outta here."

"She said she wanted to sell," Brian responded evenly. "Was that a lie, Peg? Did you just want to get Blake over here so you could fuck?"

"Shut up," Luke snarled.

Peg took a step back into the kitchen and returned holding a gun.

"What the—?" Brian started.

"Whoa, whoa." Blake put his hands up.

Blam! Blam!

"Stop! Stop!" Luke yelled as both brothers scrambled for their lives. He saw Blake go down and Brian reach behind himself for a gun.

"Wait!" Luke screamed, scrabbling for his own sidearm as he threw himself toward Brian.

Blam!

Blam!

Luke fell into Brian with a thud and both men went down. Luke grabbed Brian's arm and smashed the gun from his hand. But Brian didn't resist. He looked at Luke with dazed eyes. "She shot me."

Luke leaped up, gun in hand. He kicked Brian's gun across the room. Blake was down. Eyes open. A bullet wound in the left side of his forehead. He whipped around and saw Peg still standing, the gun down at her side. It slipped from her fingers and clattered to the floor.

She whispered, "Did I kill him? Blake? Did I kill him?"

"Peg, come here." Luke put his arm around her and guided her to a kitchen chair. Brian was groaning on the floor. Darker color was staining the front of his dark sweatshirt. He'd been shot in the chest.

"I need to call nine-one-one," Luke told her.

"Yes." She looked down at her side. Blood was turning the pink bathrobe crimson.

"Oh, Peg." Luke reached for his phone, stabbing in the numbers.

"It was worth it, you know. They killed Ted and they were never going to pay for it. Your partner tried to get them, but he couldn't."

"Nine-one-one. What is the nature of your emergency?"

"The doctors told me I had six months on the outside," Peg went on. "I've about used that up, so I decided it was time to make them pay."

"There's been a shooting," Luke said, his voice catching. "Three people down."

Peg patted his arm. "It's going to be okay now. . . ."

                              * * *

"We would like you to move to the waiting room," the nurse said to Andi and Ben, who'd already been moved to the hall.

"What if she wakes up?" Ben asked. "I want to be here."

"I'll send the doctor on call to talk to you," she said firmly.

Andi and Ben went down to the main floor. They stood in the reception area for ten minutes, but no doctor arrived. "They're not going to let us back in there tonight," Ben said angrily.

"They might," Andi responded, but she was beginning to feel tired and was seriously considering going to Luke's apartment. She thought about calling him but decided to wait till she was on her way.

"Guess I'll go home for a while," Ben said. "Get something to eat. Nothing else to do around here." He pushed against the bar for one of the double glass doors. "You coming?"

"Might as well. I'll come back in the morning."

He nodded, then added, "You came with Denton, right?"

"Yes, but I can take Uber."

"I can give you a lift. You going back to the cabin?"

She looked at Ben. "I'm still deciding," she demurred.

"What's to decide?"

"I don't know."

They looked at each other for long moments. Andi's pulse began to pound, slow and hard. Ben had been nothing but loving toward his wife, but they just had his word that he'd taken the elevator and waited around for her, not knowing she'd used the stairs.

He said casually, "No one wants to hear what I think about the Carreras, but I don't think it's such a bad idea doing business with them. They've always made money."

"They skate around the law," Andi said.

"Everyone acts like they're criminals. What they are is businessmen who know how to run profitable businesses. I know you and Emma are against them, but Carter seems to think they're okay."

"They're not okay," she said, reaching for her phone.

"What are you doing?"

"Calling Uber."

"I said I'd give you a ride." His voice was rising with anger.

"I don't need one, thank you."

She walked away from him, down a covered walk that divided the parking lot. She saw him slap the air at her in a huff and stomp toward his car. Her Uber app told her a car would reach her in seven minutes. Good.

Her phone buzzed with an incoming text.

Ambulance here. Shootout. Peg and Carreras injured. Will call soon.

"Holy God." She stared at the screen in shock. She wanted to call him. Knew she should wait for his call.

"Hey," a male voice growled near her ear.

She jumped in fear. She hadn't heard him approach.

"Don't move or I'll shoot," he said in a gravelly voice she was sure was deliberately disguised. Something hard was pressed to the small of her back.

She wasn't going to be taken hostage. She would take the risk.

But he seemed to outguess her because as she jumped forward, half-expecting the shot, he took back the gun and slammed it against the side of her head. Pain exploded inside her skull. She staggered and went down on one knee and he dragged her to a nearby car. A dark Ford sedan. She twisted to try to see the license plate, but he had her in the passenger seat too fast.

He wore a hoodie, a ski mask, and gloves. His lips were curved in a cold smile.

"Won't be needing this," he said and yanked her cell from her hand, tossing it into the bushes. Andi flung herself upward and then she was hit with a bolt of electricity that made the world disappear for a few seconds.

Tased, she thought, when she could arrange her thoughts again.

He'd zip-tied her hands and feet, buckled her into the seat, then circled the car to the driver's seat.

She focused on what she could see of his face. The laughing mouth . . . those eyes . . .

Not Ben . . . *Carter* . . .

"Hello, little bird," he purred, then lifted her limp head so he could rim her lips possessively with his tongue.

Chapter Twenty-Five

She nearly retched.

Carter was behind all of it.

Her stomach turned inside out at the thought of his disgusting kiss, if that's what you could call it.

This can't be happening, Andi thought wildly, her body still shaking, her brain rattling in her skull as she twitched in the seat of the unfamiliar car, and he stood in the open doorway, light from the interior spilling into the darkened parking lot. He was in silhouette for a second as she glanced at him. Dear God, did he have an erection?

Another surge of nausea washed over her and she wished she could leap to her feet, kick him in his nuts, and turn his own weapon on him.

She found it nearly impossible to believe that he had orchestrated it all: the threats, the misdirections, the "accidents," and the cold-blooded murders.

Traitor. Killer. Freak. And pure, raw evil.

Pain surged through her. Her nerves didn't seem connected to her mind, her arms and legs trembling wildly within her bonds. She wanted to fight, to scream, but she couldn't get out words that made any sense. The world was spinning, her eyes unable to focus on anything.

Through the dirty windshield the sky collided with the ground, then spun. Still, she caught a glimpse of the eyes staring smugly from behind his mask. She'd trusted him. Thought of him as family. Never would have believed he was the mastermind behind the terror she'd come to know. Or was that just a lie she was telling herself now? She'd always kept him at arm's length, hadn't she? She'd sensed he wasn't completely on the up-and-up.

But a stone-cold murderer?

How had she missed it? And how could she escape and warn the world, turn the tables on this cruel, perverted bastard? She shivered, as much from fear as the effects of the Taser.

Help me. Please, God, someone help me.

She thought of Luke and his last strange, chilling message: shootout here.

Was he injured? Who had been shot? Why? Did it have anything to do with Carter? The images in her mind swam and ran together, but if she could only reach Luke . . . kiss him . . . touch him . . . love him . . .

She blinked. Realized she was fading out. But she refused to fall victim to the blackouts that had once snuck up on her. She blinked. Tried to focus. Luke would be all right. He had to be.

Pain made it impossible to struggle, her muscles refusing to obey her mind's commands. She attempted to break free, somehow escape, but her body was still twitching and jolting.

"Don't," he warned. "I *will* kill you. If you scream, or so much as utter a word, I swear to God, I'll pull the trigger."

She believed him, and yet words slipped out, shaking on her tongue. "Please, Carter, don't do this!"

"You need to shut the fuck up," he said conversationally and she stopped herself from pleading with him.

Fight! Don't worry about the gun. He's going to kill you

anyway, the way he murdered the others. You know it. You'll end up dead if you don't resist. But her body wouldn't respond and her head was pounding. *Come on, come on.* She tried to kick out, but her bound legs were rubbery and useless. Was there a security camera recording this, a guard even now watching the scene playing out in this night-shadowed parking area? *Oh please!*

"One bad move and I'll tase you again, little bitch. I know you talked to Rafferty, and that just wasn't smart. You'll have to pay for that."

She studied this man she'd known for so many years, a man, she realized now, she didn't know at all. *Why?* she wondered anxiously. *Why, why, why?*

Carter had obviously killed Trini and that woman found in the Columbia River and probably Greg and maybe Emma, his own damned siblings.

Her lips still were wet with the vile saliva from his tongue. Her stomach revolted. Desperately, she tried to think of a way to save herself, but getting out of the car would be hard, running or escaping impossible. Her phone was long gone and no one, not one soul, was around.

She couldn't let him get away with it. Gun or no gun.

She opened her mouth, intent on screaming, but just as she did he shoved a rag that smelled acrid and foul deep into her throat. She couldn't help the gag reflex that followed but fought the urge to throw up.

God help me.

Satisfied with his work, Carter slammed the door shut and hurried around the vehicle. Instead of getting inside immediately, he took the time to reach into the backseat and withdraw a jacket that he shrugged into, though he was still wearing his damned ski mask and hoodie beneath it.

She tried to focus on the inside of the car. Could she lock him out? Find a way to press the lock and . . . no. What about a weapon? Or getting out of the car? Staying in the vehicle, doing what he asked, was certain death.

But she was totally helpless, bound as she was.

Fear pounded in her brain. *Think, Andi, think! You have to save yourself.*

Ignoring the bad taste in her mouth, she leaned forward, intent on using the hand bound behind her back to locate the door handle, work the right buttons and somehow escape. Before she could even try the door, he slid inside the driver's seat, the interior light casting a dim glow before he jerked the door closed again and they were plunged into darkness once more. "Don't even think about it," he warned, then leaned over to buckle her in. Not for her safety, she realized, but to disable her further. As he reached across her, she considered biting him, trying to sink her teeth into his arm, but the gag prevented her, and with a *click,* the seat belt was engaged and she had less room to move.

"Time to go," he said with a smile in his voice and quickly started the engine. "Like my jacket?" He was preening, but a deadly weapon lay across his lap. "It's the same one Ben wears."

He was driving them out of the lot. Desperately, Andi tried to free herself, but she couldn't do it. "Don't you think we'll look good on camera? A lot of people saw you walk out with Ben. He's gonna have a lot to answer for."

You son of a bitch.

If she could just get free, or find a way to use a weapon and jump him. But right now it was impossible. Her heart sank and she told herself not to give up. Just wait. Be patient. He might just make a mistake.

Then again, he might not.

He hit the accelerator. The car lurched forward. Panicked, Andi tried vainly to struggle.

"You don't listen, Andi. It's one of your biggest problems.

Try anything and I'll fuckin' tase you. Did you hear it that time?" The gun was still on his lap.

She made gurgling sounds, and he abruptly pulled the car to the curb and in one quick motion opened the glove box, removed a roll of duct tape, and tore off a hunk with his teeth. "No more noise," he warned, yanking the rag from her mouth.

She gasped, drew in a fresh breath, and tried to struggle as he slapped the duct tape harshly over her lips, the very lips he'd licked.

Again her stomach heaved, but she held back the acid burning up her throat.

Leaning close, she felt his breath against her ear as he whispered, "I've waited so long for this. We have a game to play out," he said, and for a second his voice held a far-off quality, as if he were looking into the future.

Icy fear shot down Andi's spine. She leaned hard against the door and he caught the movement.

"Oh yes, there's a game, little bird, and you'll be an active player, but if you cross me, I'll kill you." His eyes found hers for a second.

Luke's pickup fishtailed into the hospital parking lot behind the ambulance carrying Peg Bellows. Two more emergency vehicles screamed into the lot, each carrying one of the Carerra brothers. Were they alive? Dead? Mortally wounded? He didn't give a damn about them, but Peg was a different story. He remembered the blood on her bathrobe, the calm in her eyes, as if she'd already given up.

He skidded to a stop near a light pole and cut the engine.

Two EMTs pulled Peg's stretcher from the back of the emergency vehicle and met with nurses and doctors in the receiving area of the ER. Luke glanced at them, then sprinted across the lot, catching up with the ambulance in the covered

ER receiving area. "Peg," he called as the rescue workers wheeled her in.

"Don't worry," she said around the oxygen mask. "I'll see you later."

Her final tone got to him. "You're going to be all right," he said, as much to convince himself as her. "You hang in there." He tried to reach for her hand where an IV was already pumping liquid into her body, but the EMT intervened.

"Get away, buddy," the burly red-haired responder warned before barking Peg's vital signs to a waiting nurse and doctor. He shouldered Luke out of the way.

"Wait."

"Not now," the arriving doctor said calmly. "We're taking her directly into surgery. OR two," he said to a waiting nurse. "We'll keep you informed."

"But . . ."

"You heard the doctor." The EMT was all business.

Luke went inside and tried to gain access from a woman behind a wide information desk. Prim and proper, she brooked no argument, and he found himself stymied by a wall of privacy, HIPAA regulations and mountains of red tape. It didn't matter that he'd phoned 9-1-1, he wasn't kin of the patient, and the staunch receptionist at the information desk told him she could release no information on a patient. Not that he blamed her.

The wide glass doors of the emergency wing flew open and the Carrera brothers were brought inside. Luke hung close to the doors and listened to the exchanges between doctors and the emergency medical techs long enough to reason out that both Carerra brothers were probably DOA. The medical staff just had to make it official.

He was soon ordered out of the intake area and couldn't get close to the information area again. He guessed any and all emergency personnel had been called to the scene because of the multiple victims, not to mention those sitting in chairs scattered around the waiting area. A twentysomething woman with stringy hair and a bad complexion was holding a crying baby while a pale two-year-old clung to her leg. Her husband or boyfriend leaned back in a chair too small for him and played some game on his phone. An older man and woman were seated near the windows; she was cradling one arm and staring vacantly into space. Now and again she winced, but she was trying hard not to show her pain. Her husband sat next to her, arms crossed over his expansive chest, lips tight in an unshaven jaw. Other various would-be patients and loved ones whose non-life-threatening injuries were forced to wait while the gunshot victims were either treated, operated on, or pronounced DOA.

Luke's guts churned when he considered Peg, but knew there was nothing more he could do to help her. Like the others in this drab, cavernous room with its outdated magazines, well-worn chairs, and piped-in music, he would just have to wait.

He decided he had time to find Andi. She was supposed to be here, probably in Emma's room or a nearby waiting area, so he texted her again. He hung out in the ER area for a couple of minutes and looked at his screen a dozen times. No answer. Had her phone died?

A bad feeling settled in his gut, but he told himself he was overreacting because of what he'd just been through. It looked like the Carrera brothers weren't about to hurt anyone ever again, certainly not today.

But what about Bobby? Robert Fisher? Who the hell was he?

Ignoring the "No Cell Phones" signs, he tried phoning her, but the call went directly to voice mail. "Come on, come on," he said before waiting for the recorded answer to finish and leaving a message. "Hey, I'm here at the hospital, too. Call me."

He decided to leave Emergency and find her. To hell with the phone.

When he reached Emma's room he found her alone, lying on the bed, an IV in one arm, monitors surrounding her, a few bruises visible on her face. No sign of Ben or Andi.

Emma stirred. "Ben?"

"It's Luke Denton, Emma. Ben was here earlier, and Andi, but they're not now . . ."

She faded out again and he waited half a minute before he was in motion again. Andi had said she would be here, or at his apartment, but she sure as hell wasn't answering her phone.

Luke scoured the waiting areas and the cafeteria, including the separate coffee shop, and had decided she'd already left. Did she catch a ride with Ben or did she take Uber?

He walked out to the main parking lot, searching for Ben's vehicle, though he wasn't exactly sure what it looked like. Every muscle in his body tense, he speed-dialed Andi's number once more and was surprised when he heard it ringing. What?

"Andi?" he called across the dark lot.

The phone kept ringing and he headed in the direction it was coming from. Maybe it wasn't her phone. Ringtones were often the same. But then her voice mail answered at the same time the phone stopped ringing. Heart pounding, he hit Redial. Sure enough, the phone began chirping again, and this time he jogged past the main area of the parking lot to a more secluded spot.

Once more the rings stopped suddenly. "Son of a bitch." He pounded the Redial button, and within seconds the ringtone, louder now, began trilling from a clump of vegetation, part of the hospital's minimalist landscaping. Digging through the vines, he located the phone. Andi's phone. His whole world stopped for a second as all of his worst fears were confirmed.

Something was wrong.

Very wrong.

Grasping Andi's phone, he jogged around the building to Emergency and his truck. Before he got there, his own phone jangled. He yanked it from his pocket and saw it was Detective Rafferty's number.

Oh. Jesus. *Andi!*

"Denton," he answered sharply. He reached his truck and braced himself as he fished into his pocket for his keys.

"It's Detective Rafferty. I heard you called nine-one-one to report a multiple shooting and that the victims are at Laurelton General."

"I'm here, too."

"I'm on my way, so stick around. You can fill me in."

"An officer showed up with the ambulances; I told him everything I know."

"But I have more questions. It won't take long. I'm at the offices of Wren Development and was stood up by Carter."

"What did you want to see Carter about?"

"Long story."

"I'm looking for Andi. Maybe she's with him?"

"He didn't say so. My partner and I had arranged to meet him, but he wasn't here when we arrived. The receptionist was here. She thought he might be at the hospital or the resort construction site."

"I haven't seen him here." Luke was starting to feel anxious. Where was Andi?

"Why were you meeting Carter?" he asked again as he slid into the interior of his pickup and jabbed his keys into the ignition.

"A separate case we're working on. Carter was one of the lake kids who went to North Shore Junior Camp when he was a teenager. My partner and I have been trying to identify human bones that were discovered in a home not far from the lake. We believe the bones belong to a boy who lived on Aurora Lane, Lance Patten, and Carter said he and his brother and sister all knew Lance."

She was filling him in more than he expected, probably because he'd been a cop and was working the case independently. A lot of connecting dots, and he didn't like where the link of those connected dots was leading. Warning bells began to peal through his head, sharp clangs that turned his heart to stone.

"Carter said he and his brother and sister knew two of the victims back then, Patten and another girl who initially appeared to have drowned in the lake, though later it was found that she'd actually been strangled."

Luke drew in a slow breath. *What were the chances? Bodies back then, when Carter was a teenager, and now bodies of women with names of birds, some in water.*

The summer camp . . . He'd driven by it so many times. Knew it had been a place where the rich kids from Schultz Lake spent their summer vacations.

"I'll look for Carter," Luke told her. "Andi's probably with him."

"Look, Denton, I've probably said more than I should, but I haven't gone into everything. Might be best if you leave meeting with Carter Wren to us."

Fat chance. "I'll take that under advisement."

"Seriously, Denton. This is a police matter."

And I used to be the police.

"All right," he said, not meaning a word of it. He clicked off and peeled out of the parking lot.

Rafferty and her partner were working on a separate case that traced back to the Wrens. What were the chances?

Finch. Meadowlark. Wren.

His jaw tightened and he squinted into the oncoming

headlights. Traffic wasn't that heavy because rush hour was over, but he still passed a van decorated in yellow and green piping and proudly boasting University of Oregon stickers on its window and license plate. He drove another two miles and was trapped by an ancient VW that could barely chug up the hill at thirty.

His mind was on the recent killings. The women, all with names of birds who had been murdered. He downshifted and passed the Volkswagen in seconds. His truck's engine protested as his headlights cleaved the dark night. His gaze flicked to the spot where Gregory Wren had driven, or been forced, off the road.

Had that just been an accident? Who would benefit from Gregory Wren's death?

The Carreras might have, if Carter had anything to say about it . . .

"Carter."

Luke thought about that hard. His heart squeezed. If Andi was with Carter, what did that mean?

To hell with the two female detectives. If Carter knew anything, Luke was going to get it out of him first. Though he trusted the detectives to do their job, he didn't have time to wait through all the bullshit protocol. Luke was going to head to the lodge construction site first and meet up with Carter.

And if you're wrong . . . and Carter doesn't know where Andi is . . . and that bastard Robert Fisher, whoever he is, has her?

Luke pressed his toe to the accelerator, his jaw locked in concentration.

Gagged and bound, Andi watched through the windshield as Carter drove to another cabin by the lake. His cabin, she realized, as the beams of the older Ford's headlights reflected back from paned windows. Like her cabin, and a lot of others around Schultz Lake, the structure was set back from the road and hidden from the road by a wide swath of trees, but the rear end of the cabin opened to the cold waters of Shultz Lake.

"This is where the fun begins." He said it with such anticipation that she visibly shivered and her insides went numb.

During the drive her body had recovered slightly from the tasing. Her brain was clearer, and when she told her head to turn in a certain direction, she was able to. But she kept still, not wanting him to know she was gaining control of her muscles. Faking her infirmity might be her only weapon in a very slim arsenal.

Keep your wits about you. Be smart. Keep cool.

He climbed out of the car, threw off the jacket and left it on the ground, then came around to the passenger side. He'd pulled off his ski mask on the drive and now he dragged her from the car, propping her up to stand, but she dropped to the earthy-smelling ground.

"Get up!" he demanded, and she made gurgling noises behind the gag.

He pulled a knife from his pocket and put it close to her face. But then he smiled and bent down to slice the ties binding her ankles. Then he yanked her to her feet, keeping her hands bound, and half-dragged her up the two steps to the front door. It was open and he threw her inside as he flipped a switch near the door. Several lamps flickered on. The furnishings were modern and bare. A bookcase holding a flat-screen and video equipment dominated the space in front of an L-shaped leather couch.

Carter pulled a small remote from his pocket and clicked it. The wall shifted, opening to a narrow hallway. "This way," he said, grabbing her by her bound wrists and hauling her to her feet. He pushed her through the opening, along the short hallway and to another windowless room where a chair was placed squarely in its center.

Andi's heart filled with ice as she looked around the room. The perimeter was lined with several computers, two large televisions screens, a chessboard set up on a small table, and a bookshelf filled with books on puzzles, mysteries, and magic. There wasn't a speck of dust anywhere and fresh air somehow was vented inside, though the room had a deadened quality to it. She knew without being told she could scream forever and never be heard.

Andi swallowed hard. A digital clock glowed a warning red. It had been nearly an hour since she'd been abducted.

"Now, sit," he ordered, using his pistol to point to the austere ladder-back chair in the middle of the floor. She took a step that way and fell, as if her legs had given way. She didn't have to fake the trembling. She was frightened enough that her shaking was visible.

"Get up!"

She struggled into the chair and he strapped her into it, tying her with a thin, wiry cord that cut into her arms.

"You know, Andi, I've always found you attractive," he said. He glanced up from tying her ankles to each chair leg and found her eyes. "You were always too good for Greg. You should have known it wouldn't work. The bastard couldn't even get you pregnant, but he sure could Mimi. Yep, she was pregnant. I checked, and I was going to have to do something about it, but then she took care of things herself."

Finished securing her, Carter straightened and ran cool fingers along the line of her jaw. Her revulsion almost made her shrink away, but she didn't.

He walked to the front of the chair so that his crotch was only inches from her face and the bulge straining his pants was visible. He was getting off on this.

"Gregory. What made you choose him? He never had

any vision. He was a drone, working just like our father wanted him to. A drudge. I was always the one with the intelligence."

The gun. Watch where he puts the gun . . .

"And yet you fell for Greg, and now that ex-*cop*? You like 'em big and dumb? Is that it?" He shook his head, the small smile on his lips full of self-importance. "I guess it's only fair to tell you that Greg didn't really sleep around. Yes, there was Mimi. I worked to get that affair started. But there really weren't any others. Greg wasn't a player. I just told you that to keep the game going, fan the fires to keep you confused and misdirected. All part of the game."

"Want to know what it's called?"

Of course she couldn't answer.

"I named it: Cover up your misdeeds and get all the inheritance for yourself. Y'see, dead old Dad didn't trust me with the company. Thought Greg was a better shepherd of the Wren inheritance. I knew I had to get rid of Greg eventually," he admitted, slipping his gun into his belt. "He was a liability. That's why the Carreras took care of it for me."

Andi started, unable to hide her surprise.

"Oh, you didn't know that, did you? You thought it was an accident. Greg, driving away from Mimi's, in a confused state over his love for two women. . . ." Carter chuckled. "He didn't have that much emotion. He was a robot. But he did discover I'd helped myself to some company money without asking . . ."

Andi's brain burned with rage. The horror of what he was saying added fuel to the fire of her fury. Greg may not have been the perfect husband, but he hadn't deserved to be murdered. Her hands clenched and she forced them to straighten so she wouldn't give herself away.

"Of course Greg was only half of the problem; there was Emma, too."

Andi flashed to Emma's unlikely fall down the stairs, when she'd been stone-cold sober. And she thought of her lying in the hospital bed, broken and pumped up on pain pills.

"I was willing to wait, but the Carrera boys, they're impatient. Brian just gave her a little push this morning. He let me know ahead of time that he'd planned to take care of her today. Of course, he thought she'd be shit-faced drunk as usual. Who knew she'd choose today to sober up? But that's all part of the game, isn't it? Surprise."

When he looked down at the chessboard, she tested her bonds. They were tight, digging into her ankles and shoulders, her hands still tied together behind her, her arms aching. But they had feeling now, and she could command them to do her bidding.

Patience. Outwait him.

"So now we come down to you, my beautiful little bird. What am I going to do with you?"

Chapter Twenty-Six

Carter wasn't at the lodge. Luke had tried phoning both him and Ben. Ben had returned to the hospital and Emma; he'd spoken to both of them, and they'd been alarmed when he'd said Andi was missing. And then Emma had asked in a frightened voice if Andi was with Carter. His blood chilling, he'd asked her what she meant, but all she'd said was that she wanted him to find Andi soon.

Carter's phone kept going to voice mail, so after a while Luke stopped calling. He knew Carter's address, as he knew Emma and Ben's. He'd made a point of acquainting himself with Andi's family, more in case he needed to reach them for any reason, but now . . .

Something was off with Carter. Emma knew something, or thought she knew something, and that was good enough for him.

There was a reason Andi's phone was in the bushes and he was starting to fear that reason was Carter Wren.

Carter was watching Andi like a snake with a mouse.

"How am I going to come up with your demise?" he asked her conversationally. "There are just too many deaths right now, too many accidents, too much suspicion. As stupid and ineffective as the police are, they do have their means, don't they? With computers and sharing records, DNA testing, and all that forensic crap of trace evidence and the like, I have to be more careful than before.

"I miss the pre-DNA days, before iPhone cameras and microphones on every damned civilian. That's why I bought the car for cash from an illegal."

Andi watched him warily, and, when he wasn't looking, searching for a weapon or a means of escape. There had to be some way to trip him up, some way to get the upper hand.

"So, now what I need is misdirection," he said, warming to his subject. "A little sleight of hand. That's what the bird thing was all about. You were a Wren and your bestest friend was a Finch. I started this campaign long ago. Way before Greg's death. I had to plan many steps ahead. That's how you play chess, you know; plan moves way in advance of the one you're making."

She tried surreptitiously working her wrists, moving them just the slightest, trying to stretch the ties. She set her jaw, put all her concentration into forcing her hands apart.

For now, he didn't notice and kept right on talking. "Then it was simply a matter of finding other people with last names that were birds. Women I could manipulate. Not that it was easy. It had to be women, an added benefit to the game for my own personal enjoyment." He looked at Andi slyly, then walked toward the stack of board games.

Andi pulled harder at her restraints. They didn't budge. As for a weapon, the only thing she saw was a tiny screwdriver small enough to be used on a computer, left out by a stack of video games. But there was the bookcase itself, if she could find a way to topple it. Unless it was bolted to the wall, she could possibly maim or even kill him, should the heavy electronic equipment hit him just right. The gamesman killed by his own games. Or she could grab the gun and fire it in this tiny space, damning where the bullets ricocheted.

"—Belinda Meadowlark was easy," he was saying. "She was so damned hot for me, wanted it so bad she was practically panting for me when I tossed her off the ferry into the water." He licked his lips, his tongue flicking against his skin, and again his erection was hardening under his pants.

"Trini didn't know me, so she was easy. I couldn't take the chance she'd see some resemblance between me and Greg, so I always wore a disguise. She thought it was funny. Actually worked in my favor."

Carter grabbed another chair and dragged it over in front of her. He sat down and leaned forward, close enough to her that his breath ruffled her hair. "I was always worried she might go scrolling through your wedding pictures, though, and make the connection, but she really didn't like Greg much, so she had no interest in your wedding."

Oh Trini. I'm so sorry. . . . Andi's throat was hot with unshed tears.

Carter went on. "I pretended to fall for her, and because she was such a promiscuous slut it was easy to start a relationship. Too easy." He grinned, a leering, smug, king-of-the-world grin. "Poor little bird. She had a shellfish allergy. I pretended I had one, too. I really planned to sneak some shrimp into her diet somehow, but then I found out about cricket flour, that it's in the same family as shellfish. It was perfect. You should have seen the way her eyes bulged as her throat was closing. She choked to death knowing I wanted to kill her far more than I ever wanted to fuck her."

Andi couldn't stop the gasp of horror from behind her gag. Again she worked the plastic ties at her wrists. Had they given a little? Stretched? Oh please!

"And then *your* brother left his wallet at the scene of the crime!" He chortled and shook his head. "I'm telling you, it was perfect. Perfect! The best kind of surprise."

He threw his head back and roared with laughter. "I took away Trini's cell phone and dropped it into the lake miles from here. There were just too many calls to my cell phone on it. Of course, I gave her the number for one of those disposable phones, not my real cell, and supposedly untraceable, but I wasn't going to take any chances. A good player knows all the risks."

He tilted his head to one side, as if he were really thinking things through. "It did get harder and harder to find women with names of birds. There was the first one in eastern Oregon, Nightingale, and then Meadowlark, then Finch, then Tern . . . those last two were close together because you, my dear, were becoming a problem. You and that dumb cop. I followed you around, both of you. I knew we were heading to the endgame."

Andi was sweating, though the temperature in the room wasn't all that warm. She was still working her wrists, but the zip ties weren't giving a quarter of a damned inch. She glanced at the digital clock and saw that they had been locked in this tiny room twenty minutes already. Would Luke be looking for her? Surely he'd realized by now that she was missing. It was now well over an hour since she'd first been abducted. She bit her lip and Carter caught the movement.

"What's the matter, little bird? Worried? Maybe you'd like a pill for what's ailing you."

Andi gazed at him in confusion.

"You know those pills, the ones your guru shrink prescribed?" He waited, letting her wonder. "Pretty strong, weren't they? Those blackouts? I switched 'em out. I had a friend get me a key, and when you weren't home,

I sneaked into your house and looked around and found your pill bottle."

Luke had been right about the size of the pills, Andi realized. She couldn't believe the depths Carter had gone to.

"No one was picking up on my bird killings, so I decided to start leaving you notes. I had a key to your cabin, but I had to cover my tracks, so I faked the break-in. I couldn't take a chance that someone might start questioning how someone got in and left the message for you."

Behind her gag, her mouth was dry, the damned ties holding far too fast, and she had to fight to keep her spirits from flagging.

"So, now you see, it's your turn to play the game."

She watched as he set his firearm on the table, directly in front of her but completely out of reach. He was toying with her. He knew she was aware of his weapon, that she was watching it.

"I like you, Andi. I'm kind of fascinated with you and I'd love to fuck you. You'd find it pleasurable. I'm good in bed. Very good. I could really get you going."

No way in hell.

"But the most important part of this game is that I need control of the company. *My* company finances. Brian may have bungled his job today. Emma might not die immediately, but it's only a matter of time. Like Greg, she has to go."

Andi noted another fifteen minutes had passed and the ties, though giving a bit, were also cutting into her wrists.

"The beauty of it is, my darling sister has made me her beneficiary."

Andi must've changed facial expressions because Carter's eyes glinted. "News to you, isn't it? After we learned Greg had left his shares to you, Em and I made a pact to leave ours to each other. No Ben. No one else. No one else," he repeated, looking at her. "Who's your beneficiary, Andi? Oh, that's right. It's Greg. You never changed it after his death. And since he's gone, the shares go back to the company.

"Everything's in place, except you talked to Detective Rafferty. You and Denton. And she's sniffing around what happened to that suck-up junkie, Lance Patten, and probably Wendy, too.

"You don't know about them. Wendy was my first real kill." He glanced away to the middle distance, remembering, she guessed by the satisfied grin that curved his lips. "My old man had insisted I go to that goddamned summer camp. North Lake Junior Camp. I was determined to buy that piece of property even though Greg thought it was too much money, but I won that battle. Can't wait to tear down every board. Dad had some stupid notion it would be good for me to go there. I had no choice back then but to play along, so I decided I'd play by my own rules. I snuck out every night by canoe." He sighed through his nose. "Wendy was white trash. Pretty. Nice body, but white trash. I would take her out, fuck her beneath one of the willows, then sneak her back to her pathetic family on Aurora Lane. Wendy was hot for me. Too hot, as it turned out. She had the gall to keep showing up at the most inopportune times. She had no damned filter and no sense. I made her pretend we didn't know each other, but she didn't like it one bit. Had big romantic dreams. Fantasies. Thought I could be her white knight and save her from the poverty of her life."

He made a face to show how ridiculous Wendy's romantic notions were.

"I had to kill her. The last time she walked across the fields to the lake, I met her at one of the other cabins that was empty that weekend. While we were doing it, really going at it, I wrapped the willow branch around her neck and just kept tightening it. Best climax I ever had. Her face all mottled and red, her hands scratching wildly at me. After that, I never looked back. But Lance . . . he wanted what I wanted, except he didn't have the imagination. He got hooked up with a cougar on Aurora Lane, a really feisty older woman, but she wouldn't look at him after one night with me. Lance and I shared her for a while, but she wasn't good at keeping secrets. Couldn't keep her trap shut. I got lucky on that one, though. Somebody else took care of her, so all the talk about me and Lance dried up."

Andi couldn't believe the depth of his depravity. She swallowed hard and worked the ties, making slow headway. She had to keep him talking because as soon as he stopped talking about the past, he would get to the present.

And to her.

"Then Lance started getting cold feet. He knew about Wendy. He'd suspected I'd killed her and kept asking about her. Finally I told him the truth. He just stared at me, and then he tried to run away. I grabbed him and held him underwater. And then I buried him in the abandoned cabin next to my parents'.

"Except . . . the cabin wasn't abandoned forever. I knew I had to put him somewhere permanently. He'd told me about finding bones in this family's basement on Aurora Lane, the family with the hot cougar. Swore they were human. I didn't care if they were or not. I decided to add Lance to the pile. I dug him up and carried what was left of him to their house. Broke open a basement window and tossed him in. Like I said, the game always has surprises."

He suddenly grabbed her by the chin. "So now, Andi, I have another game. One more in my repertoire, and this time guess who gets to play?"

She didn't have to.

"That's right. Finally it's your turn."

She glanced at the clock. Nearly two hours had passed. Certainly someone would be looking for her.

He reached into his pocket again and withdrew his knife. Andi couldn't help herself. She shrank back as he looked at the blade catching light from the fluorescent bulbs. Slowly he slid the blade down the length of her cheek.

"Want to play a game, little girl?" he whispered in her ear, his breath hot and wet. "Want to know how you're going to die?"

Her heart thumped hard and painful.

"I brought you to the lake for a reason. A purpose. Like the others, you'll die in water. Like Belinda and Christine and Wendy and Lance. Although I pride myself on changing my modus operandi, keeping everyone guessing, I prefer the water."

Andi tried and failed to swallow back her fear. He was serious. He was going to kill her. Soon. Here. In the lake.

He let the blade travel lower, along her neck, past her carotid, sliding between her breasts. "It's no fun if you can't play, too. So if you can figure out how to escape, maybe you won't die tonight, you'll gain your freedom," he said hoarsely. She could tell he was turning himself on. "But . . . I wouldn't bet on it." He looked up at her, his tongue showing between his teeth. "Then you're mine."

Egomaniacal psycho!

She set her jaw and pulled at her wrists as his face followed the path of his knife, steamy breath blowing on her breasts and abdomen and crotch. The blade lingered at the juncture of her legs, and then, when she thought she might cry out, he moved quickly, slicing downward, cutting through her shackles.

An instant later he made short work of her manacles as well, and then, to her surprise, he pulled the duct tape from her mouth, ripping some skin, leaving some glue.

She grunted with pain, then shot to her feet. She whirled and kicked him hard but missed his crotch, her blow landing on his thigh.

"Bitch!" He hadn't expected her to be ready.

She lunged for the gun, but he was quick, beat her to it. Whirling, she threw herself at the door. If she could just get outside, into the darkness, she might be able to run, to get away. Her reflexes were sluggish, but her muscles were working again, her brain on fire.

One step. Two. The space between the fake bookshelf and wall, the opening was just a leap away. She sprang.

"Wrong move," he singsonged. Strong arms wrapped around her waist and dragged her down.

She fought, kicking and scratching, raining blow after blow upon him, but he was too strong, so much bigger, and when she smelled the malodorous stench again on the rag he was bringing toward her, she realized she was doomed.

"Ether," he crowed, smashing the rag over her face. "Old school."

She struggled wildly, but the chemical overtook her. The last thing she remembered was him hauling her off her feet and carrying her outside to his car, the one he'd bought for cash.

Luke passed a car coming from the direction of Carter's cabin. He watched its taillights in his rearview mirror, the red lights disappearing in the deep night. Had that been Andi in the passenger seat? The driver had been looking down as he passed, almost as if he'd been trying to hide his face.

Was it Carter? *Was it?* God! He was pretty sure it was.

He turned around and followed, trying to keep back far enough to stay off his radar. They were on a trajectory toward the lodge. Luke decided to stay well back and park away from the construction site so he wouldn't be seen.

Ten minutes later he was there. He killed the engine, then jogged toward the lodge, but there was no other vehicle there.

Where had he gone?

He heard the faint sound of an engine to the east and turned in that direction.

The summer camp.

Immediately he was racing back to his truck. He switched on the engine and the damn thing coughed and acted like it wasn't going to catch, but then it did. Breathing a sigh of relief, he sped down the two-lane road to the entrance to the summer camp, damn near missing it . . . except for the flattened grass he caught in his headlights.

He bumped along the rutted lane. He didn't care if Carter knew he was coming.

His headlights trapped another car in their beams, parked to one side not far from the water's edge. Broken pieces of wood from the ruined cabins lay scattered about, along with a row of forgotten canoes. Where one had been the ground was dry, even though a misting rain had started.

Luke leaped out of the car, leaving his keys in the ignition. The parked Ford was the one he'd passed on the road. It was Carter's. And Andi was with him.

He dragged out one of the canoes. In the headlights from his car he saw it had holes in the bottom. He anxiously reached for another. The second one looked good and he hurriedly pulled it out. He switched off the lights to the truck, then hauled it down to the water's edge. He faintly heard the oars of a canoe dipping hurriedly in the water.

Carter was on the water and he knew Luke was coming.

"You son of a bitch," he growled beneath his breath.

Then he was in the canoe, rowing for all he was worth.

PART IV

———◆———

CHECKMATE

Chapter Twenty-Seven

The rhythmic, rapid slap of a paddle in the water sent rage running through Carter's veins. He'd seen the headlights. Denton.

"Goddamn it." He'd known that was Denton's truck on the road.

There was no time. He couldn't have Andi the way he wanted her. The game wouldn't be what he wanted.

It wasn't supposed to be this way!

There was nothing he could do to save the moment. He looked down at the unconscious woman and gritted his teeth.

Then he leaned over her and rimmed her lips with his tongue. "Good-bye, lovely bird. . . ."

He pulled her up by the shoulders and he struggled a bit, but then she toppled into the dark water.

Luke heard the heavy splash into the water.

Andi!

He threw himself into paddling. He couldn't see through the dark and the rain, but he knew it was Carter . . . and he knew Carter had thrown Andi into the water.

If he's hurt her . . . if she's . . .

He clamped his mind shut and ground his teeth together. He could hear the other canoe paddling furiously away, but he was focused on the spot he'd seen her go under.

Oh Andi . . . please, please . . .

Ripples were reaching him. Ten feet from where he believed Carter had tossed her out, he dove into the water, down and forward. Eyes open, he could see nothing in the cold, black water.

He breaststroked forward underwater.

Andi . . . Andi . . . Andi . . .

His hand touched something.

Hair.

He surged forward and grabbed her by the hair, pulling upward. He surfaced and pulled up with all his strength, snagging part of her collar, then her arm, yanking her head above the surface. How long had it been? A minute? Two? *Three?*

He gasped for air, wrapping his arms around her chest, holding her face upward. She wasn't breathing. Treading water, he squeezed his arm hard around her and released, did it again. God. Where was the canoe?

He whipped his head around. It was there. Ten feet away but drifting away from him.

He swam with one arm toward the canoe. It felt like forever but was probably only seconds. It took all his strength to drag her upward, tumble her inside. When he tried to scramble inside the canoe tipped precariously. He threw himself in, smacked his lip and rammed his funny bone, his knee hitting the blade of the other oar, which popped up enough to ram the fingers on his left hand, but he scarcely noticed.

Andi was crumpled on her side and he turned her on her back. Immediately he began CPR, pressing her chest rhythmically, praying hard inside his mind.

"Andi . . . Andi . . ." He didn't realize he was saying her name.

His thoughts touched on Carter, but he yanked them back to the present. He would find the man and kill him if he had to. He didn't give a damn. If Andi didn't make it . . .

His mind shut down.

The rain pummeled him. He realized distantly that he was cold, that she was cold, too. He had to get them out of there . . . had to get to shore . . .

Her chest buckled. A harsh cough. A flood of water out of her mouth.

Luke quickly lifted her shoulder, turning her onto her side, joy singing through him.

"Andi! Andi . . ."

She coughed and gasped. He leaned over her, blocking the rain. She blinked her eyes and they opened dully. Her lower jaw started quivering.

"Andi, it's Luke. You went in the lake. We're in a canoe. Gotta get back to shore."

"Luke . . . ?"

"Yes, darling, it's me." He felt the burn of emotion.

"Luke, Carter . . ."

"He's gone. We're getting back to shore now." He stripped off his soaking jacket and lay it over her. Better another layer, even if it was a wet one.

He pulled out the oar and started paddling, seeing Andi's white face in the bottom of the canoe.

"Jesus," he muttered through his own chattering teeth.

By the time the canoe bumped the shore he was shaking all over. His mind was filled with black fury.

"We've got to get to my truck," he whispered in Andi's ear.

"Yes . . ."

She leaned upward, and somehow they wrangled out of the canoe. Luke half-carried her to the truck, where the keys were still in the ignition, his cell phone in the cup holder where he'd left it.

Carter had been heading north, in the direction of the Wren construction site.

He picked up the phone to call Detective Rafferty.

Fucking Denton, Carter fumed inwardly, dragging the canoe up the bank in the rain. He knew it was that fucking investigator following him onto the lake. Luckily, he'd dumped Andi and gotten away. Did Denton know it was him? How could he . . . except that Andi had talked to Detective Rafferty and he was probably there at the time, so Denton would know he was supposed to meet her and had blown her off.

He needed to meet with the goddamn detective. He should call her . . . say he went to the hospital. Explain how urgent it was to see Emma.

But now he couldn't go back to the summer camp just yet, even though his car was there. Denton had launched a canoe from the same area. He had to find a way to get back there without being seen, but he didn't trust the water, so that meant thrashing through the brush, which would take forever, or following the road, which was what he planned to do. There would be traffic, but he could stay just off the pavement and duck down whenever a car went by. There was more than enough cover for him to make it without being seen.

But Jesus . . . *fucking* Denton!

He trudged up the last thirty feet toward the lodge and pulled out his phone.

You can meet her here, he realized. *Tell her you meant to meet her at the site. Then go get your car.*

Except what if Denton's waiting for you at the camp . . .

That's what the Taser was for.

Carter scrambled up the last wet incline, his feet slipping a bit in the mud, and reached the west side of the lodge. The second story was still a skeleton of framing reaching for the sky, but the main floor's walls were enclosed by siding. Luckily, there were no doors yet, so he slipped through an open side doorway and made his way to the grand entry.

A woman was standing in the open foyer holding a flashlight.

He stopped short and the flashlight beam swung his way.

"Carter Wren?" she asked.

"Detective Rafferty?" he asked in return, adrenaline zipping through his veins. He generally loved the heightened feeling of danger, but he had to be careful here. Play the game for all it was worth. "What are you doing here?"

"Meeting you," she said in a cool tone that instantly infuriated him. The bitch thought she was in control.

"We were supposed to meet at the office," he reminded her just as coolly. "I was about to head there now. I wanted to check things out here because we've had some problems with vagrants."

"Really."

"Yes, really, Detective. And my sister's in the hospital, so we need to make this short. I told you everything I know about Lance. If only Greg had lived. They were the ones who were friends."

"What if I told you I don't believe you?"

He laughed. "What is this, some kind of shakedown?" He spread his hands, thinking about the Taser in his pocket.

"I guess it is," she said thoughtfully. "You killed Lance Patten, buried him, then moved him to the Singletons' basement. You strangled Wendy Kirkendall with a willow branch and threw her into Schultz Lake. You coerced or forced Trinidad Finch into eating an energy bar made with cricket flour because you knew of her severe allergy to shellfish. You tased Christine Tern, dragged her to the Columbia River, and threw her in. And you tossed Belinda Meadowlark over the rail of a Washington State ferry. You've been playing a killing game for a long time and you've targeted Andrea Wren as your next victim."

Carter was numb with shock. She didn't know all his moves, but she sure as hell knew a lot of them. "I don't know what you're talking about."

"I think you do."

Carter assessed his next move. Slowly, he slid his hand toward his pocket. He suspected she had a gun, but he could be on her in a flash. And from what he could tell, she looked tasty. Young, trim, smart. His cock stirred at the thought. He hadn't gotten to have Andi, but this female *detective* was ripe for the picking.

"Keep your hands where I can see them," she said sharply.

"You've got me all wrong." His fingers were inside the flap of his jacket pocket.

"Stop."

No time to waste. He rushed her.

"Fucking stop right there!" another female voice rang out from the shadows. He turned and saw the muzzle of a gun staring him in the face. "Game over, asshole," she snarled.

For a moment he almost ran, but then he calmed himself down and raised his hands. *It's never over. They don't have anything on me. I'm too smart for them. Like brilliant, untouchable, reclusive Bobby Fischer, the youngest International Grandmaster of chess at age fifteen. The best chess player of all time. And Bobby disappeared for years and years. I'll get off, and then I can, too. I'm just that smart.*

Epilogue

Luke sat on a bar stool at Tiny Tim's nursing a beer. Andi was beside him, twirling the stem on the glass of chardonnay she wasn't really drinking. She'd recovered from the near drowning, but she was still feeling scared. She knew Carter had been taken into custody, but it didn't erase the fear.

Luke's pals from the Portland PD, Amberson, Yates, and DeSantos, had gathered at the bar to send off the Carrera brothers to the great hereafter. It certainly wasn't a sad occasion, but it wasn't really a joyous one either. After all, Peg Bellows had been a victim of the shootout at her cabin.

Ray Bolchoy was there, too, quietly sitting in a corner, sporting an ironic smile. Luke had said he was actually jumping for joy. That was just Ray's style.

"It's not the ending I wanted," Luke was saying, referring to Peg Bellows's death. "And I actually would have loved facing the Carreras across a courtroom for their misdeeds."

"Rule number sixty-seven," Bolchoy said loudly. "No crying over a dead Carrera."

They all looked at him and his smile grew wider. "Not really a rule, but it should be," he admitted.

"Come back to the force," Opal said to Luke. She was tall, black, and commanding.

"I heard there're cutbacks," he responded, finishing his beer.

"They'll find a way to fit you in." She looked over at Andi and said, "Talk him into it."

"I'm doing work for my brother," he told Opal. "I kind of like being my own boss."

"You're gonna work for the defense? That'll curl Iris's hair."

Luke shrugged and smiled. He'd told Andi about his ex, and then Iris had phoned him after their interview with Pauline Kirby aired earlier that week. Luke hadn't wanted to do it, but Andi had been the one who wanted to tell her story about Carter to the world.

The newswoman had also done a segment with Detectives Rafferty and Sandler, and the overall piece had painted the Carreras as the nasty dogs in the manger they were.

An hour later they said good-bye to his pals and headed to her cabin. Luke was already half moved in; they were going to make their living arrangement permanent. Neither of them had spoken of marriage; it was too soon. But there was a subject Andi needed to talk to him about.

As Luke pulled her car up next to his in the driveway, she said, making conversation, screwing up her courage, "I'm glad Emma's going to be okay."

"If the Carreras had lived, she could have testified against Brian because she saw him."

They both climbed out of the car and walked through a misting rain to her cabin door. The willow wreath was still there, and Andi touched it softly. She swallowed and said, as they crossed the threshold, "You know what I said about not needing condoms?" His head whipped around in surprise and she added quickly, "No, not that. I'm not pregnant. I just want you to know that my pregnancy with Greg was an anomaly. It's unlikely it will ever happen again. I've been through IVF and testing and you name it, and then I lost his baby, too. What I'm saying is, no matter what happens in the future between us, that's the reality of my life."

He nodded slowly. "Okay."

They walked inside the cabin together, but Andi couldn't leave it there. "Okay? What does that mean?"

"It means I love you, Andi. I almost lost you, and that about killed me. I never want that to happen again. I'd like to have children, sure. Maybe we can, maybe we can't. But I'm not running out on you just because it might not ever happen."

She smiled. "Okay."

He regarded her steadily. "But I see your point. Maybe we don't need condoms. Maybe we just roll the dice and see what happens."

"Are you ready for that? I mean, if by some miracle it did happen?"

"Yes, ma'am."

She felt tears star her lashes. "Okay, then."

"Okay, then."

She glanced toward the bedroom, then back at Luke. For the briefest moment he was still, then he started ripping off his shirt and racewalking to the bedroom.

She was right on his heels.

"Caught you and Gretchen on television," Wes Pelligree said to September as she walked into the squad room.

"Luke Denton and Andrea Wren were interviewed, too," September protested. They teased her mercilessly about being the media darling of the department.

George swiveled in his chair. "Yeah, but Pauline Kirby

just loves you," he said. This time there was no edge to his voice. D'Annibal had called George into his office, and although she and the rest of the detectives suspected George had been reprimanded for spending too much time inside, he'd fingered Trinidad Finch's killer and helped solve the case with his research.

"How's your mom?" September asked Wes. He'd come back to work the last few days, but the situation with his mother's health was ever-changing.

"Believe it or not, great."

"Great?"

Wes spread his hands and smiled in relief. "One moment they're telling me she's unlikely to make it through the night, the next she's awake and on the road to recovery. I'm still getting used to the idea."

"I'm so glad," she said, meaning it.

"Thanks."

"It's your turn in D'Annibal's office today, Nine, right?" George asked her.

"Sure is," September answered.

All the detectives had been asked for a one-on-one in the lieutenant's office in order of the date they were hired. September was the last. She hoped her interview with Pauline Kirby didn't work against her, but it hadn't for Gretchen, who'd been right beside her. With the dental records proving Lance Patten was indeed the other victim in the Singletons' basement, and Andrea Wren's recount of what Carter told her when she was captured, the Aurora Lane case was about wrapped up as well. September and Gretchen were currently working to unravel a number of unsolved homicides that may have been Carter's doing as well. Gretchen was driving to eastern Oregon on a possible bird murder before Belinda Meadowlark's. Carter had begun his last game even before Gregory Wren's death, already planning a sick joyride of innocent victims, with Andrea Wren as the ultimate "little bird."

"Detective Rafferty?"

Lieutenant D'Annibal stuck his head out of his glass office, the walls of which were curtained. Most times the detectives could see into it because the lieutenant liked transparency in his working relations with his squad. But this week had been different. Even though he'd praised them all for solving the slew of cold cases wrought by Wren, the department's continuing financial crisis was taking a good amount of his time.

September glanced down at her engagement ring. As soon as Wren was captured, she'd gone home to Jake and said, "Let's get married tomorrow."

"Sure," he'd answered.

"I'm kidding, you know." She'd had a panicked moment that he'd taken her seriously. "But I'm ready."

He'd kissed her. "How about next spring?"

"April?"

"You don't want a June wedding?" he asked.

"Tomorrow's too soon, but I don't want to wait that long."

"April it is." And he'd kissed her and she'd felt complete. To hell with the Singletons' hateful marriage. She'd been influenced by how terrible their union must have been, and the state of her own dysfunctional family always made her wonder how long-lasting any relationship could be, but there was no way of knowing unless she tried.

"Take a seat," D'Annibal invited. As September did so, she noticed he remained standing. In fact, he walked to the exterior window and looked out. "You're a good detective. A terrier. You don't get sidetracked or categorize one case as better than another. You do fieldwork without complaint, and you rarely miss work."

September went cold inside. "But . . . ?"

"But you're the newest detective on staff and we have to cut one."

"And it's going to be me," she realized.

"Hopefully, just temporarily. I'm sorry." He looked at her, and she could tell he really meant what he said.

In a fog, September walked into the squad room. Wes and George looked at her expectantly and their faces fell at what they read in hers.

"I guess this is good-bye," she said, swallowing against the hard knot in her throat.

She sat down at her desk for the last time and began cleaning it out.